JOHN SANDFORD
ROUGH COUNTRY

**SIMON &
SCHUSTER**

London · New York · Sydney · Toronto · New Delhi

A CBS COMPANY

First published in the US by G. P. Putnam's Sons, 2009
A division of the Penguin Group (USA) Inc.
First published in Great Britain by Simon & Schuster UK Ltd, 2009
This edition published by Pocket Books, 2010
An imprint of Simon & Schuster UK Ltd
A CBS COMPANY

1 3 5 7 9 10 8 6 4 2

Simon & Schuster UK Ltd
1st Floor
222 Gray's Inn Road
London WC1X 8HB

www.simonandschuster.co.uk

Simon & Schuster Australia, Sydney
Simon & Schuster India, New Delhi

A CIP catalogue record for this book is available from the British Library

ISBN 978-1-47111-097-9

Printed and bound by CPI Group (UK) Ltd, Croydon, CR0 4YY

Pulitzer-prize winning journalist John Sandford is the author of twenty *Prey* novels, four *Kidd* novels and the stunning new Virgil Flowers thrillers. He lives in Minnesota. Visit www.johnsandford.org

Praise for John Sandford

'Sandford keeps the reader guessing and the pages turning while Flowers displays the kind of cool and folksy charm that might force Davenport to share the spotlight more often' *Publishers Weekly*

'Sandford knows all there is about detonating the gut-level shocks of a good thriller' *New York Times*

'Tough, engrossing and engaging, Sandford writes superb thrillers' *Literary Review*

'That rare beast – a series writer who reads like a breath of fresh air' *Daily Mirror*

'Few do it better than Sandford' *Daily Telegraph*

'An exciting and superbly elegant demonstration of the intelligent crime writing that has helped John Sandford to sell an estimated 33 million books' *Guardian*

'A winner in every possible way' *Independent on Sunday*

'His effortlessly fluid writing and plotting really impress and his pithy characterisation is often sensational . . . Do yourself a favour and invest in all 17 Prey novels, take a week off work and enjoy' *London Lite*

'Sandford is a cunning writer. He constantly avoids the routine or expected with intelligent and surprising new wrinkles' *Washington Post*

ALSO BY JOHN SANDFORD

Winter Prey

Mind Prey

Sudden Prey

The Night Crew

Secret Prey

Certain Prey

Easy Prey

Chosen Prey

Mortal Prey

Naked Prey

Hidden Prey

Broken Prey

Dead Watch

Invisible Prey

Phantom Prey

Wicked Prey

Storm Prey

KIDD NOVELS

The Fool's Run

The Empress File

The Devil's Code

The Hanged Man's Song

VIRGIL FLOWERS NOVELS

Dark of the Moon

Heat Lightning

For Daniel, on his birthday

ACKNOWLEDGMENTS

I wrote this book with my longtime fishing partner and fellow journalist Bill Gardner, author of the musky-fishing classic *Time on the Water*. We have been fishing for muskies together for nearly thirty years, and it was through his intercession that, in this novel, I make musky fishing out to be a much less stupid activity than it actually is.

1

THE AUGUST HEAT WAS slipping away with the day. A full moon would climb over the horizon at eight o'clock, and the view across Stone Lake should be spectacular.

All tricks of the light, McDill thought. Her father taught her that.

A full moon on the horizon was no larger than a full moon overhead, he'd told her, as a small child, as they stood hand in hand in the backyard. The larger apparent size was all an optical illusion. She hadn't believed him, so he'd proven it by taking a Polaroid photograph of a harvest moon on the horizon, the biggest, fattest, yellowest moon of the year, then comparing it to another shot of the moon when it was overhead. And they *were* the same size.

He took pride in his correctness. He was a scientist, and he knew what he knew.

McDill ran an advertising agency, and she knew her father was both right and wrong. Technically he was correct, but you wouldn't make any money proving it. You could *sell* a big fat gorgeous moon coming over the horizon, shining its ass off, pouring its golden light on whatever product you wanted to sell, and screw the optical illusion. . . .

McDILL SLIPPED across the water in near silence. She was paddling a fourteen-foot Native Watercraft, a canoe-kayak hybrid designed for stability. Good for a city woman, with soft hands, who wasn't all that familiar with boats.

She didn't need the stability this evening, because the lake was glassy-flat, at the tag end of a heat wave. The forecasters were predicting that the wind would pick up overnight, but nothing serious.

She could hear the double-bladed paddle pulling through the water, first right, then left, and distantly, probably from another lake, either an outboard or a chain saw, but the sound was so distant, so intermittent, so thready, that it was like aural smoke—a noise on the edge of nothingness. Aquatic insects were hatching around her: they'd come to the surface and, from there, take off, leaving a dimple in the water.

A half-mile out from the lodge, she paddled toward the creek that drained the lake. The outlet was a crinkle in a wall of aspen, across a lily-pad flat, past a downed tree where five painted turtles lined up to take the sun. The turtles plopped off the log when they spotted her, and she smiled at the sight and sound of them. Another few yards and she headed into the creek, which pinched down to hallway-width for twenty yards or so, and around a turn to an open spot, rimmed with cattails.

The pond, as she called it, was a hundred and fifty yards long, and fifty wide. At the end of it, where the creek narrowed down and got about its real business—running downhill—a white pine stood like a sentinel among the lower trees. A bald eagle's nest was built high in the tree, and on most evenings, she'd see one or both of the eagle pair coming or going from the nest.

From down the lake, a few minutes earlier, she'd seen one of them leaving, looking for an evening meal. She idled toward the pine, hoping she'd see the bird coming back, then leaned back in the seat, hung the paddle in the side-mounted paddle holder, spread her legs and let her feet dangle over the side of the boat, in the warm summer water.

Felt the sun on her back. Dug in a polypro bag, found a cigarette and a lighter, lit the cigarette, sucked in a lungful of smoke.

Perfect. Almost.

Perfect, if only her mind would stop running.

McDILL RAN AN ADVERTISING AGENCY, Ruff-Harcourt-McDill, in Minneapolis. Ruff was dead, Harcourt retired; and Harcourt, two weeks earlier, had agreed to sell his remaining stock to McDill, which would give her seventy-five percent of the outstanding shares.

Absolute control.

So excellent.

She'd toyed with the idea of a name change—Media/McDill, or McDill Group—but had decided that she would, for the time being, leave well enough alone. Advertising buyers knew RHM, and the name projected a certain stability. She would need the sense of stability as she went about weeding out the . . .

Might as well say it: weeds.

THE AGENCY, over the years, had accumulated footdraggers, time-wasters, slow-witted *weeds* more suited for a job, say, in a newspaper than in a hot advertising agency. Getting rid of them—she had a list of names—would generate an immediate twelve percent increase in the bottom line, with virtually no loss in production. Bodies were *expensive*. Some of them seemed to think that the *purpose* of the agency was to provide them with jobs. They were wrong, and were about to find that out. When she got the stock, when she nailed that down, she'd move.

The question that plagued her was exactly *how* to do it. The current creative director, Barney Mann, was smart, witty, hardworking, a guy she wanted to keep—but he had all kinds of alliances and friendships among the worker bees. Went out for drinks with them. Played golf with them. Lent some of them money. He was *loved*, for Christ's sakes. He was the kind of guy who could turn a necessary managerial *evolution* into a mudslinging match.

And he'd done an absolutely brilliant job on the Mattocks Motor City campaign, no question about it. Dave Mattocks thought Mann was a genius and the Motor City account brought in nine percent of RHM's billings in the last fiscal year. Nine percent. If you lost an account of that size, you lost more than the account—other buyers would wonder why, and what happened, and might think that RHM was losing its edge.

McDill wanted to keep Mann, and wondered how much of a saint he really was. Suppose she took him to dinner and simply put it on him: a partnership, options on ten percent of the stock, a million bucks up front, and no fuss when the ax came down.

In fact, he might usefully soften the blow to the people who were . . . remaindered. Maybe he could take charge of an *amelioration fund*, little tax-deductible money gifts to be parceled out as needed, to keep any pathetic tales of woe out of the media. Wouldn't have to be much . . .

McDILL DRIFTED, thinking about it.

And her thoughts eventually drifted away from the agency, to the upcoming evening, about her sneaky date the night before, and about Ruth. She'd outgrown Ruth. Ruth was settling into middle-aged hausfrau mode, her mind going dull as her ass got wider. She was probably at home right now, baking a pumpkin pie or something.

In a way, McDill thought, the takeover of the agency changed everything.

Everything.

The agency was hot, she was hot.

Time to shine, by God.

THE EAGLE CAME BACK.

She saw it coming a half-mile out, unmistakable in its size, a giant bird floating along on unmoving wings.

A thousand feet away, it carved a turn in the crystalline air, like a skier on a downhill, and banked away.

McDill wondered why: the eagles had never been bothered by her presence before. She was farther away now than she had been last night, when she coasted right up to the tree trunk.

Huh. Had the eagle sensed something else?

McDill turned and scanned the shoreline, and then, in her last seconds, saw movement, frowned, and sat forward. What was that? A wink of glass . . .

The killer shot her in the forehead.

2

FIVE-THIRTY IN THE MORNING.

The moon was dropping down toward the horizon, the bottom edge touching the wisps of fog that rose off the early-morning water. Virgil Flowers was standing in the stern of a seventeen-foot Tuffy, a Thorne Brothers custom musky rod in his hand, looking over the side. Johnson, in the bow of the boat, did a wide figure-eight with an orange-bladed Double Cowgirl, his rod stuck in the lake up to the reel.

"See her?" Virgil asked, doubt in his voice.

"Not anymore," Johnson said. He gave up, straightened, pulled the rod out of the water. "Shoot. Too much to ask, anyway. You ain't gonna get one in the first five minutes."

"Good one?"

"Hell, I don't know. Flash of white." Johnson looked at the moon, then to the east. The sun wouldn't be up for ten minutes, but the horizon was getting bright. "Need more light on the water."

He plopped down in the bow seat and Virgil threw a noisy top-water bait toward the shore, reeled it in, saw nothing, threw it again.

"With the fog and stuff, the moon looks like one of those fake potato chips," Johnson said.

"What?" Virgil wasn't sure he'd heard it right.

"One of those Pringles," Johnson said.

Virgil paused between casts and said, "I don't want to disagree with you, Johnson, but the moon doesn't look like a Pringle."

"Yes, it does. Exactly like a Pringle," Johnson said.

"It looks like one of those balls of butter you get at Country Kitchen, with the French toast," Virgil said.

"Ball of butter?" Johnson blinked, looked at the moon, then back at Virgil. "You been smokin' that shit again?"

"Looks a hell of a lot more like a butterball than it does like a Pringle," Virgil said. "I'm embarrassed to be in the same boat with a guy that says the moon looks like a Pringle."

You need a good line of bullshit when you're musky fishing, because there're never a hell of a lot of fish to talk about. Johnson looked out over the lake, the dark water, the lights scattered through the shoreline pines, the lilacs and purples of the western sky, vibrating against the luminous yellow of the Pringle- or butterball-like moon. "Sure is pretty out here," he said. "God's country, man."

"That's the truth, Johnson."

Vermilion Lake, the Big V, far northern Minnesota. They floated along for a while, not working hard; it'd be a long day on the water. A boat went by in a hurry, two men in it, on the way to a better spot, if there was such a thing.

WHEN THE SUN CAME UP, a finger of wind arrived, a riffle across the water, enough to set up a slow motorless drift down a weedline at the edge of a drop-off. They were two hours on the water, halfway down the drift, when another boat came up from the east, running fast, then slowed as it passed, the faces of the two men in the boat white ovals, looking at Virgil and Johnson. The boat slowed some more and hooked in toward the weedline.

"Sucker's gonna cut our drift," Johnson said. He had no time for mass murderers, boy-child rapers, or people who cut your drift.

"Looks like Roy," Virgil said. Roy was the tournament chairman.

"Huh." Roy knew better than to cut somebody's drift.

The guy on the tiller of the other boat chopped the motor, and they drifted in a long arc, sliding up next to the Tuffy.

"Morning, Virgil. Johnson." Roy reached out and caught their gunwale and pulled the boats close.

"Morning, Roy," Johnson said. "Arnie, how you doing?"

Arnie nodded and ejected a stream of tobacco juice into the lake. Roy, who looked like an aging gray-bearded Hells Angel, in a red-and-black lumberjack shirt, if a Hells Angel ever wore one of those, said, "Virgil, a guy named Lucas Davenport is trying to get you."

6

"You tell him to go fuck himself?"

Roy grinned. "I was going to, until he said who he was. He told me to break into your cabin and get your cell phone, since you wouldn't have it with you. He was right about that." He fished Virgil's cell phone out of his shirt pocket and passed it across. "Sorry."

"Goldarnit, Roy," Johnson said.

"Probably got no reception," Virgil said. He punched up the phone and got four bars and Roy waggled his eyebrows at him.

"I tell you what, Virgil, there ain't many things more important to me than this tournament, so I know how you feel," Roy said. "But Davenport said there's a murdered woman over at Stone Lake and you need to look at her. That seemed more important."

"You know her?" Johnson asked.

"No, I don't," Roy said.

"Then how in the heck could she be more important?" Johnson asked. "People die all the time. You worry about all of them?"

"Kinda wondered about that myself," Arnie said. To Roy: "We're losing a lot of fishing time, man."

ROY AND ARNIE MOTORED OFF and Virgil sat down, Johnson bitching and moaning and working his Double Cowgirl as they continued the drift. Virgil stuck a finger in his off-ear and punched Davenport's home number on the speed dial. Davenport answered on the second ring.

"You on the lake?" Davenport asked.

"Yeah. Two hours," Virgil said. "We've seen two fish."

"Nice day?"

"Perfect." Virgil looked around in the growing light: and he was right. It *was* perfect. "Partly cloudy, enough breeze to keep us cool, not enough to bang us around."

"Virgil, man, I'm sorry."

"What happened?"

"A woman got shot by a sniper at Eagle Nest Lodge on Stone Lake, over by Grand Rapids. Her name is—was—Erica McDill. She's the CEO of Ruff-Harcourt-McDill, the ad agency in Minneapolis."

"I've heard of it," Virgil said.

"So two things—she was a big Democrat and the governor would want us to take a look no matter what. Plus, the sheriff up there, Bob Sanders, is asking for help."

"When did they find her?"

"Right at sunup—an hour and a half ago. Sanders is out looking at the body now."

"Where are the Bemidji guys?" Virgil asked.

"They're up in Bigfork, looking for Little Linda," Davenport said. "That's why Sanders needs the help—his investigators are all up there, and half his deputies. A woman on the Fox network is screaming her lungs out, they're going nightly with it—"

"Ah, Jesus."

Blond, blue-eyed Little Linda Pelli had disappeared from her parents' summer home, day before last. She was fifteen, old enough not to get lost on her way to a girlfriend's cabin. There were no hazards along the road, and if her bike had been clipped by a car, they would have found her in a ditch. Nobody had found either Little Linda or her black eighteen-speed Cannondale.

Then a woman who worked at a local lodge had reported seeing an unshaven man "with silver eyes" and a crew cut, driving slowly along the road in a beat-up pickup. The television people went batshit, because they knew what that meant: somewhere, a silver-eyed demon, who probably had hair growing out of all his bodily orifices, had Little Linda chained in the basement of a backwoods cabin (the rare kind of cabin that had a basement) and was introducing her to the ways of the Cossacks.

"Yeah," Davenport said. "Little Linda. Listen, I feel bad about this. You've been talking about that tournament since June, but what can I tell you? Go fix this thing."

"I don't even have a car," Virgil said.

"Go rent one," Davenport said. "You got your gun?"

"Yeah, somewhere."

"Then you're all set," Davenport said. "Call me when you're done with it."

"Wait a minute, wait a minute," Virgil said. "I've got no idea where this place is. Gimme some directions, or something. There're about a hundred Stone Lakes up here."

"You get off the water, I'll get directions. Call you back in a bit."

THEY SHOT A ROOSTER tail back to the marina and Virgil showed the dock boy his identification and said, "We need to keep this boat handy. Put it someplace where we can get at it quick."

"Something going on?" the dock boy asked. He weighed about a hundred and six pounds and was fifty years old and had been the dock boy since Virgil had first come up to Vermilion as a teenager, with his father.

"Can't talk about it," Virgil said. "But you keep that boat ready to go. If anybody gives you any shit, you tell them the Bureau of Criminal Apprehension told you so."

"Never heard of that," the dock boy admitted. "The criminal thing."

Virgil took out his wallet, removed one of the three business cards he kept there, and a ten-dollar bill. "Anybody asks, show them the card."

HE AND JOHNSON walked across the parking lot to Johnson's truck, carrying their lunch cooler between them, and Johnson said, looking back at the boat, "That's pretty handy—we gotta do that more often. It's like having a reserved parking space," and then, "What do you want to do about getting around?"

"If you could run me over to the scene, that'd be good," Virgil said. "I'll figure out something after I see it—if it's gonna take a while, I'll go down to Grand Rapids and rent a car."

"Think we'll get back out on the lake?" Johnson asked, looking back again. Everybody in the world who counted was out on the lake. *Everybody.*

"Man, I'd like to," Virgil said. "But I got a bad feeling about this. Maybe you could hook up with somebody else."

At the truck, they unhitched the trailer and left it in the parking spot with a lock through the tongue, and loaded the cooler into the back of the crew cab. Johnson tossed Virgil the keys and said, "You drive. I need to get breakfast."

SINCE THE AIR-CONDITIONING WAS BROKEN, they drove with the windows down, their arms on the sills, headed out to Highway 1. Davenport called when they were halfway out to the highway and gave Johnson instructions on how to reach the Eagle Nest.

Johnson wrote them down on the back of an old gas receipt, said good-bye, gave Virgil's phone back, threw the empty Budweiser breakfast can into a ditch, and dug his Minnesota atlas out from behind the seat. Virgil slowed, stopped, backed up, got out of the truck, retrieved the beer can, and threw it in a waste cooler in the back of the truck.

"Found it," Johnson said, when Virgil got back in the cab. "We're gonna have to cut across country."

He outlined the route on the map, and they took off again. Johnson finished a second beer and said, "You're starting to annoy the shit out of me, picking up the cans."

"I'm tired of arguing about it, Johnson," Virgil said. "You throw the cans out the window, I stop and pick them up."

"Well, fuck you," Johnson said. He tipped up the second can, making sure he'd gotten every last drop, and this time stuck the can under the seat. "That make you happy, you fuckin' tree hugger?"

VIRGIL WAS LANKY and blond, a surfer-looking dude with hair too long for a cop, and a predilection for T-shirts sold by indie rock bands; today's shirt was by Sebadoh. At a little more than six feet, Virgil looked like a good third baseman, and had been a mediocre one for a couple of seasons in college; a good fielder with an excellent arm, he couldn't see a college fastball. He'd drifted through school and got what turned out to be a bullshit degree in ecological science ("It ain't biology, and it ain't botany, and it ain't enough of either one," he'd once been told during a job interview).

Unable to get an ecological science job after college, he'd volunteered for the army's Officer Candidate School, figuring they'd put him in intelligence, or one of those black jumping-out-of-airplanes units.

They gave him all the tests and made him a cop.

OUT OF THE ARMY, he'd spent ten years with the St. Paul police, running up a clearance record that had never been touched, and then had been recruited by Davenport, the BCA's official bad boy. "We'll give you the hard stuff," Davenport had told him, and so far, he had.

On the side, Virgil was building a reputation as an outdoor writer, the stories researched on what Virgil referred to as under-time. He'd sold a two-story non-outdoor sequence to *The New York Times Magazine*, about a case he'd worked. The sale had given him a big head, and caused him briefly to shop for a Rolex.

Davenport didn't care about the big head or the under-time—Virgil gave him his money's worth—but did worry about Virgil dragging his boat around behind a state-owned truck. And he worried that Virgil sometimes forgot where he put his gun; and that he had in the past slept with witnesses to the crimes he was investigating.

Still, there was that clearance record, rolling along, solid as ever. Davenport was a pragmatist: if it worked, don't mess with it.

But he worried.

"YOU KNOW," JOHNSON SAID, "in some ways, your job resembles slavery. They tell you get your ass out in the cotton field, and that's what you do. My friend, you have traded your freedom for a paycheck, and not that big a paycheck."

"Good benefits," Virgil said.

"Yeah. If you get shot, they pay to patch you up," Johnson said. "I mean, you could be a big-time writer, have women hanging on you, wear one of those sport coats with patches on the sleeves, smoke a pipe or something. Your time would be your own—you could go hang out in Hollywood. Write movies if you felt like it. Fuck Madonna."

"Basically, I like the work," Virgil said. "I just don't like it all the time."

*

JOHNSON WAS AN OLD FISHING PAL, going back to Virgil's college days. A lean, scarred-up veteran of too many alcohol-related accidents in vehicles ranging from snowmobiles to trucks to Everglades airboats, Johnson had grown up in the timber business. He ran a sawmill in the hardwood hills of southeast Minnesota, cutting hardwood flooring material, with a sideline in custom cutting and curing oversized chunks of maple and cherry for artists. A lifelong fisherman, he knew the Mississippi between Winona and LaCrosse like the back of his hand, and was always good for an outstate musky run.

Johnson wore jeans and a T-shirt. When it got a little cooler, he pulled a sweatshirt over the T-shirt. When it got cooler than that, he pulled on a jean jacket. Cooler than that, a Carhartt. Cooler than that, he said fuck it and went to the Bahamas with a suitcase full of T-shirts and a Speedo bathing suit that he called the slingshot.

NOW HE DIRECTED VIRGIL across the back roads between highways 1 and 79, generally south and west, over flat green wet country with not too much to look at, except tamarack trees and marshy fields and here and there, a marginal farm with a couple of horses. As they got closer to the Eagle Nest, the woods got denser and the terrain started to roll, the roads got narrower and lakes glinted blue or black behind the screens of trees.

"Wonder how long it took them to think of the name Eagle Nest?" Johnson wondered. "About three seconds?"

"They could have called it the Porcupine Lodge or the Dun Rovin or Sunset Shores or Musky Point," Virgil said.

"You're getting grumpier," Johnson said. "Back at the V, I was the one who was pissed."

"Well, goddamnit, I've been working like a dog all year," Virgil said.

"Except for the under-time," Johnson said.

"Doesn't count. I was still working, just not for the state."

"You oughta model yourself after me," Johnson said. "I'm a resilient type. I roll with the punches, unlike you fragile pretty boys."

"Fragile. Big word for a guy like you," Virgil said.

Johnson grinned: "Turnoff coming up."

ON THE WAY DOWN, Virgil had formed a picture of the Eagle Nest in his mind: a peeled-log lodge with a Rolling Rock sign at one end, at the bar, a fish-cleaning house down by the dock. A dozen little plywood cabins would be scattered through the pines along the shore, a battered aluminum boat for each cabin, a machine shed in the back, the smell of gasoline and oil mixed with dirt and leaf humus; and on calm nights, a hint of septic tank. Exactly how that fit with a rich advertising woman, he didn't know—maybe an old family place that she'd been going to for years.

When he turned off the highway, into the lodge's driveway, he began to adjust his mental image. He'd been fishing the North Woods for thirty years, ever since he was old enough to hold a fishing pole. He thought he knew most of the great lodges, which generally were found on the bigger lakes.

He'd never heard of an Eagle Nest on a Stone Lake, but the driveway, which was expensively blacktopped, and which swooped in unnecessary curves through a forest dotted with white pines, hinted at something unusual.

They came over a small ridge and the forest opened up, and Johnson said, "Whoa: nice-looking place."

The lodge was set on a grassy hump that looked out over the lake; two stories tall, built of cut stone, logs, and glass, it fit in the landscape like a hand in a glove. The cabins scattered down the shoreline were as carefully built and sited as the lodge, each with a screened porch facing the water, and a sundeck above each porch. An expensive architect had been at work, Virgil thought, but not recently: the lodge had a feeling of well-tended age.

There were no cars at the cabins. As they rolled down toward the lodge, the road jogged left and dipped into a hollow, where they found a parking lot, screened from the lodge and the cabins by a fifteen-foot-tall evergreen hedge. Four sheriff's cars were parked in the lot, along with twenty or so civilian vehicles, and a hearse. There were no cops in sight; a lodge employee was loading luggage into a Mercedes-Benz station wagon from a Yamaha Rhino.

Deeper in the woods, on the other side of the parking lot, Virgil saw the corner of a green metalwork building, probably the shop. Neither the parking lot nor the shop would be visible from the lodge or the cabins. Nice.

"Where're the boats?" Johnson asked, as Virgil pulled into a parking space.

"I don't know. Must be on the other side of the lodge," Virgil said.

AS THEY CLIMBED out of the truck, the lodge worker, a middle-aged woman in a red-and-blue uniform, stepped over and asked, "Can I help you, gentlemen?"

"Where's the lodge?" Virgil asked.

"Up the path," she said, and, "Do you know this is ladies only?"

"We're cops," Johnson said.

"Ah. Okay. There are more deputies up there now." To Virgil: "Are you a policeman, too?"

Johnson laughed and said, "Yeah. He is," and they walked over to stairs that led to a flagstone path through the woods, out of the parking lot to the lodge.

THE LODGE and its grassy knoll sat at the apex of a natural shoreline notch. The notch was filled with docks and a variety of boats, mostly metal outboards, but also a few canoes, kayaks, and paddleboats. A hundred yards down to the right, two women walked hand in hand down a narrow sand beach that looked out at a floating swimming dock.

Twenty women in outdoor shirts and jeans were scattered at tables around the deck, with cups of coffee and the remnants of croissants and apple salads, and looked them over as they went to the railing. Down below them, two uniformed sheriff's deputies were standing on the dock, chatting with each other.

A waiter hurried over: a thin, pale boy with dark hair, he had a side-biased haircut that he thought made him look like Johnny Depp. "Can I help you?"

Virgil said, "I'm with the Bureau of Criminal Apprehension. How do we get down to the dock?"

The waiter said, "Ah. Come along."

He took them inside, down an interior stairway, through double doors under the deck, and pointed at a flagstone walkway. "Follow that."

The flagstone path curled around the stone ledge, right at the waterside, and emerged at the dock. Two women, who'd been out of sight from the deck, were standing at the end of the path, arms crossed, talking and watching the deputies. Johnson muttered, "I've only been detecting for ten minutes, but check out the short one. And she's wearing a fishing shirt."

Virgil said, quietly as he could, "Johnson, try to stay out of the way for a few minutes, okay?"

"You didn't talk that way when you needed my truck, you bitch."

"Johnson . . ."

THE WOMEN TURNED and looked at them as they came along, and Virgil nodded and said, "Hi. I'm Virgil Flowers, with the state Bureau of Criminal Apprehension. I'm looking for Sheriff Sanders."

"He's out at the pond," said the older of the two. A bluff, no-nonsense, heavyset woman with tired eyes, she stuck out a hand and said, "I'm Margery Stanhope. I own the lodge."

"I need to talk to you when I get back," Virgil said. "I noticed that somebody was checking out when we were coming—a lady was loading luggage. I'll have to know who has left since the . . . incident."

"Not a problem," she said. "Anything we can do."

The younger woman was a small, auburn-haired thirty-something, pretty, with a sprinkling of freckles on her tidy nose; the kind of woman that might cause Johnson to get drunk and recite poetry, including the complete "Cremation of Sam McGee." Virgil had seen it happen.

15

And she was pretty enough to cause Virgil's heart to hum, if not yet actually sing, until she asked, "Are you the Virgil Flowers who was involved in that massacre up in International Falls?"

His heart stopped humming. "Wasn't exactly a massacre," Virgil said.

"Sounded like a massacre," she said.

Stanhope said, "Zoe, shut up."

"I feel that we have to take a stance," Zoe said to her.

"Take it someplace else," Stanhope said. She looked past Virgil at Johnson: "You're also a police officer?"

Virgil jumped in: "Actually, he's my friend, Johnson. We were in the fishing tournament up at Vermilion and I got pulled to look at this case. The guys who'd normally do it are on that Little Linda thing. Johnson's not a police officer."

"Pleased to meet you," Stanhope said, and shook with Johnson. "What's your first name, again?"

"Johnson," Johnson said.

She said, "Oh." Not sure if her leg was being pulled. "What's your last name?"

"Johnson," Virgil said. When Stanhope looked skeptical, he said, "Really. Johnson Johnson. His old man named him after an outboard. Everybody calls him Johnson."

Zoe was pleased, either with the double name, or the concept of a name based on an outboard motor. "You get teased when you were a kid?" she asked.

"Not as much as my brother, Mercury," Johnson said.

Stanhope said, "Now I know you're lying."

"Believe it," Virgil said. "Mercury Johnson. He suffers from clinical depression."

"Thank God Mom decided to quit after two," Johnson said. "Dad wanted to go for a daughter and he'd just bought a twenty-five-horse Evinrude."

"I don't know," Zoe said. "Evvie's kind of a nice name."

That made Johnson laugh, and, since she was pretty, laugh too hard; Virgil said, "I'll talk to you ladies later. I gotta go see the deputies."

Stanhope said, blank-faced, to Johnson, "This isn't a laughing matter. This is a terrible tragedy."

Virgil nodded and said, "Of course it is."

Virgil and Johnson turned toward the dock, and Zoe asked, "She's dead, isn't she? Little Linda?"

"I don't know," Virgil said, over his shoulder, still miffed about the massacre question. "I don't know anything about it."

"I wonder if it's connected to this death?"

Virgil paused. "Do you have any reason to think so?"

"Nope. Except that they happened only two days apart," Zoe said.

"And about forty miles," Virgil said.

"Don't you suspect it, though?" She had warm brown eyes, almost gold, and he forgave her.

"No. I don't. Too many other possibilities," he said.

She nodded. "Okay. I see that. Kind of a stupid question, wasn't it?"

Stanhope answered for Virgil. "Yes. It was."

WALKING OUT TO THE DOCK, Johnson said, "The old bag kinda climbed my tree."

"One rule when you're dealing with people close to a murder victim," Virgil said. "Try not to laugh."

VIRGIL INTRODUCED HIMSELF and Johnson to the deputies and one of them said, "You're the guy who was in that shoot-out in International Falls."

Virgil bobbed his head and said, "Yeah, I was there. I understand that the body is at a place called the pond?"

"Boy, I wish I coulda been there," the cop said, ignoring Virgil's question. "That must've been something. My dad was in Vietnam, and he must've read that story about a hundred times, about the shoot-out. I bet he'd like to meet you."

The other cop said, "Sheriff's been looking for you. He's out at the pond now. They haven't done anything but look at the body, try to keep it from floating away. Don't want to mess with the scene. One of your crime-scene crews from Bemidji is on the way. . . . I could run you out there."

"Floating away? She's in the water?" Virgil asked.

"Yeah. She got shot right in the forehead, bullet exited the back of her head." The cop touched himself in the middle of the forehead, two inches above the top of his nose. "Really made a mess. She fell backwards out of the boat—it's kinda like a kayak—but her foot got twisted under the seat and that held her up on the surface. She was still floating there, last time I was out."

"Doesn't sound like there'll be much of a crime scene," Virgil said.

"Not much," the cop said.

"Who found her?" Johnson asked.

"Guide. From the lodge. George Rainy, he's out there, too."

"Then let's go," Virgil said.

Johnson asked, "Am I coming?"

"You can," Virgil said. "Or you could wait at the lodge with Miz Stanhope."

"I'll go," he said.

THEY TOOK one of the Lunds, the standard Minnesota lodge boat, Virgil and Johnson in the front, the second deputy, whose name was Don, at the tiller of the twenty-five-horse Yamaha. The run was short, no more than a half-mile. There were no cabins along the way; Virgil could see cabins and boathouses on the other side of the lake, and down at the far end of it, but the shore elevation west of the lodge dropped quickly and became low and marshy around the outlet creek. They passed the mouth of a shallow backwater, and a line of beaver lodges, like haystacks made of small logs and sticks, turned around a point into the outlet, dodged a snag, went down a narrow channel, and emerged into the pond.

Four more boats, with seven people, were floating along the eastern shore, and Don took them that way. "The guy in the white ball cap is the sheriff," Don said. "The guy in the boat by himself is

George, the guide. The two guys in the green emergency vests are from the funeral home; they're here to pick up the body. The other three are deputies."

"How'd George happen to find her?" Virgil asked. "Anybody know?"

"Nobody saw her at dinner last night, but sometimes, people will cook something up in their cabin, though Miz McDill usually didn't do that," Don said. "Anyway, nobody really looked, but then early this morning, some of the women were going on a paddling trip and one of the boats was missing. One of them said, 'My gosh, didn't Miz McDill take one out last night?' So they went and looked at her cabin, and she wasn't there, and they knew she liked to paddle down and look at the eagle's nest"—he pointed at a white pine that stood over the end of the pond, with an eagle's nest a hundred feet up—"so George jumped in a boat and he came down here and says, 'There she was.' He came back and they called us."

Don killed the motor and they coasted down on the cluster of boats. As they came up, Virgil stood and looked over the bow, saw an upside-down olive-drab plastic boat, with a body in a white shirt bobbing in the water next to it. The sheriff stood up and asked, "You Virgil?"

"Yeah, I am," Virgil said, and they bumped gunwales and shook hands. The sheriff was a tall, fleshy man with a hound-dog face, wrinkled like yesterday's tan shirt; and he was wearing a tan uniform shirt and brown uniform slacks, along with heavy uniform shoes that weren't right in a boat.

"I read those stories you wrote for *The New York Times*," he said. "Pretty interesting."

"Couldn't miss—it was an interesting case," Virgil said.

Sanders mentioned the names of the other cops and Rainy, and said, nodding at the two men from the funeral home, "These guys are here to pick up the body."

"What do you think?" Virgil asked.

"It seems to me like a murder, but it could be suicide, I suppose," Sanders said, looking back at the body. "But you don't see women

19

like this one, shooting themselves in the head. Too messy. So . . . somebody got close and shot her. Might possibly be an accident, I guess."

"Murder," Virgil said. "Small chance it could be a suicide, but not an accident," Virgil said, looking around.

"Why's it not an accident?" Johnson asked.

"Too many trees," Virgil said. "It's too thick in here. To get a slug through the trees, you'd have to be right on the edge of them. Then you could see her. So it wasn't like somebody fired a gun a half-mile away, and she happened to be in front of it. And if it was somebody in a boat, who met her here, and they were both bobbing a little bit, they had to be really close to hit her."

Johnson nodded, looked at the white shirt floating around the body, like a veil, and turned away.

Virgil asked the sheriff, "Is there a time of death? Did anybody hear any shots?"

"Not that we've been able to find."

Virgil nodded and said, "Don, push us off the sheriff's boat, there, get me a little closer."

They got close, and Virgil hung over the boat, getting a good look at the body. He couldn't see her face, but he could see massive damage to the back of her head, and looked back over his shoulder and said, "If you don't find a large-caliber pistol at the bottom of the pond, then it was a rifle."

The sheriff nodded. "Thought it might be."

"Gotta have the crime-scene guys look for a pistol, though. If the shooter was in a boat, he might have dumped it over the side; or if it's a suicide." No other signs of violence. One shot, and the woman was gone. Virgil pushed himself upright and asked, "Where's the nearest road?"

The cops looked around, then one of them pointed. "I guess it'd be . . . over there."

"How far?"

"Probably . . . a quarter mile? There's a town road around the lake, and it crosses this creek about, mmm, a half-mile down, then hooks up a little closer to the lake and then goes on around to a cluster of cabins right on the west point of the lake. You probably saw them when you were coming in."

"Could you paddle up the creek?" Virgil asked.

"Naw. It's all choked north of the culvert," the cop said. "Be easier to walk, 'cause the creek's not that deep, but it's got a muck bottom. . . . I don't know. I don't think you could walk it, either. Not easy, anyway."

THEY FLOATED AND TALKED for a couple of minutes. They hadn't taken the body in, the sheriff said, because they wanted the BCA agent, whoever he was, to take a look and say it was okay: "We don't have a hell of a lot of murders up here."

Virgil said, "You can take her. There's enough current here to drift her a bit, and if there was any wind at all . . . no way to tell exactly where she was hit, unless we find some blood spatter." He looked around, and then said, "You might have a couple guys slowly . . . slowly . . . cruise the waterline, all the way from the channel to the far end of the pond, look at the edge of the weeds and the lily pads, see if there's any blood on the foliage. If she'd been right up against the weeds, there should be some."

The sheriff pointed at the cops in one of the boats, and they pushed off.

WHILE THEY WERE TALKING, the two funeral home guys had moved over to the body. They had a black body bag with them, and were discussing the best way to hoist the body into the boat without hurting their backs. Virgil noticed that Johnson wouldn't look at the body.

Sanders said, "I'm gonna really have to lean on you and the other guys from the BCA on this thing—all my guys are up working on the Little Linda case. That thing is turning into a nightmare. Linda's mom is some kind of PR demon; she's holding press conferences, she hired a psychic. It's driving us crazy."

"No sign of Little Linda?"

"No, but the psychic says that she's still alive. She's in a dark place with large stones around her, and she's cold. He sees moss."

Johnson: "Moss?"

"That's what he says," Sanders said.

"You're investigating moss?"

THEN ONE OF THE COPS who'd gone looking for blood called from fifty yards up the pond, toward the lake: "Got some cigarettes here." And then the other one said, "There's a lighter."

Virgil nodded at Don, and the sheriff told the rest of them to stay where they were, and Don started the motor and Virgil's boat and the sheriff's drifted up the pond. There, they could see what appeared to be a nearly full pack of Salem cigarettes floating on the surface and, a little beyond it, the bottom end of a red plastic Bic cigarette lighter.

"She a smoker?" Virgil asked.

"Don't know," the sheriff said.

"We need to mark this—this may be close to where she was killed." He called back to the guide, who motored over. "You got any marker buoys?" Virgil asked.

Rainy dug in the back of the boat and came up with a yellow-plastic dumbbell-shaped buoy wrapped with string, the string ending in a lead weight. "Toss it right about there," Virgil said.

Rainy tossed it in; the weight dropped to the bottom, marking the spot for the crime-scene crew.

"Leave the cigarette pack and lighter. Maybe crime scene can get something off them," Virgil said. To the cops: "Keep looking for blood."

BACK DOWN THE POND, the funeral home guys were hoisting the body into the boat, with some trouble. The sheriff said to the cop on the tiller, "Get me back there."

Virgil said, "I want to take a look at that other shore—where somebody might walk in. Cruise the shoreline."

"I'll be here," the sheriff said.

*

THEY STARTED where the creek drained out of the pond, moving at a walking pace. Virgil looked down the creek, and as the cop had said, it was choked with dead trees, sweepers, branches. He doubted that you could walk along it, and a boat would be impossible. They moved out, along the edge of the pond, scanning the shoreline until Johnson said, "There you go."

"Where?"

"See that dead birch, the one with the dead crown?" He was pointing across the weed flat at the wall of aspens and birch trees. "Now look about one inch to the left; you see that dark hole in the weeds? I see that all the time, in the backwaters on the river—somebody walked out there . . . over toward that beaver lodge."

"Okay." Virgil looked back at the boats around the body. "Could have set up on the lodge."

"Eighty-yard shot. Maybe ninety," Johnson said. "Looks about like a good sand wedge."

"Could be fifty, depending on how she drifted," Virgil said. "Good shooting, though."

Don said, "Not that great. Eighty, ninety yards. That's nothing, up here."

"I'll tell you what," Virgil said. "He had one shot, no warm-ups, and he put it dead in her forehead. She was probably moving, at least a little bit. And he was shooting a human being and had to worry about being caught, about being seen, about getting out of there. With all that stress, that's damn good shooting. He knew what he was doing."

Don looked from the shore back to the boats, back to the shore, then nodded, and said, "When you're right, you're right."

Looking at the beaver lodge, a low hump of bare logs, twigs, and mud just off the shoreline, Johnson said, "About impossible to get there from here. Might push a boat through to the beaver lodge, but even then . . ."

Virgil shook his head: "Better to come in from the same side the shooter did. Have to do that anyway." To Don: "Let's go see the sheriff."

★

23

THE FUNERAL HOME GUYS had McDill in a body bag and were zipping it up when they got back. The sheriff looked at their faces and asked, "What?"

Virgil said, "I think we got ourselves a crime scene."

3

WITH THE BODY OUT of the water, the sheriff talked to the two deputies who were looking for bloodstained lily pads, and told them to wait at the pond until he called them, or until the crime-scene crew arrived and sent them back. Then the rest of them pulled out, led by the sheriff in his boat, Virgil, Johnson, and Don in theirs, George Rainy, the guide, by himself, and the boat with the body.

At the pond, Virgil had only one flickering bar on his cell phone, but he had a solid four when they got back. As soon as Don cut the motor and started cutting a curve into the dock, he called the Bemidji office and talked to the duty officer.

"You got a crime-scene crew headed my way?"

"Should be there," the duty officer said. "Let me give them a call." He was back a minute later. "They ran into a closed bridge. They should be there in ten or fifteen minutes. They gotta go around."

"You still got guys up in Bigfork?"

"Oh, yeah. It's getting worse. You heard about Fox . . ."

A DOZEN WOMEN were standing on the dock, watching with the combination of curiosity and dread that you got at murders. Virgil tossed a line around a cleat and snugged the boat up to the dock and climbed out, holding it for Johnson and Don. When the sheriff had clambered out of his boat, Virgil relayed the news about the crime-scene crew and said, "Let's go see if we can spot the trail in—where the killer left the road."

"Sounds good."

To Johnson: "Why don't you go up to the lodge and see if you can get us some sandwiches; I'm starving to death."

"What're you doing?"

"I'm going to take a look at the body," Virgil said.

Johnson nodded and headed up the dock. Virgil walked over to Rainy, who was tying up his boat, and asked him to stick around until they could talk. The guide nodded and said, "Yessir," and followed Johnson into the lodge.

The funeral home guys hoisted the body bag out of the boat and Virgil had them unzip it. McDill was lying faceup, the front of her face stained red by hypostasis, the settling of blood in a dead body, under the influence of gravity. She'd gone into the water facedown, and apparently had stayed that way overnight.

The entry wound in her forehead was the size of Virgil's little fingernail, but the bone was pulped, as though the slug had exploded. The exit wound had knocked out the back left part of her skull, exposing some brain matter, which, washed overnight by the lake water, resembled gray cheese. To Virgil, it looked like she'd been shot with a small-caliber rifle, maybe a .223, or possibly a .243, with hollow-point bullets. She was wearing jeans, and he reached around to feel her back pockets, where she might be carrying a wallet, but she wasn't.

"You see any other wounds?" Virgil asked.

The funeral home guys shook their heads. "Not a thing," one of them said. "We'll check at the office, before we pack her up for the medical examiner. Let you know."

The body would be sent to Ramsey County, in the Twin Cities, for the autopsy.

"Zip it up," Virgil said. He duckwalked over to the edge of the dock, reached down, and washed his hands in the lake water.

STANHOPE HAD SEEN THEM coming in and now edged out onto the dock, and when Virgil stood up, she cringed away, unable to look, and asked, "Is that her?"

Virgil nodded and said, "You really don't have to be here. Why don't we go inside?"

She stepped away, still looking at the bag, and shuddered, and led the way along the path to the lodge door and up the interior stairs. Virgil asked, "You got the Internet here?"

"Oh, sure. Every cabin, and wireless all over the lodge."

The Eagle Nest office was a quiet suite of three rooms with two clerks at wooden desks with modern flat-screen computers and a bunch of file cabinets. Two fish replicas, framed photos of well-known guests, and a set of moose antlers hung on the knotty-pine walls. A Scots-plaid woman's beret dangled from one of the antlers. Virgil used Stanhope's computer to download and then call up Google Earth, focus on the lake, and then spot exactly where the body had been, and the shortest land-route into the pond from the loop road.

"Pretty good tool," the sheriff said, looking over his shoulder.

"Not only that, it's free," Virgil said. He grabbed the screen and printed it out.

THE SHERIFF LED THE WAY in his Tahoe, Johnson driving his truck while Virgil ate a cheese-and-bologna sandwich. Between bites, Virgil said to Johnson, "You looked a little green out there. At the body."

Johnson bobbed his head and looked out the window into the forest. "I told you about that body I found on the river."

"About a hundred thousand times," Virgil said.

"So after I found it, I called the cops. This Wisconsin river cop came over, and he knew who it was. Some guy from Lake City who fell out of his boat—"

"Yeah, yeah, you told me." He spit a piece of pimento out the window.

"What I didn't tell you was, this cop wanted to anchor the body until we could get a bigger boat out there to do the recovery," Johnson said. "So he tied a line around it, so he could pull it over closer to the shore and tie it off to a tree. But the thing is, it'd been in the river for a week, and was all bloated and full of gas, and when he pulled on the line, the body came apart and the gas came out and rolled right over me."

"Ah, jeez," Virgil said. "You know what you do in a situation like that? Course, I don't suppose you had any Vicks . . ."

"Hang on a minute," Johnson said. "Anyway, I started barfing. I barfed up everything I had and then I *kept* barfing. Nothing was coming up but some spit, but I couldn't stop. The cop was barfing, too, and I got out of there and went back to the cabin, and I kept . . . trying to barf. I couldn't get the smell off me. I took a shower and washed my hair and I even burned the clothes, and I could still smell it and I'd start barfing again. That went on for a week, and then, like three weeks later, it started again, and went on for another couple of days. So, you know, this morning, I thought a murder scene might be interesting, but when I saw her in the water . . . I smelled that gas again."

"I didn't smell much of anything, except lake water," Virgil said.

"It's not real," Johnson said. "It's stuck in my brain. That smell."

"I've heard of that," Virgil said. "People getting stuck with a smell or a mental image."

"The image doesn't bother me—never saw that much of the guy's body," Johnson said. "But when I saw you get your face right down on top of her, and her hair floating out like that, I about blew my cookies. I don't see how you do it."

"Job," Virgil said.

"Yeah, well . . ." Johnson sighed, turned around, dug a Budweiser out of the cooler, popped it open. "Think you better find yourself a ride, Virgil. I'm going back up to the V. This murder shit— I'm done with it. I thought it would be interesting, but it's just nasty."

AT THE CLOSEST APPROACH to the pond, they pulled off onto the shoulder of the road, and the sheriff and Virgil walked one way, and Johnson the other, because Virgil knew that he'd spot the trail, and so would Johnson, but he wasn't sure about the sheriff. He and the sheriff had walked thirty yards along the gravel road when he saw it: "There." He turned and shouted, "Johnson!"

Johnson jogged over and Virgil said, "Stay back from it—we'll want the crime-scene guys to walk it."

There'd been no way the killer could have gotten in without leaving a trail: the soil was firm enough underfoot, but damp, and the plants were the soft, leafy, easily broken kind that you saw in the shade, on the edges of wetlands.

"The question is, where'd he leave his car?" Virgil asked. The road was narrow, and there were no obvious turnoffs. "Couldn't park it here; too many people would have seen it."

The sheriff said, "There's some empty cabins up the way. He could park back there, and not get seen. But what if he dropped off a gun, then parked up at the lodge? You could walk down here in fifteen or twenty minutes. Gravel road like this, you could hear a car coming. A little care, you could just step into the woods before it went by."

"A guy would be noticed at the lodge, a stranger," Virgil said. "Maybe a woman?"

Johnson said, "If it was a woman, especially if it was one who was staying at the lodge, she'd see McDill going out in the boat. She might even have asked her where she was going . . . run down here, boom."

Virgil looked into the woods. "If that's right, the gun might still be in there. Unless she came down last night and picked it up, but that'd really be taking a chance. If they saw her, people would remember."

"We'll check everybody on this road," the sheriff said. "Every swinging dick."

Car coming; they heard it before they could see it, and when they saw it, it was an oversized white van. "Crime scene," Virgil said.

THERE WERE FOUR GUYS with the crime-scene crew, led by Ron Mapes, who'd last run into Virgil while they were looking at the murder of an Indian cop from the Red Lake Chippewa reservation.

Virgil ran them through what had been done, including the marker buoy out on the lake, and all four of them looked down the track toward the lake. "We're gonna need head nets, metal detectors . . ." Mapes began.

Virgil said to Mapes, "Could you guys go in there right now, take a quick look at the track? See if anything pops up? At Red Lake, you told me the killer was a small guy, and that got me started in the right direction."

"We can look," Mapes said.

The crew all had fifteen-inch rubber boots and head nets and cotton gloves to protect against the mosquitoes, and they took it slow, pushing down the track, looking for anything along the way, checking for metal. While they were doing that, Virgil, the sheriff, and Johnson walked farther down the road, looking at the driveways branching off to the sides. The driveways were gravel-and-dirt tracks leading uphill, away from the lake: hunting cabins, the sheriff said, usually empty until the fall.

THE CRIME-SCENE CREW had been in for ten minutes, out of sight, when they got back, and the sheriff called the Grand Rapids airport Avis and reserved an SUV for Virgil. He'd just rung off when they heard somebody coming in, and then Mapes pushed delicately through the brush beside the killer's track, still searching it with his eyes. When he got out on the road, he pulled off his head net and said, "The mosquitoes are thick in there . . . gets wet about a hundred yards in."

"So . . ."

"I can't promise you that she's the killer, but I can tell you that whoever walked back there is a woman," Mapes said. "She maybe went in more than once, or maybe there were a couple of them, because it's tracked up."

"Scouting tracks," Virgil said.

"Anyway, we got three partial footprints so far, the instep of a woman's boot or shoe. Maybe a shoe, because there's a low heel," Mapes said. "We won't be able to give you an exact size because we're mostly seeing that instep, but it also looks to me like there's a capital M in the instep, a logo. One of the guys thinks it's for Mephisto shoes. He said Mephisto shoes run about three hundred bucks a pair."

"Not something you'd see every day," Virgil said.

"Heck, I don't even know if you could buy any locally, I mean, closer than the Cities," Mapes said. "Though you could order them on the Internet."

"What else?" Virgil asked.

"Well . . . nothing. But I thought that was quite a bit," Mapes said.

"Nothing on the beaver lodge?"

"Not there yet. I'm going back in."

"Done good, Ron," Virgil said.

The sheriff looked at Virgil and said, "Gotta be somebody at the lodge. A woman, shoes from the Cities." Sanders had relaxed a notch: this was more of a Cities problem than a local deal, and he was happy to have it that way.

"Let's go back and talk to Stanhope," Virgil said. "Then if you could have one of your guys give me a lift down to Grand Rapids, we could let Johnson go."

"I can do that," the sheriff said.

ON THE WAY BACK to the lodge, Johnson said, "I feel like I'm ditching you."

"You're not. This isn't your job. Catch a fish for me, up there," Virgil said.

"Not gonna catch any fish," Johnson said gloomily. He ducked his head over the steering wheel, looking up at the bright sky. "This trip is cursed."

At the lodge, Virgil hopped out, got his duffel bag, walked around to the driver's side, and said, "You stay off that Budweiser when you're driving."

"Yeah, yeah . . ."

"I mean it, Johnson. I got enough goddamn dead people on my hands."

Johnson cracked a smile: "First turn I get around, I'm gonna throw a beer can out the window. I'll call it the Virgil Flowers memorial beer can. It'll still be there when the next glacier comes through."

And he was gone.

*

VIRGIL TOLD SANDERS that he needed to talk to Rainy, the guide, and then to Stanhope, and then to anyone that they might suggest. "Gonna be a while," he said.

The sheriff shrugged, "Well—it's a murder, so I guess that takes a while," and a couple of seconds later, "You're not gonna get much from George."

"Yeah?"

"George is a drunk," Sanders said. "Every day that he works, he stops at the liquor store and picks up a fifth and he takes it home and drinks it. He's trying to drink himself to death. He did that last night. He was in no shape to ambush anybody."

"Any particular reason he's doing that?" Virgil asked.

"Not as far as I know. I think he's tired of being here," Sanders said.

THEY FOUND RAINY and interviewed him in a room called "the library," a cube with three soft chairs and a few hundred hardbacks with sun-faded covers, and six geraniums in the window, in terra-cotta pots. Rainy lived fifteen minutes away, toward Grand Rapids, but outside of town. He worked a half-dozen lakes in the area, guiding fishermen in the summer, deer and bear hunters in the fall. He got a hundred dollars a day plus tips, had worked on another lake the day before the killing, and had been scheduled to take out a couple of women in the morning and teach them how to fish for walleye.

"Got down to the dock, and they was runnin' around like a bunch of chickens with their heads cut off. They thought Miz McDill might of gone down toward that pond. So I says, 'Well, why don't I go take a look?' So I jumps in a boat and runs down there, and there she was. Wasn't like I investigated—I come out the pipe and there she was. I spotted her as soon as I come out, the boat and her shirt."

"You touch her?" Virgil asked.

"Shit no. I watch TV," the guide said.

Virgil nodded. "Okay. No ideas?"

Rainy shook his head: "Nope. Well . . . one. Don't mention it to Miz Stanhope; I need to work here."

"I can keep my mouth shut," Virgil said, and the sheriff nodded.

"The women here, you know, a lot of them are singing on our side of the choir," Rainy said.

Virgil looked at the sheriff, who did a little head bob that suggested that he agreed, but hadn't mentioned it out of politeness.

"You think . . ."

Rainy nodded. "Rug munchers," he said. "The thing is, you know, they'd go on down to the bars—the Goose in particular—and you'd hear that there were some fights when they got the liquor in them. I don't mean like, out in the parking lot, but you know, screaming at each other. Fighting over who was munchin' who. So . . . it could be a sex thing."

Virgil asked the sheriff, "Miss McDill . . . ?"

"Don't know. I *do* know that a lot of the women who come up here aren't gay," Sanders said. "Margery told me once that a lot of them want to come up here without having to put up with macho North Woods bullshit. Don't mind men, they just want to get away for a while, get back to nature on their own."

"How'd that come up?" Virgil asked. "About who was gay?"

"Somebody made a comment at the Chamber of Commerce, and she was steamed about it," the sheriff said. "I bumped into her, purely by accident, and she let it out. We've known each other since grade school."

"Huh."

The sheriff chuckled. "You just said, 'Huh,' like a cop."

"No, no . . . but you wonder, if this was done by an outsider, somebody who was staying here at the lodge, how'd they know exactly how to walk in there? To the pond?" Virgil asked.

"Could have looked on Google Earth, like we did," Sanders suggested.

"One possibility," Virgil admitted.

"Could have scouted it," Sanders added.

"Or it could be a local," Virgil said.

"Look, if you'd asked me how to get in there, to the pond, off the road, I'd have to take a long look at a map and maybe get a compass, and I've lived here all my life," Sanders said. "The killer either knows this exact area a lot better than I do, or she looked at Google Earth. Or a map. Maybe used a GPS. *And* probably scouted it. So it's just as likely to be an outsider as a local. Either way, they'd have to scout it."

"Or was a deer hunter," Rainy chipped in. Virgil and the sheriff turned back to him. "After it freezes up, it's not so bad back there. No bugs, no mud. You go a couple hundred yards back, and you can see the pond. John Mack has a couple of tree stands maybe a five-minute walk west of there. Guys around here'll push that piece of woods, from the road over to the lake, up toward Mack's place."

"Must take a lot of guys to push it," Virgil said.

"Naw, it's not so bad. Like I said, you can see better. You get six, eight guys across that neck, about noon on opening day, and push 'em west, the deer'll funnel between two little ponds," Rainy said. "The kids on the stands will usually take one or two. The guys put their kids up on the stands, to give them a crack at a good one."

"I'll keep that in mind," Virgil said. "Thank you."

As they were leaving the library, the sheriff leaned close to the guide and said, "Long as you're working here, I'd go easy on that 'rug muncher' business."

Rainy's Adam's apple bobbed a couple of times. "I'll do that. I will."

OUT IN THE MAIN LODGE, Sanders said to Virgil, "I don't want you to get the idea that people up here are antigay. Some of the women at the lodge might be gay, but it doesn't bother anyone. We *want* them to come into town, shop, go to the restaurants— these women have *money*. This resort's gonna cost them two thousand dollars a week, and some of them come up for a month. It's not like they buy a bucket of minnows and sleep in the back of the truck."

Virgil smiled. "You mean like me and Johnson?"

"Well—you know, they hang out at the Wild Goose, like George said. Tom Mortensen, he's the owner, if you told him he was going to lose his gay business, he'd have a heart attack," Sanders said. "They keep him going. He likes having them, and they like being there. Hell of a lot less trouble than a bunch of cowboys."

THEY WENT by the office to find Stanhope. Zoe, the woman who thought Virgil had perpetrated a massacre, was sitting at a computer, wearing a pair of black librarian glasses, which meant that Virgil would almost certainly fall in love with her; the near-sighted intellectual look did him in every time. If she'd had an overbite, he would have proposed.

Stanhope was standing behind her, looking over her shoulder and at a piece of paper in her own hand, and said, "I'm sure we paid him off before July first. The Fourth of July fell on a Friday, payday, and I remember that he wasn't here for the fireworks, because he usually helps set them up—"

"You see the problem, though," Zoe said, tapping the computer screen. "If he slopped over into July, then he has to go on the third-quarter numbers, too."

Stanhope sensed them at the doorway, turned, and said, "Hi. We're trying to figure out an accounting problem."

"When you got a minute," Virgil said, "I'd like you to walk me over to Miss McDill's cabin, talk a bit about her."

"Go right now," Stanhope said.

The sheriff said, "I'll leave you to it, Virgil. I gotta go talk to the TV people."

Virgil nodded: "Go. I would like to fix a ride down to the Avis dealer, though."

Zoe said, "My office is in town—I could ride you down there. I'll be another half-hour here."

"That'd be great," Virgil said.

ALL THE CABINS had names: McDill had been in the Common Loon, one bedroom, with extra sleeping space up a ladder in a second-story loft. The loft also had a doorway out to the sundeck.

In addition to the bedroom, the cabin had a segregated space, like a den, with a computer desk complete with an Ethernet cable and a wall notice about wireless connections, a Xerox laser printer, a high-end business chair, and a two-line phone; a small, efficient kitchen; and a living/sitting room with a fieldstone fireplace. McDill's Macintosh laptop was hooked to an Ethernet cable.

"No television," Virgil said.

"We've got a thing about that. If you want to watch television, you've got to come up to the theater at the lodge. But the basic idea here is you get away from TV and all that," Stanhope said.

"But you've got—"

"We found out that most of the people who come here want to get away from the absolute *crap*—TV—but a lot of them can't afford to completely isolate themselves. They're businesswomen and they need to stay in touch. You'll notice that your cell phone works here."

"I did," Virgil said.

"Because we've got a low-power repeater in the lodge, which goes to our antenna—it's out by the shop, you can't see it from here—that is line-of-sight to a cell out on the highway," Stanhope said. "So we're all hooked up, we have all the conveniences, but you can't see it. We're looking for *feel* that's a little more rustic."

Virgil dropped into an easy chair and pointed her at the couch next to it. "I've got some questions that you can probably answer. . . ."

McDILL HADN'T BEEN seen the night before, but that wasn't unusual, Stanhope said. Some of the women put in strenuous days on the lake, and with a lot of sun, many of them were pooped by the end of the day and went to bed early. Others went into town, and to a bar called the Wild Goose. So exactly who was where, and when, was not an easy thing to pin down.

"To tell you the truth, I didn't even know that nobody saw her last night, until we were talking about it this morning," Stanhope said.

"Was she pretty social?"

"Oh, I'd say . . . average. A little more aggressive about it when she was being social. She liked to dominate the talk, but there are other women up here who are no cream puffs. So, I'd say, she fit in."

McDill did like to go to the Wild Goose.

"Was she gay?"

"Mmm-hmm," Stanhope said, nodding. "She was, but she really didn't come up here for romance. She has a life partner down in the Cities—she's been notified, she should be coming up—but Erica really came up here to get away. To think. To relax a little bit. She was one of the girls who sometimes drank too much. I mean, not crazy, but she wouldn't be your designated driver down to the Goose."

"I want you to believe that I don't have a problem with gay women," Virgil said, "but I've got to ask: as far as you know, was she involved in any kind of stressful sexual entanglement?"

Stanhope shook her head: "Not as far as I know."

"No kind of sexual competition with another woman up here?"

"I don't think so. She'd been up here for a week, she was going to be here for one more week. She was participating, yoga in the morning, nature hikes and boating in the morning and afternoon, but I didn't see her pairing off with anyone." She put her hands to her temples, pressing. "I can't figure it out. Believe me, if I had any idea of what happened, I would tell you in an instant. But I didn't see anything."

"Okay. Have you ever had anybody die here?"

She nodded. "Twice. One woman actually came here to die—she loved nature, she loved the place. It was in the fall, after we were pretty much closed down, and we'd wheel her out on the deck so she could see the lake. Then she died, from pancreatic cancer. We had another woman who had a heart attack, this was four or five years ago. We actually got her to the hospital alive, but she died there."

They talked for a few more minutes, but Stanhope seemed befuddled by the killing. Her confusion was genuine, Virgil thought: it was too muddled to be faked.

Last question: "Who was that checking out when I was coming in?"

"Dorothy Killian from Rochester," Stanhope said. "She was scheduled to leave. I don't think you'd be interested in her, but what do I know? She's seventy-four. She's on some kind of art board down in Rochester and they have a meeting tomorrow afternoon, so she had to go."

"Okay. Well, let me spend a few minutes here in the cabin, and then we'll need to lock it up again, until the crime-scene crew can go through it," Virgil said.

Stanhope stood up, sighed, and said, "What a tragedy. She was so young, and active. Smart."

"Well liked?"

Stanhope smiled and said, "Well, she was well liked by the kind of people who'd like her, if you know what I mean. She didn't take any prisoners. So, she put some people off. But anybody who's successful is going to get that."

VIRGIL SPENT TEN MINUTES in the cabin, giving it a quick but thorough going-over.

McDill had brought up two large suitcases. One was empty, with the clothing distributed between a closet and a chest of drawers. The other was still partly full—a plastic bag with dirty clothes, and other bags and cases with personal items, perfume, grooming equipment. None of the clothes, either clean or dirty, had paper in the pockets.

Her purse contained a thin wallet, with a bit more than eight hundred dollars in cash. A Wells Fargo envelope hidden in a concealed compartment had another three thousand. He went through the wallet paper: a new Minnesota fishing license, bought just before she came up to the lodge, insurance cards, frequent flyer card from Northwest, five credit cards—he made a note to check her balances, and her finances in general—a card from Mercedes-Benz for roadside emergency service, and membership cards from a bunch of art museums, including the Minneapolis Institute of Art, the Walker Art Center, the Museum of Modern Art and the Metropolitan Museum of Art in New York, the Norton Simon Museum in Pasadena, the Art Institute of Chicago.

An art lover.

Tucked in with the other cards, he found a folded-over paper, and when he opened it, a lipstick impression of a woman's lips . . . nothing else. He put the card on the dresser. Interesting.

She had a digital camera; he turned it on and paged through two dozen photos. Most were shots around the lake, but a half-dozen had been taken in a bar, women having a good time, getting loud, like women do when they're loose and safe in a group of friends.

He took the SD card: he'd read the card into his own computer. He put the camera back on the dresser, next to the card. Picked up her keys, including a big black electronic key with a Mercedes-Benz emblem, and dropped them in his pocket.

The computer was password protected. He tried a few easy workarounds, then decided to leave it to the crime-scene guys.

McDill's cell phone was sitting on the desk next to the computer. He brought it up and found three dozen calls made in the past week, the week she was at the lodge, mostly to one number in the Cities, a 612 area code, which was downtown Minneapolis—the agency?—and several others, both incoming and outgoing, to a separate number with a 952 area code.

He checked her driver's license. She lived in Edina, which would be right for 952, Virgil thought. So, home and office. He took out his pad and jotted down all the numbers she'd called while at the lodge, and all the incoming calls. Nothing local.

Thought about local and picked up the phone on the desk and got a dial tone. All right; she had a direct dial phone. He would have to get those calls from the phone company. . . .

After a last look-around, he wrote a quick note to crime scene, explaining the lipstick card and the cardless camera, and left it on the chest of drawers.

He wrote, *DNA on the lipstick? What do you think?*

4

VIRGIL WALKED BACK TO the lodge, nodding to a couple of women along the way, picked up his duffel bag, found Margery Stanhope, and asked, "Have you heard anything from Miss McDill's friends?"

"They called from the air. They decided to fly up, which wound up taking longer than driving would have."

"Maybe I'll see them at the airport?"

She shook her head. "No. One of the things that took so long is that they apparently had the impression that we're way deep in the woods. They got a floatplane out of St. Paul; they'll be coming straight into the lake."

Virgil looked out at the lake, which was not an especially large one, a couple of thousand acres at most, cluttered with islands. Pretty, but not exactly a landing strip. "You land floatplanes?"

"From time to time," she said. "It annoys people—one cranky old man in particular, who'll be calling me tonight and the county commissioners tomorrow."

"All right. Well, if I can find your accountant . . ."

"She's down at the shed—you get there through the parking lot."

"I saw it. Okay: I'll see you later. I'll want to talk to Miss McDill's friends," Virgil said.

"You find out anything?"

"Maybe," Virgil said, going for the enigmatic smile.

ZOE TULL WAS TALKING to a Latino man who'd been working on a gas-powered weed whip, which he'd disassembled on a workbench. She saw Virgil and waved, went back to talking to the Latino. Virgil fished McDill's keys out of his pocket, pushed the unlock button, and saw the lights flash on a silver SL550.

He popped the driver's-side door, squatted, and looked inside: car stuff, Kleenex, a cell phone charger plugged into the cigarette lighter, a bottle of Off!, a box of Band-Aids, breath mints, chewing gum, two lipsticks, an ATM receipt that showed a checking account balance of $23,241 at Wells Fargo, pens, pencils, a checkbook, a utility knife, an LED flashlight, two empty Diet Pepsi bottles, a sweater, a cotton jacket, an umbrella, a dozen business cards in a leather case.

He was thinking, *What a pile of shit,* when Zoe said over his shoulder, "She keeps her car pretty neat."

Virgil stood up, said, "I was hoping for a blackmail note. You all done?"

"Yes. Getting more numbers."

Virgil glanced over at the Latino, who'd gone back to working on the weed whip. "He illegal?"

"Would you arrest him if he was?" she asked.

Virgil laughed. "If I started arresting illegal Mexicans, I wouldn't have anyplace to eat."

"Well, he's not—I think Margery runs a few illegals in and out, paying them off the books, but since Julio's name was right out there, I wanted to get his green card number," Zoe said. "That way, the feds'll think we're on the up-and-up."

"I don't want to disillusion you, but the feds don't think *anybody* is on the up-and-up."

"And they wouldn't be wrong about that," she said. "I know a judge who deducted a wife and daughter as dependents for three years after the divorce and they moved to California."

"He do time?" Virgil asked.

"He never got caught," she said, adding, "He wasn't a client of mine. I heard about it from an accountant friend who was reviewing his returns. He was like, 'Well, I didn't know.' Idiot."

"Seems to be the excuse *du jour* when you've committed a major crime," Virgil said.

"My," she said, "he knows French."

ZOE DROVE A RED HONDA PILOT with a metal file box behind the driver's seat, and a clutter of empty water bottles and ice cream wrappers in the passenger-side foot well. She put the file folder in the metal box, snatched up the ice cream wrappers and bottles and threw them on the backseat, and they took off.

"So—who did it?" she asked. "Any ideas?"

"Some," he said. "But let's not talk about the murder—let's talk about you. Your life and your boyfriends, and all of that. Say, those are nice shoes. Are they Mephistos?"

She glanced at him, puzzled, and said, "What?"

"Just trying for a little friendly conversation," Virgil said. Sitting shoulder to shoulder with Zoe, he could smell a floral scent, light and vanilla-y.

"Virgil, are you on drugs? Is this something I should know about?"

"They're not Mephistos, are they?" She glanced at him again, then lifted her left foot off the floor so he could see the Nike logo. "I wouldn't know a Mephisto if one bit me on the ass," she said.

"Now *there's* a war crime for you," Virgil said.

She smiled and said, "Bob Sanders told me that you were sort of full of it."

"I'm shocked," Virgil said, the uninterest set deep in his tone. "*Shocked.*"

"You don't seem like somebody who would have perpetrated a massacre," she said.

"I didn't."

THEY'D GOTTEN TO THE END of the driveway, and when Virgil looked left, he saw the crime-scene van rolling toward them. He said, "Hold on for a second, will you? I want to see if these guys got anything else."

He hopped out of the car, and when the van driver saw him, he pulled off onto the shoulder of the road. Mapes climbed out of the passenger seat carrying a small plastic bag, which he handed to Virgil. Virgil held it up to the sky, to get some light on it.

"A .223," he said. The shell's brass was still bright.

"Hasn't been there long—I could still smell the powder burn," Mapes said. "It was caught in some logs, a couple inches above the water. The shooter couldn't have looked for it long—it was right there."

"Off to the right? Like it was thrown out by an autoloader?"

"Ah, yes—off to the right, but the extraction marks look like they came from a bolt action. I'm sending Jim"—he jabbed his thumb back toward the truck—"back to Bemidji with it, see what we can see. The other guys are still working the beaver lodge."

"Good going, man."

"Well, it was right there—even you could have found it," Mapes said. Pause. "Maybe."

Virgil handed him McDill's car keys and said, "I knew you were going to insult me, so I carefully contaminated the car. See if you can find something anyway."

VIRGIL GOT BACK in the Pilot and told Zoe about the shell. "Now all I have to do is find a rifle and some Mephistos, and we've got it."

"You'll be able to tell the rifle from just one shell?"

"Not me, the lab. But, yup. Extraction marks. And if we're lucky, she pushed the cartridge down in a magazine with her thumb, and there'll be a big ol' thumbprint. Brass takes good prints."

"Mmm. Well, I for one have no Mephistos," she said. "Why'd you ask?"

"Because the woman who killed Erica McDill may be local—she knew exactly when and how to get into the pond to catch McDill alone. And she may wear Mephistos."

"You thought I did it?"

"You've been sort of hanging around. A psychopath might do that," Virgil said.

"I've been hanging around because I'm curious," she said. "Also, I'm not a psychopath. I'm an obsessive-compulsive."

"That's what a psychopath would say," Virgil said. "The case of the curious accountant—a woman for whom blood was just another cocktail."

She brushed the chatter away, as though it were a fly. "You know for sure it's a woman?"

"Pretty sure," he said.

"And local."

"Possibly. You could make a good argument that it comes from the lodge, too," Virgil said. "Would you like to suggest a name or two?"

"No, no. But it makes you think," Zoe said.

"It *does* make you think," Virgil agreed.

After a moment, she asked, "Should you be telling me all of this?"

"Why not?" Virgil asked. "I've got nothing to hide."

"Well, God. What if I blabbed to everybody?"

Virgil yawned, tipped his seat back a couple of inches, leaned back, and closed his eyes. "Go ahead," he said. "I don't care."

AT THE AIRPORT, Zoe pointed him at a metal building; inside, he found a guy with a pilot's hat half asleep on a couch, who got groggily to his feet and asked, "You the state trooper?"

"Close enough," Virgil said. He rented a Chevy Trailblazer, got his duffel from Zoe's car, and threw it in the back of the SUV.

"How come you don't have a gun?" she asked, through her open car door. "Aren't cops required to carry guns? I read that somewhere."

"In my experience, bad things can happen if you carry a handgun," Virgil said. "For one thing, it causes your shoulder to slope in the direction of the pocket you carry it in. Over the years, that could cause spinal problems."

"I can't tell whether this is some hopeless attempt to be charming, or if you're just being weird," she said.

"Can you tell me where the Wild Goose is? I want to take a quick look."

"Well, follow me. I'll take you over," Zoe said. "It's mostly a women's bar. You might feel a little odd being there by yourself. Lonely."

*

THE WILD GOOSE was a mile or so north of the Grand Rapids city limits, a standard North Woods country bar—orange-stained peeled-pine logs set on a rectangular concrete-block foundation, a pea-gravel parking lot, a tin chimney, a low wooden porch outside the front door, and a carved wooden upright black bear guarding the front door, an American flag in its paw.

There were four other cars in the front lot, and two more that Virgil could see around the side. Probably the bartender's and the cook's, around to the side—at most country bars, the employees tried to park where their cars wouldn't get hit by drunks.

Inside, the bar was a little softer than most, with lots of booths and only a few freestanding tables, four stools at the bar, and a small stage on the other side of a dance floor; a jukebox. Three of the booths were occupied by women, two in one, three in another, four in the third. One of the bar stools was occupied by an elderly man who was peering into a half-empty beer glass.

They stopped at the bar, and Zoe said, "Hey, Chuck," to the bartender, who took a long look at Virgil, not unfriendly, and Zoe ordered a beer and Virgil got a Diet Coke. Zoe asked, eyebrows up, "Little problem with alcohol?"

"No, I just don't drink much," Virgil said.

The old man at the bar said to Virgil, "If you gotta ask, it's half empty. Not half full."

"Looks more like four-fifths empty to me, partner," Virgil said.

The drinks came, and they carried them to a booth. Virgil checked out the women, and the bar in general, saw the bartender watching.

"What do you think?" Zoe asked.

"It's a bar," he said, smiling. "Must pick up at night—mostly people from Eagle Point?"

"Eagle Nest."

"Right, Eagle Nest. Mostly women from the Eagle Nest? Or half-and-half with locals, or . . ."

"More locals than Eagle Nest. It's just that if you're at the Eagle Nest and you want to get out, you probably come here."

"Gay or straight?"

"Gay or straight," Zoe said. "Same with locals—mostly women, gay and straight. They can come down here, do some serious drinking, and not have to put up with being hit on, or pushed around. Chuck keeps all that runnin' smooth. Most local guys know that this isn't where they want to go."

"You come down here?"

"Sure. Like I said, it's safe and friendly," she said.

A woman came in the door wearing cutoff jean shorts, a tight halter top, cowboy boots and a cowboy hat, and sunglasses. She was short, but well rounded, with dark hair twisted in a single braid. She had an Andy Warhol "Marilyn" tattoo on one tanned shoulder. She looked around once, scratched herself between her breasts, wandered over to the bar, and asked, "Seen Wendy?"

"Not in yet."

"Ah, man—we were supposed to meet down at the Schoolhouse," the woman said. She glanced over at Virgil and Zoe, her gaze lingering on Virgil for a moment, then flicking to Zoe, and her mouth turned down. The two women stared at each other for a moment, then the other woman turned back to the bartender. "We're working up 'Lover Do.' If you see her, tell her we're down there, waiting."

Virgil watched her go, and when she was gone, Zoe leaned forward and said, "She's a drummer."

"My type, too," Virgil said.

"Not your type," she said. "She lives with the lead singer."

"Yeah? Maybe they're breaking up," Virgil said, hitting on the Diet Coke. "Musicians lead tumultuous lives."

"The lead singer is Wendy—it's an all-girl band," Zoe said.

Ah, he thought. "Okay."

"You're supposed to say, 'What a terrible waste.'"

"Hey, I'm sophisticated—I went to college," Virgil said. "Anyway, the way you sounded, it's not being wasted."

"Ahhh, poop." Zoe finished her beer in a gulp.

"Ahhh poop, what?" Virgil asked.

"Ahhh . . ." She wiped her lips with the back of her hand. "Wendy. The singer."

"She's pretty good?"

"Very good. Country, some crossover jazz stuff," Zoe said. "Mostly country, though, Dixie Chicks."

"*Really* not my type, then, even if she wasn't gay," Virgil said. "Give me a choice between listening to a whole Dixie Chicks album, or sticking a gun in my ear, I'd have to think about it."

"Well, she's my type," Zoe said. "And that's my big problem."

Virgil looked at her for a few seconds, then dropped his forehead on his arms. "No."

"Well, it was gonna come out sooner or later, Virgil," Zoe said, laughing. "We're getting friendly, but I don't want you to get any ideas."

"Poop," he said.

He looked toward the bar and saw the bartender smiling and shaking his head, then hold up a finger, pull another Diet Coke, and bring it around the bar. "On the house," he said, when he put it on the table.

"Coulda put a little rum in it," Virgil said.

VIRGIL SAID TO ZOE, "You know, I can usually pick up on it? I apologize if I've offended you along the way."

"No, no, you were fine," Zoe said, "and I've had boyfriends. Maybe that's why you didn't feel it. But I . . . like women better. Always did and I finally admitted it to myself. I can still be attracted to some men. I mean, you're attractive in an obvious, superficial way. When I'm attracted to a guy at all, they usually have strong feminine characteristics. Like you, with the long blond hair, and you've got sort of a delicate face."

Virgil said, "Okay—you've guaranteed my shrink's income for another two years."

"You've got a psychiatrist? I think that's very interesting. It shows an unexpected psychological sensitivity."

"I don't really have one," Virgil said. "I was lying."

"Really?"

"Yeah. I lie a lot," he said.

46

She said, "Sorry about this. I mean, the lesbian thing. I didn't mean to lead you on, if I did."

"That's okay. The band doesn't have a straight saxophone player, does it?"

HE GOT HER LAUGHING AGAIN, then asked, "Why don't Minnesota women wear makeup? There are ten women in here, and a couple of them are pretty good-looking, including you, and none of you wear lipstick. Is it some kind of Minnesota thing? An efficiency thing? An egalitarian thing? What is it?"

"Not many people wear lipstick anymore," Zoe said. "It's a pain to keep it looking good. You wind up chewing it off. But . . . people will put on a touch when they go out."

"Even gay women?"

"Not so much, maybe," she said. "But . . . some. The girly ones."

He thought about that for a moment, then said, "Ah, man. Well, I've got to get back and talk to Erica McDill's friends from the Cities. I thank you for the tour. Maybe I'll come back tonight, take a look at the band. See if I can figure out your type."

"Wendy . . . Whatever. She's a slut. But she turns my crank. If I had a crank."

Virgil laughed and asked, "Why don't you pay for the drinks?"

OUTSIDE IN THE PARKING LOT, she walked with him to the Trailblazer and asked, "You really don't care if I tell some friends about this? About . . . that a woman did it?"

He shrugged. "No, go ahead. Something to talk about. Better than the Internet. But be careful about who you talk to—we *are* dealing with a nutcase."

THE CRIME-SCENE CREW was eating dinner at the Eagle Nest, and Mapes said, "We think she braced the rifle across a four-inch log. Looks like she moved the log for that reason—to get a rifle rest. There were a couple of other logs she might have braced her hands or her arms on, and we've bagged all that and we'll look for prints and DNA. Haven't found any hair, but we did find some cotton fibers that may have come from her shirt. No more shells, so there might have been only the one shot."

"Any possibility that more might have gotten thrown into the water?" Virgil asked.

"We checked with a metal detector. Never got a flicker," Mapes said.

"So it's basically prints or DNA and the Mephistos," Virgil said.

"I wouldn't count on prints—I took a long look at that cartridge, and it looked clean and a little oily. I should have been able to see a print. But, maybe not. Maybe the lab will bring something up. And I've got to believe that if she came through that swamp, and knew what she was doing, she was wearing gloves. It's not so bad out in the open, but coming over the margins of the marsh, the mosquitoes were so thick they were clogging up our head nets. If she knew what she was doing, she would have covered up. Gloves, maybe even a head net."

He left them to finish eating and went looking for Stanhope. A woman Virgil hadn't met was turning off lights in the office. She said, "She took them up to the library."

"Uh, who . . . ?"

"The people from the Cities. Miss McDill's friends."

LAWRENCE HARCOURT, whose name was on the agency, was a slender man with close-cropped white hair, quick blue eyes behind military-style gunmetal glasses, and a face that seemed oddly unlined for his apparent age—a face-lift? The second and third of McDill's friends, Barney Mann, creative director for the agency, and Ruth Davies, McDill's partner, always called him Lawrence, never Larry, and though neither deferred to him, they always listened carefully when he spoke.

Mann was a fireplug of a man with a liquor-reddened face and blond hair going white; he had an Australian accent. Virgil thought he might be forty-five. He was noisy and argumentative and angry.

Davies was stunned: not weeping, but disoriented, almost not-believing. A short, not-quite-dumpy woman with brown hair and wire-rimmed glasses, she looked like a church mouse. Her mouth was a thin, tight line: whoever had given McDill the lipstick note, it hadn't been Davies.

All three, Virgil thought, after the introductions had been made and some questions answered, were intensely self-centered. They were not so concerned about the existential aspects of McDill's death, but rather, *what it means to me*. They had also been concerned with image, Virgil thought, to the point of silliness. They could have driven up from the Twin Cities, individually, in three hours. Instead, they'd rented a floatplane, apparently to demonstrate the urgency of the matter, and after soaking up time in arranging the flight, and getting together, and making the flight, they'd taken six or seven hours.

Harcourt had checked Virgil quickly, eyes narrowing a bit, and he asked, "Have you had any experience with this kind of investigation?"

"Yes," Virgil said.

"He's the one who killed the Vietnamese," Stanhope told them.

They all looked again, and Mann asked, "Do you have any ideas about how it happened? About who did it?"

Virgil opened his mouth to answer, and Davies broke in. "I just want to *see* her. What if there's been a mistake?"

"She's been identified by people who knew her," Virgil said, as kindly as he could. "The photograph on Erica McDill's driver's license is a picture of the woman who was killed."

"I still . . ." she began, and she turned in a circle, and Stanhope patted her on the shoulder.

Mann: "You said you have some ideas . . ."

"It seems to me after some investigation that the killer is a woman who knows how to handle a rifle and knew the territory. Could be local, or could be an outsider, a guest at the lodge. If I knew *why*, I'd be closer to a complete answer."

Mann rubbed his nose and then looked at Harcourt and said, "That's not what I expected to hear."

Harcourt nodded, and Virgil asked, "What'd you expect?"

He shrugged: "That it came like a bolt out of the blue and nobody had any idea. If that were the case, I could probably give you the why."

Virgil spread his hands. "I'm all ears."

Mann said, "Lawrence told me on the way up that he and Erica had agreed that she would buy his stock in the agency. That would have given her about three-quarters of the outstanding stock, and total control. Ever since Erica took over, she's been agitating to make the agency more . . . efficient."

"She wanted to fire people," Harcourt said. "As many as twenty-five or thirty. A lot of them have been with the agency for a long time. They've been protected by the board. Erica had the authority to fire them, as CEO, but then her actions could be reviewed by the board, and there are a number of people on the board who already didn't like her. There would've been a fight—"

"What did you think about the firings?" Virgil asked him.

Harcourt stepped back and sat in one of the library chairs and crossed his legs. Virgil noticed that even though he was wearing jeans and ankle boots, he was also wearing over-the-calf dress socks. He said, "I was generally against them—I could see a couple of them, but no reason for a top-to-bottom housecleaning."

"But you were gonna sell?"

Harcourt sighed, and looked around the room at all the faded old books. "I kept the stock in the first place because the agency pays a nice dividend. But I'm seventy-one and I've got a bad ticker. I need to get my estate in order," he said. "The thing about an ad agency is, its property is mostly intellectual. It's a group of talents, a collection of clients. We don't really own a damn thing, except some tables and chairs. We even lease our computers. So, if I passed the stock down to my children, and Erica got pissed, she might just cherry-pick the talent and start her own agency, and my kids would get screwed. They'd get nothing. But bolting would be a big risk for Erica, too. Big start-up costs, diminished client list. She'd be much better off keeping things as they are. All of that gave me an incentive to sell, and Erica an incentive to buy. We made a deal a couple of weeks ago. We never closed on it."

Mann said, "The point being, there are about thirty scared people down in the Cities who think they might lose their jobs. Some of them have worked at the place for twenty-five or thirty years. They'd have no place to go. Too old. Burned out. Some of them, or one of them, might have . . . you know . . . killed her to stop that. That was my first thought, when I heard she'd been killed."

"Would killing McDill actually stop the firings?" Virgil asked.

Mann scratched his head. "I don't know. For a while, probably. I don't know who gets her stock, now. Her parents are still alive, I think. . . ."

"They are," Davies said. "I won't get a thing. Not a thing."

"She didn't leave you anything in her will?" Mann asked her.

"I don't think she had a will," Davies said. "She was pretty sure she'd live forever."

"She had a will somewhere," Harcourt said. "She was too . . . not calculating, but rational . . . not to have a will."

"Oh, for Christ's sakes, Lawrence, the woman was calculating," Mann snapped. To Virgil: "They called her the SST at the office. Stainless Steel Twat."

Virgil asked Mann, with a smile, "So . . . were you on the list? To be fired?"

"Oh, fuck no," Mann said. "She went out of her way to let me know that."

"Barney runs our major accounts and they're pretty happy with him. If *he* were to leave, he might take some of them with him," Harcourt said. He added, "I had reason to believe that Erica was planning to offer him a partnership. Or a share."

Mann cocked his head. "Really? Well, that's a shot in the ass."

Virgil threw his hands up. "So? What happens now? With the agency?"

Mann and Harcourt looked at each other, then Mann turned back and said, "I don't know."

Harcourt said to Mann, "We need to make arrangements here

51

and get back to the Cities. We need a board meeting. Immediately. We have to have a new management in place by Monday, before the clients start calling."

"What's going to happen to me?" Davies asked. "What's going to happen?"

Again, Harcourt and Mann looked at each other. Neither one said, "I don't know," but Virgil could see it in their faces; and so could Davies.

VIRGIL GOT OUT his notebook and jotted down a few thoughts, then talked to Harcourt, Mann, and Davies individually. Harcourt and Mann both said that they'd been in the Cities the day before, and gave Virgil a list of people they'd seen during the day. Unless one of them was telling a desperate lie, the alibis would eliminate them as the killer, because the Cities were simply too far away to get back and forth easily.

Davies, on the other hand, had no alibi. She'd been sick the morning before, she said, and when she finally got out of bed, it was almost noon. She went grocery shopping at a chain supermarket where they'd be unlikely to remember having seen her. Still feeling logy— "I think I ate something bad"—she'd spent the day cleaning, watching a movie on DVD, and then had gone to bed early, with a book. Neither a DVD nor a book would leave an electronic trace.

She picked up on the direction of the questioning and protested, "I wouldn't ever do anything to hurt Erica—I love Erica. She was the love of my life. We've been together for six years. . . . I don't know anything about guns. I've never been here. I didn't even know exactly where it was. . . ."

"Did you or Erica have outside relationships? Was your relationship, uh, an open relationship?"

"No. No, it wasn't open," she said. "I mean, back at the beginning, we both were dating other people simultaneously, if you see what I mean . . ."

"I know what you mean," Virgil said.

". . . but once I moved in, we were committed."

Virgil nodded. "Okay. I believe you when you say you wouldn't want to hurt Erica, but I had to ask—you know, if there had been another person, if there was a sexual tension, if she'd started pulling away from the other person, to stay with you."

"Why wouldn't the other person have shot me?" Davies said. "Why would you shoot the one you want?"

"Because you shoot the one who rejects you," Virgil said. "Hell hath no fury . . ."

Davies slumped. "Oh, God. You know, there might have been one fling. She might have had one relationship, but she broke it off a year ago."

"With who?"

She shrugged. "I don't know. I was afraid to ask. I was afraid if I asked, it would precipitate something. Instead, I just went out of my way to . . . attach myself more firmly."

"You must at least suspect a person, a name . . ."

She said, "Look. I only suspect a relationship. I'm not even sure there was one. It could have been a bad time at work. We didn't talk about her work. She didn't want to. Our relationship was her way of getting away from work. So it's possible that what I thought was a distracting relationship was actually something else. So, no. I don't have a name. Or a suspect."

SHE LOOKED SO TIRED and beat-up that Virgil let her go. Mann and Harcourt had gone with Margery Stanhope to call the funeral home, to see if the body had already been shipped to the medical examiner at Ramsey County, or if further arrangements had to be made. Virgil lingered down the hall from Stanhope's office until he saw Mann emerge, turn away, and head toward the front of the lodge. He caught him just as Mann stepped into the bar.

"Mr. Mann . . ."

Mann looked back over his shoulder, then nodded to the bar. "I need a drink."

At the bar, the bartender looked at him and said, "Sir, this bar is basically ladies only—"

"Just give me a goddamn drink, honey," Mann said.

"Sir—" Still apologetic.

Mann cut her off: "I came up here to take care of Erica McDill. If you don't give me a drink, I'll sue you for discrimination in so many different directions that you'll be an old woman before you get out of court. A martini, a double, two olives, and I want to see you make it and I don't want to see you spit in it, because then I'd have to throw you out the fuckin' window."

"Relax," Virgil said. The bartender, anger on her face, stepped away, picked up a shaker, and scooped up some ice.

"Relax, my ass. As soon as I get a couple drinks under my belt, I'm gonna go rent a car, and me and Harcourt are headed back to the Cities," Mann said. "What a waste of time. What are we doing up here? We need to be down *there*."

"You'll take Miss Davies with you?"

"Yeah, I guess, if she wants to go," Mann said. He watched as the bartender finished making the drink. "But she's sort of a prune."

The bartender pushed the martini across the bar and said, "Choke on it, motherfucker."

Mann grinned at her, then at Virgil, said, "They got a tough brand of bartender up here." He sipped the drink. "Make a pretty good martini, though." He'd put a ten on the bar, and the bartender slapped five dollars back in change. He pushed it into the bar gutter as a tip.

The bartender, a bottle-redhead with dark-penciled eyebrows, with a name tag that said *Kara*, looked at the money, then at Virgil, and said, "You're the police officer. People said it was the surfer-looking guy."

"Yes," Virgil said.

Mann looked him over and said, "You *are* sort of surfer-looking."

"Cute, for a cop," the bartender said, softening a bit on Mann.

"He *is* cute," Mann said. "I'd fuck him myself, if I were gay."

"Guys," Virgil said. "Shut up."

The bartender looked at him for a beat, then another, then made a tiny dip of her head toward the back of the bar, and wandered away. Mann had been concentrating on his drink, said, "What a day."

"When you're on the way back, and I expect either Miss Davies or Mr. Harcourt will be driving, because you'll have done this drinking . . ."

Mann grinned again and said, "You're an optimist, son."

". . . so when you're on the way back, make up a list of the people who would have been fired. Especially the ones who'd be most bitter, and the women."

"You really think a woman did it?"

"At this point, it's the best bet," Virgil said. "Though I take you seriously about those people down at the agency. I've been thinking about it, and looking at Google Earth, and the maps, and the fact that people down at the agency knew where Erica was going, and when, and she probably talked about what she did up here. I've recalculated. It might be fifty-fifty on whether the killer was from up here or down there."

"You think?" Mann sucked the life out of an olive, then popped it into his mouth.

"Which brings me to ask, who did McDill have that affair with, last year? Ended about a year ago. Somebody at the agency?"

There was about one long suck of alcohol left in the martini glass, and Mann paused with the rim of the glass an inch from his lip, stared straight ahead for a minute, thinking, then turned to Virgil and said, "So . . . Ruth knew about it, huh?"

Wasn't a guess: he'd figured out where Virgil had gotten the information. Smart guy. "She did," Virgil said. "But she doesn't know who it was."

"Abby Sexton, editor at a specialty home-furnishings magazine down in the Cities," Mann said. "She never worked at the agency, but her husband does."

"Her husband. Okay. Was he gonna get fired?"

"That's possible. The word was, Erica would have left Ruth for Abby, but Abby sort of blew her off. Had her little fling, went back to Mark, and promptly got pregnant. Erica was *really* hosed about the pregnancy. That was one thing that Erica couldn't have given Abby. Anyway, Mark's an account guy. He's okay, not great. Firing him would have been a nice little piece of revenge, what with them having the new kid. Magazines don't pay enough to feed a canary."

Kara the bartender was at the far end of the bar, and Mann held up another finger. She rolled her eyes and started putting together another drink.

Virgil took out his notebook, wrote *Abby Sexton* in it, asked, "What magazine was that?"

Mann said, "*Craftsman Ceramics*, something like that. They specialize in Arts and Crafts tile and pottery and so on."

"You're a smart guy," Virgil said. "What else should I know?"

"I don't know. The Abby thing hadn't occurred to me, because I don't think like a cop. But I do take this hard, this murder. If I think of anything, I'll call you."

Virgil nodded and said, "Thanks—and I'll give you a call tomorrow morning about that list. If you could get me a phone number for Abby Sexton, that'd be a bonus." He caught the eye of the bartender, drifted out of the bar, turned left, and walked down toward the restrooms.

THE BARTENDER pushed through the back door a moment later, stepped close, and said, "You could lose me this job, and there aren't any more jobs like it. Not around here. So, I'd appreciate it if . . . you know."

Virgil nodded. He was like the Associated Press—lots of sources, all anonymous.

"I saw you with Zoe, getting in her car," Kara said. "You know she's gay?"

"Yeah."

"Well, the thing is, I like her fine—I'm straight, by the way—but I thought you should know that Zoe has had two short, mmm, involvements, with a girl named Wendy Ashbach, who's a country singer down in Grand Rapids."

"Sings at the Wild Goose," Virgil said.

She nodded. "Zoe told you? Anyway, Wendy has this longtime girlfriend named Berni Kelly . . ."

"The drummer?"

"Yes. You know, you're smarter than you look, picking up all this stuff."

"Thanks, I guess," Virgil said. "So there's a love triangle with Zoe and Berni and Wendy."

"Up until night before last," Kara said. "Then it became a rectangle. Or a pentagon."

"Yeah?"

"There were some women in here late, getting loaded. My deal is, I stay until they leave. So I got out of here late and walked down to my car when I saw Miz McDill's car pull into the parking lot. They didn't see me, I was down at the far end of the lot, where the employees park. Miz McDill and Wendy Ashbach get out of the car and walk around to the end of it, and Miz McDill throws a lip-lock on Wendy and Wendy gives it right back to her. So they're fooling around for a minute, which made me kinda hot, I gotta admit, and then they go sneaking off through the dark, toward Miz McDill's cabin. I don't know what happened the next morning, or if they snuck out early, or what."

"You didn't mention this to anyone?" Virgil asked.

"No, but if somebody saw them the next morning, the word would have gotten around," Kara said. "A lot of the lesbos know Wendy, and they know she's hot and likes girls, and if McDill got her in the sack, everybody would have been interested."

"Huh."

"That's *exactly* what I thought. *Huh*." She glanced down the hall. "I gotta go . . ."

"Listen, Kara . . . don't tell anybody about this. There's a crazy woman around here and you don't want to attract her attention."

"No shit, Sherlock," she said. "My last name's Larsen. I'm in the Grand Rapids phone book. If you need to ask me any more questions, call me. Don't talk to me here."

VIRGIL FOUND MARGERY STANHOPE in the main office, alone, staring out the window at the darkening lake. She turned in the chair when Virgil stepped in and asked, "Figured it out?"

"Not yet. Margery: if you knew anything at all that might put some light on this thing—or even if something unusual happened with Miss McDill in the last day or two, behavior-wise, you'd be sure and tell me, right?"

She said, "Something happened. What happened? Why did you ask that?"

"I'm wondering who spent the night in McDill's cabin, night before last, and why nobody's telling me about it," Virgil said.

Stanhope sat up straight: "Night before last? I know *nothing* about that. I don't spy on people—but I should have heard. I *would* have heard, if it were true."

"You don't think it's true? I've got it on pretty good authority."

She said, "Let me go talk to people. I'll find out."

"Do that," Virgil said. "Let me give you my cell phone number. Call me anytime."

5

NINE O'CLOCK, AND VIRGIL rolled out of the resort into the dark, called Zoe Tull. She answered, and he picked up a soft Norah Jones–style sound behind her. "You going to the Wild Goose tonight?" he asked.

"I could, but . . . I usually stay away on nights when Wendy is singing. She likes to come over and pull on my tits. If you know the expression."

"I don't, actually. I mean, I've pulled on a few tits, both human and bovine, but I've—"

"She comes over and chats, like she thinks there's no problem and we're still good friends, and she pushes Berni in my face," Zoe said.

"Berni's the drummer? The one with the cowboy boots and the nice whachacallums."

"Yeah. She calls herself Raven. Like the Edge, or Slash."

"Well, if they come over, you could come slide in the booth next to me and put your hand on my thigh," Virgil said.

"I don't think that'd mean anything to her," Zoe said.

"Mean a lot to me, though," Virgil said. "I miss the woman's touch."

After a moment of silence, she laughed long, and said, "I really like that crude shitkicker side of you. All right. I'll take you to the Goose."

"Good. I've got a question I need to ask you," Virgil said.

"Can't ask on the telephone?"

"Cell phones are radios," Virgil said. "You never know who's listening."

"That's paranoid," she said. "But . . . I wouldn't mind going. Pick me up at the house, or meet me there?"

"Since there's no chance I can get you drunk and take advantage of you, I'll meet you there," Virgil said. "Be quicker, and I'm going south tonight."

"The Cities?"

Virgil nodded at his reflection in the windshield. "Yeah."

"I thought you'd be up here for the duration," Zoe said.

"I need to get some stuff—I'll be back tomorrow."

"Fifteen minutes," she said. "Wait for me in the parking lot if you get there first. We can go in together."

He stuck the phone back in his pocket, caught the yellow-white-diamond eyeblink in the ditch at the last possible moment, and stood on the brakes. A doe wandered into the headlights, stopped directly in front of the truck, fifteen feet away, and looked at him, then hopped off toward the other side of the road.

He waited, and another doe, and then a third, crossed in front of him, like ladies going first through the supermarket door. When he thought the last of them had crossed, he eased forward again, keeping watch: saw a half-dozen more deer in the ditches, but had no more close calls.

HE WAITED FIVE MINUTES for Zoe. She pulled in, hopped out of her Pilot, came across the parking lot wearing a frilly white low-cut blouse that showed her figure, tight jeans that showed the rest of her figure, and fancy dress cowboy boots made out of the skins of chicken testicles, or some such, with embossed red roses.

"Nice boots," Virgil said into her cleavage.

"My eyes are up here," she said.

"Yeah, yeah," he said, as they crossed the parking lot to the door. "I've only heard that line in about eight movies."

"What's your favorite movie?"

He paused at the door, thought, and then said, "That's too important a question to settle on the front porch of a bar."

"You don't have to defend your choice—just name it," Zoe said.

"*The Big Lebowski*," Virgil said. "The dude abides."

"I was afraid of something like that," she said.

"I could've said *Slap Shot*," Virgil said.

"Ah, Jesus. Let's go drink." Inside the door, she said, "If you'd said, *Hannah and Her Sisters*, you might've got laid tonight."

"I was gonna say that," Virgil said. "Honest to God."

"I was lying," she said. "I lie a lot. Like you."

THE BAND WAS ON, singing a Dixie Chicks song which, like all the other Dixie Chicks songs, Virgil didn't like. Not so much that he didn't like them, it was just that they affected him like the Vulcan nerve pinch, and caused him to crumple to the ground and drool. They got the last booth and Virgil checked the crowd—probably fifty women and eight or ten men—and then the singer.

Wendy was a fleshy blond beauty in the Janis Joplin mold—not crystal-pretty, like the blondes big in Nashville, but stronger, with breasts that moved in their own directions when she turned, over a narrow waist and long legs. She was wearing a deliberately fruity cowgirl suit, a white leather blouse and skirt with leather fringes, and cowboy boots like Zoe's. And lipstick: she had a large mouth, with wide lips, coated with deep red lipstick that glistened in the bandstand lights. Here was the source of the kiss-card that he'd found in McDill's cabin, Virgil thought.

She could sing. Again, not the currently popular Nashville

crystal-soprano, but a throwback to the whiskey-voiced singers of an older generation. Virgil actually listened to the song, although the words themselves threatened to lower his IQ. When she finished, Wendy said, in the whiskey voice, "One more song this set, for those of you who like to dance, a little old northern Minnesota slow-waltz, 'The Artists' Waltz.' I wrote it myself and I hope you like it."

Virgil did: like it.

A dozen couples, all women, danced to the music, as Chuck turned the rheostat and the lights dimmed, a real slow-waltz and terrifically romantic. Virgil listened all the way through, alternately watching Wendy, and then watching Zoe, whose face was fixed on Wendy's, and whose hands were clenched on the table, the knuckles white. She *had* lied to him, Virgil thought. Even if he'd said, *Hannah and Her Sisters*, he wouldn't have gotten laid, because the girl was already in love.

Wendy finished and said, "We're gonna take fifteen minutes, back to you then with another hour of the finest Wild Goose music. Thank you . . ."

THE SOUND LEVEL DROPPED, and Zoe, halfway through her beer, leaned forward and asked, "What's the question you couldn't put on the cell phone?"

Virgil shook his head. He almost didn't want to ask it, now that he'd seen her reaction to Wendy. On the other hand, unasked questions didn't often solve murders.

"Look," he said, "I was watching you watching Wendy, and I didn't realize how attached you were. Are. Whatever."

"I'm not attached. We're all done," Zoe said.

"If she'd take you back, would you go?" Virgil asked.

She said, "No," but her hands were doing their twist again. Virgil shook his head, and she said, "All right—yes."

"That's better," Virgil said. "You're really a horseshit liar."

"What does that have to do with the question?"

Looking right in her eyes, Virgil asked, "Did you know Wendy spent the night before last with Erica McDill, at her cabin at the Eagle's Lair?"

61

"Eagle Nest, and I don't believe you," Zoe said. She was looking straight back at him, and he felt that she was telling the truth. Then she said, "Why would you try to tell me something like that? Are you trying to get me to spread the lie around?"

Virgil opened his mouth to answer, when Wendy dropped in the booth next to Virgil, her thigh against his. She looked across the table at Zoe, said, "Hey, babe," and then at Virgil, then back to Zoe, and asked, "Who's the hunny-bunny?"

"He's the cop investigating the murder at the lodge," Zoe said.

Wendy tensed just a hair; Virgil saw and felt it.

Zoe added, "He's the guy who massacred all the Vietnamese up at International Falls. He looks like a surfer boy, but he's a stone killer."

"Hey," Virgil said. "I . . ."

The drummer, Berni/Raven, came up on Zoe's side of the table, looking first at Wendy, then at Zoe, and said, "I thought you might be over here."

Wendy tossed her hair back, like Marilyn Monroe might have done, and said, "Oh, God, don't be evil."

"I know, you're just punkin' me," the drummer said. She was dressed in black jeans, with a sleeveless black jean jacket over nothing, and heavy dark eye shadow. The name *Raven* was stitched into the front of the jacket. She looked down at Zoe: "Wish you'd find a friend. He ain't it, is he?" she said, looking at Virgil.

"He's a cop," Wendy said. "Asking questions about the murder."

Berni said, "So ask me a question."

Virgil shrugged. "Where were you at eight o'clock last night?"

"Eight o'clock. Mmm, lying in bed, rubbing myself, thinking about Wendy," she said. She checked Virgil to see if he was embarrassed. He wasn't. He did think, *No alibi*.

"Do me," Wendy said. "Give me a question."

Zoe blurted, "Don't do it."

"Do what?" Wendy asked, but Virgil was looking into Wendy's eyes now, and saw that she knew. So he asked.

"I need to know what Erica McDill said to you night before last. Whether she said anything that might have to do with the murder."

"She didn't see Erica McDill the night before last," Berni said. "She had to run over to Duluth. . . ."

THEY ALL STOPPED TALKING. Zoe was staring at Wendy, who looked from Virgil to Berni and back to Virgil. Berni was focused on Wendy, saw the truth on her face, shouted, "You bitch," pulled back her fist, and plugged Wendy in the left eye.

Virgil wasn't moving fast enough; saw the punch coming and started to move, but the punch was already coming and landed with a solid thwack, and some tiny backward part of his brain thought, *Good punch*.

Wendy rocked back, her skull bouncing off the back of the booth, her mouth twisting, and then she came out of the booth in a hurricane of fingernails and teeth and the two women surged together and then went straight down to the floor, punching and screaming.

That answered one of Virgil's questions: the drummer hadn't known.

ZOE WAS SCREAMING at Virgil, "Stop them, stop them."

Virgil was reluctant. In his experience, when women break down the social barriers so far that they begin physically tearing at each other, they are dangerous. Men learn social fighting as children; the posturing, the dominance routines, the punch in the nose, the threats to "get you someday," and everybody goes home satisfied. Women don't learn any of that: when they fight, they'll rip the gizzard out of anyone who gets in the way.

But something had to be done. The women in the room were surging around like a lynch mob in a movie, as Chuck the bartender's head bounced through them like a fishing bobber on a windy day. Virgil reached into the whirlwind of twisting flesh and grabbed a cowboy boot and yanked Berni out of the pileup.

Wendy came crawling after her, blood on her face. Berni tried to kick Virgil, and her boot started to come off, and Virgil grabbed her other boot; then Chuck grabbed one of Wendy's boots and instead of trying to kick him, she did a pure abdominals sit-up, which put her within range, and she slashed him across the forehead with her fingernails. Chuck stumbled back but held on to the boot, and Wendy went with him. Berni was trying to kick Virgil again, so he twisted her feet once, and she flipped over onto her stomach and he put a knee in the middle of her back and pinned her, like a turtle: legs and arms still flailing, but the body was going nowhere.

The mass of women now got between the two fighters, and Berni was yelling, "Let me up, you motherfucker," and Virgil could hear Wendy screaming. A bunch of women were looking at Virgil and he said, "Could you help? Please? Hold on to her. Don't hurt her, just tangle her up."

So they piled on, and the women closer to Wendy saw what they were doing, and they piled onto Wendy, which freed up Chuck, who staggered to the bar and pressed a wet towel to his bloody forehead.

Zoe shouted over the crowd, "Good going."

Virgil wasn't sure how to take that, and shrugged.

"We leaving?" she asked.

"She never answered the question," Virgil shouted back.

Zoe elbowed her way to his side. "Now might not be the best time," she said.

"Fuck her," Virgil said.

Both the fighters were on their feet again, but pressed away from each other by the crowd of women, and, as in other bar fights that Virgil had witnessed, everybody seemed to be enjoying themselves, other than the two or three horrified liberals.

Virgil pushed his way through to Wendy and said, "Back of the bar. Back of the bar." He gave her a shove, and when a drunk woman brayed, "Who the hell do you think you are?" he snarled, "I'm a cop. If you don't want to get handcuffed to the bumper of my car, you best get the *fuck* out of my way."

She stepped back; she wasn't *that* drunk.

CHUCK PUT THEM in the storeroom, which was full of beer cases and a few kegs. Virgil stacked three sets of two cases. Wendy had a bruise under her eye and was dabbing blood from one corner of her mouth; her lower lip was protruding a bit, from a tooth cut. Virgil said to Wendy and Zoe, "Sit," and they sat on the beer cases, and he went back into the bar and got a couple of clean towels, wrapped fist-sized lumps of ice in them. Berni was still in a swirl of women, who were looking at a fingernail gash on her forehead. She'd started to cry, and was telling her tale of infidelity.

In the back room again, Virgil gave the ice packs to Wendy and said, "On your lip and on your eye, for half an hour. Won't be too bad in the morning."

"Not the first black eye I've had, probably won't be the last," Wendy said.

"So. You spent some time at Erica McDill's cabin the night before last. Were you sexually involved?"

She grinned at him, and he realized that she really wasn't much shaken by the fight. "Sure. What'd you think we were doing, playing Pinocchio?"

Zoe said, "That'd be pinochle."

Wendy shrugged. "Whatever."

"Where were you yesterday afternoon, between six and eight?"

"At the Schoolhouse, working up a song," Wendy said. "For most of it, anyway. There was some coming and going. Out to get a sandwich, and stuff."

Zoe: "The Schoolhouse is a recording studio."

Virgil nodded. "How many of you?"

"Me, the keyboards, a guy from the college who's an arranger, an engineer, our manager, uh, a pizza guy came and chatted for a while . . . might have been one or two more."

"So, quite a few, and I could check your story," Virgil said.

"Sure. Listen, I didn't hurt Erica. I mean, she was gonna set my career on fire," Wendy said. "She knew everything about advertising and promotion. She was going to take me to Nashville, or Austin, or someplace. She knew people."

"You were sleeping with her because she knew people?" Zoe asked.

"Well, yeah," Wendy said. "Duh."

Virgil said, "That's nothing personal against you, Zoe."

Zoe said, "No, no, that makes perfect sense to me."

"Someplace along the line, you gave her a souvenir of the night, right?" Virgil asked.

Wendy went blank. "What souvenir?"

"A little kiss mark?"

"You mean, a hickey?"

Virgil said, "A lipstick kiss on a card?"

She shook her head. "No. Nothing like that." She pulled the ice pack away from her face and looked at it; there was a little bloodstain where it had been pressing against her mouth, but not much. Her face was red from the cold.

"You didn't make a lipstick impression on a card?" Virgil asked.

"No . . . you found one?"

"In her purse. I assumed it was you," Virgil said. "I mean, if it was you, there's no reason to deny it—nothing wrong with it," Virgil said.

"Yeah, but . . . I didn't do it," Wendy said.

"Huh." Virgil thought she was lying—there was a feral quickness about her eyes—but didn't know why she would. Maybe because she could? They all thought about it a minute, and then Virgil asked, "She didn't mention any other relationships?"

"She said she had a woman in the Cities, but that relationship was all but over," Wendy said. "She said she'd already decided to get out, but she wanted to let the other person down easy. She was going to give her some money. I mean, Erica had a lot of money. She was talking about putting together a syndicate to sponsor me. She said that in three years, I could be making a million bucks a month."

"Ah, girl," Zoe said.

"You've got no idea of what might've happened to her?" Virgil asked.

"I really don't. It freaked me out," Wendy said. "I was kind of hoping that nobody knew about us, that she hadn't mentioned it to anybody. I mean, you know, me going with her had nothing to do with her getting killed, but it looks bad."

★

THE DOOR CREAKED OPEN, and Berni peeked in. She squeaked, "Wendy?"

Wendy stared at her for a minute, then grinned and said, "How're you doing?" and she strode over and they wrapped each other up, and they both started crying, and Wendy was stroking Berni's hair, saying, "It's all right, it's all right . . ."

OUTSIDE, Virgil looked up at the stars; bright and cool, full night now.

Zoe said, "Well, that worked out really well. I thought they were gonna go for it, right there on the floor."

"Got me a little hot when they started kissing each other," Virgil said. Zoe put her fists on her hips and he held up his hands and said, "Joke, joke. Jesus."

"I'm gonna go home and cry," Zoe said.

"I'm heading south," Virgil said.

"Good night for driving."

Virgil put his arm across her shoulders. "Get a few beers or a little weed, listen to some LeAnn Rimes. You'll be okay."

"That a promise?"

"Well . . ." He thought about his three ex-wives. "No. But LeAnn's always good."

6

ZOE PUTTERED AROUND THE house, waiting—did the few dishes that she'd left in the sink that morning, vacuumed in the living room, cleaned up the guest bathroom, put out a hand towel. She was neat, tidy—an accountant even in her household chores. The only place she wasn't an accountant, she thought ruefully, was in her sex life. If she could write off Wendy, life would be easier. Take her as a loss, depreciate her, call her a toxic asset, and unload her at twenty cents on the dollar . . .

And she thought about Virgil. Virgil was good-looking, in the way she liked men to be—shoulders and arms, big hands, small butt, long hair, cheerful. But that, she thought, was misleading. His attitude and appearance were natural enough. It's what you got with a good-looking small-town jock who'd grown up with an intact family and enough, but not too much, money. There was nothing faked about his attitude—but beneath the attitude, she thought, there was something cool, watchful, calculating. Hard, maybe.

An emotional accountant, with brass knuckles.

She smiled at the thought; and the doorbell rang. She glanced at the mantel clock: eleven o'clock, right on the dot. She popped the door and said, "Hi. Come on in."

Margery Stanhope stepped in, let her shoulders slump, and said, "This day . . ."

"Something, huh? You want a margarita?"

"Yes, I do. Make it a large one," Stanhope said.

"Did you hear about the fight?" Zoe asked, as she led the way to the kitchen.

"The fight?" Stanhope tossed her purse on the kitchen table.

"At the Goose . . . Wendy and Berni got into it."

Zoe put the margaritas together—a couple ounces of Hacienda del Cristero Blanco, a bit of Cointreau, lime juice; she wetted the rims of the glasses with the lime juice, spilled some salt on the countertop, rolled the rims in it, shook everything with ice, doing it proper—and got Stanhope laughing about the fight.

". . . we left them standing there, and she had her tongue so far down Berni's throat, Berni's lucky to be alive . . ."

"Oh, dear; I know how you feel about her," Stanhope said.

"Yeah." Zoe handed Stanhope her glass: "Luck."

Stanhope said, "Luck," and took a sip and said, "Make a damn good margarita . . ."

They went and sat in the living room and Stanhope said, "So. Virgil."

"He's going to catch whoever did it," Zoe said.

"You think it'll be a guest?" Stanhope asked.

"We've got to hope not—if it is, it'll all come out, about the gays and so on. You know what the TV stations will do with it."

"I keep thinking about Constance. Should I have told Virgil?"

"If there's any other indication that the killer's a guest, we probably have to. If we don't . . ." Zoe shrugged. ". . . I don't know. *We* might be in trouble."

"I'm not sure how many people know, other than us," Stanhope said.

"Some people do. I'm pretty amazed that Virgil hasn't heard yet—some of Wendy's band members must know. Wendy does, for sure," Zoe said.

"But that makes it look like the band is involved," Stanhope said. "They wouldn't want that."

"And *we* think it makes it look like the lodge is involved, and *we* don't want *that*."

They sipped at their drinks for a minute, thinking, and then Zoe sighed and said, "If nothing comes up, I'll probably tell him when he gets back. I'll just tell him that we don't know anything about it, but it was another murder, and she did stay up here. . . ."

"Mention the band," Stanhope said. "The more he looks at the band, as the cause, then the less it looks like the lodge."

"Mmmm."

"So what *I* want to know," Stanhope said, "is *your* position, if it does involve the lodge."

"I'm ninety-five percent go-ahead," Zoe said. "It'd have to be really awful before I'd back out. I'm already moving money, I'm talking to Wells Fargo about a loan, and they're telling me it's no problem. I'll continue the accounting business—I'll move Mary up to partner, and let her run the office—while I set up the lodge."

"Gonna have a lot of balls in the air," Stanhope said.

"What else have I got to do? I've got no life," Zoe said.

"Somebody'll come along," Stanhope said.

"Maybe I ought to jump in bed with Virgil," Zoe said. "It'd never work out, but maybe I could have a baby before it blew up."

"There's an idea," Stanhope said, her tone dry as sandpaper. "A lodge *and* an accounting business *and* a baby *and* no husband to help out . . ."

"Ah, I'm not going to jump in bed with Virgil," Zoe said.

THEY SAT for another minute, then Stanhope said, "Look me in the eye and tell me you didn't have anything to do with McDill getting shot."

"Margery!"

"Well . . . I wouldn't tell. But you've got this thing about Wendy, and I guess some people at the lodge knew Wendy stayed over with Erica the night before she was shot," Stanhope said. "You could've heard, and I know you can shoot, because I've seen you do it."

"I didn't shoot Erica McDill," Zoe said.

"And you didn't have anything to do with Constance . . ."

"No! God! Margery!"

"I'm sorry. I believe you. Even if I didn't . . . I'd let it go. You're a good person, Zoe."

"I was down at the U that weekend, with some friends. I didn't even know Constance was dead until I got back up here."

"I'm sorry," Stanhope said again. "I just . . ." She rubbed her forehead. "This whole thing . . ."

She held up her glass, looking through the cut glass at the ceiling light, and asked, "You got another one of these?"

WENDY ASHBACH had a new forty-two-inch LCD television and Blu-ray DVD player and she and Berni were halfway through *Pretty Woman* when her father banged on the trailer door and pulled it open and asked, "Whatcha doing?"

"Movie," Wendy said, through a mouthful of microwave popcorn. Wendy was lying on the couch, with Berni sitting on the floor, her back to the couch. Her father came in, uninvited, waved at his daughter's legs. Wendy pulled her knees up to make a space at the other end of the couch, and Slibe Ashbach dropped into the opening.

"What's this shit?" he asked, looking at the TV.

"Richard Gere and Julia Roberts," Wendy said.

"Oh, yeah." He stared at it for a minute, then asked, "Doesn't she blow him or something?"

"You don't see anything," Wendy said. She reached out with the remote and paused the movie. "So what's up with you?"

"Tell me about the cop," Ashbach said.

"I only talked to him for five minutes," Wendy said. "He's a cop."

"What's he think?"

"He doesn't know what he thinks. Some people think the murder was because McDill was taking over her advertising agency and might fire people; some think it was because of a gay thing at the Eagle Nest, a sex thing. And he wanted to know if it was because of me. I told him it wasn't, and gave him my alibi, and he said he'd check it; which is okay with me."

Ashbach looked closely at them, at the scratches on Berni's forehead, and Wendy's bruised eye socket, and asked, "What happened to you guys?"

"Me and Berni got in a fistfight down at the Goose," Wendy said.

"She slept with McDill, night before last. Night before she got killed," Berni said.

"What? Does the cop know?"

"Yeah, he asked me about it, with Berni standing there. That's what set her off," Wendy said. "She hit me right in the eye, before I had a chance to say a thing."

"Witch. I'm gonna have nightmares, about you and McDill," Berni said.

"He's talking to Zoe Tull," Wendy said. "They're hanging out."

"Did you mention Constance Lifry?" Ashbach asked.

"No way," Wendy said. "Let him find out for himself."

Ashbach looked at the two of them for a minute, then said, "You didn't say a word."

Wendy rolled her eyes: "Dad, we're not talking to him. Okay? We said we weren't, and we're not."

"But you both lie like motherfuckers," he said.

Berni leaned toward him and asked, "Gee, what's a motherfucker lie like, Mr. Ashbach?"

Wendy said, "This doesn't have anything to do with us. Lifry was up at the Eagle Nest, like McDill. Another gay murder, if it comes to that."

"Another gay murder of somebody who was talking about helping the band, which is pretty fuckin' weird, if you ask me," Berni said.

"I'll tell you what, you little bitch, talking like that . . . your goddamn alligator mouth could get your butterfly ass in trouble," Ashbach said.

"Is that right?" Berni asked, staring him down. "I'll tell you what, SA, we just hope the fuck that *you* didn't have anything to do with those murders. You or the Deuce."

"Dad, take off, okay?" Wendy said. "Get out of here."

"Watch your mouths," Ashbach said. He jabbed a finger at Berni. "Watch your mouths." He gave them a last look, turned, and headed out, letting the door slam behind him.

When he was gone, Berni said to Wendy, "I hope to fuck *you* didn't have anything to do with McDill."

Wendy shook her head: "I'm cool," she said.

"Okay. I'm not so sure about Slibe Two, though," Berni said. "Every time I look at the Deuce, I get the feeling that somebody smacked him on the side of the head with a coal shovel. He ain't right."

"He wouldn't hurt anybody," Wendy said about her brother. "He's . . . you have to understand him. He's out there."

"Watches me. All the time. Creeps me out," Berni said. "I wonder what would happen if I showed him my tits?"

"Don't do that," Wendy said.

"Don't worry—I won't." Berni shivered. "He'd probably go off like a bottle rocket. I wonder if he touches himself?"

Wendy snorted, then said, "You gotta be careful about the way you talk to Dad. You piss him off, he might throw your ass out of here."

SLIBE II WAS SITTING outside the back window, listening, and thrilled to the fact that they were talking about him. And he *had* seen Berni's tits, lots of times.

He had a concrete block that he put down at the end of the trailer, and if he stood on it, he could just get one eye overlapping the screen window. He'd gone in the trailer while they weren't there and bent one blade of the venetian blind, to help things along, and now he spent his evenings with them, watching and listening.

Berni liked to run around with her shirt open, and sometimes— well, once—without her pants. If he'd missed that . . . he didn't like to think about it. That was the best thing that had ever happened to him in his entire life. Better than finding his old man's stash of *Hustler*.

He didn't know what he'd do for company in the winter, though, and had started worrying about it. Couldn't use his concrete block— they'd see his foot tracks in the snow and figure it out.

Maybe something good would happen; there was time before the snow started.

And they were *talking* about him.

7

SUNDAY MORNING, getting up.

Virgil could always wring a few more hours out of a night if he had to. With four hours in bed, he could make it through the next day, and since most investigations happened during the daylight hours, when other people were available for interviews, the night was available for travel and introspection; and retrospection, as far as that went.

Virgil left the Wild Goose a little after ten o'clock at night, pulled into his garage in Mankato a few minutes before three o'clock in the morning. He set his alarm for eight, thought about God for a few minutes, and what place McDill's death might have in His Great Scheme—nothing much, he decided—and went to sleep.

The next morning, he was up before the alarm, threw his clothes in the washing machine, opened the mail, wrote some checks for the bills, moved his clothes to the dryer, and went out to drop the mail, to get breakfast at a Caribou Coffee, to return the rented truck to Avis, and to catch a cab back.

He got a *Star Tribune* outside the coffee shop. The McDill story was on the front page, above the fold, with a two-column headline and a photograph. Nothing on the murder, except that it happened, and a few details. The rest was biography and expressions of shock from parents, friends, and business and political associates.

He had his clothes folded and put away, his working clothes packed, and was on the road in his own truck, pulling his own boat, by nine-thirty. He had taken down Barney Mann's cell phone number the day before, and on the way out of town, headed toward the Cities, rang it. Mann answered on the third ring and Virgil asked, "Had your meeting yet?"

"It's at one o'clock," Mann said. He sounded tired. "I'm just getting up and I'm hungover. . . . Are you coming to the meeting?"

"I don't know—am I invited?"

"I couldn't speak for the board, but I can tell you, the meeting's in the agency's main presentation room," Mann said. "I can tell them that you invited yourself."

"Give me the address—I'll see you there. I'd like to get that address and phone number for Mark and Abby Sexton."

Mann chuckled: "Boy, I'll bet they'll be happy to hear from *you*. 'Tell me, Mr. and Mrs. Sexton, was there anything about Mrs. Sexton's venture into muff-diving that might have elicited this response?' Like one of those intellectual BBC cop shows, huh?"

"You got the number?" Virgil asked.

"Getting my book now," Mann said. "You know what? You gotta loosen up. You strike me as tense."

Virgil called the Sexton number as he was coming into the Cities. Abby Sexton answered the phone and said, "We read about it at breakfast. This is awful. But why would you want to talk to us?"

"I'm filling in as much background on Miss McDill as I can. I understand the two of you had a relationship that ended badly."

"Oh, God, are people still talking about that? Well, come on ahead . . ."

The Sextons lived in a big brown-shingled bungalow on a narrow lot, with a garage in back accessed from an alley, in the St. Anthony neighborhood, a nicer residential area of old homes north and east of the Minneapolis downtown. The porch had a swing; a strip garden in front of the porch was divided between flowers on one side, and vegetables on the other, including eggplant. Virgil hated eggplant, even chicken-fried eggplant, and took this as a sign of the Sextons' decadence.

He clumped up the stairs to the front door and rang the doorbell. Abby Sexton's blue eyes popped up behind the cut-glass diamond in the door, and she pulled it open and asked, "Virgil?"

She was a dishwater blonde, slender and athletic and pretty, wearing a white long-sleeved blouse with the sleeves pushed up, khaki capri pants, and sandals. Her husband came up behind her as she invited Virgil in: he was a dishwater blond, slender, athletic, and pretty, wearing a blue shirt that vibrated with his blue eyes, and khaki surfer shorts and sandals. He was eating an apple and shook hands with his free hand, and said, "Come on in—should we have our lawyer here?"

Virgil said, "This is more of an interview than an interrogation. I can't tell you not to get a lawyer, so . . ."

"We'll trust you, at least for now," Abby said with a toothy smile. "I might have to run and get the baby now and again. He's in his pen right now, not making a peep."

They arranged themselves in the front room, Pottery Barn couches and overstuffed chairs with a scattering of antiques and new Stickley-style oak tables and bookcases. Abby Sexton put a plastic box on the table and said, "It's an intercom, so we can hear if the baby cries."

Virgil didn't quite know how to open the conversation, with Mark Sexton sitting there, and said, "I don't know exactly how to get into this . . . ?"

"If you're worried about Mark, he knows all about it. He knew about it at the time," Abby Sexton said.

Mark Sexton nodded; he didn't seem put off.

"All right," Virgil said. He still felt uncomfortable—this wasn't exactly a country-western scenario. "I've interviewed a number of people, and it's been suggested that the murder may have originated here in the Cities. That Miss McDill was about to get full control of the agency, and that she planned to fire a number of people. I've been told that Mark might have been one of them, not because of job performance but as revenge for . . . the unpleasantness at the end of your relationship."

"We didn't know that she'd gotten control of the agency," Mark Sexton said. "I read that in the paper this morning, and called up some other people. One guy had heard rumors, but most of us were clueless. I don't think I would have been fired anyway, because I'm pretty on top of the job. But who knows?"

"Who heard the rumors?" Virgil asked.

The two glanced at each other, then Mark shrugged and said, "Barney Mann. He's the creative director for the agency. He's sort of the information central."

"What was Mr. Mann's attitude toward Miss McDill?" Virgil asked.

"They got along," Mark Sexton said. "Barney's really good at what he does. So was Erica, in a way. She wasn't any threat to him."

"Like Hitler," Abby Sexton said. "Good at what she does, if you don't mind working with a Nazi."

"But you had a relationship with her," Virgil said.

"That was sex," Abby Sexton said. "Even a Nazi can be good in bed." Mark Sexton smiled indulgently at his wife. Like Ward Cleaver finding out that June had just dropped an oatmeal cookie on the good carpet, Virgil thought.

He said, "Huh." Virgil didn't like either one of them, and struggled to hide it. "When you and Miss McDill broke up, was there any kind of an aftermath? Did she come around to see you? Were there any threats? Or scenes?"

"Phone calls. But it was typical breaking-up kind of stuff," Abby Sexton said, wrinkling her nose. "The problem was, she didn't want to share. I mean, *she* wanted to stay with Ruth while we went out—you know about Ruth?—but she didn't want me with Mark. But I like men and told her I was going to stay with Mark. So then I suggested that we share Mark, that we three get together. But she wasn't into that. She'd be happy enough to share a man, but not an employee, if you can believe that."

"Huh. So she wasn't strictly gay?"

"Not strictly—technically a bi, I guess, like Mark and me," she said.

He digested that for a moment, then smiled at them, apologetically, and asked, "Where were you the evening before last? Here in the Cities?"

"We got a babysitter, Sandra Oduchenko, who lives down the street, and she came at seven o'clock, and we went out clubbing with some friends," Abby Sexton said. "We are completely alibied, up to our necks. That's why we didn't call a lawyer. Do you want everybody's names?"

Virgil took the names down, and then asked, "Who do you think did it?"

Abby Sexton rolled her eyes up and took a deep breath. Her husband deferred to her, and she said, "We definitely think it's possible that it was somebody with the agency. If we had to take a guess—you're not going to tell anybody that we said this, right?—we'd say Ronald Owen."

Ronald Owen, she said, was in his late fifties and for the past five or ten years, had slipped from being one of the top account managers to being something less than that: the guy who got small stuff, and who no longer did much with it.

"He burned out," Mark Sexton chipped in. "But he's got kids and alimony and a second wife and he can't afford to quit. The other thing is, he's one of those veteran guys you see around—he was in Vietnam toward the end of the war, and all of that. He's bitter about the way everything turned out. He's also got good sources, so I suspect he knew about McDill taking over. And he hunts. Every year. People kid him about it, but he goes off and shoots antelope in

Montana, and deer in Wisconsin. He's really into guns. He's always talking about how the rest of us don't know about real life. He says we get life from Whole Foods. He calls us Whole Foodies."

They had another suggestion, a John Yao, "An Asian, who's always creeping around. He runs some Asian business accounts, local stuff, Hmong businesses. He's another gun guy. I get a really bad feeling from him," Mark said. They had nothing specific about Yao—no suggestion that he was about to get fired, except that his accounts were "ratshit stuff. Small, insignificant. McDill might have decided to get rid of them."

VIRGIL BROUGHT THE TALK BACK to the Sexton-McDill relationship. "From what you knew of her, was she sexually predatory? When she was with you, was she drifting away from Ruth, and looking for another long-term relationship? Or was she really going out on the town?"

"Mmm. She definitely didn't like me leaving—but I think her relationship with Ruth was about done. And I knew that our relationship wouldn't have lasted, and she was smart enough to know that, too."

"Might there have been another relationship after you? Somebody that Ruth didn't know about?"

She shook her head: "I don't know. I'd tell you, but I don't know."

"If she did," Mark said, "it wasn't with anyone associated with the agency. Word would have gotten around—there are no secrets in that place."

VIRGIL ASKED a few more questions, but basically had written them off as suspects: their alibis would be too easy to check, so he doubted that they'd be lying. He ran out of follow-up questions, asked them for any last thoughts, and stood up.

As he did, the baby started crying, its voice squeaking out through the intercom.

"You're up," Abby Sexton said to her husband, and he hurried off. "We try to split the baby chores exactly fifty-fifty," she said.

She trailed Virgil to the door, and as he went out, he said, "Listen, thank you for your help, and I may get back to you."

She stepped a foot too close and put a hand on his triceps and said, "Do you do any clubbing? Here in the Cities? I notice you're not wearing a wedding ring."

"I'm, uh, mostly down south of the Cities," Virgil said, edging away.

"Well, give us a call if you're in town," she said. "We enjoy creative relationships."

He bobbed his head and hastened away. *Creative relationships, my ass.* He *really* didn't like them—and he really didn't think they were involved in the murder of Erica McDill.

Ruth Davies? That was a more interesting proposition. . . .

Virgil glanced back. Abby Sexton was still on her porch, and she waved.

He waved back, and was gone; and thought to himself, as he turned the corner, *Do not* imagine Mark Sexton naked in bed.

NOON. He called Mann from his truck and asked, "How long is that meeting going to last?"

"I don't know, but it'll be a while. People are freaking out. Everybody'll want to talk for eight minutes, so that'll be an hour and a half of bullshit before we get to the hard stuff."

"Do you have a number and address for a Ronald Owen?" Virgil asked.

"Sure. What does Ron have to do with this?"

"Don't know. I want to ask him," Virgil said.

"That fuckin' Sexton pointed you at him," Mann said. Not a question. "That little weasel. Listen, I'll vouch for Ron, if that means anything."

"What about John Yao?"

"Jesus. Pointed you right at the two non-yuppie fucks in the office," Mann said.

"Would McDill have fired them?"

After a minute of silence, Mann said, "Ron, probably. She didn't like him and he didn't like her back. John Yao, probably not. He's got good connections in the Asian community here, and they do a surprising amount of business with us in one way or another."

"Mark Sexton said that his accounts didn't amount to anything," Virgil said.

"That's because Mark's a dumbass," Mann said. "None of John's accounts are huge and they don't do TV or glamour stuff—it's all business-to-business work—but taken all together, they bring a nice lump of change."

"So Yao was safe, but Owen, probably not," Virgil said.

"Yes. And Erica and John get along," Mann said. "Don't know why—chemistry or something. They got along."

"What's Owen's address?" Virgil asked.

"I feel like a rat giving you all of this," Mann said.

"I'd get it anyway," Virgil said. "If Owen didn't do it, might as well clear him out."

OWEN LIVED TWENTY MILES northeast of Minneapolis, in rural Grant Township. Virgil headed that way, got a buzz on his cell phone, looked at it: Davenport.

"Yeah?"

"You still in Grand Rapids?"

"No. I'm in North St. Paul, headed out toward Mahtomedi, talking to a guy who didn't like McDill." Virgil filled him in on what he'd learned, and what he planned to do the rest of the morning, before heading north again.

"Stacy and her crew started processing McDill's house last night," Davenport said. "They should be out there for the rest of the day. Her father's there, you might want to check in."

"That's in Edina, right?" He'd written McDill's address in his notebook; either Edina or Eagan.

"Yes. Her girlfriend got back last night and made a fuss, but that's straightened out now," Davenport said. "What's the story on the girlfriend?"

"Still thinking about her," Virgil said.

"Okay. Stay in touch."

OWEN'S HOUSE SAT at the crest of a hill. A fifties-era ranch-style, the house had a later wing stuck on one end, with a garage and a shop building in back, on what Virgil thought might be ten acres. At the top of the gravel driveway, Virgil saw a man in jeans and a T-shirt watching him from the edge of a stand of sweet corn in a sprawling hillside garden. *Owen*, he thought.

He parked beside a Chevy pickup, got out, looked around—the whole country smelled like fresh-cut hay and dry gravel—then walked up to the front door. The inner door was open, and he knocked on the screen door. He could hear music playing inside, but couldn't identify it. A fiftyish brown-haired woman came to the door, wiping her hands on a towel, and peered through the screen. She smiled and asked, "Can I help you?"

"I'm with the Bureau of Criminal Apprehension," Virgil said. "Is Mr. Owen around?"

"Oh, boy," she said, the smile sliding away. "Is this about Erica?"

"Yup. I'm interviewing people from the agency," Virgil said.

"All of them, or some of them?"

"Several of them, anyway," Virgil said. "I just came from talking to Mark Sexton."

"That little shit," she said. "He probably told you that Ron did it."

"No, he didn't—but . . ." Virgil scratched at the screen. "I really need to talk to Mr. Owen. You're welcome to listen in, if you want. I'll tell you that Barney Mann says that Mr. Owen had nothing to do with Miss McDill's death."

"He's right—well, I do want to listen in." She pushed through the door and said, "C'mon. He's out in the garden."

OWEN WAS SHUCKING the last of the summer's sweet corn. He was wearing Oshkosh overalls and a T-shirt, a self-conscious hobby farmer. He nodded when Virgil and the woman walked up, and asked, "Police?"

Virgil identified himself, and the woman said, "The Sextons."

"That figures," Owen said. He asked Virgil, "You want some

sweet corn? We've got too much for the two of us, and not enough to freeze."

"I'd take a few," Virgil said. The corn smelled sweet and hot in the light breeze playing through the plot; but it was a shade too yellow, and might be a little tough. Good, though. He said, "You know what I'm doing. Were you here in the Cities night before last?"

Owen nodded. "Yeah. I worked until six at the agency, then came home." He named a few people who'd seen him working late. "I wouldn't have killed her anyway. I wouldn't kill anybody, for any reason."

Virgil nodded. "The Sextons said you hunt. Whoever killed Miss McDill was good with a rifle."

"How did it happen, exactly?" Owen asked. Virgil told him, and Owen said, "Sounds local, to me. You can look at all the Google Earth you want, and it won't tell you about wandering around in the North Woods. And one shot, right between the eyes?"

"Yeah."

"The thing about that is, it was either an accident, or maybe there was another shot that you don't know about, and she looked at it, and caught the second one . . . or the guy's crazy," Owen said, shucking the green leaves off another ear of corn. He exposed a corn worm, cutting down through the kernels, snapped off the worm-eaten end, dropped it, and crushed it with a boot. "Why would you take a high-risk shot like that, when her whole heart-lung area was right there?"

"Don't know," Virgil said. The question hadn't occurred to him. "Maybe she was an amateur, and thought the head was the natural place to aim."

"She?"

"We think the shooter might have been a woman," Virgil said.

"So you really didn't think it was me?" Owen asked.

"Nope. But everybody said you didn't like her, that she might be planning to fire you, so I had to check," he said. He glanced at the woman and said, "I mean, maybe your wife shot her."

The woman said, "I don't even kill mice. I take them outside and let them go."

"And you were here the night before last?"

"I was at work until five, at Highland Junior High," she said. "I'm a teacher. I had after-school volleyball."

Virgil smiled: "I thought it was local, myself. . . ."

To Owen: "If you had to pick out one woman, that you know of, who was most likely to shoot McDill, who'd you say?"

Owen thought for a couple of seconds, scanning Virgil's face, and then said, "Jean."

"Who's Jean?"

"That's me," the woman said. "I really didn't like that bitch."

They talked for a few more minutes: Owen didn't know anybody at the agency, he said, who'd kill McDill.

"It's some backwoods redneck antigay thing," he said. "I'll bet you a hundred bucks that some backwoods guy did it. I was watching a football game once, at Palachek's up in Milaca, and somebody said something about one of the quarterbacks being gay, and this redneck guy said, 'I'd kill a queer,' and he meant it."

"Wonder if he'd think the same about a lesbian?" Virgil asked.

"Why would a lesbian be different?"

"Lesbian's not a threat to a straight guy," Virgil said. "Some straight guys have fantasies about lesbians."

Jean checked him: "Sounds like you have personal experience in that area."

VIRGIL ASKED, "It's been suggested that I might check into the whereabouts of a John Yao. Do you know . . . ?"

"John? John wouldn't hurt a rabid rat. The Sextons suggested him, right? Those fucks . . ."

VIRGIL LEFT with a brown paper bag full of sweet corn and cucumbers.

Why the head shot? Maybe a personal passion, and the killer wanted to mutilate McDill's face? That happened in male homosexual murders of passion, but he wasn't sure about females. Owen was right, though. The head shot had made the killing harder, and no more certain. Something to think about.

Did he have fantasies about lesbians? He considered the proposition and decided that he did not. He had fantasies about women; he'd never considered the lesbian angle. Maybe he'd give it a try, the next time he needed a fantasy.

VIRGIL LEFT the Owens's place behind, headed back into the core of the Cities. First to McDill's house, then to the board meeting, to see what that might produce. He should put more pressure on Davies, he thought, to see if he could squeeze something out of her; and talk to the crime-scene crew working on McDill's house.

He'd just gotten back inside the I-694 loop when he took a call from the duty officer at BCA headquarters in St. Paul. "You know a woman named Zoe Tull, up in Grand Rapids?"

"Yeah—what happened?"

"I don't know if anything happened. But she called and said she needs to talk to you, and it's urgent. Actually, she said, 'kinda urgent.'"

VIRGIL PUNCHED in Zoe's number and she answered on the second ring, fast for a cell phone. "Virgil?"

"What happened?"

"Somebody was in my house last night, while I was in bed," she said.

"Ah, jeez—why?" He had an image in his mind's eye, a killer at night in a dark house. "Why do you think there was somebody in the house?"

"I couldn't sleep last night. I lay awake forever, thinking about everything," Zoe said. "After that fight, my brain was going around in circles. Then, really late—two o'clock—I thought I heard something. In the kitchen. Or maybe, in the office. So I sat up and I turned on the light, and then I got up, and I couldn't see anything, because it was so dark in the rest of the house, so I yelled, 'Hello, I've got a gun.' After a minute, I didn't hear anything, so I peeked out and I saw the cat in the hallway, and I thought it was the cat, and I walked through the house, and didn't see anybody. Then this morning, the back door was open, maybe a quarter inch. I didn't even see that it was open until I went out. I mean, I reached out to open it, and it opened as soon as I touched it. It won't even close now, because they broke the wood around that hole-thing where the lock goes in."

"The strike plate."

"Whatever. I looked at it, and somebody had pried it. They broke some of the wood around the lock."

"Did you call the cops?" Virgil asked.

"Yes. I told them the whole thing, about how I'd been talking to you, and they said the door definitely had been pried, but they couldn't tell when," she said. "They didn't do anything, though. They said I should get better locks. They said I should tell you."

"Okay. Get better locks. Is there anyplace else you can stay overnight? A motel . . ."

"I could stay with my sister if I had to," Zoe said. "Her husband is out of town."

"Go to your sister's," Virgil said. "The crime-scene crew is probably still there, so I'll have them look at your back door. Did the cops screw around with it, looking at it?"

"No, no. I don't think they touched it," she said. "They looked at it pretty close, though."

"All right. I'm going to give the crime-scene guys your number, and they'll call you, and talk to you about it," Virgil said. "Don't touch the door again. Go to your sister's until you get the locks changed."

"Okay."

"What kind of gun do you have?" Virgil asked.

"I don't have a gun. I've got a baseball bat. Also, I've got one of those Wave radios and a CD of a Doberman barking," she said. "But I forgot about the bat and the CD last night. I'm such a twit."

"Get the locks. Go to your sister's. I'm coming back up this afternoon. I'll call you when I get there," Virgil said.

HE CALLED MAPES, with the crime-scene crew, and had them send a guy to Zoe's. Called Zoe back and told him the guy was coming. Next he checked with the medical examiner: "We got all the usual stuff, Virgil, and I can tell you she wasn't drunk or doped up, to any significant extent. There's a messy entry wound in her forehead, which I guess you saw . . ."

"Yeah . . ."

"I'm calling that a .223. Won't know for sure unless you find a slug, but we can see the rim of the impact hole, and judging from the damage it did, it sure looks like a high-powered .22 of some kind—.223 would be the best bet, could be an old .222. I don't think it's one of the small hyperspeed ones. . . . I'm going with .223."

"Thank you."

Independent confirmation. The .223 was one of the more popular shooter's guns in the state, the same caliber used in current military assault rifles, low recoil, relatively cheap ammo, very accurate in the right gun. All he had to do was find the gun; preferably with attached fingerprints and a map of the murder scene.

And he thought: If the killer had broken into Zoe's house, then the killer was local, from Grand Rapids; she would have to have been hooked into a local gossip network to know that Zoe had been talking to Virgil.

ERICA McDILL HAD LIVED in an area of million-dollar homes with quiet suburban streets, big yards, tall trees, and swimming pool fences in the backyards, where the backyards were visible. McDill's home was a low, flat-roofed midcentury place, showing steel beams and glass, ugly, but probably architecturally significant, Virgil thought. The driveway wound around back and ended at a four-car garage. A guy named Lane, from the crime-scene crew, let him in: the house had been professionally decorated, from the carpets to the ceiling paint.

Ruth Davies was there with McDill's father, sitting on the floor in the living room, surrounded by twenty square feet of paper.

He took Davies first, and got nothing. She simply dithered, until it began to drive him crazy, and eventually she went into the kitchen and began baking something with peanut butter.

McDill's father, Oren McDill, looking down at all the paper that summed his daughter's life, was distraught, depressed, shaken. He was a tall, thin man with a gray buzz cut, simple gold-rimmed glasses, wearing a T-shirt and jeans. He said that McDill did have a will, and that he was the executor. "I'll get you a copy as soon as I can get to my safe-deposit box," he said. He gestured at all the paper. "It wasn't supposed to end like this. She was supposed to do this for *me*."

McDill's mother lived in Arizona with a second husband, and she and her daughter were not close, McDill said. "It goes back to the divorce. We got divorced when Erica was in high school, and she couldn't believe that her mother would dump both of us. Mae wanted her freedom. Didn't want a husband—at the time, anyway—didn't want a kid. She told us that. Erica never got over it."

"I don't want to . . ." Virgil looked around; they were sitting in a four-seasons porch, alone, but he could hear Davies babbling on somewhere. "Look, I don't want to be an asshole, is what I don't want to be. But I have to ask: If you've looked at the will . . . would Erica's mother be in line to inherit anything?"

McDill shook his head. "Not a penny."

"Huh. How about Ruth?"

"Ruth will get a hundred thousand," McDill said.

"That's not bad . . . she thought she'd get nothing," Virgil said.

McDill frowned at that: "I think she knew. I think she knew the terms. Did you ask her?"

"I did, but maybe I wasn't clear," Virgil said.

"It's been in the will for three years," McDill said. "Erica had a new will made when she took over as CEO, and got a kick in salary. Hard to believe that they didn't talk about it at all."

THE CRIME-SCENE CREW, led by Stacy Lowe, had almost finished processing the house—looking at phone records, calendars, computers, and anything unexpected that might point to a killer.

Virgil took Lowe aside and asked, "Have you finished with Ruth Davies's room?" He'd learned that the two women had separate bedrooms.

"Yes. Looking for something in particular?"

"I'd like to look at her shoes. . . ."

Lowe cornered Davies, to confer, and while they were doing that, Virgil slipped into Davies's room and checked the closet. Davies had a shoe rack, with nine different pairs of shoes mounted on it. He looked through the shoes and found no Mephistos. Went into McDill's room, found perhaps twenty pairs of shoes, including a pair of Mephistos. He found Lowe. "Process the shoes. The guys up north say the killer might have been wearing Mephistos. Look for dirt. Swamp muck."

"Okay. Cool." She bent close to them, then said, "They look clean."

"Do your best." He checked sizes: eight and a half. Back in Davies's room, he checked sizes: eight. Davies could have worn a pair of McDill's Mephistos. Even if those in the closet had never been in the swamp, he knew that McDill owned Mephistos. . . .

Lowe told him, "There were no guns of any kind. No rifles."

Virgil held up a finger, to quiet her, as he tried to catch a thought: Ah. Yes. McDill wore Mephistos. Wendy was in McDill's room the night before the killing, where she might have had access to McDill's shoes. . . .

Something to check.

"What?" Lowe asked.

"No guns, huh? Interesting."

DAVIES HAD NO ALIBI—she'd been sick, she said—had a monetary and maybe even an emotional reason to kill McDill, had access to Mephisto shoes. May have lied about McDill's will. She might well have an idea of what McDill did at the resort; might have heard about the solitary visit to the eagle's nest, might even have had it pointed out on a chart or on Google . . .

On the other hand, her behavior was simply too . . . unparsed. Davies hadn't thought of answers in advance. She hadn't calculated her behavior. Everything about her was raw and unrehearsed.

Unless, he thought, *she was crazy.*

He had, in the past, encountered a crazy serial burglar who

seemed the soul of innocence because after the burglaries, he some-how forgot that he'd done them. Virgil didn't think that he was lying—because of his peculiar psychological problem, he really for-got. Of course, that hadn't prevented him from selling the stolen stuff on eBay, America's fence.

WHEN HE WAS DONE with the talk, Virgil cruised one last time through the house, had a thought—the walls weren't bare, but they didn't seem quite right, either. He walked through again, trying to be casual about it, and saw a couple of empty nail holes at picture-hanger height. He asked Lowe, "Did you find anything in her paper about art that she owned?"

"There's a file of receipts somewhere. I could find it," Lowe said.

"Do that, and check it off against the paintings here." He ges-tured around the room. Each wall was hung with either an oil painting or a print, and they didn't look like they came from a deco-rator's back room—they looked like stuff he'd seen in galleries: col-orful, idiosyncratic, even harsh. "See if there's anything missing. I don't know how much it's worth, but . . . that's what I want to know. What it's worth, and where it is. If it's missing, I want to know what it could be sold for."

When Virgil left, Davies and Oren McDill were stacking Erica McDill's clothing in the hallway, preparatory to packing it; a dismal task, Virgil thought, and both of them stopped occasionally to cry. He left them like that, in a house of misery, and headed downtown to the agency board meeting.

THE AGENCY WAS HOUSED on the fifth floor of the Laughton building in Minneapolis, a fashionably international lump of blue glass and steel. Mann introduced him to the board, a group of well-dressed men and women who were snarling at one another around a maple table.

Virgil made a brief presentation of what he'd found, and one of the men blurted out, "I was at a Twins game," and, one by one, without being asked, the other members provided alibis, most of which would be easy to confirm. One guy didn't have one, but he was six-five and his shoes must have been thirteens, Virgil thought. He made a note anyway. If any of them had done it, it was going to take a break from somewhere else, from somebody else, to prove it.

By four o'clock, he was on his way north again.

Kept thinking about what Owen had said: a backwoods gay-basher making a point.

Could be, but he doubted it. It usually took something more specific to trigger a murder; not always, but usually. Money, sex, obsession, competition, alcohol . . . something. Something he was missing.

8

ZOE TULL'S SISTER'S HOUSE was more like a cabin than a real house, and sat on a shallow bay down a dark dirt road on Fifty-Dollar Lake. Zoe'd talked Virgil back to the place by cell phone, and was standing in the yard when he pulled in.

"The crime-scene guy who came to my house couldn't find any fingerprints but he said the door had definitely been forced," she said. And, "Hello."

"Hi. Yeah. I talked to him," Virgil said. "He said your locks wouldn't have kept a small child out."

"That situation will be fixed tomorrow." She wrapped her arms around herself and shivered. "I don't like this. I don't know if it was a coincidence, or if it's because I'm talking to you, or if it's some goof who kills women."

An older woman pushed out of the house: Zoe's sister. She looked a lot like Zoe, slender but more weathered, with cool, distant green eyes and a nose that was a bit too long. She was wearing a plaid shirt with the sleeves rolled up over her elbows, and jeans. She looked at Virgil for a moment, nothing shy about it, then looked past him for a minute, and said, "Nice rig."

"Works for me," Virgil said.

"You all best come in before the bugs eat you alive," the sister said.

"My sister, Sig. Signy," Zoe said. And to Signy, "This is Virgil."

SIGNY'S HOUSE SMELLED like pine wood and maybe a hint of bacon and pancakes; had a tiny kitchen, a small living room with a couch and a couple of easy chairs on an oval hooked rug, a woodstove in one corner, and a hallway that apparently led back to a couple of bedrooms. Virgil took one of the chairs and Zoe asked, "So what'd you find out?"

"Not much. Talked to a couple of people who didn't like McDill, but they didn't do it. Found out that Ruth Davies will inherit a hundred thousand dollars, and that she knew that McDill had had at least one affair, so I guess it's possible that she thought that their time was ending. Oh. She has no alibi."

Signy had gone to the kitchen and came back with three bottles, handed one to Virgil. Negra Modelo. Virgil took a swallow and said, "I'm sorry, ma'am. I can't drink when I'm on duty."

"That's a goddamn shame," Signy said. She handed another bottle to Zoe, and had one for herself. "You don't think this Davies woman did it?"

"I didn't say that," Virgil said.

"You sound like it," she said.

"Okay. I don't think she did it."

"Who do you think did?" Signy asked.

"I don't know enough of the players," Virgil said. "I'll be up for a few days, figure that out."

Signy smiled at him and showed a chipped front tooth. "Got an ego on you, I'll say that."

SIGNY'S HUSBAND was in Alaska. "One time he went out for a loaf of bread and wound up in Churchill, on Hudson Bay. This time, it's Alaska."

"Sounds confused," Virgil said.

"He *is* confused. A nice guy, but confused. I don't believe he'll be back," she said.

"He *could* come back," Zoe said.

"I don't think so," Signy said. To Virgil. "He keeps moving further north. Last time, he barely made it home. This time, he's over the horizon. I don't think he'll make it at all."

"Life," Virgil said.

"Show Virgil the picture he sent you," Zoe said.

Signy got up, went to a table in the front hall, picked up an envelope, and carried it back to Virgil; Virgil slipped out a photograph and tipped it toward the lamplight to see it better. It showed a thin, dark-haired man standing on the bank of a creek, looking at a bulldozer that had about sunk out of sight in what appeared to be a bog, or maybe quicksand. A chain led down to the dozer from a second bulldozer; the second dozer was apparently trying to pull the first one out of the muck.

"Guess what he got a job driving," Signy said.

"The bulldozer?"

"He has accidents," Zoe said.

Virgil gave the photo back to Signy, who asked, "You want another beer?"

"I shouldn't," Virgil said. She went and got him another one, and said, "I'd give you a sandwich, but I don't have anything in the house. I usually eat out."

"Got a bag of sweet corn in the truck," Virgil said.

Signy's eyes lit up: "I could do some sweet corn. That's just boiling water, right?"

VIRGIL GOT THE CORN and she looked in the bag and said, "Cucumbers. I could put together a salad. I've got some apples and lettuce. . . ." Virgil got the impression that she wasn't big on cooking.

Signy wandered off to the kitchen and Virgil sat down again and said to Zoe, "Tell me all about this band. Tell me about Wendy and Berni and whoever else. . . ."

★

ZOE TOLD HIM that the band had been around for two or three years, but that Wendy had been something of a Grand Rapids celebrity since middle school. "She's always been the best singer that anybody ever knew. When she was a little kid, she used to sing with a polka band, and even travel around with them. Around the Iron Range, I mean. Not all over."

Wendy and Berni became best friends in middle school, and Berni learned the drums because she wasn't any good at other musical instruments. Together they played in a high school rock band that later became a country band when Wendy decided that she had more of a country voice. She also decided that women got a better break in country music than in rock.

After high school, she worked for a while at a local convenience store, and then for her father, breeding dogs. "Nasty hairy yellow-looking things," Zoe said. "Though I guess they get a lot of money for them. They're some kind of rare dog, or something."

"I wonder if she literally breeds them," Signy said from the kitchen. "She breeds everything else."

"Shut up, Sig," Zoe said.

All the time she was working, Wendy had a band. The band was getting better—they were shedding the old high school part-timers, and were picking up some pros—and Wendy's voice was getting richer. So was her love life.

ZOE SAID, and Signy agreed, between bouts of looking into the corn kettle, that Wendy was a heartless slut who played her lovers off against each other, and sometimes slept with men to demonstrate her independence.

"But she's really talented. You heard her," Zoe said, her face alight. "She's got this magnetism that pulls people in. Even McDill. That's what all the big stars have. You can't figure it out, but you can feel it."

Berni, on the other hand, was a below-average drummer, Zoe said. "She can do it, but she's not so creative. Wendy told me that."

"You think Wendy'll dump her?" Virgil asked.

Signy said, "If Wendy thought Berni could cost her a recording contract, she'd drop her off the bus on the side of the interstate."

WENDY KNEW THAT she had to move—Taylor Swift, Zoe said, was two years younger than Wendy, and was already a huge name with the best-selling album in the U.S.

"But you know what? Taylor Swift is like Grace Slick. You know who Grace Slick was?"

"Jefferson Starship?" Virgil ventured.

"Yeah, and another band, Jefferson Airplane, before that. Everybody thought that she was going to be the queen of rock and roll. Then along came Janis Joplin, and Janis Joplin *was* the queen of rock and roll. Wendy is Janis Joplin. But she's got to make a move. She knows it. Time is pressing on her."

WENDY AND BERNI LIVED together in a double-wide out at Wendy's father's place, Zoe said. Berni and Wendy's father were tight.

"I think he's the one that got Wendy back with Berni, instead of with me," Zoe said.

"Are you still in love?" Signy asked.

"Well, what do you think?"

Signy said to her sister, "I think it might be a lack of other opportunity. If you were down in the Cities, with lots of other women, you'd be fine. But up here, what're you going to do? Go out with Sandy Ericson? I mean, Wendy's what you got."

Zoe faked a shiver and said to Virgil, "Sandy goes about twotwenty in her boxer shorts."

"And it ain't muscle," Signy said. To her sister: "You know why Wendy was plucking your magic twanger? Because you're an accountant, and she thought she might learn something about handling money. That's why."

"Sig—shut up," Zoe said.

VIRGIL ASKED, "If Berni thought Wendy was going to dump her because of McDill, would Berni have shot McDill?"

Signy and Zoe looked at each other, and then simultaneously shrugged. Zoe said, "I don't know if Berni knows anything about guns. I could ask."

"Don't do that. You already had one nut creeping around your house." Signy said, then, "Water's boiling. I'm gonna drop that corn in there for one minute and then we're gonna eat, so you might as well come now."

AS THEY STOOD UP, Virgil said to Zoe, "I can't think why somebody would break into your house, that would be connected with this killing. Can you?"

She shook her head. "No."

"On the other hand, we have a violent crime, and you know all the main local people around the dead woman, and you've been seen hanging out with me, and somebody breaks into your house. Is this the first time you've had a break-in?"

"Oh, yeah—I mean, we had some kids who were breaking into houses in my neighborhood, a couple of years ago, stealing stuff to buy drugs, but they caught them right away."

"There *are* burglaries," Signy said. "It's not like this place is totally crime-free."

"But the time link makes it interesting," Virgil said. "She's been up around the crime scene, she's seen with me, and we get the break-in."

"On some of the crime shows, you get people who don't know what they know, and that's why they're in danger," Zoe said. "You think that's like me? I don't know what I know?"

Virgil grinned at her and said, "Crime shows and mystery novels are totally different things than real life, you know? What I'm thinking is, you had somebody come in there, planning to threaten you, or even hurt you, or to find out what you were saying to me, or to find out what you knew, and he came in with a pipe or just his fists, and this voice says, 'I've got a gun,' and he says, 'Fuck it,' and takes off."

"Or she," Zoe said.

"Or she. And if you knew something, I think you'd know it. Wouldn't you?"

Signy said, "Well, we had that secretary of defense, who was always talking about known unknowns, and unknown unknowns, and all that—maybe Zoe could have an unknown known."

Virgil looked at her for a second, then said, "Two beers might have been one too many. I didn't understand a thing you said."

SIGNY HAD a tiny kitchen table, and three mismatched chairs. As they sat around, working on the mediocre salad and terrific sweet corn with real butter, Virgil asked Signy what she did, and she said, "I've got a quilt store in Grand Rapids."

"Ah. That's pretty cool. I like quilts," Virgil said. "My mom makes them and I've got three of them."

"Damn near can't make a living at it," Signy said. "You can get so close . . . but then you always need an extra fifty dollars for something. You'll think everything's working this week, and then you tear up a tire or something."

Zoe said, "Signy went to the U in Minneapolis. In art."

Virgil reevaluated, and so obviously that Signy said, "*What?* You thought I was a hillbilly woman, right?"

"Nah. I come from a small town myself," he said.

"It's Joe that's dragging you down," Zoe said to Signy. "You oughta get a divorce. Like, next week."

"Divorces cost money and he's not bothering me, so . . . when I get the money," Signy said.

"I don't even know why you married him; he's such a loser," Zoe said.

"Well," Signy said, and she picked up one of the corn cobs on her plate and held it erect, contemplated it with slightly crossed eyes. *About ten inches long*, Virgil thought. "I don't honestly know why," she said after a minute.

Zoe fell into a coughing fit, and Virgil asked, "Can you breathe?" and she patted herself on the chest and said, "I inhaled a corn."

"'Zat what it was," Virgil said. And he asked her, "Are you staying here?"

"Until the locks are on," Zoe said. "The lock guy is coming tomorrow morning."

"What're *you* going to do tomorrow?" Signy asked Virgil.

"Push on people," Virgil said. "I'm going to run around and push on people."

"I'd like to see that," she said; her head was tilted, and she stroked her cheek with the fingers of one hand. "I really would like to see you work."

VIRGIL CRASHED at a chain motel on Highway 169 South, the kind where they don't bother with drywall, but simply paint the concrete blocks a dusty shade of yellow; but offered double-length parking for customers pulling boats. When he checked in, the desk clerk asked him how long he'd be there, and he said, "Three or four days."

Before he went to sleep, in the time he usually thought about God, he thought about Wendy. One problem with looking at a talent in isolation, he thought, was that it was almost impossible to judge exactly how good they were.

Wendy was as good as anyone he'd heard in a small bar in Minnesota—but on the other hand, those bands *were* in small bars in Minnesota, and that was the problem. Put Wendy up against Emmylou Harris, and she might sound like Raleigh the Talking Bulldog.

Of course, that didn't mean so much if the people around her were convinced that they stood at the edge of a gold mine; on the one hand, you had life in Grand Rapids; in the other one, the possibility of Nashville and Hollywood and . . . whatever.

Then he thought about God and, after a while, went to sleep.

IN THE MORNING he put on a fresh, but vintage, Nine Inch Nails T-shirt, took five of the eight remaining free miniature Danishes in the complimentary breakfast, and two cups of coffee, and ran out to the Eagle Nest. Another good day, sun creeping up into the sky, almost no wind. He wondered if Johnson was fishing, or if he'd given it up and gone home.

That God-blessed Davenport.

The problem with Davenport, Virgil thought, was that he tended to think in very straight lines. Brutally straight. We have a murder in Grand Rapids, the victim's prominent, the BCA agent with the highest clearance rate in the agency happens to be on a lake nearby, so what do you do? Send in Flowers.

Was there anything creative in that? Was there a break for a new guy, somebody who could use the experience? Did it take into account the agent's emotional state, or need for respite?

Virgil thought not.

Just drop in that fuckin' Flowers, and forget it. Let him sink or swim.

MARGERY STANHOPE was leaning against a railing, looking out over Stone Lake, when Virgil came up beside her. "Still bummed?"

"I can't shake it," she said.

Virgil looked out over the lake and said, "Well . . . another month, and you can take the winter off."

She sighed and asked, "What are you up to?"

"I'd like to talk to people who are still here who knew McDill. I need some names."

"You want to talk one at a time, or all together?"

"Both," Virgil said. "I'd like to have the whole group in, and then, when we're done, I'll ask if anybody has anything they'd like to follow up with me, privately. Give them my cell number to call."

"A bunch of them went on a bear-spotting trip to Steven's Island. They'll be back for lunch. How about right after lunch?"

Virgil patted the rail. "See you then," he said.

HE CALLED ZOE. "Get your locks?"

"The guy's here now. He'll be done in an hour," she said.

"Where'd I find Wendy and Berni and the rest of them?" Virgil asked.

"Probably down at the Schoolhouse. They've rented it for the month; they're working on a record."

THE SCHOOLHOUSE was east of town, and had once been a one-room schoolhouse. A red-brick cube with a chimney at one end and a door and bell tower—no bell—at the other, it was surrounded by a gravel parking lot with a half-dozen SUVs scattered around in no particular pattern. When Virgil got out of his truck, he could see through a glass-brick wall the flailing arms of a drummer, but he could hear not a sound. He climbed the steps, went through the front doors, found himself in an entry room facing a skinny, nervous blond woman who was sitting on a desk, reading what looked like a manuscript, but turned out to be a musical score, and chewing gum in rhythm with the faintly audible bass.

Virgil said, "I'm looking for Wendy Ashbach."

The woman chewed and asked, "Who're you?"

"The cops," Virgil said.

He must've said it in a cop-like way, because she nodded and said, "Virgil. I heard about you. You were at the fight last night."

"Yeah . . ."

"They're laying down the basic tracks for 'Lover Do,' and they'll be greatly pissed if you mess it up."

"I don't want to mess anything up, but I need to talk to Wendy and maybe Berni and anybody else who might have something to chip in," Virgil said.

"Okay. You ever been in a recording studio?"

"Nope."

"Follow me in, and sit on the couch against the back wall," she said. "You don't have to be real quiet, but be a little quiet. They're working."

The control room was probably twenty feet long and fifteen feet deep, with a long window facing a room full of women musicians— a bass guitar, a lead, keyboards, a violinist, all wearing headphones, playing a fairly simple song. On the other side of the musicians' room was another, smaller room, also with a window, and Berni was inside, pounding on her drums.

Under the window, on Virgil's side, two men crouched over a control board that must have been fifteen feet long; the music flowed into the control room through speakers on either side and above the control board. Wendy was in the control room itself, standing behind the engineers, wearing headphones and a microphone, half singing, half humming the words to the song, and behind it all, a metronome-like click was parsing out the beat.

Nobody looked at Virgil or the blonde. They stayed with the music, and the blonde pointed Virgil at a couch against the back wall, and when he sat down, she sat down beside him.

"They're laying down the basic tracks," the blonde said quietly. "They'll record the solos later, and overdub them. When they've got that perfect, then Wendy'll come in with the real vocals and they'll overdub that. She's doing scratch vocals now, to keep everybody tuned in to her."

Virgil nodded.

The blonde asked, "Are you here about Erica McDill?"

"Yeah."

"That was a bad break. We needed somebody like her. She knew her shit."

"Who're you?"

The woman stuck out her hand and said, "Corky Saarinen. I'm the manager."

As Virgil shook it, the band clattered to a sloppy stop, and one of the engineers said, "Okay, guys, let's pick it up right at the top of the fourth verse. Sin, lead us in, and Wendy can pick it up. . . ."

They started again, and Virgil whispered, "Why'd you need McDill?"

Saarinen leaned closer and said, "I can handle all the detail stuff—the road stuff. Making sure everything gets where it's supposed to, on time. And I can find other people to work for us, lawyers, accountants, and so on. But some of it—contacts, agents, advertising, publicity—so much counts on talent. You don't know when people are bullshitting you, or if you're getting what you're paying for. And you know, if you come out with a bad initial image, you could be dead for years. It's something you've got to get right, right off the top. That's what McDill could have done for us."

"So what'll you do now?"

She shrugged: "McDill talked to some people down at her agency, about the band. I'll track them down, find out what they think. Maybe they can give us a lead to a new PR guy."

"You guys were going to hire McDill? Could you afford her?"

"Nah. Wendy and McDill were bumpin' each other. McDill was doing it because it made her feel hip. Edgy. Out there. I mean, she was married to a fat housewife, and along comes Wendy, you know?"

"You knew they were involved?" Virgil asked.

"Yeah, me and Sin did. We tried to keep it quiet, because we figured Berni'd go off, like she did. Have you seen Wendy's eye?"

Virgil hadn't; hadn't seen anything of Wendy but the back of her head. He shook his head: "No."

Saarinen giggled: "She looks like she went six rounds with Rocky."

"How long were Wendy and McDill involved?" Virgil asked.

Saarinen glanced at the singer, then said, "A few days—since about . . . mmm . . . Tuesday. Maybe Tuesday. McDill and some other women introduced themselves on Saturday night, at the Goose, and they got to talking. McDill came around and watched us work on Monday, and on Tuesday, we were talking about PR and I realized that they'd been talking during the day, when the rest of us weren't around. You could tell *something* was about to happen."

THE BAND got to the end of the song, then played the end again, and again, and finally one of the engineers leaned into a microphone and said, "That's got it, guys."

Wendy pulled her headphones off and turned and spotted Virgil and did a double take, then grinned and said, "Hey, guy." She had a black eye as big as a silver dollar, startling under her blond hair.

"Wendy," Virgil said. "That black eye looks pretty interesting."

"You like it? We did a couple of publicity photos this morning. Might use it for the album cover."

THERE WAS AN EMPTY wheeled office chair pushed under the control board, and she rolled it over to Virgil and plopped down, with her feet overlapping his, their knees almost touching. She did it deliberately but good-naturedly, poking at him, to see how he'd react. He said, "I need to talk to you and the band about which one of you killed McDill."

That stopped her: "You know . . . one of *us* did it?"

"No, but you're the best I've got, and I've got to work with what I got," Virgil said, poking her back.

"Well, let me see . . . I guess it was Wednesday when we decided to kill her. I said, 'Girl, you gotta get it on. Gotta get the six-gun and shoot Erica McDill right in the ear.'" The smile vanished and she cocked her head: "So what in the fuck are you talking about?"

"McDill could have been killed for business reasons, but when I dug into that, I couldn't find any," Virgil said. "Most everybody needed to keep her alive. Her getting killed is going to cost a lot of people a lot of money. Then, I thought maybe her girlfriend did it—but her girlfriend needs written instructions to walk across the street, and I don't see her figuring out something this complicated. Then I've got a whole band full of people whose love lives are all twisted up, with you in the middle of it. A lot of emotion going around. People fighting in bars about it. Most of you are small-town girls, and I bet more than one of you has her own rifle, and could figure out how to get through that swamp into Stone Lake. That's how I figure it."

Wendy looked at him for a minute, then backed up to the control board. On the other side of the glass, the musicians were chatting as they took down music and put their instruments away, and Wendy pushed a button on the control board and said, "Everybody, come on in: there's a cop here who thinks we killed Erica."

IN A MINUTE or so, the room had filled with a half-dozen queru-lous women, none of them, with the exception of Berni the drum-mer, especially small. Virgil watched with interest as Wendy put on her outraged mask. It went on like a Halloween face, and Virgil thought, *I've got a crazy one.*

Not knowing exactly what was going to happen, Virgil eased to his feet as the women pushed into the control room, as though he were being polite; they brought the odor of overheated bodies with them, and he noticed that a couple of them were sweating, from the session just ended—harder work than it seemed.

Wendy said, "Well, he says one of us did it—who was it? Cat? Did you do it?"

"Not me," said the keyboard player. She looked at Virgil, storming up. "Did he say it was me?"

Wendy turned to Virgil, ready to say something, but Virgil snapped, "I didn't say it was anybody. But we've got a lot of women swarming around Wendy here, and Wendy was sleeping with McDill. You're where we look. Everybody who doesn't like Wendy, raise your hands: you can go."

They all looked at one another, and a couple of women flashed amused smiles. No hands went up.

Berni said, "You know, people could get sued if you go throwing these accusations around."

"If you think you see an accusation, sue me," Virgil said.

"Maybe we ought to kick your ass," the lead guitar said, and she sounded serious.

More quick glances, people checking to see how far this was going, and Virgil took a step to his right, to open the distance by three feet and to get his back against a wall. One of the engineers said, "Whoa, whoa, whoa, we got equipment in here."

Virgil said to the lead guitar, "Well, roll it out, honey. Let's see what you got," and he said it with enough ice that he caught their attention.

"You think you can take all of us?" the lead guitar asked.

"I think so," Virgil said. "Maybe not. I'll have to hurt a couple people bad, maybe blind you."

"You're fuckin' crazy," one of the engineers said.

"I'm a BCA agent investigating a murder. If you guys take me on,

I'll beat as many of you as I can, and all of you will be going to prison for assault on a peace officer, which is a felony in the state of Minnesota," Virgil said. "You think a murder is fuckin' funny, you should have come down and looked into McDill's dead empty eyes, the back of her head all blown out. She wasn't laughing. You want a couple of years in prison to think about that, bring it on."

That turned them off, quick as a light switch. The woman who'd been playing the violin said, "This is nuts. I've got nothing to do with this. I don't want to fight a cop. My dad's a cop."

"Pussy," Wendy said.

"Hey, you wanna come out in the live room and say that?" the woman snarled at Wendy.

The engineer, a burly guy with heavy-rimmed black-plastic Hollywood hipster glasses, pushed into the woman and said, "Get out of here. You're gonna start breakin' stuff, goddamnit. Wendy, that board's a hundred and fifty thousand and if you bust it, you pay for it; or your old man does."

"I'm outa here," said the violinist.

"Nobody's out of here," Virgil said. "I came here to interview you, one at a time. Take five minutes each."

"Outside," the engineer said. "Do it outside."

THEY WOUND UP doing it in the drum booth, Virgil sitting on the drummer's stool, the women, Wendy last, moving in and out of a metal folding chair.

Berni Kelly, who called herself Raven, drummer: "Like I told you the other night, I was by myself, but I didn't do it. I was home, waiting for Wendy. Her dad was there, over at his place, part of the time, anyway. I didn't see him—I saw his truck and I'm sure he must've seen mine. I didn't know about Wendy and McDill. I guess I was the last to find out."

"You're pretty upset?"

"Well, she's gone off before," Berni said. "She always comes back. But I was pretty upset. I mean, last night, I hit her as hard as I could."

"Pretty good shot, too," Virgil said with a grin.

"Thank you."

"You're back together?" Virgil asked.

"We are. Yes. Listen, I really don't have anything against you. I hope you find out who killed Erica, even though I didn't like her. Us guys got this rock 'n' roll attitude about cops, but it's a TV thing, it's not real. I'm on your side, really."

"What do you think about Zoe Tull?"

"I don't think about her," Berni said. "She and Wendy had a thing, but Zoe's so straight, Wendy couldn't stand it anymore. I mean, Zoe wanted to exchange Valentine's Day candy-heart boxes, for God's sakes."

CATHY (CAT) MATHIS, KEYBOARDS: "We could have taken you."

"Maybe—you had total weight on your side and you might have taken me down, but I would have hurt a few of you, and the more I hurt, the more room I'd have to go after the rest," Virgil said with a smile. "It'd be an interesting thing to try out, except that we'd have to hurt people to do it. If I didn't have the job I have, I'd be willing to try it out."

Her head bobbed up and down a couple of times, and then she said, "Really?"—a genuine question.

"Yeah. Really," Virgil said.

"You like to fight?" she asked.

"*Like* is the wrong word," Virgil said. "I find it intense. My life lacks intensity."

"You killed all those Vietnamese. Was that intense?"

"I didn't personally kill anybody—but yeah: it was intense," Virgil said. Before she could ask another question, he asked, "Where were you when McDill was killed?"

"I don't know exactly when she was killed, but I heard it was late afternoon. I have a karate class at six o'clock, and I was in class."

"Karate. You like to fight?" Virgil asked.

"My life lacks intensity," she said.

"How many people in the class?" Virgil asked.

"Probably eight or nine people, plus the sensei," Mathis said.

"Then, another class came in while we were finishing. If you want to check the alibi, you should do it quick—today—before people start to forget. I sparred with a guy named Larry Busch."

"If you had to pick out one person that you know who might have killed Erica McDill, who would you pick?"

But she was already shaking her head: "Not a fair question. I have no idea who might have wanted to hurt McDill. I knew that she and Wendy were fooling around, but I figured that was their business."

"Have you had a relationship with Wendy yourself?"

"Yeah. She pays me to play keyboards. I'm an employee," Mathis said.

"But . . ."

"I'm straight."

"All right; so you had no . . . love interest in the situation . . . with either McDill or Wendy or Berni or whoever."

"Nope."

BERTHA (BERT) CARR, the violinist: "You're looking at the wrong place. The only person who might have wanted to get rid of McDill for romantic . . . or sexual reasons . . . would be Berni, and Berni really didn't know. I mean, I know she didn't know, because I was talking to her about Wendy and she asked me if I thought McDill was a threat. She knew McDill had an eye on Wendy, but didn't know how far it had gotten."

"When did you figure it out?"

"Tuesday night. Nobody said anything, but we were sitting around here and Wendy's dad brought some pizzas and McDill and Wendy were sitting right next to each other, were touching each other all the time; right there with Dad watching."

"Tuesday."

"Yes. I counted back."

"If I shouldn't be looking here, where should I be looking?" Virgil asked.

"At the Eagle Nest," Carr said. "That place . . . you know that there are a lot of us who stay there, right?"

"Us?"

"Gays. Lesbians," she said.

"Sure. I've been told that."

"That's not the whole story," she said. "Did you notice that there are quite a few little boy-toy waiters up there?"

"Boy toy . . . Are you . . . ?" He thought of the waiter who'd taken him down the steps to the water, and his cutting-edge hairdo.

"Yes. There are any number of hasty romances going on up there, and they're not all gay. I'd heard that McDill would rent one of the boys every once in a while. She had this dominatrix thing going. You know, I don't mean leather or vinyl or any of that, but she sort of liked getting a little boy to kneel down for her, if you get the picture."

"Ah, man. Did Wendy know that?" Virgil asked.

"Wendy . . . Wendy would inhale a boy every once in a while," Carr said. "That was something she and McDill shared. I wonder if there was a boy there that night, when Wendy stayed over?"

"Ah, man," Virgil said.

"What? You weird about sex?" Carr asked.

"No. But everything just got more complicated," Virgil said. "So where were you when Erica McDill was murdered?"

"I think—this is just from what I heard on TV—that I was right here, working on 'Lover Do' with Wendy. There were a few people here, Gerry, Corky, our manger, that guy Mark . . ." She pointed through the window to one of the engineers, who was disconnecting a microphone in the live room.

"Okay. Enough to nail down an alibi."

"Yes. I believe so. I mean, people were coming and going, we went out to eat for a while. . . . But, generally, we were around," Carr said.

"It's only ten minutes out to the Eagle Nest."

"Well . . . what can I tell you? I don't know where everybody was, for every ten minutes. The dinner break, some people were out for an hour. . . ."

CYNTHIA (SIN) SAWYER, the lead guitar. She came in carrying a saxophone, tooted it once, then put it on the floor beside her chair.

"Gay or straight?" Virgil asked.

"Me? A little of both," she said.

"Do you think Wendy and McDill ever shared a male companion?" Virgil asked.

"I doubt it. Wendy would have been bragging about it, if they did," Sawyer said. "And she hasn't. Been bragging."

"You ever hear about male companions working up at the Eagle Nest?"

"Sure. It's a high school joke around here," she said. "If you've got a certain look, apply at the Eagle Nest for a summer job. Depending on the length of your dick, you might get overtime."

"You believe it?"

"Yep." She smiled.

"The place is starting to sound like a whorehouse," Virgil said.

"What, you thought women came up to look at loons all day? Believe me, you can only look at a loon for so long," she said. "You get up, you do some yoga, drink some body-cleansing green tea, look at some loons, paddle some canoes, drink some martinis, get your brains banged loose, go to bed. All part of the package."

"Do you have any feeling that anybody in the band might have wanted to hurt McDill?"

She leaned forward and tapped his knee. "No. And I'll tell you why. I'm a good goddamned lead guitar; I'm a pro. Gerry is a terrific bass player—she's not from here, she's from the Cities, and moved up here to get with Wendy's voice. And she's got a good backup voice. The violin is fine, the keyboards are okay; if we can find a decent drummer, we could go a long way with Wendy. McDill could have been part of that plan. I listened to McDill talk, and I'm a believer. She knew her shit. She was somebody we needed."

"But you'd have to dump Berni, right?" Virgil asked.

"Well, yeah—but she doesn't necessarily know that," Sawyer said. "Or maybe she does. That's life. Maybe she could be an assistant manager or something, a roadie, or a spare drummer, or she could do some other percussion shit—tambourines. She can sing a little, and she's got really great tits, so she'd look good up front, I mean, she could stay . . . but the point is, McDill could have put us on that road, you know? She had contacts all over the place: she knew how to get it done."

"You liked her?"

"Oh . . . no. But that didn't make any difference to me," Sawyer said. "It's like you've got a terrific music teacher, and he puts his hand on your ass. You don't like him, but hey—he teaches you to play a killer guitar. You like *that* part. Same with McDill. I'm not going to sleep with her, but she can do my PR all day and night."

She had been running around to a grocery store and to a Wal-Mart when McDill was killed: "I guess that's not exactly a great alibi, but that's what I was doing. I was in and out of here, while they were trying to figure out 'Lover Do,' but I didn't have anything to do with killing McDill."

Virgil believed her.

GERRY O'MEARA, BASS, didn't seem to have a nickname; she'd been working on the "Lover Do" song with Wendy and the others when McDill was killed. "Yeah, there'll have to be some personnel changes in the band, and I guess she probably knows it. I mean, this is what I do for a living, and I'm good at it, and I've played with some heavy people. Now I need to cash it in. I'm almost thirty, and if I'm going to make it, it's got to be soon."

"But you don't think the changes might somehow lead to this murder?" Virgil asked.

"I don't see how. McDill was going to help with PR, and with contacts in Nashville and so on, but . . . I don't see how the changes would wind up with her getting shot. I think it was something at the Eagle Nest. Somebody heard about her sleeping with Wendy and got jealous. I mean, who else would know where Erica was going in that canoe?"

"Good point. Have you heard that McDill had anything going up here, other than Wendy?"

"No, I haven't heard anything. I don't hang with the gay chicks. I'm straight. But McDill getting killed has to be one of two things, right? Business—I mean, money—or sex. Jealousy. One of those two things. You just have to figure out which one."

"Thank you," Virgil said.

WENDY.

"I think maybe I want a lawyer when I'm talking to you," she said.

Virgil said, "Okay. Get a lawyer. If you can't afford a lawyer, I'll arrange to have the court appoint one. . . ."

She threw her hands up. "Wait-wait-wait. You got me. I don't want a fuckin' lawyer," Wendy said. "Ask your questions."

"When you slept with McDill the other night, was there a man around? Did you share a man? In any way?"

She looked at him for a minute, then did a reflexive grin, shook her head, and said, "You know about the boys, huh? But no, it was just the two of us, bumpin' cunts." She said it casually, no longer trying to shock him.

"Had McDill been playing with any of the other women up there? Or any of the men?"

"They're not really men—they're boys. Everybody calls them boys. And I don't know about McDill. I went up there because we'd been talking and doing some cocktails, and we were sneaking around Berni to do this, which got me kind of hot, so when Erica says, 'Come on up to the lodge,' I said, 'Okay.' It was that quick. Nothing planned. We went up there, had a few more cocktails, and got naked. I can give you the details of that, if you'd like."

"Sure, go ahead," Virgil said.

She looked at him for a moment, then said, "Fuck you."

"Do I make you nervous?" Virgil asked.

"You're not like other cops I've known—the thing that worries me is that you might be nuts," she said. "We don't need a nut. We need somebody who can clear this up, not a big cloud over the band."

Virgil said, "I'd like to talk to your father."

"Why's that?"

"Because from what I've heard, he's virtually a part of the band. And I've got this thing going in my head: maybe somebody didn't want McDill to mess with the band. Maybe somebody saw her as a threat, who'd either take you away from them, or maybe force some people out of the band. . . . I understand from some people that your father has been pretty central to your career."

"Well, he's . . . I don't know what he is. He's not an official member or anything," Wendy said. "He's the one guy I know who has my best interests at heart, and I don't have to worry about that. I don't have to worry that he's up to something."

"He's got your back," Virgil said.

"That's it: that's what he does."

"Still need to talk to him," Virgil said. "I'm told he's sort of a backwoods guy. A good shot."

She didn't react to the "good shot." She said, "Well, go on out—he's around."

9

BEFORE GOING TO TALK to Slibe Ashbach, Virgil called Zoe again, and she was still at her house. He got directions and went over, and looked at the locks.

"The locks are fine," he said, when he'd looked.

She lived in a modest bungalow, two bedrooms, and one of the bedrooms had an antique folk-art crucifix over the bed, and he wondered about it but didn't ask.

"The doors, on the other hand, are crap," he said. "A child could kick out those bottom panels, and the windowpanes are too big. Somebody with a gun could stick the gun barrel through the glass, knock it out, and unlatch the door. When you get the money, buy new doors."

She was anxious about it, but also an accountant: "There's usually no problem . . ."

"This is the twenty-first century, the problem's always out there," he said. He put his fists on his hips: "Now, why'd they break in? Why?"

"I still can't figure it out. I keep thinking about it—I can't get away from it," she said. "But I know one thing. I've lived here for thirty years with no problems, and then I hang out with a cop on a murder case for one day, and somebody tries to get in. . . . That doesn't feel like a coincidence."

"No, it doesn't. So think about it," Virgil said. "All the time. Work something out. Call me."

THE ASHBACH PLACE was an early twentieth-century farmhouse eight miles out of town, down a country road that pushed past a couple of lake turnoffs, dropped from blacktop road to gravel, and finally ended at Ashbach's. It could be a hard place to get to in the winter, Virgil thought as he drove in; a place where you'd *need* snowmobiles.

The two-story farmhouse looked like something from Grant Wood: white, with a picket fence around a neat patch of green lawn, clumps of zinnias and marigolds along the fence, fifty yards off the road. Closer to the road, a brown double-wide trailer sat on concrete blocks that had all been neatly painted gray. Farther back, at the end of the drive, was a newer metal barn, and off to the right of the barn, an open shed, covering two Bobcats—a backhoe and a front-end loader—and a larger Caterpillar shovel. A lowboy was parked beside the shed. Across the drive from the farmhouse, an open half-shed was two-thirds full of split firewood.

The house sat on what Virgil thought was probably twenty acres, with a pine plantation at the far end, and a half-dozen apple trees clustered in a back pasture. At the driveway entrance, a home-painted sign said ASHBACH KENNELS. Under that, an older sign said SLIBE ASHBACH SEPTIC & GRADING. And under that, a newer metal sign said NO TRESPASSING.

As he turned in the drive, Virgil noticed that the metal barn had a series of chain-link enclosures protruding from the sides, each with a half-grown yellow dog inside. A neat and expansive vegetable garden ran parallel to the driveway, filled with corn, beans, cabbage, some used-up rows that probably had been greens and radishes, earlier in the year; and a plot of dark green potato plants, enough to feed a family for a long northern winter. The back side of the garden was bordered by a raspberry patch.

A nice place, Virgil thought, if a little low, dark, and isolated.

A man was working next to the firewood shed.

SLIBE ASHBACH WAS FIFTY or fifty-five, weathered, stocky, with a sandy three-day beard and dishwater blond hair worn long from a balding head. He was dressed in a T-shirt, jeans, and muddy camo boots, working over a hydraulic log-splitter, splitting and piling firewood, which he stacked in the shed.

Virgil got out of his truck and walked over. Slibe didn't stop working for a minute, finished off three logs, threw them on the stack of split oak, then cut the motor and looked at Virgil and asked, "You see that no trespassing sign?"

"Yeah, but I ignored it," Virgil said. "I'm with the Bureau of Criminal Apprehension, looking into the murder of Erica McDill."

Slibe picked up his chain saw, popped the oil cap, paused, and asked, "What's that got to do with me?"

Virgil said, "I'm talking to everybody associated with Wendy's band. Your daughter had a sexual . . . interlude . . . with McDill the night before she was murdered. It turns out that McDill was involving herself in the affairs of the band. Some people don't like that, so it seems that we should check on the band."

He was blabbing on, he realized, and cut it off, and asked, "Where were you when McDill was killed?"

Slibe said, "Well, from what Wendy told me, I guess I was feedin' the dogs, or trainin' them. Or in the house, or somewhere. I was around."

"Anybody else around?" Virgil asked.

"Berni was over in the trailer for a time. . . . The Deuce was around somewhere, probably out in the woods. And somebody might have drove by, but I didn't notice. You could check back down the road. See if anybody saw me."

"Who's the Deuce?"

"Slibe Junior. He's called the Deuce."

At that moment a dark figure, in a long-sleeve blue shirt and jeans and a yellow ball cap, slid from behind the double-wide, looked at them for a moment, then slid back behind it. Big guy.

"Your son wear a yellow hat?" Virgil asked.

Slibe turned and looked at the double-wide, and said, "Yeah. Big kid? He ghosts around here like a . . . ghost. Spooks me, sometimes. Don't have much to say for himself."

"Huh. Well . . . you got a rifle?"

Now Slibe showed an improbably white smile—false teeth, Virgil thought—though it was as thin and nasty as a sickle blade. He asked, "You think you could find anybody around here who doesn't? Doesn't have about six?"

"How about a .223?"

"Yes, I do. Hasn't been shot for a while," Slibe said.

"I'd like to take it with me, if I could—I'd give you a receipt for it," Virgil said.

"Get a warrant," Slibe said.

"Well, I'll do that," Virgil said. "But things could get pretty inconvenient for you, to do it that way. But if that's the way you want to go, it's up to you."

Slibe asked, "What's that supposed to mean?"

Virgil shrugged. "If we get a warrant for weapons . . . they'll take all of them. No skin off our ass. Wind up sending in a crime-scene crew, search everything out here."

"Aw, fuck. The goddamn government." Slibe screwed the oil cap back on the chain saw and said, "All right. In the house."

"Let me get my notebook," Virgil said. "I'll write you out a receipt."

He walked over to the truck, got a notebook, dug his pistol out from under the seat, and clipped it under his jeans in the small of his back. Turning out of the truck, he saw the Deuce slide back behind the double-wide.

He followed Slibe to the house; up close, it looked as neat as it did from the road. The kitchen was like Signy's, small, with a two-chair table, with a dog-fancier newspaper folded on the table. Slibe went to a kitchen drawer, pulled it open, rattled some forks around, came up with a small key, walked down a hall to a closet, and opened it, to reveal a steel gun safe.

He popped the safe, which had at least four rifles and two shot-guns, and, on the top shelf, showed the stock of a large-frame hand-gun. He pulled out a rifle and handed it to Virgil—a military-look semiautomatic Colt AR-15 Sporter II with open sights. More than enough to take out McDill. He hadn't heard back from Mapes on the extraction marks, but Mapes had thought they were probably from a bolt action, not from a semiauto.

Virgil said, "Thank you," pulled the bolt, sniffed, and smelled the distinctive cut of gun solvent. "I'll get it back to you as soon as I can." He poked back into the safe. "These all Thirties?"

"Except for the .22," Slibe said. "A .308, .30-06, and the .22."

Virgil pulled out the pump .22, checked it, put it back. A long-rifle slug would have killed McDill if it had hit her right, but wouldn't have done the damage.

"I thought she was shot in a swamp," Slibe said.

"She was," Virgil said, turning around to face him.

"But you found a slug? That's why you need the rifle?"

"No slug, but we've got a cartridge. We can do some tests of the shell . . . and we'll test fire your rifle, and then, if we ever do find a slug, we'll have it." Virgil shrugged. "But what we'll probably do is some metallurgy, check metal remnants in the rifle against the metal frags in McDill's skull."

It was very quiet in the house, and Virgil became aware of a buzz-ing sound; a bee had gotten in. Slibe was staring at him, then blinked like a gecko and said, "Well, do what you got to do. I'd like the rifle back, soon as you can get it. We might go out to Wyoming and shoot some prairie rats in October. It's something we do."

"Do our best," Virgil said. Coming out the door, he said, "I hear you run a kennel out here."

"Best dogs in Minnesota," Slibe said. "English Crème Golden Retrievers. I'm the biggest breeder in the Upper Midwest; you want one of my dogs, baby-trained, gonna cost you three grand."

Virgil whistled. "You get three grand?"

"And I got a waiting list long as your arm," Slibe said. He pulled a can of Copenhagen out of his jacket pocket, stuck a pinch under his tongue. "Ask anybody."

"What did you think about McDill?"

"Didn't know her. From what Wendy said, she might have had some good ideas. Wendy's pretty anxious to get the show on the road."

"What do you think about that?" Virgil asked.

Slibe poked a finger down toward the kennels. "You see them dogs? They're solid gold. That's where the money is. Aren't nobody in Nashville going to pay any attention to a poor girl from Grand Rapids, Minnesota. Maybe twenty years ago, but not now. She wants to do it, but Wendy's a little crazy. I told her that a hundred times."

"So you think she should stay with dog breeding."

"That's what I think. But kids get crazy ideas. I mean, it's all right here. Everything she needs. I spent my whole life building this place up so she could take it over. And the Deuce, too, but the Deuce ain't got what it takes to run it. She knows that, but all she thinks about is that CMTV shit," Slibe said. "Now—you got the gun. You want anything else? I got some logs to split."

Virgil nodded and headed for his truck, then turned and said, "Wendy's a little better than good. I don't know if she's good enough, but she's better than good."

Something shifted in Slibe's face. "Don't go telling her that. She'll go sliding off to Nashville or L.A. and wind up on the street, selling her ass. She ain't a bad singer, but that's not why she's here."

BY THE TIME VIRGIL got back to town, it was late in the day. He called the Bemidji office and arranged for a guy to pick up Slibe's rifle the next morning, looked at his watch, and headed out to the Eagle Nest, still dragging the boat. Margery Stanhope was sitting in her office, alone, sad, and pensive, as she had been the last time he'd seen her; the murder was working on her. Virgil went in, closed the door, and she looked up as he crossed the office and took one of the visitor chairs.

She glanced at the closed door and asked, apprehensively, "What happened?"

"I have some embarrassing questions to ask, Margery," Virgil said.

Her brow beetled: "What?"

"Is it true that some of your waiter boys provide additional services to the guests?"

She leaned back and said, "Oh. Damnit. Well, I'll tell you what, Virgil, I have heard that, but I do not make any inquiries. What our guests do, as long as they don't do it in the parking lot, is up to them. They are adults."

"Yeah, but Margery . . . you hire them," Virgil said. "The boys."

"You ever been to a Hooters?" she asked.

"No, I haven't."

"I have. They didn't hire those girls on the basis of their master's theses." She actually smiled. "Have you seen Kevin?"

"No . . ."

"Nineteen. Sophomore at UMD next year. Half the people in town think Kevin might be gay, because he goes around with these French haircuts. He even gets them done in a ladies' salon down in Grand Rapids. Looks like he came out of one of those science fiction movies. The women up here eat him up like a big ice cream cone. But I don't know anything about it."

"Did McDill sleep with any of the boys?" Virgil asked.

"I have no idea. Well, let me change that. *Maybe*. From what I understand, she'd do a little bit of everything," Stanhope said.

"I was told that she might like to do a little domination routine with the boys," Virgil said.

Stanhope shrugged. "Don't know."

"Did you ask whether anybody knew about McDill and Wendy?"

"Yes, I did, and I couldn't find anybody who'd admit it; and I get up early, earlier than about anybody, and I never saw Wendy heading out to the parking lot."

"And it doesn't bother you that you're running a high-rent, ecologically sensitive whorehouse?"

"But I'm not," she protested. "I don't get a penny of anything that changes hands. I don't make any arrangements. I simply don't interfere when nature takes its course."

"Although you arrange nature a little bit," Virgil said.

"Hooters," she said. "Look. Are you going to put this in the newspapers? I mean, you'd wind up embarrassing a lot of fairly important people for no good reason, and probably wrecking a pretty good business."

"I'm not interested in doing that, Margery. I leave that to our administrative people, and my boss," Virgil said. "But it's possible, even likely, that all of this sex stuff had something to do with the murder. People get killed for money, sex, and drugs—cocaine and alcohol—and sometimes simply because of craziness. I don't see much money here, and not much in the way of drugs. That leaves sex and craziness."

"The sex here doesn't involve competition . . . it really doesn't," Stanhope said. "The boys . . . I don't interfere with the boys, or make any arrangements for them, or anything like that. But everybody knows that the boys are here, and what they might do for you. Word gets around. But there isn't a competition for them—why would you compete, when a couple of hundred dollars would get you what you want?"

"What if you want love?"

She sighed and said, "I've got no answer for that, Virgil. Now, you want to see McDill's friends?"

THE DISCUSSION LEFT A bad taste in Virgil's mouth. Sex was terrific; sex for money, at least in the American culture, was brutally destructive. He didn't care what Stanhope said: it *was* a whorehouse

*

HE MET WITH SEVEN WOMEN in the library; gay or straight, he had no idea. All of them were aware of McDill's sexual orientation, but none of them had seen her with Wendy Ashbach. One woman said that McDill seemed interested in a dock boy named Jared—nobody knew his last name, and Stanhope had gone off on an errand—whom they described as blond and thin and, one woman added, "girly."

When they were done, Virgil took that woman aside and asked, "Did McDill have a sexual relationship with Jared?"

"Maybe. We didn't talk about it, but I'm pretty sure she liked his looks."

"Have you seen him today?"

"No. I haven't seen him for a couple of days, but I haven't been looking," she said.

Virgil found Stanhope and asked, "Who's Jared?"

"Jared? Jared Boehm? He's a dock assistant."

"One of the boys?"

She looked exasperated: "Yeah, I guess."

"Is he working today?" Virgil asked.

"No. He had to take some kind of a test. Over at the university in Duluth. He's trying to get in there. He last worked on Friday."

"I'm gonna need his number."

VIRGIL CALLED JARED BOEHM on his cell phone, got no answer, went back to the motel, got a Coke from the machine in the lobby, and lay on his bed and thought about Slibe and Margery and Jared and the boys.

Just as an everyday, walking-around matter, nothing Slibe said had sounded crazy—if every music wannabe stuck with his old man's business, the world would probably be a better place, Virgil thought. If you didn't mind raising dogs and digging septic systems and splitting wood for winter heat. . . .

Margery. She didn't look like a madam, and he supposed she wasn't, technically; but she did get money from the boys, if only because the boys pulled in the women who wanted a little nocturnal carnality to go with their diurnal snipe hunts.

Jared: the problem was, if Jared was the age Virgil thought he might be, then his "hasty relationships," as somebody had called them, might constitute statutory rape under the laws of Minnesota if the female partner was old enough; or child abuse. If he was getting paid for sex, it was prostitution. If it were any of those things, and there had been an attempt at blackmail, if there had been threats or counterthreats . . .

He needed to talk to Jared.

And he felt bad about Margery. She was a type he liked: tough old ornery woman yanking a good livelihood out of the North Woods. Who ran a few whores.

He remembered the camera memory card he'd taken from McDill's camera. He'd looked at them on the LCD on the camera, but not closely. Had there been a male face anywhere along the way? He rolled off the bed, got the card, read it into his laptop, started paging through the photos. Not much, women at the Wild Goose, pictures taken out on the lake, some down by the swimming beach . . . and a young boy on the dock, standing with a couple of women, apparently telling them something about a boat.

He was tall, thin. Girlish? Maybe; but with some thin, hard muscle, like you might see on a cyclist or a runner. He was subtly at the center of the photograph . . . Jared . . .

HE WAS STILL THINKING about Jared when the motel phone rang. Almost anyone he wanted to talk to had his cell phone number, so he contemplated it for a moment, then picked it up: "Hello?"

"This is Signy. I'm thinking about ordering out for a pizza, but I'm out of beer. Are you up for an emergency beer run?"

"Sounds fine," Virgil said. "Give me twenty minutes."

He was surprised; but then, on second thought, not totally surprised. He and Signy had shared a little spark. He got up, brushed his teeth and shaved, thought about it for three seconds, then jumped in the shower and scrubbed down with Old Spice body wash.

He went out in the night: still hot. Could be thunderstorms lurking somewhere, but the stars were bright overhead, and he heard no thunder anywhere. Signy had given him a Negra Modelo the night before, so he got a six-pack of the same, already cold. He got lost again, on the way out to Signy's, and she talked him in on the cell phone.

WHEN HIS HEADLIGHTS PLAYED across the front of her house, she was waiting outside the door, looking up at the sky, and she came to meet him. "I just ordered it a minute ago, when you called. I didn't want to get stuck with a whole meat lover's if you had to cancel."

"'S okay," he said. "Probably ought to put the beer in the fridge."

He followed her inside, took a couple of bottles out of the six-pack, put the rest in the refrigerator, very aware of her moving around him in the narrow space of the kitchen, and she said, "We ought to take these out to the gazebo."

"You got a gazebo?"

"Last thing Joe did before he went to Alaska—built me a gazebo. Never got the screens in, so I had to do that part. C'mon . . ."

She got a flashlight and led the way out the back door, down a flagstone path, over the lip of the lake bank, and down to the water. The night was dark enough that he couldn't see much but the cone of the light over the path, from the flashlight, and then the greenish timbers of the gazebo. They went inside, and she wedged the door shut, to keep the bugs out. There were two aluminum lawn chairs and two recliners, and she took one of the recliners and Virgil folded into a chair.

"Great night," he said. "Million stars."

"Lot of great nights in August," she said, turning off the flash. The lake was quiet, with still some blue in the west, stars in a thick crescent overhead, and dots of light that were cabin windows on the far shore. Far down to the right, a more golden dot, a weenie-roast fire on a beach. "So what happened with the murder? Did you get anywhere?"

"I don't know. I went around and pissed off a lot of people, hinted that I knew about stuff that I don't know about. See what I could stir up."

"Zoe told me how you massacred the Vietnamese."

"I didn't—"

"Yeah, I know. So does Zoe. She's figured out that talking about it is a way to get on top of you," Signy said. She pulled up her knees, draped her hands over them.

"Fuckin' women," Virgil said.

THEY SAT AND DRANK their beers and Virgil told her about his encounters with Berni and Cat and the others, and with Slibe, and the boy toys. She said, "Slibe. Now there is a wickedly mean guy. Slibe did it."

"You think?"

"He could definitely kill someone," Signy said. She burped. "He's a sociopath. Came up dirt-poor and his old man used to beat him like a cheap carpet. He never saw anything wrong with that, so that's what he did with his wife and son. His wife took off one day, and nobody's heard from her since, but Slibe was pretty hosed. His kid, Junior, is another one to keep your eye on. He might not be violent, but he's not right."

"How about Wendy? Did Slibe abuse her?"

She said, "You know, I don't think so. Wendy is the apple of his eye. Probably the only apple his eye has ever had. Except maybe for his wife."

"Does everybody around here know about the boys going up to the Eagle Nest?"

"I don't know if everybody does," she said, "but I suppose quite a few people do. The word leaks around."

"The sheriff didn't tell me anything about it."

"Well . . . nobody's going to tell the sheriff. He's *really* straight," Signy said. "He'd probably think he had to do something about it."

"And you don't think so."

She shrugged. "Hey. It's a little goddamn squirt in the dark. People having a good time, nobody gets hurt. So why would you care?"

"I know most people don't think about young guys this way, but if they were under eighteen, there could be some legal issues with older women. Statutory rape, child abuse . . ."

She said, "I don't believe the boys would be thinking that way."

"A lot of female hookers think they're in the entertainment industry—you know, like movie stars," Virgil said. "But they're not."

SIGNY GOT ON HER CELL PHONE, pushed a speed-dial button, identified herself, and asked about the pizza, said, "Uh-huh, uh-huh. When do you think, then?" When she hung up, she said, "Jim's on the way. Probably ought to get back."

He trailed her back up to the cabin, and she flopped on the couch and he arranged himself cross-legged on the carpet and asked, "Hear anything more from Joe?"

She laughed and said, "Yes! Today." She jumped up, went out to the kitchen, and came back in a moment with an envelope and took out a picture, laughing as she did it. The picture showed two men, one of them Joe, looking down at a furry black lump; it took Virgil a moment to recognize it as a dead black bear. "He was sleeping in his car and a bear tried to get in with him," Signy said. "This was at a campground by Fairbanks, and he started yelling and the bear started running around knocking everything over and somebody came out and shot it."

Virgil shook his head, feeling bad for the bear, and gave the photo back to her. "I've been to Fairbanks. I was told that in the winter, it's the coldest place on earth."

"Well, Joe hasn't been there for a winter, yet," she said. "He's thinking of going to Anchorage and getting a job on a fishing boat."

A PAIR OF HEADLIGHTS swept the house and she said, "Pizza," and went and got it. They ate it in the living room, sitting close enough that he could feel the warmth from her arm. Virgil asked her about Grand Rapids, and the schools, and her friends, and the Eagle Nest, and the Wild Goose, and Wendy and Berni and Zoe.

About halfway through the pizza, when Virgil was thinking about declining the next piece, she said, "Actually, I have a piece of information for you—I thought of it one second ago. I don't know if it'll mean anything to you, or not. Because, I don't know . . ."

"I accept all information," Virgil said.

She said, "Erica McDill wasn't the first lesbian who was murdered after messing around with Wendy's band. Or who stayed at the Eagle Nest."

Virgil forgot about the pizza. *"What?"*

10

SIGNY ONLY HAD BITS and pieces of the story. A woman whose name was Constance Stifry, Lifry, Snifry, something like that, had two years earlier come up to the Eagle Nest on vacation from Iowa—Iowa City, Sioux City, Forest City, Mason City—"Something-City, I can't remember which, but it was definitely Iowa."

"I can find it," Virgil said.

Signy added, "I think somebody said she'd been here before, but I'm not sure about that."

Wendy's band was playing the area, Signy said, and did a one-week stand at the Wild Goose, but was not yet the house band. Constance whatever-her-name-was was an older woman, but knew a lot about country music. She was also friends with a guy who ran a major country-western nightclub, one of the circuit clubs where the about-to-be-big acts often played, and she suggested that Wendy might want to talk to the guy.

When she went back to Iowa, she did, in fact, talk to somebody, who was, in fact, something of a big shot. There was talk of a gig, of opening for one of the big hat acts.

"And then," Signy said, "she got killed. She got murdered and people were running around looking for the killer, and the whole idea of playing this nightclub kinda went away."

"How do you know this?" Virgil asked.

"From Zoe, who got it from Wendy, and Margery knows about it, too, because Constance whatever-her-name-is, Nifly, Gifly, something like that—Constance stayed at the Eagle Nest, and she was a lesbian."

"Why didn't Zoe tell me?" Virgil asked, running one hand through his hair. Couldn't believe it.

Sig said, "I don't know. I guess maybe . . . The woman was killed down there, in Iowa, and nobody really knew what happened to her. Somebody heard about it, probably one of the lesbians, and people at the Eagle Nest knew her, so the word got around. But it was quite a while ago, a couple of years, anyway. Nobody saw any connection with anything up here. I think the word was, it was a robbery. Maybe. I'm not sure about that part."

Virgil said, "Well, now there's a connection. Goddamnit, Sig, I'm gonna have to scream at your sister. Does she know all the details?"

Sig said, "I don't know what she knows. Really, it was sort of vaguely interesting . . . like you once met somebody who crashed in an airplane, but, you know . . . not all *that* interesting."

Virgil had come over for the pizza, feeling that there was an excellent chance that he would finish the evening with his boots off. Sig was an attractive woman who was apparently suffering the tortures of involuntary abstinence. Even if Virgil wasn't able to solve that problem this very night—misplaced and poorly considered Midwestern courtship manners usually demanded an acquaintanceship of longer than three hours before commissions of adultery—he might have hoped to establish a forward base camp from which to organize an attack on the summit.

But now *this*.

"Ah, man," he groaned. He pulled out his cell phone and found Zoe's number and punched it up, and when Zoe answered, he shouted, "Why didn't you tell me about Constance what's-her-name from Iowa?"

She said, "Oh, God."

"I'm coming over there. Goddamnit, Zoe . . ." He clicked off.

"You're leaving?" Sig asked.

"I gotta . . ."

She tilted her face up at him. "Well, shoot. I was enjoying our talk."

She was definitely standing inside his circle of friendship and he edged a little closer and said, "So was I—I mean, enjoying the talk, but, hell, Signy . . ."

"I know," she said, her eyes resigned. "The woman got murdered. So, maybe sometime . . ."

Virgil eased a bit closer and leaned over and kissed her on the lips and she pushed into him enough that he felt authorized to give her butt a squeeze, and what a glorious appendage it seemed to be. . . .

She pushed off and said, "Goddamnit, your own self. Go see her. Maybe you could call me tomorrow. If you want . . ."

"I want, definitely," Virgil said. He looked around, checking to see if there were any excuses flying through the air that he might grab and use to avoid going to Zoe's, but there were none. "I'll call you," he said.

Signy had been wearing a sweet-tasting lipstick, and a little perfume, and Virgil could taste and smell her halfway over to Zoe's.

ZOE WAS WAITING in her living room, anxious, a twisted sheet of paper in her hand. Virgil thought she might have been pacing, rehearsing whatever she was going to say.

"Virgil, I'm sorry. I didn't really think it was important enough—"

"You're smarter than that," Virgil snapped. "So don't give me any bullshit. Tell me what happened."

"I didn't know exactly, but I went online and found an article in the Cedar Rapids *Gazette*. She was from Swanson, Iowa, near Iowa City. Between Iowa City and Cedar Rapids, anyway . . . I got the article."

She handed Virgil the sheet of paper and he unrolled it.

Sept. 29—Forty-nine-year-old Swanson restaurant owner Constance Lifry was found strangled Saturday night in the parking lot behind Honey's, 640 Main in Swanson, Johnson County Sheriff Gerald Limbaugh said Sunday.

Lifry was a well-known civic activist and a member of several local gardening clubs, and an expert on heritage roses.

Limbaugh said that Lifry was last seen alive by two cleaning women who worked at the restaurant. The women said that Lifry had worked in her office until about 10 P.M. Saturday night, after the 9 P.M. closing, and they found her body when one of the women went outside to smoke a cigarette.

"We are processing a good deal of crime scene information and hope we can settle this quickly," Limbaugh said. "I knew Constance most of my life and everyone who ever met her would tell you that she was a wonderful woman, involved with her community and with the American Heart Association, somebody who worked hard and made jobs for twenty or thirty people. This is a tragedy, and we'll be busting our butts to bring her killer to justice."

He said that Lifry had been strangled with "a cord of some kind, but the killer apparently took it with him."

No witnesses to the murder have been found, he said, "But we're talking to several people, and we're also processing videotape from Larry's Exxon across the street."

THAT WAS THE HARD INFORMATION: the rest of the article was testimonials and history.

"That's all?" Virgil asked. "There was never an arrest?"

"It's not in the paper. I never heard that there was."

"When was she up here?" Virgil asked. "She stayed at the Eagle Nest, right? Did she go to the Wild Goose? What'd she have to do with Wendy?"

Zoe shook her head; she'd been twisting her fingers and sidling around him as he read the article, and now she produced some tears and said, "God, I feel awful about this."

Virgil softened up a notch: "Zoe . . ."

"She was here two summers ago, in August. And some other years, I think. She went to the Goose, she met Wendy, they talked," Zoe said. "There's this big country-western place near Iowa City, called Spodee-Odee. It's pretty important, you know, as a showcase. Lots of big bands play there. Willie Nelson used to play there and Jerry Jeff Walker. Those Texas guys."

"Okay."

"So she . . . I mean, Constance . . . knew the guy who owns the place, whose name is like, Jud. That's all I remember. But they were supposed to be pretty close, and she told Wendy that if Wendy wanted to do it, she'd, uh, recommend the band to Jud. Actually, she didn't like the band so much as Wendy. You know, her voice. She was right—the band back then sorta sucked, but they're a lot better now."

"So she was going to get Wendy a gig," Virgil said.

"More than a gig. A big deal, really. If you play Spodee-Odee, I guess, it's like a badge. You're that good," Zoe said.

"Who would have a problem with that?" Virgil asked.

"With what?"

"With Wendy getting a gig in Iowa City?"

She shook her head. "I don't know. Why would anybody have a problem with it? It's a *good* thing."

"But now we have another woman who was going to do a good thing for Wendy, and she's also murdered," Virgil said. "Right?"

"Right," she said.

"Was Lifry gay?"

"I think so," Zoe said. "I never met her. She was out of my age range. But, that's what I heard."

"From who?"

"I don't know. Wendy, maybe," she said. "Wait: I don't want to get anybody in trouble. I don't know who I heard it from, but I remember that I heard it."

"Okay. From what you know, then, she was right down the line, like McDill," Virgil said, ticking the points off on his spread fingers. "Gay, stayed at the Eagle Nest, talked to Wendy about her band, went to the Wild Goose. And was murdered."

"Yeah, but . . . not murdered for quite a while after she was here," Zoe said.

"Why didn't you tell me?" Virgil asked.

She looked up at him and misted up again: "Because . . . I was afraid that this is all going to blow into the newspapers and television, as some kind of perversion thing, lesbians killing each other, and drag the Eagle Nest down. I was worried about Margery. She's worked her whole life to build up that place, and if it turns out that killers go there, or killers stalk her customers . . . See?"

"Not exactly," Virgil said. "I would have found out sooner or later, and your not telling me delayed things by a couple of days. That's all it did. Let the trail get a little colder."

"I'm sorry," she said. "I'm sorry."

VIRGIL GOT DAVENPORT, who was out for a nighttime walk with his wife. Virgil told him what had happened, and said, "I've got to get down to Iowa City. There's no airline that will get me there faster than a car would, but it's nine hours, and I don't want to drive nine hours, and nine hours back. Can I rent a plane? It's maybe a grand."

"Is it absolutely necessary?"

"It's pretty necessary," Virgil said.

"Tell you what—drive down here, bag out in a motel, and I'll get Doug Wayne to fly you down first thing tomorrow. Tell me a time."

Wayne was a highway patrolman who'd flown Virgil on other trips. Virgil glanced at his watch, did some arithmetic, and said, "Seven o'clock tomorrow morning at St. Paul."

"I'll call somebody right now. You're still in Grand Rapids?" Davenport asked.

"Yeah."

"Okay, uh, you'll be here by two. Five hours of sleep. That good enough?"

"That's fine," Virgil said. "Listen, call the patrol and tell them I'm coming down I-35 with lights. If they'll let me roll, I can get an extra half-hour."

"Plan on it. But I'll call you."

ZOE SAID VIRGIL could drop the boat in her driveway, and when that was done, he headed back to the motel, told the clerk to hold his room, got his bag, and took off. Davenport called as he was pulling out of the parking lot, said, "You're clear all the way down, but don't hit any deer or you'll be all over the place. You're not pulling a boat, are you?"

"No, I'm not pulling a boat," Virgil said. "Why're you always so suspicious?"

"'Cause I got you working for me, for one thing," Davenport said. "I talked to Doug; he'll be ready to fly at seven o'clock."

Then he was driving fast through the starry night, past the hamlets and small towns and widespots, Blackberry, Warba, Swan River, Wawina, Floodwood, Gowan to the Highway 33 cutoff, south to I-35, then hammering down I-35, into Minneapolis by one o'clock. He crashed at the Radisson University, with a wake-up call for six-thirty.

Thought little about God that night; but, still, some.

WAYNE WAS IN HIS FLIGHT SUIT, reading a Walter Mosley paperback and eating a peanut butter cookie. Virgil came in, five minutes late, and Wayne said, "We're rolling."

They were in the air in ten minutes, heading for an airport south of Cedar Rapids. Hertz had promised to have a Chevy Impala waiting for him.

"So tell me about what happened after I dropped you off last time," Wayne said.

Virgil told him about the shoot-out in International Falls, about who did what, and how they set up the ambush, and about the Vietnamese team coming in, about the firefight at dawn.

"Man, people were so proud of you guys," Wayne said. "Nobody was talking about anything else. Fucking North Vietnamese commandos, man, and you guys took them down."

"Didn't feel proud at the time," Virgil said. "Still don't. And we missed their main operator."

"That chick. Yeah. But man, that was something. . . ."

ON THE WAY DOWN, passing from cell tower to cell tower, Virgil talked to the chief deputy for Johnson County, whose name was Will Sedlacek, and who said the sheriff was fishing in Minnesota. "If you tell me he's in Grand Rapids, I'll kill myself," Virgil said.

"I don't know where Grand Rapids is—I thought it was in Michigan, to tell you the truth—but he's on Lake of the Woods."

"That's quite a way from Grand Rapids," Virgil said. "Look, I'll be down there at eleven, and I need to talk to somebody about the murder of Constance Lifry and this country-western bar you got down there—"

"The Spodee-Odee," the deputy said. "Tell you what: call me when you get here, I'll take you over and talk to Jud."

"Deal," Virgil said.

Two hours to Cedar Rapids, clear skies all the way. Wayne said he'd catch a movie up in Cedar Rapids. He'd brought a bag, and was prepared to stay overnight, if Virgil had to.

"I don't think we'll have to," Virgil said. "I mostly need to look at the case file and talk to a few people, and we're all set up on that."

SEDLACEK WAS A BURLY, dark-haired man who pointed Virgil at a visitor's chair and asked, "Have any trouble finding us?" and half listened to Virgil's reply as he poked a number into his office phone and said, "He's here," and hung up.

"Yeah, I got tangled up by the river and went the wrong way around the university . . . nothing to speak of," Virgil said.

Another deputy stepped into the office, carrying a paper file, and Virgil stood up to shake hands with Larry Rudolph, and they all sat down and Sedlacek asked, "What the heck happened up there?"

Virgil ran them through it, both men listening closely, and when he finished, Rudolph said, "That's a hell of a coincidence, if it's a coincidence, but boy, it doesn't *feel* like our guy. Our guy did it with a rope, up close and personal. Gun's a whole different thing."

"Both wound up dead," Sedlacek said.

"Yeah, but I know what he means," Virgil said. "I'll tell you what: I've got all this stuff in my head, not much of it written down yet, so if it's okay with you, I'd just like to go through your file and see if anything pops up."

"Okay with us," Sedlacek said, "but, there's not much there. I mean, all the reports and everything, but we never got the first hint."

"Pissed off Jerry," Rudolph said. "He was good friends with Constance."

"Jerry's the sheriff," Sedlacek said. "He was pushing us like dogs."

"Did it look to you like somebody deliberately ambushed her?" Virgil asked. "Did they rob her? Rape her? Anything?"

"Took her purse, so it could have been a robbery—especially outside her restaurant. Wasn't raped or anything. Wasn't beat up. Whoever did it jumped her with the idea of strangling her. Might have figured she was taking the day's receipts home," Sedlacek said.

"But then they'd have to know about her," Virgil said. "They'd probably be local."

"Pretty much," Sedlacek said.

Rudolph added, "The thing about Swanson is, it's this tiny little town halfway between Cedar Rapids and Iowa City and it's got seven businesses—one gas station, one restaurant, Constance's, and five bars. It used to be where the kids went to drink, but we cleaned that up. But still, it's a honky-tonk town, and a lot of folks still go up there for the atmosphere."

"Is that where the Spodee-Odee is?" Virgil asked.

"Naw. That's in Coralville, out on the strip. That's right next door, here."

THEY TALKED for a few more minutes, then they gave Virgil a table and chair, and he spent an hour combing through a thick but nearly information-free file. All of the technical work looked good, but the technicians simply hadn't found anything except one nylon fiber buried in Lifry's neck, and more under a couple of broken fingernails, which suggested that she'd been strangled with a nylon cord.

Which—except for one thing—was like discovering that the killer wore pants. Useless.

When he was done, he carried the file back to Sedlacek's office to ask about that one thing. Sedlacek asked, "Crack the case?"

"I didn't even bend it," Virgil said. "One thing. The cord that Lifry was strangled with, nylon, I guess, but the ME says that it cut way into her neck muscles. You figure it was a guy?"

"Oh, yeah. That oughta be in there somewhere, but that was our operating assumption," Sedlacek said. "A guy with some muscle: she was not only strangled, she actually bled quite a bit."

"Doesn't fit with us," Virgil said. "We found those tracks, women's boot or shoe . . ."

"You breed some big women up that way."

"But none of the ones I'm looking at could do that," Virgil said. "They're healthy, but I don't see them cutting somebody's head off with a rope."

Sedlacek flipped his hands up. "Can't help you. Anyway, you had anything to eat today? We could get a sandwich and head out to Jud's. He'll be there at one o'clock. . . ."

THEY GOT A BURGER, fries, and a shake at a student bar. Virgil was wearing a Breeders T-shirt under his jacket and a thin blond woman, standing in line for food, leaned toward him and asked, "Are you a musician?"

He grinned at her: "Nope."

"I really admire the Breeders," she said. "Kim Deal is awesome."

"I'd give you the shirt," Virgil said, gesturing across the table at Sedlacek, "but this guy's a cop, and he'd probably bust me for exposure."

"Maybe I could give you a phone number, and you could drop it off," she said. But she was joking, and she twiddled her fingers at him and moved up the line.

"I've been working downtown for ten years and I've *never* been hit on by a college girl," Sedlacek said, looking after her. "What have you got that I don't?"

"Good looks, personality . . . cowboy boots."

"Fuck me," Sedlacek said. "I've been trying to get by on intelligence."

"Well, there you go," Virgil said.

THE CORALVILLE STRIP was a fading business/motel district outside Iowa City, motels, service businesses, insurance companies, a few clubs, and the Spodee-Odee, a big log-sided bar with an acre-sized gravel-and-dirt parking lot and a useless hitching post in front of the doors; and a life-size painting of a John Deere tractor splayed across one side wall, juxtaposed against a Sioux Indian on a pinto horse. A tangle of prickly pear cactuses climbed out of two pots on the front porch, and behind one pot was a sign that said, "Pee on these plants, and you will be shot; survivors will be shot again."

Virgil had followed Sedlacek out to the place, and they got out in a swirl of dust, hitched up their pants, and looked around. Another sign, inside the barred front window, said, CLOSED, but the door was open, and in the dim interior, a bartender was doing paperwork. He looked up and said, "We're not open until four," and Sedlacek answered, "Johnson County sheriff. We've got an appointment with Jud."

"He's in the office," the bartender said, pointing with his pen. "Go on back, right there in the corner."

They followed the line of the pen, across a dance floor and past a twenty-foot semicircular stage. Virgil was impressed: he'd been in a lot of country bars, but the Spodee-Odee was maybe the biggest. In the back, down the hall, was an office suite, a secretary behind a big wooden reception desk, and two more women poking at computers behind her. The secretary said, "Deputy Sedlacek?"

JUD WINDROW POPPED OUT of the back office, a tall, thin, dry-faced guy in a Johnny Cash black shirt with mother-of-pearl buttons, jeans, and cowboy boots; brush mustache, nicotine-stained fingers. He said, "Come on back, y'all want a coffee or a beer?"

"Just ate," Sedlacek said, and Windrow said, "How you doing, Will? We don't see you much anymore."

"Ah, you know, got the kids, I'm so damn tired by the time they get to sleep all I want to do is sleep myself."

"Can't go through life that way," Windrow said. "Get a babysitter. Come out and dance. Your old lady would love you for it. . . . You must be Virgil."

They shook hands and all took chairs and Windrow said, "By the way, I invited Prudence Bauer to come down and talk with us."

A woman stepped through the door, probably fifty, Virgil thought, with small prim features, and gray hair swept up on top of her head in an old-fashioned bun: Prudence, all right. She must have been right behind them, in the parking lot.

"And there she is," Windrow said. He stepped over to Bauer and they air-kissed, and Windrow said to Virgil, "This is Connie's sister. She took over Honey's when Constance passed away."

"Was murdered," Bauer said. She had a low, grainy voice, the voice of the third-grade teacher in Virgil's nightmares.

"Sure," Windrow said.

They all sat down again and Virgil asked Windrow, "What was your relationship with Constance?"

He nodded: "We were probably best friends. Wouldn't you say so, Prudie?"

Bauer said, "I believe so."

Windrow added, "We grew up like twins. Born a week apart, next door to each other in Swanson, raised together, went to school together, talked to each other most every day. When she was killed, it broke my goldarned heart."

Virgil knew of such things, and had old friends in Marshall, Minnesota, whom he might see once a year, but were still close, even intimate, and always would be. "Okay. What—if anything—did you guys have to do with a band run by a singer named Wendy Ashbach from up in northern Minnesota? Or with a resort called the Eagle Nest?"

"Nothing," Bauer said. "I knew Connie went to the Eagle Nest, and she told me a little about this Wendy, that she was a wonderful singer, but I never went up there, and never met Wendy."

"I heard about Wendy from Connie," Windrow said, looking at Virgil over a steeple made of his fingers. "She said there was this terrific country act up in Grand Rapids, and thought I might want to bring them down here. I was planning to go up and listen to them, but then Connie got killed, and that broke the connection. I never followed up."

His affable country-western personality had disappeared behind his businessman's face, Virgil thought—not that he'd ever doubted that the businessman was back there. Running a successful bar was not something done by fools.

"Was there a contract, or an offer . . . ?"

"Nothing official. Connie had an ear for all kinds of music, and if she said this woman was good, then I'd listen," Windrow said. "Also, the woman and her band would probably be cheap. What I do is, I have a house band that plays four nights a week for a month, which are the slow nights. Then the headliner plays on Friday and Saturday, with the house band playing as the opener on those nights. We're closed on Sundays, of course. I would have brought this Wendy in for a one-month gig as a house band. If they were good enough."

"But only if she was cheap," Virgil said.

Windrow wagged a finger at him: "The money would pay for their keep, and a little more. The main thing is, they'd be heard by big-time music people. If a new band does good at the Spodee-Odee, people hear about it. I mean, people who run country music. That's worth more than any money I could afford to pay them."

"But you never . . . nothing ever happened," Virgil said.

"Nope. That was two years ago, almost. Connie's been gone almost two years," Windrow said.

Bauer jumped in. "When I heard why you were coming down here, I looked on the Internet and found the story on this other murder. You know my sister was a lesbian?"

Virgil nodded. "Yes."

"There has been some speculation about this Miss McDill," she said.

"She was a lesbian, or bisexual, businesswoman who stayed at the Eagle Nest, like your sister," Virgil said.

Bauer leaned back in her chair: "Then that's the connection. I prayed to the Lord for two years to give us something. Anything. Connie's murder couldn't have been a random act. The Lord wouldn't allow it."

"That argument might not hold up in court," Sedlacek said.

She waved him off. "I don't care about that. I want to know *why* some animal took Connie's life. If I can find out why, I'll find some peace. The way it is now, I think about it all the time. I have no peace."

Virgil went back to Windrow and pressed him on Wendy, but Windrow insisted that he knew nothing at all about her. "So tell me," he said, "you got that music shirt on, and you've heard her . . . what do you think?"

Virgil thought about it for a moment, then said, "Have you seen the Rolling Stones film *Shine a Light*?"

"'Bout twenty times," Windrow said.

Virgil said, "Think Christina Aguilera. But country."

Windrow tipped back in his chair, raised his eyebrows, and said, "Really."

"Really," Virgil said.

"That's pretty damn interesting," Windrow said. "I'm hunting for a September band. The guy who was coming in hurt himself bad and had to cancel."

"She's good," Virgil said. "Her band's got a couple of soft spots."

"We can fix that," Windrow said. He tipped forward and wrote a note on his calendar, and added, "Backup people are like lamp plugs—plug them in, pull them out. A good one can play anything."

Bauer said, "I believe this will have more to do with sex than with music."

Virgil nodded at her and said, "Well, Miz Bauer, Wendy Ashbach is a little bit gay. She's living with a gay drummer, and spent the night with Miss McDill, the night before McDill was shot to death—so you may be right."

HE TOLD THEM ABOUT the investigation so far, and about the fistfight between Berni and Wendy, and when he did, Windrow made another note on his calendar, then said, "I'm going to run up there and take a look at her."

"You like the idea that she fights?" Virgil asked.

"Yeah, I do," he said. "People like that have an authenticity that these crystalline chicks can't fake. The fans can feel it; they're starved for it."

"Take it easy when you get up there," Virgil said. "We got enough dead people."

AS THEY WERE LEAVING, Bauer said to Virgil, "We saved all of my sister's papers; I thought there might be something in them for an investigator, but nobody saw anything. If you want, I could make them available to you."

Virgil looked at his watch. "I'd like to get out of here before dark—how far are the papers from the Cedar Rapids airport?"

"Five or six minutes," she said. "Swanson is a little way south of the airport."

"Good deal," Virgil said. "I'll follow you up there."

"And I'll probably see you up in Grand Rapids," Windrow said. "How far is it?"

"Nine hours by car, probably. You can fly in, commercial, but there aren't many flights. Bar is called the Wild Goose."

"I fly a little Cessna. Love to do it, don't do it enough," Windrow said. "If the weather's good, I'll head up there in the morning, maybe."

OUT IN THE PARKING LOT, Sedlacek and Virgil shook hands, and Sedlacek said, "Prudence is okay. A little dry, but she's smart, like her sister."

"Seems okay," Virgil said.

"I was worried that she might seem a little crazy, going on about the Lord this and the Lord that, that he wouldn't allow Constance to be murdered at random."

"Who can tell about that," Virgil said, looking over at the woman as she got into a Ford Taurus. "She might even be right."

11

JANELLE WASHINGTON WENT TO WORK in a candy store to pick up extra cash when her husband, a greenskeeper, hopped down off a tractor and tore his ACL. He was out of work for weeks, and they were living on worker's comp payments, and something had to be done.

The candy store barely paid minimum wage, but that was fine. The work wasn't onerous, and they were only bridging the gap between worker's comp and what they needed, so they didn't need a lot. Then, after he got back on the tractor, she decided she liked the contact with other people during the day, and she stayed on with the candy store.

There was a problem, though\. Janelle couldn't stay out of the chocolate. She'd always prided herself on her figure, which wasn't perfect, but her husband, James, seemed to like it a lot, and when she gained two pounds in the first week, and another in the second week, then two more . . . something had to be done.

First, she resolved to eat only two pieces of fudge a day: five hundred calories. Then, during the summer, at least, she'd ride her bike from her house, out in the countryside, all the way into town, eight miles each way, which took her about forty-five minutes each way, and burned, according to an Internet calculator, about five hundred calories. Also, she learned, she'd be building muscles, and more muscles also meant more calories burned.

Now the question was, should she use the extra calories for another piece of fudge? Or really turn herself into a raging piece of super-fit muscle? Staying at two pieces a day was hard, with the owner in the back cooking up all that chocolate. . . .

On this day, she'd finished up, cleaning off the counters, had said good-bye to Dan, the owner, and took off. The first few blocks were stop-and-go, getting out of town, watching the traffic; but once she was on the other side of the river, the traffic disappeared and she started to pump; started to sweat.

She'd never been an athlete, but the bicycle had turned something on, and she was getting addicted to the flow of the thing. . . .

MCDILL'S KILLER SAT in a copse of trees that grew on a natural mound at the intersection of the county road and a trail that led back to a canoe-landing on the Mississippi. From a nest at the top of the mound, both the landing and the road were visible. No canoeists had come along in an hour, and none were visible in a half-mile stretch of the river above the landing.

Washington should be coming around the corner at any minute. Shooting her would do two good things. First, it'd confuse the issue. The killer would carefully leave behind a shell, so they'd know that McDill's killer also shot Washington. But since Washington had no connection to lesbians or Wendy's band or the Eagle Nest, maybe they'd go for the idea that the killings were random. Maybe; but if not, it'd at least be confusing.

The other thing the killing would do is get rid of Washington. Nobody would remember it after she was dead, the killer thought, but Washington knew a little too much about Slibe Ashbach Jr. and his father. . . .

WASHINGTON CAME AROUND the corner a mile away, not pedaling hard, but moving right along. The road was smooth blacktop, and she was clear and steady in the four-power scope. She was wearing a scarf, as a babushka, to keep her hair neat. Her face was clear in the glass . . . four hundred yards, three-fifty, three hundred, and closing . . .

A truck came around the corner behind her. Not moving fast, sort of idling along, and the killer took the gun down, forehead beaded with sweat, breathing hard from a sudden shot of adrenaline. Not good. Not good.

TOM MORRIS SAW JANELLE pedaling along and thought about what might have been if he'd moved a little faster after high school.

They might have hooked up. The possibility was out there, for a while. He knew it, and she knew it, and that made them like each other all their lives, even if nothing happened, and they both wound up happily married to other people.

He slowed, ran the window down, grinned at her, and called, "Still pedaling your ass around town . . ."

"You shut up!" she said.

"No, I think it's a good thing," he said. "I saw James downtown yesterday. He said you guys were going out to Moitrie's on Friday. We might be out there, we're thinking about seven."

She stopped, straddling the bike, moved it over to the truck, and said, "I'll call Patsy. Maybe we can get a table together."

They talked for a minute about a snowmobile club that wanted to take out some unused field crossings, and the culverts that went with them, and if that would put too many snowmobilers on their road, and about the growing flock of crows that were hanging around, and how Morris had hired an exterminator to get the squirrels out of his attic—routine neighbor stuff—and then he said goodbye: "Talk to Patsy. See you out there."

THE PICKUP MOVED ON, slowly, paced by the bike for a hundred yards or so, and then pulled away. By this time, Washington was opposite the killer, then passing, and the truck was still there, moving slow as white paste down the highway, and Washington was farther and farther down, the crosshairs first on her head, but then the head shot became uncertain, and then on her back, on her white blouse . . .

The truck went over a low rise and disappeared. The killer glanced back: nothing from the other direction. But this wasn't as clean as the other killings, there could be somebody . . .

"Ah . . ."

White blouse in the scope, squeeze . . .

The shot was almost a surprise.

WASHINGTON FELT AS THOUGH she'd been hit by a meteor. She was down, and bleeding, in the ditch, her bicycle on top of her, and looked down and found blood gushing from her rib cage, and she began to crawl up the side of the ditch, not thinking, not knowing what happened, wondering if she'd been hit by a car. She began to grow weak, understood that she was going to die if something didn't happen.

One last push and she was on the shoulder, and she tried to hold herself together, tried to think, still not understanding, rolling up, blood on her hands, blood on her blouse, no car, what happened? She could hear herself making a growling noise, and felt the gravel on her face and under her hands, sticky with blood. . . .

Some time passed, and she was mostly aware of the blue of the sky above her, and then the wheel of a car was right there by her head, and she heard the crunch of gravel. A face appeared in her field of vision, and she heard the man's voice:

"Jeez! Janelle! What happened, oh, my God," and she focused on Tom Morris's face and he was on his cell phone screaming, "We've got a woman hurt bad . . . bleeding bad . . . Get some help out here, my God, we need an ambulance, we need an ambulance. . . ."

12

PRUDENCE BAUER HAD FIFTEEN or twenty sealed cardboard moving boxes full of her sister's life, consolidated in a back bedroom, and when Virgil opened the first one, he was hit in the face by a dusty lilac-scented perfume that smelled more like death than death itself. Two of the boxes contained papers taken from Connie's desk within a couple days of her death, including a diary, and an appointment book from the Louvre.

"Was she an art enthusiast?" Virgil asked Bauer, thinking of the museum membership cards he'd seen in McDill's wallet.

"No, not especially—she used to get those from the Barnes and Noble store up in Cedar Rapids. There's another one around, but I think it was on the theme of *cats*."

She left him sitting in a rocking chair, in the bedroom, on a braided rag rug, flipping through the paper and getting nowhere. She came back fifteen minutes later with a Diet Coke: "Found anything?"

He took the Coke. "Not so far. But it all helps: even if I don't see anything now, maybe something relevant will pop up later. It's a matter of getting the most information that you can, into your head."

"You know, you should look at the phone receipts, to see who she was talking to at the time. They're in here somewhere. . . ."

She started digging through boxes of records, looking for the phone receipts, as he paged through the diary, which was fairly bland: who did what to whom, in Swanson, and none of the things done were dramatic, except that a man named Don left his wife, Marilyn, and moved to Marion, wherever that was, to be around a woman named Doris.

"Whatever happened to Don and Doris?" Virgil asked Bauer.

She looked up, her eyes distant, for a moment, and then she said, "I think they moved to Oklahoma. Lake Eufaula."

"So Don never got back with Marilyn?"

"No. Marilyn's still alone. Sometimes I see her standing in her window, looking out. She lives just down the street and around the corner," she said.

"Maybe she's looking for Don coming back," Virgil suggested.

Bauer looked at him and smiled: "That's going to be a long wait. Don and Doris are in love."

HE'D FOUND NOTHING at all when Bauer handed him a stack of phone bills: "There are four calls to northern Minnesota right before she died. Three to one number, one to another."

He took the bills, checked through them, copied the numbers into his notebook, held up the bills, and said, "I'd like to take these. I'll give you a receipt."

"I don't really need—"

"Legal niceties," Virgil said.

He was curious about the numbers, though, got on his phone,

called the office in St. Paul, read the numbers off to Davenport's secretary, and said, "Get somebody to run those down. They're two years old."

"How soon do you need them?"

"I'll be back tonight. You could leave them on your desk, if you get them."

When he'd finished with the paper, he called Doug Wayne, the pilot, arranged to meet him at the airport. Bauer walked him out to the rental car, touched his elbow, and said, "I think you'll find him, whoever he is. When you asked about Don and Doris, that gave me confidence that you're interested in things."

Virgil nodded. "I will find him. I *will* run him down."

"And if you kill the sonofabitch, I would shed no tears at all."

"Why, Prudie," Virgil began, intending to shine the light of his third-best smile on her, but his phone rang and he fumbled it out, looked at the phone number, unknown, but from northern Minnesota. Like a cool breeze down his shirt: he punched up the phone and said, "Yeah?"

"Hey, this is Mapes . . ."

"I was gonna call you, man, but I'm down in Iowa. What happened with that shell?"

"The shell came from a .223 bolt action, but hey, Virgil, shut up for a minute. Listen: a woman got shot, an hour and a half ago. Named Jan Washington. Was she part of your investigation?"

"No, never heard of her," Virgil said. "Where was she shot?"

"In the back, the bullet exited outa her—"

"No, no, where in Minnesota?"

"Oh—right outside town. Outside Grand Rapids. The thing is, since we were still working here, the sheriff asked us to go out and take a look. We came up with one, single .223 shell, fired from a sniper's nest. And I'll tell you what, Virgil—it's going to take the lab to tell us for sure, but I will kiss your ass in Macy's front window if it didn't come out of the same gun as killed McDill."

Virgil didn't react immediately; let it percolate down through the lobes of his prefrontal cortex. Then he said, "Shit."

"Yeah."

"Is the woman dead?" Virgil asked.

"No, she isn't. She's hanging on," Mapes said. "Not talking, but hanging on, and they say that she's got a good possibility of making it, though she's lost most of one kidney and her spleen."

"I gotta get up there."

"See ya," Mapes said.

HE TOLD BAUER ABOUT IT, and she asked, "What does this mean?"

"I don't know," Virgil said. "I'll call you and tell you, when I find out."

HE GOT TO THE AIRPORT before Wayne, and called Sanders, the sheriff, who was driving back toward Grand Rapids from Bigfork, where he'd been looking for Little Linda, and asked, "How is Washington connected to the Eagle Nest?"

"As far as I can tell, she's not," Sanders said. "Her husband said neither one of them has ever been there."

"Her husband—so she's not gay?" Virgil asked.

"Not gay or bi, either one," Sanders said. "At least, that's what I believe, from knowing each other all our lives."

"Does she know Wendy?"

"Probably. Most people do. I asked James—he's the husband—and he said they don't know her well. Know her to see her on the street. They don't go to the Goose."

"Gotta be something there," Virgil said. "This shooting is different enough that if we can see the connection, we'll know who did it."

"We'll ask her when she wakes up," Sanders said. "The thing I thought was, if she was shot because she knows something about all this, and she lived, maybe the guy'll try again. So I got three people around her. They'll stay long as it takes."

"Good idea, man. Listen, I'm heading that way. Talk to you in the morning," Virgil said.

★

145

HE GOT UP IN THE AIR with Wayne, called Davenport, filled him in, and took a call from Zoe: "Have you heard?" she asked.

"Yeah, I heard. How did you hear?"

"Everybody in town knows," Zoe said. "There were only about ten deputies out there, and they're blabbing all over the place. They say your crime-scene crew said it's the same guy who shot Erica."

"Could be. Damnit. You know anything about this woman?"

"Works in a candy store. She's more Sig's age than mine, but she seemed nice enough. Her husband works at the golf course, and they organized a deal to put some cross-country ski tracks around the course in the winter, and Jan raised the money for a tracking machine. She just seems . . . nice."

"Is she part of the gay community up there?"

"Oh, God, no. And I'd know. Nope. She was not—is not," Zoe said.

"Maybe I'll stop by Sig's when I get up there. Think she'd know any more?" Virgil asked.

"No, but I wouldn't doubt that she'd like to tell you what she knows."

She said it with a little snap, and Virgil thought, *Uh-oh.* And didn't pursue it. "Okay. Well, see you up there. Probably coming in late."

THEY WERE BACK in St. Paul before dark, landing into the setting sun, the prop beating through the pulsing orange starfire as they touched down. Virgil thanked Wayne, threw his bag in his truck, and drove over to the BCA headquarters on Maryland Avenue, climbed the stairs and walked back to Davenport's office, checked his secretary's desk. A file folder sat squarely in the middle of the work space, and *Virgil* was scrawled across the folder with a Sharpie.

He opened it and found a single piece of paper, with a name, Barbara Carson, and an address in Grand Rapids, attached to the number that had been called once. The other number, which Constance had called three times, was for the Eagle Nest.

On the way out the door, he ran into the BCA's resident thugs, Jenkins and Shrake, coming through the door. They were both big guys, in sharp suits and thick-soled shoes, whose faces had been broken a few times. Jenkins said, "It's that fuckin' Flowers."

Shrake asked, "Has he got on one of those fruity musical shirts?"

Jenkins looked at it and said, "Hard to tell. It says, 'Breeders.'"

Shrake: "Christ, if he's breeding, now, we gotta find a way to stop it."

Jenkins: "I read your stories in *The New York Times*, and I was wondering, could I have your autograph?"

"Envy is a sad thing to see," Virgil said. "But I suppose my proximity might bring a little joy into your humble lives."

"Weren't you dating a little Joy a couple of years ago? Played sandlot beach-ball bingo or some shit?" Jenkins asked.

"She was a professional beach volleyball player and was highly skilled," Virgil said. "And her name was June, not Joy."

"I believe the skilled part," Jenkins said. "She looked like she had all sorts of skills."

"A maestro on the skin flute," Shrake said.

"The old pink piccolo," Jenkins added.

Shrake asked, "So what's happening up north? You figure it out?"

"It's a little nuts," Virgil said. He gave them a quick outline of the situation, and they all drifted over to a snack machine behind the atrium and rattled some coins through it, dropping out bags of corn chips. Virgil realized he hadn't eaten since lunch, and was close to starvation.

When he finished telling them about the two shootings, Shrake said, "You know, you're right. It is nuts. You've got a nut. One of your problems is, none of this other stuff—the lesbians, the resort, the band, Wendy—might have anything to do with it. Even the murder down in Iowa. It might just be some weird high school kid with a rifle, getting his rocks off."

Jenkins said, "The first woman who got shot, in the canoe—shooting her like that was pretty unprofessional, you know? If he's four inches off at eighty or ninety or a hundred yards, on a moving target, he misses clean, and she's over the side and under water. He could have shot her in the chest, which is twice as big a target. So the thing is, he was either showing off, or . . . well, there isn't an *or*. He's proud of himself. Proud of his ability to do that."

"So why'd he shoot the other woman in the back?" Virgil asked. Something was tickling at the back of his brain, a thought, but he couldn't catch it.

"We don't know, but I bet there's a reason. Bet the shot was longer. You said she was riding a bike. If she was moving fast, and it was a long shot—that might have been one hell of a shot," Jenkins said. "Not moving, between the eyes, eighty yards, is an easier shot than hitting something that's moving fast, bouncing maybe, at two hundred yards. We need to know how far away he was. . . ."

"So you think he's a shooter. A marksman."

"He thinks he is," Jenkins said. "Or he's like Lee Harvey Oswald—he's trying to prove something."

VIRGIL HAD BEEN LEANING against a wall, and now he straightened and said, "I've got to get my ass back up there."

"She out in the car?" Shrake asked.

"Who?"

"Your ass," Shrake said, and he and Jenkins faked laughs and bumped knuckles.

"Listen, boys, if I get to the point where I need to beat the answers out of somebody, I'll give you a call," Virgil said.

"Always happy to protect and serve," Jenkins said.

Virgil left, still trying to catch the thought that the two thugs had stirred up; still didn't catch it, but it was back there, and felt like it did when he went to the supermarket and forgot to buy the radicchio.

A thought that itched.

VIRGIL HEADED NORTH, up I-35, stopped more or less halfway at a diner called Tobie's. Hungry as he was, he didn't feel like diner meat, so he got a piece of blueberry pie and a cup of coffee, pushed on, north and then west, and pulled into his motel in Grand Rapids at ten minutes after ten. He carried his bag up to his room, and found the phone blinking. A message from Signy: "I talked to Zoe a minute ago and she thought you might have a question for me, about Jan Washington. I'm always up until midnight, so come on over if you want."

He thought about it for a minute—he was tired, but not too—and headed out, stopped at a supermarket and got a hot whole-roast chicken and a six-pack, and drove out to Signy's. He saw her shadow on the window when he pulled in, and then she pushed the door open, a wry smile on her face, saw the supermarket bag, and said, "Oh, you brought me roses. You shouldn't have."

"Bought you something better than roses—I bought you a roast chicken," Virgil said.

He went through the door, and she said, "You must think I'm sitting out here starving."

"No, but I have the feeling that you're not much interested in cooking," he said. "Maybe that's why Joe left; he wanted a pork chop."

"You could be onto something," she admitted. She opened the chicken bag and the scent filled the room, and she said, "You cut up the chicken, I'll open the beer."

They ate at the little table, facing each other, and he asked her about her day, and she told him about the quilt group that couldn't talk about anything but the McDill murder, and how, halfway through the quilting bee, Zoe had called her to tell her about Jan Washington, and how the group had freaked out.

"They really, really couldn't figure that out. We all decided that there's a crazy man loose. You're going to start getting some pressure, I think. People want this guy caught right away. They don't want to hear how it's hard. And if you can't, then bring in more cops until everybody's got their own cop."

Virgil told her about his day, and asked about the woman Barbara Carson, whom Constance Lifry had called before she was murdered. "Barbara," she said. "Hmm. I know her, she used to work for the county in human services or something like that—welfare, I think. But she's an older lady . . . if you wanted me to swear that she's not gay, I couldn't. I couldn't swear that she was, either. Zoe might know."

"How about Jan Washington?" Virgil asked. "We think it's the same woman who shot McDill . . . or the same person anyway. The same gun. What's the connection?"

"Beats me," she said. "We all live in the same town. But Barbara . . . Everybody else involved in this, like Margery and McDill and this Constance woman and Wendy and even Zoe, are worker-types, and they're gay. Jan is a housewife who never wanted to work, but she had to, because her *husband* got hurt. I can't think of *anything* she really has in common with the others. She goes to the First Baptist Church, and she helps organize food-shelf drives, and I don't think any of the other ones go to *any* church. Not one of them."

"Huh." He looked at her, and she brushed hair out of her eyes.

"What?" she asked.

"Do you have a gun?"

"You think *I* shot them?" She was incredulous.

"No, no, of course not. I was thinking, you're out here alone, your sister is seen hanging around with a cop, and her house gets broken into," Virgil said. "Now the cop investigating the murders is hanging around you. . . . I don't want you to be a target. If you already are, I'd hope you'd be able to defend yourself."

"How do you defend yourself? He shoots you in the back when you're riding your bike, or when you're sitting in a canoe, bird-watching. He's a sneak."

Virgil got up, rinsed his hands and face in the kitchen sink, and dried himself with a paper towel, and said, "The Washington shooting could be the critical one that breaks this, because it'll bring light from an entirely different direction. Unless he's a nut . . ."

He went out and dropped on the couch, and she brought her beer along and dropped next to him, and he put his arm around her shoulders and she said, "It's a little scary, all right."

"It's a little scary when you think that somebody broke into Zoe's place."

"Well, I do have a gun, a shotgun, a twenty-gauge that Joe bought me," she said. "It's under my bed. My windows are pretty good—I was thinking I could stack some beer cans behind the doors, and if they fall over . . ."

"Lock yourself in the bedroom with your cell phone and scream for help," Virgil said.

"Mmm," she said.

Virgil stroked her hair and she leaned closer, and he kissed her; and events moved along, as they do, and at some point down the line, he popped the catch on her brassiere and slipped his hands around her breasts. They were, in the whole world of breasts, on the smaller side, but that was fine with Virgil. He'd seen more than one of his mother's friends go from 38C to 38-Long, and that was not a problem with the slender ones. . . .

"Mmmm."

They were both breathing hard, and he was in the precise process of squeezing her left nipple between his thumb and forefinger, like picking a blueberry, and she had a hand on his belt buckle, when his cell phone went off.

She jumped and said, "Virgil . . . For God's sakes, you left your phone on?"

The curse of being a cop, and not the first time this had happened to him. He groaned and thought about letting it go, but curiosity got the better of him and he slipped it out. The sheriff. He groaned again.

"Who is it?"

"The sheriff," he said.

"Well . . . answer it. Better than wondering what he wants," Sig said.

Virgil clicked up the phone and Sanders asked, "Where are you?"

"Just got some gas, I'm gonna turn in," Virgil lied.

"Head over to the hospital," Sanders said. "One of my guys called two minutes ago and said Jan Washington woke up, and she's talking. You need to talk to her—just in case."

"In case . . ."

"She dies," Sanders said.

"Of course," Virgil said.

He hung up and looked at Signy for a minute, and said, "I can't help it."

He told her what happened and she stood up and said, "Then you really do have to go. Come on. Get up."

They went to the door, and she was tangled up in her shirt and brassiere, and Virgil stopped to kiss her good-bye and she said, "I'm a mess," and she stopped fighting the tangle of clothing and simply took it off, and Virgil asked, "Aw, man, did you have to do that?" and he crowded her into the corner between the door and the wall, and they were in there for a minute or so and then she pushed away, laughing, and said, "Take a good look, buster, and get out of here."

He got out.

Preceded by what he believed to be the most substantial erection he'd had since junior high.

13

THE HOSPITAL WAS A sprawling flat red building south of town; Virgil found a parking space near the emergency room, and jogged across the tarmac and through the door. A nurse spotted him as he came through and he blurted, "Virgil Flowers, Bureau of Criminal Apprehension—I'm here to see Mrs. Washington."

"Have to hurry. She's sort of in and out," the nurse said.

JAN WASHINGTON'S HUSBAND was an overweight balding guy who wore Wal-Mart glasses and a pathetic mask of fear, choked by the violence to his wife. He was sitting in the hospital hallway outside the intensive care unit, in a metal-and-plastic chair, while Sanders squatted beside him, one hand on Washington's shoulder. When Virgil walked up, Sanders stood and said, "Virgil: James Washington, Jan's husband."

Virgil shook Washington's hand and said, "We're sorry about your wife, Mr. Washington. How is she?"

"She's hurt bad; hurt bad," Washington said.

Sanders said, "We've got one of our investigators in there talking with her; she's pretty drowsy."

Virgil said, "I'll step in and listen. . . ." He turned to the door, then stopped and said, "Mapes told me about that .223 shell. How far was the shooter from where Mrs. Washington went down?"

"Two hundred and forty-four yards," Sanders said.

"And she was riding her bike at the time?"

"Yes . . ."

Jenkins and Shrake had been right, Virgil thought. The shooter was showing off, or proving something . . . or maybe was just really, really good with a rifle.

INSIDE THE ICU, Washington looked like everybody looked in an ICU: on her back, head propped a little forward, eyes closed, electric monitoring lines running under her hospital gown, drip lines running into her arms, a catheter draining her bladder, the urine collected in a bag visible under the sheet on one side of her bed.

A cop sitting near her head looked up at Virgil, who said, "BCA—Virgil Flowers," and the cop nodded and said, "She comes and goes."

"She have any ideas?"

The cop shook his head. "None. No ideas at all . . ."

Without opening her eyes, Washington said, in a rusty-sounding voice, "I'm here."

The cop said to Virgil, "I don't have a lot more to ask . . . if you want to talk to her."

Virgil said, "Mrs. Washington, I'm from the state police. Did the deputy tell you that we think the man who shot you also shot Erica McDill, the woman who was killed at the Eagle Nest?"

No response for a second, then a slight nod, and the slow words, "Yes . . . I don't know . . . why."

As far as she knew, she had no connection with Erica McDill—had never even heard the name, she said—and not much with the Eagle Nest, though she did know Margery Stanhope somewhat, through a gardening club. She knew Wendy and other band members by sight, but not really to chat with, and had known Slibe Ashbach and his wife twenty years earlier.

"Were they close—did you have a falling-out, or something?"

"No, no, nothing like that. I worked for the county for a while, in permits, and Maria Ashbach would come in for permits. We weren't friends or anything, we'd just chat when she came in. Then, she ran away, and that's the last I know."

"Mrs. Washington, when you were shot, were you riding fast, or slow?"

"I think . . . I can't remember right when I was shot, but I think I was riding regular . . . about twelve miles an hour is my regular."

"Twelve miles an hour. You know that?"

"That's my regular. I have a speedometer on my handlebars."

Twelve miles an hour, two hundred and forty-four yards: heck of a shot. The shooter, Virgil thought, knew his capabilities, went for the bigger target at the longer distance, and pulled it off. There was something here, Virgil knew, but he couldn't pin it down. Something that he knew . . .

"Mrs. Washington, I have one more question, and you being in your condition, I hate to ask, but I have to . . ."

She said, "I'm not having an affair. Neither is James."

The cop grinned at Virgil and said, "We covered that territory."

"Okay. I had to ask. Listen, I deal with wounded people, and you're gonna be all right. You'll hurt for a while, but they'll fix you up good as new."

She nodded again, and a few seconds later, drifted off.

OUT IN THE HALL, Virgil spoke to her husband, again with the apology for having to ask. James Washington said, "Hell no, I'm not messing around with anybody. Why does everybody ask that?"

"Because when a married woman gets shot under unusual circumstances, the first guy we look at is the husband, and most of the time, he did it. In this case, we don't think you did—never did—but we have to push a little, we have to let you know that if you were fooling around, you better tell us now, and explain that, because we'd find out sooner or later," Virgil said.

"Did all my fooling around before I married Jan. Nothing since," Washington said.

He had no more idea of where the shot might have come from. They were talking about that when another man, who looked something like Washington, heavy and balding, stuck his head down the hall and said, "James—how's she doing?"

The sheriff said to Virgil, "This is Tom Morris. He's the one who found her and called the ambulance. He saw her just before she was shot."

Morris told his story:

"I was driving up behind her on that stretch along the river, right outside of town, and I stopped to talk for a minute, and then went on my way. I went over this little hill and couldn't see her anymore, but then there's a little bigger hill and when I got to the top, I looked in the mirror and I thought I saw her layin' on the road. She was wearing this white blouse and she looked like she was on the road, so I stopped and looked out the back window, but I was a long way away, and it did look like she was down, so I turned around and went back. . . ."

Virgil dug into the story and between the four of them, and knowing where the shot came from, they worked out a sequence: the shooter was waiting for Washington to get close on her bike, and probably planned to shoot her as she came up to his sniper's nest, or immediately after she'd passed him. But then Morris came along, and he couldn't shoot until Morris was out of sight. Then Morris went over the hill, and he shot Washington and probably ran down to his vehicle, and took off in the other direction, back toward town.

Morris said, "I thought about it, and the guy was taking a hell of a risk. He had to be parked down on that canoe-landing, and then walk up on that hump. He could see a long way to the west, but he couldn't see no more than a half-mile to the east, and if he'd pulled the trigger and then a car had come around the curve to the east, he'd have been screwed. He'd have had to kill that guy, too. If I'd come around the corner one minute later, it'd have been me."

"Not a lot of traffic out there, though," Sanders said.

"No, but there's *some*," Morris said.

"Could he have been in a boat?" Virgil asked.

The other three men looked at one another, then the sheriff said, "We asked that question, but we don't have an answer. The thing is, if he was in a canoe, the river bends away from the road about right there, going west. It's really more like a big creek than a river right there . . . but he could have gotten lost pretty quick, and a mile or so upstream, another road comes along on the other side, where he could have left his car. There are places along there, back in the trees where it'd be completely out of sight. . . . It could be done."

"It'd take some serious stones," Morris said. "The problem is, in a canoe, he's moving slow. And if he's seen, he's got no way to run. It'd be a hard fifteen-minute paddle back to his car."

"Or her car," Virgil said.

"Doesn't feel like a woman anymore," Sanders said. "I could go with a woman on the McDill thing, but this doesn't feel like a woman to me."

"The guys in Iowa think their killer is male," Virgil said. He filled in Morris and Washington on the Iowa murder, and warned them that it might not have anything to do with McDill and Jan Washington.

BEFORE LEAVING, Virgil took Sanders off down the hall and asked, "You know a woman named Barbara Carson? Lives here in Grand Rapids?"

"Sure . . . she's an older lady, she's about six blocks from here. Used to work for the county."

"The woman who got killed down in Iowa called her before she came up here. I need to talk to her, I guess. Tomorrow."

"I'll get you an address."

"How about a kid named Jared Boehm? Works out at the Eagle Nest."

Sanders pulled back a bit. "Jared? Sure. His dad's a manager at the paper plant. Why?"

"I need to talk to him, too," Virgil said.

"About this stuff?"

"Some people think that Erica McDill might have been fond of him," Virgil said.

Sanders stared at him for a minute, then said, "Oh, shit."

"Hey, I don't know if it's serious—I just picked up a rumor, and he hasn't been back to work since the killing," Virgil said.

"I'll run him down tonight," Sanders said. "Call me first thing tomorrow."

"Good kid?" Virgil asked.

"Yeah. You know—he wears shirts like this." Sanders tapped Virgil's Breeders T-shirt. "He's got a funny haircut."

"Girls like him?"

Sanders said, "I never thought about it, but now that I think about it, I expect they do. Good-looking kid."

"There you go," Virgil said. "I'll call you."

VIRGIL WENT BACK to his lonely motel room, thought about Signy, lying unfulfilled in a lonesome bedstead in her rural cracker-box, and himself, lying unfulfilled in his concrete-block motel, and about God, and about how God was probably laughing his ass off. Virgil laughed about it himself for a couple of moments, then thumbed the switch on the motel lamp and went to sleep.

HE'D CRACKED HIS EYES in the morning, had thought about how the pillow smelled funny, and had considered the possibility of getting up, when Sanders called. "Jared Boehm is at home, with his mother, who is an attorney. Susan isn't sure they'll talk to you, but you can go over."

"When they say they're reluctant, does that mean they're reluctant because Jared might have been up to something? Or reluctant because it's a knee-jerk response from Mom?"

"I tend to think knee-jerk. She thinks she's smarter than anyone in Grand Rapids, including her husband and any cops, and she went into full oh-no lawyer mode when I told her you wanted to talk to her son."

"Did you tell her why?" Virgil asked.

"Nope. I said you were talking to everyone who knew McDill."

"Find Little Linda yet?"

There was a moment of silence, then Sanders said, "No."

Virgil laughed, though he knew it was wrong.

VIRGIL GOT THE BOEHMS' ADDRESS and directions on how to get there, and an address for Barbara Carson, cleaned up, got out a Stones shirt from Paris, 1975, his most formal T-shirt, suitable for talking with attorneys, and pulled it on. Gave his boots a quick buff, and headed out: another good day, a good fishing day, just enough wind to keep cool. He was officially on vacation. He had his boat, right down at Zoe's . . .

The Boehms lived out of town, on Lake Pokegama, in a tree-thick neighborhood of ranch-style houses, long driveways, and boats. Virgil pulled his truck into the Boehms' place, glanced at a beat-up sixties Pontiac sitting on a trailer—he wasn't a gearhead—and knocked on the front door.

Sue Boehm looked like an attorney: dark brown hair, dark brown suit, beige blouse, practical heels, panty hose. A real estate attorney, Virgil thought, as she asked, "Could I see some ID?"

He showed her his identification, and she said, curtly, "Okay," as though she were still suspicious, and, "Come in."

Inside, no sign of Jared. Boehm backed off a few steps and asked, "What's this about?"

"I need to talk to Jared about Erica McDill."

"Is this informational, or do you see him as a suspect?" she asked.

"I'm interviewing a pretty broad group of people," Virgil said. "Is there any reason that I should treat him as a suspect?"

"Of course not," she said. "He's a teenager and a good kid. He graduated from high school near the top of his class."

Virgil spread his hands in a placating gesture: "Then . . . there should be no problem. But let me ask you, are you a criminal attorney?"

"No. I do mostly property law," Boehm said.

Virgil nodded. "My concern is, if you're not familiar with criminal procedure, you'll unnecessarily block the investigation, when a criminal attorney would recognize the questions as routine. And I have to treat Jared as a potential suspect: read him his rights and so on. I think . . . if you think an attorney is a necessity, that you'd be better off getting a criminal attorney. I could come back later, if you wish."

"He doesn't need to be defended against a crime," she said. "He needs to be defended against somebody who's trying to pin something on anybody available."

Virgil shook his head: "We really don't try to do that, Mrs. Boehm. A criminal attorney would probably know that. Maybe you should call somebody."

She looked at him for another moment, then said, "In here."

JARED BOEHM WAS A TALL, thin boy—young man—with a fashionably gelled upright haircut that gave him a permanent look of surprise and irony. He was sitting on the living room couch, wearing jeans and a T-shirt that said, "Make tender and awkward sexual advances, not war." He was nervous; over his shoulder, through the window, a Hobie Cat had been dragged onto the lawn, and a runabout was hanging off a wooden dock.

His mother said, "This is Officer Flowers."

Virgil shook hands with him, sat down, said, "Like the shirt," and Boehm nodded and asked, "Want to trade?" and Virgil said, "I'll stick with the Stones, I guess." He opened his notebook and explained about rights, and read the Miranda card to the kid. Boehm nodded that he understood, and Virgil made a note of the time and circumstances, and then asked, "Could you tell me where you were when Miss McDill was killed?"

"He was in Duluth," Susan Boehm said.

Virgil waved her down: "I really have to get this from Jared, okay? Your answers don't work for me."

Jared said, "I was in Duluth. I worked until three, and Erica—Miss McDill—was up at her cabin when I left, and I said good-bye and went home, and got my bag, and started off to Duluth. Driving. I got to the campus about five and checked into the dorm—there was an orientation, and I ate with some other guys in the cafeteria. There was a guy named Rusty Jones who took us around."

"How many people in the group?" Virgil asked.

"Maybe . . . ten. Or eleven. Something like that."

"Okay. And if I talk to Rusty Jones, he'll tell me that you were there around five o'clock?"

"He should. I was," Jared said.

Virgil doodled, and then asked, "Did you see anybody hanging out with Miss McDill, or did you ever see any kind of conflict, any trouble?"

He said, "No, not really."

"Was she popular in the camp?"

"I guess. She had friends . . . I never really saw any hassles. I've been thinking about who might have something against her, but all I can think of is that sometimes people disagreed about stuff, you know? One wants to do this, the other wants to do that. . . . But not something that would get anybody shot. I've seen people pissed off, but never like I thought there'd be a fight."

"Okay." Virgil shut his notebook, turned to Susan Boehm, and said, "I'm going to call this fellow Rusty Jones and confirm that Jared was there—but I really don't think Jared would be dumb enough to lie about it . . ."

"He isn't," she said, still cold, but relaxing.

". . . and since we believe it's the work of one person, that would rule Jared out. At this point."

"So are we done?" Jared asked.

"Not quite," Virgil said. "I'd like to talk to you for a minute, privately."

Susan Boehm snapped, "No way."

Virgil said to Jared, "If you're eighteen, you can ask your mom to step away."

"Okay," Susan Boehm said, standing up. "That's enough. Out of the house."

Virgil shook his head. "This is why you should have had a criminal attorney," Virgil told her. "I need to finish my interview with Jared. The law says I can do that. You invited me in. Time is of the essence. I would like to talk to Jared privately. If you both refuse, I'll talk to him with you in the room. It's up to you two."

"About what?" Jared asked.

"I think you might know," Virgil said.

Jared looked at him for a moment, then turned to his mother and said, "I think you better leave."

"No fucking way," she said.

Mother and son dueled for a minute, and Jared caved: "I can't do anything without you getting all over me."

She said, "It's for your own good."

"No, it isn't," he said. "It's because you're a fucking control freak."

She recoiled: "You can't speak to me that way!"

Jared ran his hands through his hair: "Ah, God." Then, to Virgil: "Go ahead."

"You had a sexual relationship with Miss McDill?"

Susan Boehm looked as though Virgil had slapped her. She stared at her son: "What?"

With perhaps a glimmer of satisfaction, Jared said, "Yes."

"Did you . . . see her often?"

"Twice. She came in on Saturday, and I went over there on Wednesday and Thursday evenings."

"Was anybody else there when you were?" Virgil asked.

"No. Just us."

Susan Boehm's head was going back and forth like a spectator's at a tennis match.

"Did you hear that she'd spent time with anyone else?" Virgil asked.

"I heard that like on Tuesday, she was there with Wendy Ashbach. Tuesday night."

"Who'd you hear it from?"

"I don't know, really. I was working the dock and I heard these two women talking, joking, about Wendy and Erica," Jared said. "I don't even know that Wendy was there, just that they were hanging, you know, but I got the impression that Wendy was there. But I'm not sure about that."

"What's going on here?" Susan Boehm asked her son. "You were *dating* this woman? Wasn't she a lot older than you?"

Virgil: "Mrs. Boehm—"

"Don't *Mrs. Boehm* me," she said to Virgil. To her son, "Why would he ask you if there was anybody else there while you were, were . . ."

Virgil said, "Listen, I don't think we need—"

Jared said, "Because, Mom, she paid me three hundred dollars a time to fuck her."

This time, Susan Boehm went down for the count, standing there, her mouth flapping. Jared said to Virgil, "You knew that, right?"

"Yup. You have to kick any of that back to Margery Stanhope?" Virgil asked.

"No . . . jeez, she'd kill us if she found out about it."

"Okay . . . was Miss McDill paying anyone else?"

"I don't think so," Boehm said. "She picked up on me right away, and she was flirting with a couple other women there."

Susan Boehm, still flapping, "Other women?"

"Yeah. She was a bi," Jared said. To Virgil: "I'm telling you the truth. I don't know what happened. I don't have any ideas. I sat around thinking about it, but I couldn't think of anything. If I had, I would have come to talk to you, or somebody. As it was, I decided to keep my mouth shut and see if I could slide through."

"Wasn't going to happen," Virgil said. "People joke about 'the boys.' You were toast."

"Didn't know that," Jared said.

Virgil asked, "Were there any other women interested in you, who might have become jealous when you went with Miss McDill?"

162

"No . . . there was a woman the week before, named Karen something or other, but she was gone," Boehm said.

"Okay. Did you see or hear anything about Wendy Ashbach or her band when you were hanging around with Miss McDill?"

Boehm jabbed a finger at Virgil. "Yes. She talked about that. They had a deal. She asked me what I thought about Wendy's band, and I told her I didn't like country music, but that Wendy had a good voice and I thought she could go somewhere. And she told me she was going to take Wendy there. She patted some papers. Like, she had some papers there, and I thought they might be a contract or something, but I didn't ask. But: she was deep with Wendy."

"Have you ever had any kind of relationship with Wendy?"

"No. Nope. If I had a chance, I wouldn't," Boehm said. "You ever seen her brother? The Deuce? There's one scary guy. He's goofy, and he could pull your arms off, and I think he's hot for Wendy. I'd like to know what that's all about. . . ."

"Hot for Wendy. Is this a rumor, or something you know, or what?" Virgil asked.

"Just from school. He dropped out as soon as they'd let him, and they were happy to see him go. Didn't make any difference, he wasn't going to graduate anyway. He was a couple years behind me, so he must be about sixteen? People used to say, you didn't want to mess with Wendy or the Deuce would kill you. They meant it: kill you."

"Tell me one person who said that."

He thought a minute, then grinned and said, "Tommy Parker. He's still here, he works at Parker Brothers motors in the summer, for his dad. He goes to the U. I saw him yesterday. You catch him, ask him what happened when he asked Wendy to go to the prom."

Virgil made a note of the name. "Anything else?"

Jared shook his head. "No. Who are you going to tell about all this?"

Virgil stood and said, "At this point, nobody. I'll tell you, Jared, I'll check your alibi for the time of the murder, but right now, I believe you. And if I were you, I'd keep my mouth shut about your summer job. You really don't want to be in the newspapers."

"So you're not going to do anything?" he asked.

"Not at this point," Virgil said, "I was mostly concerned about whether there might be a sexual conflict involving the boys that led to the murder. You don't seem to think that there was."

"I don't think so," he said. "She showed up, she let me know she was interested, I don't think any of the other guys were cut out, or anything. She didn't seem interested in a three-way . . . and that was about it."

"Okay. Listen, you take care of yourself," Virgil said. "We don't know what's going on here, but . . . be cool. Watch TV. Go to Duluth. Don't go wandering around by yourself until we get this guy."

AS VIRGIL WAS LEAVING, he heard Susan Boehm ask, "A three-way?" and he thought to himself, *I just said "this guy." That feels right. The killer's a he. So who made the Mephisto prints?*

He was getting in his truck when Susan Boehm blew through the front door and shouted, "Wait a minute! Wait!"

He got back out and she steamed up and said, "Something has to be done."

Virgil shrugged. "I don't know exactly what."

"But this is . . . sexual exploitation. This might be statutory rape."

"It's prostitution, is what it is," Virgil said. "My problem is, I know one boy—your son, and he certainly wouldn't testify against himself—and one patron, Erica McDill, who was murdered. So who do I charge?"

"You mean . . . ?"

"I thought about going after Margery Stanhope, but she denies knowing anything about it, and your son confirms it. I don't necessarily believe Margery—that she doesn't know anything about it—but if everybody agrees she wasn't part of it, what am I going to do? None of the women will testify against themselves, and none of the boys would. All we could do is send in a woman agent, get one of the boys to proposition her and mention a price, and then bust him for prostitution, but . . . I don't even know if that would work. Or if we could get a conviction."

"So nothing's going to get done," she said.

"If a group of parents had a quiet word with Margery, it might end. Or maybe not. You're talking about a bunch of horny college boys who need the money, and you heard what Jared said: three hundred dollars a time to have sex with her. Who knows? He might make thirty thousand dollars a year, tax free, if he works at it. . . . Of course, he's a prostitute."

She started to blubber and he patted her on the shoulder. "Listen, talk to your husband. Figure something out. Tell me what you want to do, if anything, and I'll try to help out. But I'm not sure this is a problem the law is very well equipped to deal with."

Still blubbering, she headed back toward the house.

VIRGIL BACKED HIS TRUCK out of the driveway and thought, *The killer's male. What's this about the Deuce?*

He thought about the Deuce, but then switched back to Susan Boehm, and for a moment felt very, very sorry for her, and for her son; not bad people, probably. And he hadn't been exactly diplomatic about it: *Of course, he's a prostitute. . . .*

He drove to Barbara Carson's, suffering from the knowledge that he'd been an asshole. Maybe, he thought, looking for an excuse, the realization of assholedom was the beginning of wisdom.

But probably not.

14

BARBARA CARSON WAS A bust. An elderly widow who got around with a walker, she lived in a tiny rambler with a yard full of nasty-looking rosebushes.

"I did know her quite well," she said. She looked like Santa Claus's wife, with curly white hair and pink cheeks. "We corresponded regularly about our heritage roses."

Virgil learned that heritage roses were old varieties no longer grown, but often found around abandoned farmsteads. A few thousand people scattered around the country were dedicated to saving them—Lifry had been one, and so was Carson.

"Everybody was shocked when she was murdered. She was the nicest lady, that's all we talked about for weeks, her murder," Carson said.

"Who's we?" Virgil asked, one foot out the door.

"Well, the rose people, on the Internet. That's how I heard: I got an alert. Another one of our people down in Cedar Rapids put out all the information."

She knew Lifry came to Grand Rapids to "be with her gay friends at that resort."

"So she made no secret about being gay?"

"Why should she?" the little old lady asked. "Nobody would care but a bunch of stuffy old men."

VIRGIL DROVE BACK to the sheriff's department, tracked down Sanders, filled him in on Boehm without mentioning the whole prostitution snarl, and on Carson, and asked, "You ever heard of Slibe Ashbach Junior? Call him the Deuce? About sixteen, has a reputation for being a little flaky?"

Sanders shook his head: "Can't say that I have. We've got forty-five thousand people in the county, and I only know about thirty-eight thousand of them."

"So he's not big on your felony list?"

"Not that I've noticed," Sanders said. "He live up there with Slibe?"

"I guess. I'd like to check your records."

"We can do that—let me call the deputy who runs that area. He might know him."

ITASCA COUNTY—the Grand Rapids police department, actually—had run into Slibe II on two occasions, after fights at the junior high school. There'd been no charges out of either fight, and nobody had been seriously injured. The police had been called because both of the fights had been on the school grounds, and the cops had written reports mentioning Slibe as one of the combatants.

Sanders said a dozen or so similar reports came in every year, either through the sheriff's department or the Grand Rapids Police—"Everybody's screaming at us to stay on top of the schools, ever since the school shootings at Red Lake. We don't let anything go anymore."

When Virgil finished reading the reports, the deputy who might know Slibe II hadn't shown up, so he walked kitty-corner over to a coffee shop, and was sitting there, looking at a cup of coffee, and listening to an orchestrated, Muzak version of "Hells Bells," when the deputy came in and offered a hand and said, "Roy Service."

Service got a cup of coffee, and the waitress behind the counter said, "Pretty fast service, huh, Service?" and cackled and went off with her coffeepot.

"Honest to God, she's said that to me three hundred times," Service muttered to Virgil. "One of these times, I'm gonna take out my gun and shoot her. Or myself."

"Don't think I would have lasted this long," Virgil said. "Don't tell her my name is Flowers. . . . So, you know a Slibe Ashbach Junior? They call him the Deuce?"

Service nodded. "I've met him. You think he might be involved in these shootings?"

"I don't know. I've only seen him once. . . . He seemed a little odd," Virgil said.

Service chuckled. "Yeah, you got that right. He's a little odd." He stirred some nondairy creamer into his coffee, then said, "You like movies?"

"Sure."

"You know *Jeremiah Johnson*? Robert Redford as a mountain man?"

"Sure. One of my favorite movies, aside from *The Big Lebowski*."

"Well, the Deuce is like Jeremiah Johnson. A mentally impaired Jeremiah Johnson. He goes sliding around the woods and the lakes up here, popping up here and there . . . don't know what he eats, if he always does . . . fish, I guess, squirrels, eats at home sometimes, I suppose. But he walks all over the place. I've seen him out twenty or thirty miles from home, on foot. Carries a gun. He sleeps out there, in the woods."

"You know what kind of gun he carries?"

"Depends. Sometimes, a single-shot shotgun, when he's shooting grouse. Sometimes an old pump .22. A DNR guy told me once that he shoots deer with his .22—slides right up next to them and shoots them execution-style, ten feet, one shot to the brain."

"A .223?"

Service shook his head. "I've never seen him with anything like that, with a centerfire. He may have one. Probably could get one. But I don't think he really needs one—getting really close is part of his game."

Virgil took a sip of coffee and thought about it, about the way the shooter found his way into the back-bay, the pond, off Stone Lake. "Does he drive? Does he work?"

Service said, "He did. He's got a Chevy pickup, and he used to work out at a junkyard on Highway 2, tearing down cars for salvage parts. He was the yardman for a few months, but then he quit. I don't know why. I guess he works for his old man now, at the kennels. His old man does septic-system excavation, and he helps with that."

"You think he could hurt somebody?" Virgil asked.

Service said, "Going back to movies. Have you ever seen *Of Mice and Men*?"

"Yeah."

"Lennie, you know, who kills the guy's wife. The Deuce is like that," Service said. "He could get excited and kill somebody by accident, but I don't see him planning it out."

"How about if he popped a couple of people because he got the urge?"

"Maybe," Service said. "He's had enough shit shoveled on him, all his life. He could be pretty angry under all of it. Kids gave him a hard time in school, old man gives him a hard time at home, doesn't have the brains to deal with it. He just heads for the trees."

Interesting, Virgil thought, when he said good-bye to Service. *A good suspect whom he had no good reason to suspect.*

FROM HIS CAR, he called Mapes and asked him about Slibe's AR-15, and was told that they'd done test shots with it, and whatever it might be, it wasn't the weapon that had produced the shells at Stone Lake or the Washington shooting.

"Could you get that back to me? Is there some way I could get it back this afternoon?"

"Let me check around. We'll figure out something."

The gun, Virgil thought, was an excellent reason to go back out to Slibe's place.

HE WAS ON HIS way to the hospital, to check on Washington, to see if she was awake and had anything else to say, to ask if she or her husband knew anything about Jared Boehm or the Deuce, when Sanders called. "I got a woman who wants to talk to you. She says she might have some information."

"Yeah? Who?"

"Iris Garner. She's Margery Stanhope's daughter."

IRIS GARNER was a tall redheaded woman in her mid-thirties who lived not far from the Boehms, in another sprawling ranch house, but on the precise edge of town, off the water, with an actual ranch in the back. Not *exactly* a ranch, but a training ring for horses, with a small horse barn behind it, and a pasture that extended out to a tree line that marked the edge of the real countryside.

She smiled in a tired way when she answered the door, said, "Come in," and as they walked through to the living room, she said, "I wasn't sure I should call you. I had to think about it. But after Jan Washington . . . I'm not even sure that this amounts to anything. . . ."

"I take everything," he assured her.

"Mother doesn't know that I called you," she said. "Please don't tell her, unless it's necessary. She'd be really upset."

She sat down in a red armchair next to a flagstone fireplace, and Virgil settled onto a couch. "That's not a problem. The only time the specifics of an investigation get out is when they get into court. At that point, of course, things are pretty serious."

She understood that. "All I want to say, that I think you should know, is that Mother told me that you were a little friendly with Zoe Tull. Is that right?"

"A little. She gave me a ride from the Eagle Nest to the airport, to pick up a rental—and she showed me the Wild Goose, so I could interview some of the people who hang out there," Virgil said.

"Wendy and her band. I know about that." Garner sighed, then asked, "Did you know Zoe wants to buy the Eagle Nest from Mother? That she's been trying to do it for a couple of years? And that Erica McDill is . . . was . . . another possible buyer?"

A moment of silence, then Virgil said, "Nobody mentioned it to me."

"Here's the thing," Garner said. "Mother would like to retire. Earl and I—that's my husband—think she should stay on for a few years. The real estate market is falling to pieces, and five years from now, she could probably get a lot more. Unless we're in a depression, or something. Anyway, Zoe is pushing her to sell. Zoe would like to market the place more to lesbians. She thinks that lesbians are a rich specialized market. Mother has never really done that. We had lesbians, but we had a lot of straight women, too. Heck, when I was a kid, we were a family resort. My folks only started the all-women thing when every Tom, Dick, and Harry from the Cities started building fishing resorts."

"About McDill . . ."

"Mother mentioned to Erica McDill that she might want to sell the place, and Erica right away said that she might be interested in buying it," Garner said. "Mother told me at dinner Sunday before last. I don't know how serious Erica was, and I don't know what became of it."

"You're saying that Zoe might have had competition for the place," Virgil said.

"Not just that . . . by the way, I do like Zoe, even if she is gay. What I'm saying is that Zoe works really hard, and saves her money, and really has her heart set on this. Then Erica comes along. A bidding war would push up the price, and Zoe can't afford that. A bidding war would be the end of her. Erica, as I understand it, has a *lot* of money. Had a lot of money."

"When's the sale supposed to take place?" Virgil asked.

"Well, if it does, this winter. Usually, that sort of thing happens in the off-season. It would have happened last winter, but Zoe couldn't get the financing together, and asked Mother for another year."

"Why wouldn't your mother have told me this? Or Zoe?"

"I suppose because . . . they didn't want you to suspect them," she said. "I'm only telling you because . . . well, what if it *is* Zoe? What if she's gone a little crazy? What if Mother's on her list?"

"Huh. All right. Interesting," Virgil said. "You did well to tell me. I will keep your name under my hat, but I will look into it."

AT THE HOSPITAL, he found Jan Washington had been moved to Duluth.

"When did this happen?" he asked the nurse.

"About an hour ago. They think she might be bleeding again, inside, and they need better imaging equipment. They're probably going back in."

"Is she . . . how serious is this?"

"Serious, but nobody thinks she'll die. I mean, she might—but it's mostly getting inside to see what's happening. She's pretty strong."

VIRGIL STOPPED AND KNOCKED on Zoe's door, but nobody was home. He called the sheriff's department, identified himself, and asked for an address and directions. He got them, found Zoe's business office at the end of a strip mall, ZOE TULL, CPA.

Inside, he found a waiting room, with a half-dozen comfortable chairs with business magazines, two people waiting, and a secretary-receptionist who said Zoe was with a client, behind one of three closed office doors down a short hallway. A bigger operation than Virgil had expected.

Virgil identified himself and asked, "Could you break in, tell her that I need to talk to her for a minute? It's somewhat urgent."

The secretary was reluctant, knocked on the last door, then went in; a moment later, she came back out and said, "Just one minute."

Zoe came out a minute later, and Virgil tipped his head toward the door, and they stepped outside.

"What happened?" Zoe said.

"Why didn't you tell me that you were competing with McDill on the purchase of the Eagle Nest?"

Zoe pulled back a bit, watching him, judging, then said, "Because it had nothing to do with the murder, and it was a complicating factor. Besides, she wasn't serious. When Margery told her that she might sell out, she said something like, 'I could be interested in something like that.' But she never came back to it. Never asked any serious questions."

"I needed to know, Zoe."

"Why? It's a distraction. It has nothing to do with these killings," she said.

"Because there's a few million dollars in play there. That's enough for a murder," Virgil said. "Her daughter, and her husband, want Margery to stay on, because they think the resort'll bring a better price once we get out of this market slowdown. And the reason they want that is because they'll probably inherit, eventually. So it's not just you."

"You don't really think Iris and Earl would kill somebody to stop a sale?"

"How would I know? I don't know Earl. Or Iris," Virgil said. "I do know that McDill was shot and somebody broke into your house. I have to look at them—and I have to know about them before I can look at them."

She nodded. "Okay, okay. So, I was dumb. But it didn't seem related. Erica wasn't serious. . . . I'm sorry."

"Is there anything else that you don't think is important, that *maybe* I should know?"

"No. No, there's nothing. Jeez. I thought for a minute that I might be back on the suspect list."

"You never really left it," Virgil said, shaking his head at her.

MAPES CALLED: the rifle was on the way to Grand Rapids with a highway patrolman. "He left here ten minutes ago, but it'll be better'n an hour before he's down there. He'll leave it with the sheriff's office."

"Thanks, man. I'm gonna use it as an invitation to get back into a place."

"Piece of shit, I can tell you. Been shot a lot. Our gun guy put it on a bench out at the range and couldn't keep it inside four inches at a hundred yards," Mapes said. "Suppose it'd be a good self-defense weapon."

AN HOUR TO KILL.

He'd get some lunch, he thought, pick up the gun, and go roust Slibe. There was something in the whole mess that seemed to want to pull him toward Wendy and her band, including her old man and her brother. An ambient craziness.

He headed out to the highway, to a McDonald's, got a call from Johnson Johnson, who was back home: "Fished the V one more day, never did see a thing. You solve the murder yet?"

"Not yet."

"I was thinking, since they peed all over your vacation, why don't y'all come along to the Bahamas this fall? Get you in a slingshot, put you on some bonefish."

"Johnson, the chances of getting me in a slingshot are about like the chances of you getting laid by a pretty woman."

"Aw, man, I been laid by lots of pretty women," Johnson said.

"Name one."

After a long silence, "This woman . . . she gotta be pretty?"

Virgil laughed and said, "Johnson, I'll call you when I get back. But count me in. Goddamnit, they can't pull this shit if they can't find me."

SITTING OVER A BIG MAC, fries, and a strawberry shake, he took another call, this one from Jud Windrow, the bar owner from Iowa.

"You in Grand Rapids?" Windrow asked.

"I am," Virgil said, through the hamburger bun. "Where're you?"

"About three thousand feet straight up . . . just coming in. Wendy's playing the Wild Goose tonight. I'm gonna stop by and take a look. You gonna be around?"

"Could be," Virgil said. "You got something?"

"Huh? Oh, no. You told me to be careful, and I thought if you were around, with a gun, that'd be careful," Windrow said. "Besides, you were wearing that Breeders T-shirt."

"Well, hell. What time you going?"

"First set at seven o'clock," Windrow said. "If she's decent, I'll stay until she quits. If she's not . . ."

"See you at seven o'clock," Virgil said.

VIRGIL BACKED out of his parking place, drove a block, pulled over, and got on his cell phone. Davenport's secretary answered, and Virgil asked, "Lucas in?"

He heard her call back to Davenport's office, "It's that fuckin' Flowers."

Davenport picked up, said, "Virgil," and Virgil said, "Sometimes I get tired of that 'fuckin' Flowers' stuff."

"I'll let her know," Davenport said. "But it's part of the growing Flowers legend. Or myth, or whatever it is. What's up?"

"Wanted to fill you in," Virgil said.

"Shoot."

Virgil spent five minutes filling him in. When he finished, Davenport said, "You know what I'm going to say."

"So say it."

"Go see this band with the guy from Iowa, stay up late, have a couple beers, and in the morning . . ."

"Say it . . ."

"Go fishing."

"I wanted it to be official," Virgil said. "So I could say that you ordered me to."

THE HIGHWAY PATROLMAN HADN'T gotten to the sheriff's office yet, so Virgil hit the men's room, then wandered outside, not wanting any more food or coffee, and so at loose ends; standing there, with his fingers in his jeans pockets, he saw the liver-colored patrol car turn a corner, and walked out to meet the driver.

The patrolman's name was Sebriski, and he wanted to hear about the shoot-out in International Falls. Virgil told him a bit about it, and Sebriski said, "Better you than me, brother."

He'd handed over the rifle and Virgil had signed a receipt for it, and they talked for a couple more minutes about Department of Public Safety politics, and the prospect of raises, and then Sebriski slapped Virgil on the back and went on his way, and Virgil threw the rifle in the back of his truck.

Sebriski had been sucking up a little bit, Virgil thought.

In the immediate wake of the shoot-out in International Falls, in which three Vietnamese nationals had been killed, and another wounded, Virgil, who had a second career going as an outdoor writer, had been invited to write two articles for *The New York Times Magazine*.

There'd been some bureaucratic mumbling about it, but the governor's chief weasel, who was using the episode to pound his Republican enemies, did the algebra, got the governor to clear the way, and the *Times* published the articles, the second one two Sundays earlier.

The effect had been greater than he'd anticipated—the Minneapolis papers subscribed to the *Times*'s news service and reran the articles, and that had put them in every town in the state. He was, Davenport said, the most famous cop in Minnesota.

Which worried him a little.

He'd always been the genial observer—that was most of his method—and having other people looking at him, questioning him, watching his moves, was unnerving.

He'd mentioned it to Davenport, and Davenport's wife had said, "Well, somebody's got to be the tall poppy."

He hadn't known exactly what she'd been talking about until he looked it up on Wikipedia.

Then he worried more . . . and now fellow cops were sucking up to him, which made it worse.

He'd have to fuck something up, he thought, to get back to normal. Shouldn't be a problem.

SLIBE WASN'T HOME when Virgil got there.

The pickup was gone, and when he knocked on the door, he got a hollow echo, the kind you get when a house is empty. Virgil had the rifle case in one hand and stepped back from the door and turned toward his truck and saw Slibe II standing in the doorway of the kennel, with a half-bag of Purina dog chow in his hand. The sun was illuminating him, a Caravaggesque saint set against the black velvet surround of the barn's interior.

Virgil went that way, called out, "How ya doing?"

The Deuce didn't say anything; stood in his camo coveralls, one hand in a pocket, and watched Virgil get closer. Virgil thought about the pistol under the front seat of the truck, but kept walking anyway, smiling, called, "Your dad around?"

The Deuce said, "No trespassin'."

"Bringing your dad's rifle back to him," Virgil said.

The Deuce was an inch taller than Virgil, with melancholy, deep-set dark eyes under overgrown eyebrows and shaggy dark hair that looked as though it had been cut with a knife. He was slender, under-fed, with hard, weathered hands and a short beard. He wore a Filson canvas billed hat the precise color of a pile of dog shit somebody had shoveled out of the kennels. He considered Virgil's comment for a moment, then grunted, "You can leave it."

"Can't. Need to get your dad to sign a receipt," Virgil said. He turned casually toward the kennels and asked, "How many dogs you got here?"

"Some," the Deuce said. He smiled, said, "Get 'em going at it, we'll have some more."

"The kind of business you want," Virgil agreed.

"Them bitches want it all the time, when the heat's on them," the Deuce said. He spat in the yard, but in a conversational way, not as an insult.

"You know when your dad's coming back?" Virgil asked.

"Nope."

"I'm a cop, I'm looking into that shooting up at Stone Lake."

"Wendy . . ." The Deuce lost his thought for a moment, as though his mind were wandering through corridors labeled "Wendy," then found it again. ". . . told me."

"Yeah? You know that country? Up around Stone Lake?"

"The Deuce knows all the country around here." He dropped the bag of dog food by a foot, stepped out into the driveway, turned slowly around, as though sniffing the air, looked north, then northeast, then pointed with his chin and said, "Off that way. About, maybe . . . I could walk there after breakfast, get back here for lunch, if I hurried."

"You ever do that?"

"Oh, I went by there a few times, but it's not a good spot," the Deuce said, turning his dark gaze back on Virgil. "The trails don't lead in there."

"The trails?"

"Indian trails. I follow the Indian trails. But the lake is there, cuts the trails off. . . ." He looked north again, then gestured. "See, the trails go this way, and that way, but they don't go straight, because the lake cuts them off, so they bend."

"But if I needed somebody to take me in there, you could do it," Virgil said.

"Could. Probably wouldn't," the Deuce said.

"Yeah? You don't like cops?"

"Not much," he said.

TALKING TO HIM, Virgil understood what people had meant when they described Slibe II as not quite right. He thought too long about his words, though the words, when they arrived, were appropriate enough; it was the measure of his sentences that was wrong. And he had an odd sideways gaze, not shy, but shielded, as though he were trying to conceal an unhealthy curiosity, or passion, or fear.

Virgil had met people like him a few times, and he knew for sure that if he accused Slibe II of stealing a ham sandwich, a good prosecutor could get him sent to prison for life.

The Deuce oozed guilt.

VIRGIL WAS ABOUT to go on with the questions about Stone Lake, but Slibe Ashbach turned into the driveway in his pickup, bounced down past the garden, and rolled to a stop fifteen feet from the kennel. He climbed out and Virgil said to Slibe II, "Nice talking to you," and walked over to his father. "Dropped by to return the rifle."

Slibe took the gun case, looked at Virgil a little too long, then said, "Clean bill of health, huh?"

"It's not the gun that killed McDill or shot Jan Washington," Virgil said.

Slibe turned his head toward his son a bit, then asked, "They was both shot with the same weapon?"

"We think so," Virgil said. "That's what the lab people tell us."

"Told you it wasn't me," Slibe said. Once again glanced toward his son and then asked, "So what'd the dunce have to say?"

The Deuce backed into the kennel and out of sight.

"We were talking about Indian trails," Virgil said.

"Mmm. Well, he knows them," Slibe said. He hefted the gun: "You done with us?"

"Not completely," Virgil said, with a smile. "Me'n a friend are gonna go see Wendy tonight. He's sort of a big shot in the country music world, wants to take a look at her."

"Yeah, well," Slibe said, and he walked up to the kennel door, then looked back and said, "You know what I think about that horseshit."

HE DISAPPEARED into the barn, after his son; Virgil waited for a moment, thinking they might come back out, but then he heard them knocking around, and doors started opening down the side of the barn, and fuzzy yellow dogs began moving into their separate cages.

Virgil turned and left. *Fuck 'em*, he thought, *I know where they are if I need them*.

Nothing to do; nobody to talk to—Sig was working, Zoe was pissed off. And he had things to think about, so he went back to the motel and took a nap.

GOT UP GROGGY, looked at the clock: time to move. But toothpaste was critical, he thought, smacking his lips.

Virgil and Jud Windrow hooked up at the Wild Goose at ten minutes to seven, found a booth, talked to Chuck the bartender for a couple of minutes, were comped the first two beers on grounds of good-bar fellowship, and paid for two more before Wendy went on.

Virgil had briefed Windrow on the exact nature of the band, the crowd, and the bar, and when Wendy and the other women climbed on the stage, he said, "They got a good look. That dyke vibe works. Is that black eye from the fight?"

"Yeah. You'll notice a big scratch healing up on Berni's cheek. . . ."

Wendy growled into the microphone, "It's been a heck of a week, so instead of getting everyone riled up all over again, we're going to start out slow. So grab a hunny-bunny and let's do the 'Artists' Waltz.' . . ."

They did and Virgil watched Windrow sit back in the booth, a skeptical sideways tilt to his head, and watched the skepticism drain away as Wendy did a number on him. When they finished, they went into some soft-rock bullshit that Virgil didn't know, and Windrow leaned across the table and said, "She can do it."

"You think?"

"Oh, yeah. Gotta do something about the drummer," he said. "She sort of hits around the beat, but not exactly on it."

Virgil nodded. "Everybody says that, but she and Wendy are, you know, whatever."

"She's the one who punched her out?"

"Yeah. Right in this very booth," Virgil said.

Windrow did a low coughing laugh, like a bear, looking at Berni pounding away on her drums, and said, "I could get a big old hard-on thinking about that. Wish I'd been here."

"No, you wouldn't. This wasn't a wrestling match, this was like watching a couple of bobcats go after each other," Virgil said.

Windrow turned back to the band, listened for a bit, then asked, "The first song—where'd they get that? Is that local up here?"

"She wrote it," Virgil said.

"Better and better," Windrow said. "Gotta do something about the drummer."

"Somebody told me that she's okay as a backup singer, and her tits are good enough to put her out front, singing. Maybe with a tambourine or something," Virgil said.

"Could do that, if you had to keep her," Windrow said.

Wendy finished the bullshit soft-rocker and looked out over the crowd at Virgil and Windrow, and said, "Here's another one of ours; we were just working it out today . . . it's called, 'Doggin' Me Around.'"

She had Windrow playing the air drum before she finished, and he said to Virgil, "Goddamn. I kinda didn't believe the story, but I'll sign her up if I can."

THE FIRST SET LASTED forty minutes, ending with a quiet cheek-to-cheeker ballad, and then they climbed off the bandstand and Virgil saw Wendy heading straight for them. When she came up, they both stood and she asked Virgil, "This the guy?"

"How'd you know?"

"Daddy said you were bringing up some guy. . . ." And she said, as they sat down, and she slid in beside Virgil, "You're Jud Windrow. I looked you up on your website."

"You got a nice act," Windrow said. "Let me buy you something."

Chuck comped them another three beers and Windrow interviewed her about the band: who everybody was, how long they'd been playing together, how many country songs they could cover, what else they could play.

Wendy told him about her mom dragging her around to polka fests and about singing in polka bands, and Windrow's head was bobbing, and he was saying, "That's good, that's good, nothing is better than playing a lot, especially when you're young."

"I was doing that—when Mom was taking me around, I was singing twice a week for two years," Wendy said. "She was going to take me to Hollywood."

"What happened?" Virgil asked.

"What happened was a guy named Hector Avila. They had an affair, and everything blew up and they took off. Went to bed one night with a mom and dad, and woke up with a dad and a note. Blew us off. Went to Arizona. Never even called to say good-bye."

"How old were you?" Windrow asked.

"Nine," she said. "It was like the end of the fuckin' world. The Deuce cried for three days, and Dad wouldn't talk to anybody. He went out and started the garden and worked in it day and night for two straight months and wouldn't talk to anyone. I thought he was going to take us to an orphanage or something. Then, you know, it got better. Took time."

"Hard times make good singers," Windrow said. Then, "You got a problem with your drummer."

Wendy winced. "I know. That can be fixed, if we can find somebody better."

"I got drummers," Windrow said. "I know a female-person drummer from Normal, Illinois, who can drum your ass off, and she's looking for a new band. The one she's got ain't going nowhere: they shot their bolt."

★

VIRGIL HADN'T SEEN ZOE come in, but suddenly she was standing next to Wendy, and she said over Wendy's head, to Virgil, "You're so mean. I've been crying all afternoon."

"I'm sorry. I was too harsh. But I was pissed," Virgil said.

Zoe said to Wendy, "He says I'm still a suspect, because I'm in love with you and because I want to buy the Eagle Nest and McDill was sleeping with you and she might have bought the Eagle Nest out from under me, and . . ."

She started to blubber, and Wendy patted her thigh and said to Virgil, "Asshole."

"Hey . . ."

"You can solve the murder without being an asshole," Wendy said.

"That's r-r-right," Zoe said.

Berni came up and said to Wendy, "Get your hand off her ass."

"Shut up," Wendy said. "We got a problem here."

Zoe said to Berni, "If she wants to put her hand on my ass, she has my permission."

Berni backed up a step and Virgil said, "Aw Christ . . ."

Wendy shouted, "No!"

Berni was about to smack Zoe, and Zoe's teeth were bared—she was ready to go, Virgil thought, as he tried to push past Wendy to get out of the booth. Wendy lurched forward and put herself between Zoe and Berni, and Virgil got out and put an arm around Zoe's waist, and Chuck the bartender came running over and Windrow laughed out loud and cried out, "Rock 'n' roll . . ."

VIRGIL GOT ZOE out the door, kissed her on the forehead, and asked, "Are we made up now?"

"No."

"I won't call you a suspect again unless I've really got something on you," Virgil said, which he thought was a reasonable compromise.

"Thanks a lot, jerk," she said.

"Look: go home, take a Xanax, go to bed. It'll be better in the morning."

"That's right: take drugs. That's everybody's solution," Zoe said. "Nobody takes responsibility for their feelings."

She rambled on for a while, and Virgil lost the thread, because he noticed a moth the size of a saucer flapping around one of the bar lights, and he'd always had an interest in moths. He kept nodding and watching the moth, in silhouette, circling toward the light, and she said something and he said, "I hope so. Look, get some sleep," and whatever she'd said, his response was apparently okay, because she said, "Thanks . . ."

A flash of green. A goddamn luna moth: he hadn't seen a live one in years. Late in the year for a luna. Were they producing two generations now, in Minnesota? He had a friend at the University of Minnesota who'd know. . . .

". . . tonight?"

"Yeah," Virgil said. "Call me anytime . . . let's get a cheeseburger or something."

She looked at him oddly, and he wondered what she'd said— there'd been a little chime in his head, when she said whatever it was—and she headed off to her car, turning to wave.

The luna flapped around the light, beating against it. Virgil tried to edge up close, but the bug must've spotted him, because it flapped wildly off into the night, toward the third-quarter moon hanging overhead.

HE WENT BACK INSIDE, told Windrow he had to run, and Windrow nodded and the band started playing and Windrow lifted his voice and said, "Thanks for reminding me about these girls. I owe you one."

Virgil left. He had a plan; he'd go fishing in the morning, and while he was out in the boat, he'd solve the crime.

In his head, anyway.

But he might get a late start. Tonight, he was gonna drop by Sig's place. There was, he thought, an excellent chance that he might not be in any shape to get up at five A.M.

An *excellent* chance.

HE GOT TO SIG'S PLACE at eight-thirty. Zoe's Pilot was parked outside, with a couple of other cars, and he could see lights down at the gazebo.

He groaned, and heard the chime again, the one that'd gone off when Zoe was talking.

Quilting bee, she'd said. Sig's having a quilting bee. . . .

15

ROBERT PLANT AND ALISON KRAUSS were working their way through "Please Read the Letter" as Virgil backed his boat down the ramp into Stone Lake. The music suited the morning and his mood, and he sat and listened to the last bit of the song before he cut the engine.

Another day with flat water, but the sky had turned, showing a flat gray screen of cloud that could make some rain before the day was gone. He climbed down from the truck, into the smell of fish scales and backwater, clambered up on the trailer tongue and walked out to the bow of the boat, grabbed the bow line and pushed it off. The boat slipped off the trailer and he pulled it around to the side of the ramp and tied it off to a bush.

After parking the truck and trailer, he locked up, unlocked again, got his raincoat, peed on a shrub, climbed in the boat, pulled it out with the engine, then swung around and headed for the south shoreline.

There were muskies in the lake, but he wasn't going to worry about that. Instead, he went looking for a weedy bay, something with lily pads and snags, found one and started flipping out a weed-less bass lure, looking for either northern pike or bass. He wouldn't keep anything, so he didn't much care what he caught, or, indeed, whether he caught anything at all.

*

FISHING CALMED HIS MIND, slowed him down: the sheer, unimportant repetitive quality of it, flip and reel, flip and reel, worked as a tranquilizer, but the possibility of a strike kept him alert. The combination of alertness and quietude was good for thinking in general. Sometimes, when he was buried in facts, he couldn't see the forest.

And he knew how to work that state of mind.

Instead of attacking the facts, he let them float across his consciousness as he worked the bait around the flat purple-and-green lily pads. Halfway down the bay, a white heron watched him with its yellow-rimmed snake eye, until it decided that Virgil wasn't a threat and stalked on after a breakfast frog.

A wise man—a cop named Capslock—once observed that he'd never seen a murder with a large amount of money attached to it, in which the money wasn't important. On the other hand, Virgil hadn't ever seen a murder that involved an intense sexuality in which the sexuality wasn't involved.

The same was not true with the mentally challenged: he'd seen lots of cases that involved obviously crazy people, the first suspects in everyone's minds, in which the crazy people weren't involved at all. But that was no guarantee—sometimes obviously crazy people *did* do it.

SO: he had a murder case in which there was large money involved in at least two unrelated ways.

1. McDill's lover, Ruth Davies, was apparently about to be dumped and disinherited by McDill. By killing McDill, Davies would inherit a hundred thousand dollars and whatever she could loot from the house, which, Virgil thought, might include a few expensive artworks. If McDill had lived, she wouldn't have gotten a dime.

2. Zoe Tull was apparently trying to scratch together enough money for a bid on the Eagle Nest, and McDill may have been a threat to that plan. Though Virgil liked Zoe, he couldn't eliminate her as a possibility. She'd complained about the door of her house being

forced, but there was no apparent reason that anyone would do that. Had she faked the break-in as a naive tactic to distract him, to suggest another agency working in the murder? Possibly. But, he had to confess to himself, he didn't think she'd killed anyone. He simply liked her too much to think that.

AND: sex was all over the place.

Zoe and Wendy. Wendy and Berni. Wendy and McDill. McDill and Davies. McDill and Jared Boehm. The Deuce and the dogs? Maybe not. But how about one of the Slibes, and Wendy? Odd things happened on those remote farm sites in the long dark winters. . . .

Berni might fear that she was about to be dumped by both her employer and lover; she must have some idea that if the band was going to make it, she wouldn't be making it with them . . . or with Wendy. And she had no alibi for the time of the McDill killing; and Constance Lifry had been a threat to move the band, as well.

Virgil had also gotten a bad vibration from the Deuce, when the strange man had talked about the dogs. What had he said? "Them bitches want it all the time, when the heat's on them."

Sounded like a line from a rap song. And he'd said it with a little too much relish.

Of course, he *was* talking about bitches. Virgil had noticed in the past that country people tended to use specific words for the different sexes of specific animals: goose and gander, ram and ewe, boar and sow, dog and bitch, words generally felt to be archaic in the now-urban populace.

Or maybe they just like using the word *bitch* in public.

FINALLY: he had at least one, and perhaps two, people with uneven mentalities, to be politically correct about it. The Deuce and Wendy, brother and sister. The Deuce wore his problem like a cloak. In Wendy, Virgil had only seen it as a quick flash, but it was there, he thought.

Which meant that Slibe I should be on the list as well, since he was probably the force that bent Slibe II and Wendy.

Slibe.

Slibe had said something that had tickled Virgil's brain a couple of times. He thought about that, about what he'd been doing when he heard whatever it was, still couldn't find it, and let it go.

HE LET ALL of it cook through his brain as he worked down the bay, around the corner of it, past the docks of a half-dozen lake cabins. Mind drifting.

A fish of some kind took a slash at the lure, but Virgil missed it, went back to the same spot a minute later, got hit again, but this time, hooked up. Small bass, maybe a foot long. He unhooked it, slipped it back in the lake, leaned over and rinsed his fingers in the cool lake water.

And thought: *Davies.*

I can eliminate her, if I stop fucking around.

He looked around, trying to figure where he was from the Eagle Nest. Not far . . . He checked his cell phone and got two bars, looked at the time: 7:45. Davenport wouldn't be at the office yet. He called Davenport's home, got his daughter, Letty, told her to take the phone back to Davenport's bedroom.

"This better be something," Davenport groaned into the phone. "Do you know what time it is?"

"Yeah. Time to get up. Everybody else has been up for hours: so shut up, and call Jenkins or Shrake. I need those guys to lean on somebody for me."

"Aw, man . . . all right, all right. I'll get one of them to call you back. You're on your cell?"

"Yeah. Quick as they can."

HE HUNG UP and at that instant, he got it—what Slibe had said that tickled him.

Slibe had said that he was thinking of going to Wyoming to shoot prairie dogs. Said it like he'd done it before. But a real dog-shooter wasn't going out there with a worn-out semiauto .223 with open sights that couldn't shoot inside four inches at a hundred yards. Nor would he be taking the pump .30-06, or the twelve- or the twenty-gauge shotgun, or the .22 or the old Ruger pistol that had also been in the gun safe. Could possibly take the .308, he supposed, but that wasn't usually used on prairie dogs. Too big, too expensive.

So Slibe had a prairie-dog shooter. Very likely a .223, but a bolt action with a big scope on it. Nothing like it had been in the gun safe.

Slibe, Virgil thought, had another gun. And since he should not have known what kind of gun was used to kill McDill, he shouldn't have had any reason to hide it.

And he *was* hiding it.

Virgil started to whistle. The ice was going out. . . .

What else?

HE FISHED HIS WAY past the Eagle Nest dock and was coming up on the pond where McDill got shot, when his phone jingled. Shrake. "Whatcha need, big guy?"

"I need you and Jenkins to lean on an emotionally fragile lesbian."

"We can do that," Shrake said. "What do you want from the miserable bitch?"

Virgil told him, and Shrake said, "Okay. Now, let me ask you something, since you're the resident cop-genius. I'm thinking if I got some fake stainless-steel braces for my teeth, you know, that I could put on and take off, they'd make me look *way* crazy. I saw a guy my age yesterday, walking through the skyway, talking on a cell phone, with braces. He looked like a complete fruitcake. If I got some and grinned at people, showing these things off . . ."

"Two thoughts," Virgil said. "One: people already think you're nuts, so it'd be a waste of effort. Two, if you put braces on, and somebody busted you in the mouth, they'd break off all your teeth, instead of maybe one."

A moment of silence. Then Shrake said, "Maybe I should reconceptualize my attack persona."

"Whatever," Virgil said. "You wanna break down this woman for me?"

*

OKAY.

Suppose that Jenkins and Shrake eliminated Davies as a murder suspect, by pinning down where she'd been when Washington was shot. There remained the possibility that the murders were coming out of the advertising agency, but the Washington shooting—for which nobody had been able to find any connection to anybody— could hardly have been coming out of Minneapolis . . . unless it was simply done at random, as a diversion. So: set that slim possibility aside, simply on the grounds that he didn't know how he'd approach a solution.

He scratched his chin, and thought, *Although* . . .

Mark and Abby Sexton were definitely off center. Mark might have been facing dismissal, and Abby might have harbored some unknown sexual grudge against her former lover; there might be a murder somewhere in that snarled-up psychology, with Washington done as a diversion, at random. If they were both involved, and alibied each other, and were clever about it . . . he'd never catch them.

So: set it aside.

THAT LEFT THE GRAND RAPIDS/Eagle Nest complex. Wendy, Zoe, Berni, Slibe, the Deuce, maybe another band member, maybe another unknown lover from the Eagle Nest.

The unknown lover seemed least likely, especially with the thread leading from Constance Lifry, down in Iowa, through McDill, from Minneapolis, to Jan Washington, in Grand Rapids.

And the Iowa cops thought Lifry's killer was male, and Virgil tended to think they were correct. So where did the women's Mephisto shoes come from?

Stray thought: Was it even barely possible that McDill had landed her boat at the beaver lodge, had walked out to the road, and then back? To meet somebody in secret? And that somebody had followed her back in and killed her?

Hadn't thought of that—and that would definitely put the Cities back in play. Who would she be meeting secretly, outside a swamp in northern Minnesota?

Drifted a little farther, line slack in the water, ignored . . .

Thought, *That's fuckin' ridiculous.* She could have gotten in her nice comfortable car and driven to any one of a thousand places, within five miles of here, for a secret meeting. She didn't have to wade through a swamp.

And he made a mental bet with himself: Slibe. Slibe and the unknown rifle.

One way or another, Slibe was involved. He was willing to bet that Jenkins and Shrake would clear Davies, and that he could draw a line through the possibility of involvement from the Cities. The killer was here. . . .

He started whistling again, reeled the lure in, flipped it back out. Virgil fished on, hard at work.

16

THERE WAS A LOT to think about, and Virgil worked at it hard, all morning; and in the early afternoon, found a place with a SAND-WICHES sign in the window, facing the water, and an ancient Pabst sign hanging below it, and a dock. He'd put in for forty-five minutes or so, got a Coke and a hamburger, read a two-day-old *Herald-Review* at the bar, and talked to the bartender, who thought the killings were the work of a nut from the Twin Cities.

"Take my word for it—I'm very rarely wrong about these things," the bartender said.

His name was Bob, and Bob had no reason to think what he did, except that, in his opinion, the Twin Cities were chock-full o' nuts. He also had, Virgil thought, a variety of bad opinions on sports, women, beer, fishing, and Sebring convertibles.

"The thing is," Bob said, laying his fat forearms on the bar, "that place is known for having lesbians going through there. I bet it's all tied up with a Twin Cities lesbian thing, whachacallum—covens?"

"I believe that's an assemblage of thirteen witches," Virgil said.

"Same difference," Bob said. He pulled a toothpick out of his mouth and closely examined the chewed end. "Maybe it's some kind of sacrifice thing."

VIRGIL WAS BACK on the water before two, working down the waterline opposite the Eagle Nest. At three, he took a call from Shrake: "We shook her up and I can tell you two things: she had an alibi for the Washington shooting—she was at the funeral home, making funeral arrangements. And, she took three paintings away for safekeeping, and she will now be bringing them back. She claims that McDill gave them to her as gifts, but she's got no proof of that."

Virgil was no longer interested, but he asked, "How much were they worth?"

"Hard to tell, but McDill paid around ninety thousand for one of them, and thirteen thousand or so for the other two," Shrake said.

"So they were worth stealing."

"Hard to tell. I asked a pal who runs an art gallery, and he says they're worth what somebody will pay you for them. The big painting, which is like a lot of color splotches, was done by a woman from Washington, D.C., who hung out with some abstract big shots in the fifties, but wasn't a big shot herself. Maybe she will be someday, and the picture will be worth a lot more. Maybe everybody will forget her, and then it'll be worth nothing."

"Wait, wait, wait, back up there," Virgil said. "You've got a pal who runs an art gallery?"

"Fuck you. Anyway, that's what we got," Shrake said. "If Davies is involved, she's pulling strings, but she's not pulling the trigger. She was down here when Washington was shot."

"Thank you. That helps," Virgil said.

And he thought, *Slibe*.

AND HE ALSO THOUGHT, *I've got nothing to take to trial.*

*

HE HAD SOME PIECES of forensic evidence: two rifle shells, and a shoe impression. The shoe impression was worse than useless, since it pointed at a female killer. If the shooter had an accomplice, then it might work into something. . . . The rifle shells were better: if he could find the rifle, he'd have something. And the rifle could have DNA, fingerprints, a history.

But if Slibe was the shooter, the best thing he could have done, at this point, was to have thrown the rifle in a lake somewhere. If he'd done that, and lain low, and kept his mouth shut, Virgil couldn't get at him.

HE FISHED FOR ANOTHER ten minutes, coming up to the launch ramp, put the rod down, kicked back in the captain's chair, and called Sig. "You want to get something to eat?"

"I'd do anything to avoid my cooking," she said. "Was that you that turned around in my driveway last night?"

"Yeah. Quilting bee. I forgot," he said.

"I'm not quilting anything tonight," she said. "A steak and a bottle of wine could get you somewhere."

"Seven o'clock?"

"See you then."

AND HE CALLED SANDERS, who was back in Bigfork. "Could you have one of your deputies go around and pick up Berni Kelly? She's the drummer with Wendy Ashbach's band. I want to talk to her, but I want her treated like a suspect. No handcuffs, but put her in the back of a squad car. Make it feel bad. Sit her down in a hallway outside an interview room and let her stew. She's probably down at that Schoolhouse place, the music studio. If she's not there, try out at Slibe Ashbach's place."

"You think she did it?"

"I don't think anything in particular, except that the scope of suspects seems to be narrowing," Virgil said. "The one that bothers me, though, is Washington. Have you guys got even a hint of anything?"

"Nope. One of my investigators drove over to Duluth to talk to her again, and she says she's mystified. She just can't think of *anything*. She's no help."

"That happened when I was down in Iowa. I'd told some people where I was going—I'm wondering if she was shot at random, to take the attention away from Iowa, from Lifry. From the band and the Eagle Nest?"

"Hate to think that. Hate to think that we got somebody that crazy. But I guess we do," Sanders said.

"Know how you feel. Listen, get Berni Kelly, call me when you got her. I'm heading back to town now."

"Where you at?"

"Been out investigating," Virgil said.

VIRGIL PUT THE BOAT back on the trailer and hauled it to Zoe's driveway, unhooked it, and dropped the tongue on the ground. Knocked on the door, but Zoe was still at work. Drove over to her office, was told that she'd be with a client for another fifteen minutes or so. Went down the street to an ice cream parlor, with a pistachio cone in mind, checked his gut to see if he was pick- ing up any flab, decided he hadn't, and ordered a hot fudge sundae instead.

A couple had come in the door behind him, had gotten cones after trying three different samples, and had left, and the wide-eyed girl behind the counter asked, "Are you that state policeman?"

"Yes, I am."

"You think you'll catch him, whoever did it?" she asked. She was self-consciously wiping down the countertop, working to keep the questions casual.

"Count on it," Virgil said. "We made a lot of progress today. I figure we ought to have him in another day or two. Three at the outside."

"Really?"

"Really."

She looked at him, doubtfully, he thought, and then asked, as Zoe had, "Why are you telling me this?"

Virgil shrugged. "Why not? You're a taxpaying citizen. Your money is paying for this investigation, and I'm keeping you up-to-date."

"Can I tell my mom? She's pretty worried, and if she knows you're going to catch him, she won't worry so much."

"Sure, go ahead," Virgil said.

She looked at his shirt: "Why does your shirt say Gourds? Do you grow gourds?"

VIRGIL, REELING FROM HIS EXPOSURE to the ignorance of the young people of Grand Rapids—she didn't know the Gourds? The world's best (and only) country cover of Snoop Dogg's "Gin and Juice"? What kind of education were they getting, anyway?—walked back to Zoe's and was sent down to her office.

Zoe said, "I'm going out to Wendy's in a couple minutes. She wants me to look at the contract with the guy from Iowa."

"I've seen his place—it looks pretty substantial to me," Virgil said, pulling a chair out. "He had pictures of the bands in his office. Big-time stuff."

She said, snippy, "So what've you been up to? Harassing innocent females?"

Virgil thought about Davies and said, "Well—yes." He told her about eliminating Davies, and that he hadn't really thought that the mousy stay-at-home would have done it anyway.

"But you still suspect me. At least, one percent, you do," Zoe said.

"Nope. I decided I like you too much to consider you a suspect," Virgil said.

She shook her head. "You know, if you were an accountant . . . never mind."

"Say it."

"People would run all over you," she said. "You can't do somebody's books, and tell them that they're okay, because you *like* them. Things have to be *right*. They have to be *logical*."

"Maybe. Now, tell me who you think did it," Virgil said. "It's got to be somebody no more than two degrees from Wendy."

She looked at him, then at a wall calendar, then at a picture of a herd of white horses running across a pasture, then back to him, and said, "Slibe."

"I don't have a single damn thing that points at him." Not quite true: he had the prairie dog comment.

"Let me tell you about Slibe," Zoe said. "He had this wife, whose name was Maria Osterhus, and they had Wendy and the Deuce, and he had this business that was doing okay, S&M Septic & Grading, and then . . . she fell in love with this other guy. She took off. Didn't want the business, didn't want the kids, she wanted Hector what's-his-name. He quit his job and they took off, one night, and went to Arizona, and haven't been back since. She ditched them, and Wendy and the Deuce were brought up by Slibe. Slibe really loved Maria, and that got transferred over to Wendy. . . ."

"How do you know all this stuff? How old were you when it happened? Ten?"

"I got it from Wendy. We were together for a while. It was the big thing in her life."

"Slibe never . . ."

"No, no, no . . . they didn't. At least Wendy said they didn't," Zoe said. "I asked, too. But: I don't think he wants her to leave him. I think he wants to keep her. I think Slibe believes he *owns* her. Like he owned Maria. She's his."

"He seems to be pretty cool about the fact that she's a lesbian," Virgil said.

"Well—he's got the man attitude. If she was hooked up with a guy, that guy would own her. The ownership would go from Slibe to the guy. He doesn't want that. Lesbians, in his eyes, it's just chicks being chicks. But a guy . . ."

Virgil said, "Huh."

"What's that mean?"

His phone rang, and he fished it out of his pocket and looked at it—the sheriff's department—said, "Virgil," and Sanders said, "They got her, and she's madder'n a hornet."

"You don't sound too worried."

"Naw, if anything goes wrong, I plan to blame it on you," Sanders said.

"Good plan," Virgil said. "I'll go on over there."

He stood up, and Zoe asked, "Is there any possibility you'll be seeing my sister tonight?"

Sig must have talked, Virgil thought: "I might drop by, have a beer."

"Yeah, have a beer. She went to shave her legs," Zoe said.

"Well, shoot. I was gonna offer to do it for her," Virgil said.

Zoe laughed and then said, "Slibe."

BERNI KELLY WAS EXACTLY as mad as a hornet. She was sitting in an orange plastic chair looking at a guy behind a desk reading a newspaper. Virgil came up from slightly behind her and thought he could hear her buzzing; and she was—she was doing an angry hum, like his first ex-wife used to do.

He put an offensive smile on his face and said, "Berni! Thanks for dropping by."

She turned in the plastic chair and said, "You motherfucker," and came up out of the chair and Virgil thought she might be going for his eyes. The cop behind the desk felt it, too, and stood up, but Virgil put his hands up and said, "Whoa, whoa. Just want to talk."

She started to cry, and he saw that she'd already been crying, and that her eyeliner had started to run. "I think Wendy's gonna kick me out of the band."

"Really?"

"Aw, that guy who came up here with you, Jud, he's telling her that she needs a better drummer."

"You talked to Jud about it?"

"No, he told her, and she's telling me. They say they haven't made a decision, but they've made a decision . . . and then you go and get that fuckin' deputy to drag me outa there."

"Still got a mouth on you," the cop said.

She turned around and said, "Shut up, Carl," and to Virgil, "Carl's wanted to fuck me since he was in the ninth grade and I was in the fifth. Isn't that right, Carl?"

Carl said to Virgil, "You want to take her in the interview room? I don't want to put up with her anymore." And to Berni, "Who knowing the judgment of God, that they which commit such things, are worthy of death."

"Oh, yeah, I heard you got born again," she said. "Which you needed, since they fucked up the first time."

Virgil edged her toward the interview room. "C'mon, let's go talk," he said, and to Carl, who'd pissed him off, "The soul of Jonathan was bound to the soul of David, and Jonathan loved him as his own soul."

"That didn't mean they were queer," Carl called after them, as they went into the interview room. He sounded anxious about it.

Berni asked, "What was that all about?"

"I'm a preacher's kid," Virgil said. "I know all that stuff, for and against."

"Was David queer?"

Virgil said, "Who knows? Donatello apparently thought so."

"Don who?"

VIRGIL SAT HER DOWN on the opposite side of the conference table and said, "Berni, we've been through all the evidence, the sheriff and I, and it's pretty obvious that you're involved in these killings somehow."

She started to protest but he held up his hands. "Hear me out. First of all, we've had two band-related killings, plus a third shooting, which was done with the same rifle that killed McDill. You have no real alibis. So we started putting together a case, including the tracks back into the sniper's nest, which were left by a woman—"

"I didn't do it," she groaned. "I never went back there."

"Look: we can make our case, and what we're really looking at now is state of mind. If you feel that you were . . . upset . . . that could always be worked into a pretty good defense. If you were emotionally unstable because of McDill's relationship with Wendy—"

"I didn't know about that," she said.

"We've got the tracks," Virgil said.

"*Not mine.*"

"But everybody else has an alibi," Virgil said. "And you gotta admit, these killings are tied to the band."

"McDill's woman, down in the Cities . . ."

"Has an absolute watertight alibi," Virgil said. "Look, I don't know how familiar you are with the legal system. If you cooperate, this will count toward some leniency, if that's the way the court wants to go. You don't have any prior record—"

"*But I didn't do it.*"

"Well . . ." Virgil threw his hands up; he was helpless, apologetic. Getting to the point. "We believe you're involved. I mean, you say you didn't do it, but if you didn't, who did?"

She looked sideways, and then said, "Oh, God, I was hoping you'd catch him yourself. Wendy's gonna kill me."

"If it wasn't you . . . I mean, if you know something, you better speak up. He seems to be shutting down everybody who knows something," Virgil said.

She looked up: "You think?"

"I don't think anybody's safe," Virgil said. "This person is unbalanced. He, or she, needs help. If you did it, that's the way we'd go: get you some help."

"*I didn't . . .*" She turned away and began humming again, thinking, and then said, "I don't know. I don't know a single thing about it, but I think you need to look at the Deuce."

"The Deuce? Not Slibe?"

"Slibe . . . I don't know. I do know that the Deuce has this sex thing going for Wendy, and always has. Ever since they were little. If you get Wendy off by herself, she'll tell you that. Deuce would never want her to go away. *Never.*"

"Is the Deuce sexually active?"

"Oh, hell yes, all the time. With himself. Him and his little Hormel."

"I meant, does he have a girlfriend?" Virgil asked.

"As far as I know, he's a virgin," she said. "If he's not, he paid for it. But he's . . . *really* . . . different. He watches you, all the time. Pretends like he isn't, but you can see that his eyes are on you."

"Maybe he's interested in you, not in Wendy," Virgil suggested.

"I think he's all slobbery interested in sex," she said. "I mean, God, he's seventeen, you know he wants it—but Wendy's the center of the universe."

"Huh."

"What does that mean?" she asked.

"Wendy seems to be the center of a lot of universes," Virgil said.

"Yeah. Including her own," Berni said.

Virgil tried to look like he was thinking it over. Then he said, "I don't know, Berni. I admit we haven't been looking at the Deuce. I don't know what his alibi is, but you have to admit that there's good reason to think you might be involved."

He continued to push her around, coming back for more about Wendy, Slibe, and the Deuce, whenever she gave him the opening. Cranking her up.

Setting her up.

She'd talk to Wendy, Wendy would talk to everybody . . .

And the killer would hear; and might do something.

HE LET HER GO at five o'clock, told her to stay around town.

Back at the motel, he took a short nap, showered, shaved again, put on a fresh T-shirt, jeans, and a sport coat. For the T-shirt, he was torn between two of his newest, a Blood Red Shoes and an Appleseed Cast, and went with the Appleseed after deciding that in the circumstances, Blood Red Shoes might be in poor taste.

Sig was ready when he got there; came skipping out the door, wearing a cotton dress, kissed him in the driveway, slipped a couple fingers under his belt as she did it, then said, "Steak! Burnt!"

"Where're we going?"

"The Duck Inn. Back downtown. They are so cool that they've got little individual packets of sesame crackers on every table."

Virgil laughed: "Can't pass on that."

*

SIG TURNED OUT to be pretty funny, when he actually talked to her. She knew almost everybody in town, and their foibles; and she told him about finding out that Zoe had been experimenting with a female friend of hers. "I was absolutely not shocked. For me, you know, if they don't got that thang, it doesn't make any sense. But I found out that Zoe liked women, it seemed perfectly normal."

Sig and Virgil had overlapped at the University of Minnesota, and, they thought, might have even had a common acquaintance, a woman who was methodically working her way through every art form known to mankind. Having demonstrated little ability in painting, sculpture, ceramics, architecture, botanical drawing, music, and dance—she'd played the classical guitar, badly, and the dance instructor had suggested that her true métier might involve a pole—she'd moved on to creative writing, where Virgil thought he'd met her.

"Can't remember a single thing she wrote, though," he said.

"I can remember one piece of art," Sig said. "She had a boyfriend who hunted, and she did an engraving of a skinned rabbit. Scared the shit out of everybody who saw it."

"Maybe it was good, then? If it had that effect?"

"No . . . it didn't look like a skinned rabbit, but you could tell it was, you know, an animal that something bad happened to," Signy said. "But it looked like a mutant. A mutant that had been beaten with a hammer or something . . . But you know, maybe you're right. I can't think of any other art that I remember that well, for that long. Maybe it was good. But she quit, anyway."

THE DUCK INN was a fake log cabin with a neon duck sign with flapping red-blue-green wings and a gravel parking lot planted with sickly pines. Going in the door, they met Jud Windrow, coming out.

"Hey, Virgil," Windrow said, taking a long look at Signy. "You going up to the Wild Goose tonight?"

"Probably have to pass. I have a forensics conference tonight," Virgil said. "The case, you know."

"Yeah, well, I'm heading over there now. We had a meeting out at their trailer-home, and Wendy's gonna sign up."

"You fix the drummer thing?" Virgil asked.

"Yeah, I think. Berni told us about talking to you this afternoon. She was pretty upset."

"People are dead," Virgil said.

"I hear you, brother." Windrow looked Sig over again and said to Virgil, "Don't do anything Willie wouldn't."

"I'll keep that in mind, partner," Virgil said.

Windrow laughed: "Yeah, partner. Well: better get my young ass over there."

SIG WAS MILDLY INSULTED by the exchange and, when they got inside, asked, "What was that about?"

Virgil told her about Windrow, and she said, "He was pretty . . . presumptuous."

Virgil leaned across the table and said, "You don't know how good-looking you are. The guys in this place have their tongues hanging out. That's what he was reacting to."

She said, "Well . . ."

They got on famously. She ate a burnt steak with mashed potatoes and drank two-thirds of a bottle of Santa Barbara Pinot Grigio and told him the joke about the minister checking in at the motel ("I certainly hope the pornography channel in my room is disabled"—"No, it's just regular pornography, you sick fuck") and he told her about how his aunt Laurie on his mother's side ran away with a minister, and how his father tormented his mother for a week by suggesting he might preach on the topic.

An hour and a half slipped away, and when they finished, she insisted on a walk through the downtown, so she could show him around. They looked in at a couple of bars, and she said hello to a couple of people, and a half-hour later, back at the truck, she asked, "Have you got your cell phone?"

"Sure—you need to make a call?"

"No. But this time, leave it in the truck, huh?"

"Yes!" He took the cell phone out of his pocket and put it in the cup holder. "You are a woman of great practicality."

"Damn right," she said.

BACK AT HER HOUSE, she popped a Norah Jones album in her Wave CD/radio and went off to the bathroom, and when she came back out Virgil put a hand on her hip and said, "Dance," and they danced around the room to "Come Away with Me," "One Flight Down," and "The Nearness of You," and she said, "Oh, God, Virgil," and licked his earlobe, and he pushed her against a handy wall. . . .

Headlights swept through the front windows, the automatic yard light came on, and Virgil moaned, "No!"

Sig pushed free and went to the window and peered out through a curtain and said, "It's Zoe. She knew you were coming over. We'll tell her it's inconvenient. She'll take off."

Virgil wrapped her up from behind and said, "Honest to God, and not to be crude about it, but if I don't get you on the bed tonight, something could break. I mean, something might fall off."

Sig reached back and squeezed his thigh: "We'll just get rid of her."

Zoe knocked.

17

THE DOUBLE-WIDE SMELLED LIKE Dinty Moore beef stew, coffee, sweat, and the vagrant vegetable odor of marijuana. Jud Windrow leaned back in the beanbag chair, scuffing his boot heels across the shag carpet; sucked on a Budweiser, tried to stay alert, and listened to Wendy, Berni, and Slibe snarl at one another.

He'd seen all this before. You had artists who'd spent thousands of hours learning how to play a musical instrument, who could tell you anything you might want to know about writing a song, about bridges and transitions and about single specific words that you couldn't use in a song. Cadaver? Had anyone ever used *cadaver* in a song?

They knew all that, worked it, groomed it, smoothed it out, sat up all night, night after night, doing it—and they didn't know a single fucking thing about business. They were in a business, but they didn't know it. They thought they were in an art form.

He sighed and let them fight it out.

HE'D PUT THE SKUNK among the chickens when he mentioned the necessity of recruiting another drummer, and possibly somebody different on the keyboards. Berni had gone ballistic, and he'd thought for a few seconds that she might come after him, physically, but then she had started pleading with Wendy, trying to save her job, and when Wendy had looked away, Berni began to cry.

"I . . . I . . . I get this asshole cop who drags me down to the police station and tortures me, and now you guys are kicking me out of the band . . . No, don't say you're not."

Windrow then suggested that she could help front the band: play a rhythm instrument of some kind, sing backups, and she'd quieted down a bit.

"As long as I get to stay . . ."

Wendy defended the keyboard player: "We put too much weight on her, is all. She's fine on recordings, but hasn't got an act, you know? She stands back there and plays and looks kinda dead. We can work on that."

"She *can* play," Windrow said. "But you don't see many big bands without everybody having some kind of personality."

"We'll get her a hat," Wendy said. "I'll work on her. The thing is . . . she does the melodies on the songs. She made the 'Artists' Waltz' into a waltz . . . used to be a straight-up ballad."

"Okay," Windrow said. "So she's okay. Get her a hat."

THEN THEY MOVED ON to the terms of the contract, and that's where Slibe jumped in with both feet. There were terms which,

Windrow admitted, were favorable to him. After the initial month-long house-band gig, they agreed to play the Spodee-Odee for a week in each of the next five years, at Windrow's option. If they refused, they'd agree to pay Windrow the equivalent of fifteen percent of the royalties from any records released during that period. On the other hand, if Windrow didn't want them, in any particular year, he could cancel them without penalty.

Slibe shouted at Wendy: "You see what happens? This guy takes a cut out of everything. He owns your ass."

"Not her entire ass," Windrow said. "Fifteen percent of it."

"That's how these guys steal from you," Slibe said. "They get you all tied up in legal contracts that you can't get out of."

Wendy wanted to sign anyway, for reasons that Windrow told her were good.

"Listen: you can stay up here and be a ratshit band and play at the Wild Goose or maybe get a couple gigs down in the Twin Cities, or wherever, but you aren't going to break out that way. You won't," he said.

"They could get people to listen to them up here—" Slibe began, but Wendy said, "Shut up, Dad, let him talk."

Windrow went on. "If you wanna break out, you gotta put it on the line. That means I bring you down for a month, expose you to some of the top acts and top managers and agents in the business. And I pay you. What do I get? I get a new band that nobody knows—but you're pretty good, and my big payoff comes if you do well. You make a couple records and they sell okay. So then you gotta come back and play the Spodee-Odee for not much money, but hell, that won't hurt your reputation any. It's one of the top slots on the circuit. I pack the place for a week, and you get to keep all the money from your albums."

They heard a car turn in at the driveway, and Slibe got up to look. "It's that Zoe," he said.

"I called her," Wendy said.

"What the fuck for?" Berni asked.

"Because she's smarter than we are, and she knows about things like contracts and taxes," Wendy said. "And besides, she's in love with me, so we don't have to pay her."

"She's a pain in the ass," Slibe said. "And she hates my guts."

Zoe knocked, and Slibe let her in. She said, "Slibe," and he said, "Zoe."

ZOE TOOK THE CONTRACT, saying, "I'm not a lawyer."

"Just read the thing," Wendy said.

Zoe went into the kitchen to do that.

Slibe said to Windrow, "But if you don't want them, even if they do make an album, but it doesn't sell that well, then you can throw them away."

Windrow nodded: "Absolutely. The contract is written in my favor, because I'm the one taking the risk here. Show me a bank mortgage where it says the buyer doesn't have to pay, if he doesn't feel like it. Bullshit, there are no bank contracts like that. They *all* favor the bank. In this deal, I'm the bank."

THEY WERE ALL SITTING in the living room area of the trailer-home, Windrow closest to the exit, which was near the middle of the trailer, Wendy and Berni on a long couch against the end wall. Windrow was looking at Berni when he thought he saw something move behind the venetian blind, where the bottom blade of the blind was bent. Something like an eye, but then it was gone, leaving nothing but the gathering darkness.

Zoe came back, handed the paper to Wendy, and asked, "What do you want to know?"

"Basically, if I should sign it," Wendy said.

"I can't tell you that. Depends on what you want to do. I don't know anything about this Spodee-Odee. Is it a big deal?"

"Pretty big deal," Wendy said.

"According to this guy," Slibe said, nodding at Windrow.

"We're not the biggest club in the country, but we're up there," Windrow said.

"Well, I've seen a few contracts with writers, and it looks like those. Mr. Windrow is sort of acting as an agent here. That's the fifteen percent part. Of course, if you get another agent, he'll also want fifteen percent . . . but you don't have to pay Mr. Windrow if you play, you know. Depending on how much money is involved at that point, you could decide to go either way. Unless . . ."

Wendy: "Unless what?"

"Unless the band breaks up and you quit singing," Zoe said. "I don't see what happens then."

"One of two things," Windrow said. "If she wins the lottery and is worth a hundred million bucks and doesn't want to sing, I sue her, hoping to get a piece of the hundred million bucks. The second thing would be, she doesn't win the lottery, the band breaks up, she quits singing, goes to work in a diner, and what the fuck would I sue her for? Half of her next cheeseburger? If that happens, I wave it off. There's no profit in going after what doesn't exist."

"That's some pretty fancy tap-dancing right there," Slibe said.

Wendy started flipping through the contract. "What about this chick O'Hara? It says we've got to take O'Hara while we're with you. How about if we kept Berni for that month?"

Windrow said, "Bite the bullet, Wendy. O'Hara's the best female drummer out there, who's loose. She'd fit you guys like a glove. Divorced, no kids, and she's looking for a new band. I'll make the deal with her, she'll come up here and work out with you. And Berni can start working on her front act, right up on stage with you, singing backup, showing off, playing the tambourine, maybe. Struttin' her stuff."

"Fuckin' tambourine," Berni said, and she dropped her face into her hands, and again, Windrow saw the flash behind the venetian blind. Was there somebody out there?

Wendy put her hand on Berni's thigh and said, "We can do it. We can make you into the hottest thing on the stage. I've got these big cow tits, but you're what every cowboy wants. . . . It'll work."

Slibe said, "Something else about this contract . . ."

*

SO THEY ARGUED into the evening, watching the clock, and finally Wendy turned to Slibe and said, "We gotta get down to the Goose. But I'm gonna do it. I gotta talk to the other guys, but I'm gonna do it."

And to Windrow: "Are you in town overnight?"

"Yup."

"So let's get together at the studio tomorrow, we can talk to everybody at the same time, and I'll give you the contract. You coming to the Goose?"

"Gonna get something to eat first, if you got a recommendation."

Wendy looked at Zoe, who said, "Probably . . . the Duck Inn. Right downtown."

"This is bullshit," Slibe said. "I say we take the whole thing to a lawyer tomorrow. What's the rush?"

"No big one-day, two-day rush," Windrow said. "But I've got to get somebody lined up, quick. I got a hole I'm trying to fill. You take it, fine. You don't—well, we're lining up people for next summer and fall. That'd be your next shot with us. If Johnny Ray hadn't drove his Mustang into a ditch, there wouldn't be this hole."

"I'm doing it," Wendy said. "I'm doing it."

18

ZOE SPOKE.

Virgil put his hands on his head and asked, "What the hell you mean you can't find him? We talked to him. We saw him coming out of this place. . . ."

Sig said, "The Duck Inn."

". . . three hours ago. He's probably back at his motel—"

"He's not," Zoe said. "I went over there and knocked on his door. I even went out to the airport and talked with Zack."

"Airport guy," Sig said.

"And Jud's plane is still parked there."

"Probably in a bar."

"I cruised all the downtown bars. He was supposed to be there right at seven."

Virgil looked at his watch and turned to Sig. "I must've picked you up about then."

"I looked at the clock just before you got here and it wasn't quite seven."

"So we must've got down to the Duck place at . . ."

"Maybe ten after."

"So he was already running late," Zoe said. "He doesn't know anybody in town, he told us that. I couldn't find him. Wendy and Berni and Cat are out looking for him. . . . I mean maybe he's drunk out in a ditch somewhere. . . ."

"Wasn't drunk when we saw him," Sig said, picking up some of her sister's anxiety.

Virgil said, "Aw, fuck me. If that guy's off on a toot somewhere . . . Do we know what kind of car he was driving?"

"It was a red Jeep Commander," Zoe said. "He was out talking to Wendy this afternoon, when I went out there. I left at the same time he did, so I saw the car."

Virgil went out to his truck, got his phone, and called Sanders. "This may be a complete false alarm, but maybe not: we need to get your guys looking for a red Jeep Commander driven by a guy named Jud Windrow. . . ."

SIG SAID, "Virgil—go."

He didn't want to. "This isn't an investigation, it's a search," he protested. "All I could do is go out and drive around."

"I can see what's going through your head, okay? We can't do this, not with you all cranked up, looking at your watch every two minutes. You're going to be getting phone calls. So go. Find the guy. I'll be here." She smiled at him. "I don't really think anything'll break off."

★

HE WOUND UP in the driveway with Zoe, and said, "Thanks a lot."

"Well, what was I supposed to do, Virgil?" she asked.

"Yeah, yeah . . ."

She said, "I do feel bad. Siggy likes men, and since Joe's been gone . . . and Joe . . ."

"What about Joe?"

"Joe's a heck of a guy," Zoe said. "He wanders off, like this, and it's no way to have a marriage, but he was a heck of a guy and she misses having a guy around. You know, if he'd been an asshole or something, maybe she'd want to sign off men. But Joe wasn't. Isn't. He's funny, he's hot, and he's sort of . . . out there. And I know she needs something like that. You guys are going to be good together."

"Christ, maybe *you* should have married Joe, if he was such a heck of a guy."

"Virgil . . ."

"All right. I'm going," Virgil said. "And you know what? Fuck a bunch of Joes."

DRIVING BACK TOWARD TOWN, he had a thought, pulled into a driveway, found his notebook, and called Prudence Bauer, in Iowa. She picked up on the second ring, and he identified himself: "I hate to bother you, but Jud Windrow didn't call you this evening, did he?"

"No. Why would he?"

"Well, I got the impression that you were friends; I thought he might have given you a ring. He's going to sign up Wendy."

"Virgil, we're friends, slightly, but he was really friends with Connie," Bauer said. "Now tell me the truth: have you lost him?"

"Temporarily," Virgil said.

She said, "Oh my God, no," and he regretted calling.

"We don't know that anything happened," he said.

"But you think that, or you wouldn't have called," she snapped. "Don't lie to me, young man."

"We'd like to find him," Virgil conceded.

"You should call his ex-wife. Her name is Irma Windrow, and she still works at the Spodee-Odee as the bookkeeper. They're very close," she said.

VIRGIL DID THAT.

"We're trying to get in touch about this, uh, contract he was working out with Wendy Ashbach," Virgil said.

"Haven't heard a thing—he usually calls around ten o'clock. It's past that, so, you know, he doesn't *always* call . . ."

She knew nothing—but Windrow hadn't called in.

Virgil's annoyance was shifting to alarm.

THE SHERIFF CALLED BACK. "We got the tag number from the rental place, and did a quick run-through in town, didn't find him. We're gonna spread out. What're you doing?"

"I'm going out to Ashbach's place. That's where he was before he disappeared—this whole damned thing has to do with the Ashbachs. I don't know which one, but it's one of them."

"Where you at?"

"Just going past the Arby's."

"Pull in there, at Arby's. If you're going out to Ashbach's. I'm going to send a couple guys along with you."

VIRGIL PULLED IN, left the motor running, and three or four minutes later, a sheriff's car pulled in and he got out to talk.

The two cops were called Ben and Dan, both large, beefy guys with blue eyes and butt-crack chins, and Virgil said, "It's my personal opinion that one of the Ashbachs is involved in all this. I want to keep everything calm when we go in there, because this shooter knows how to use a weapon and he's crazy. Okay? Got your vests? When we get there, I want you to behave like it was a 'shots heard' situation. Don't get right next to each other so he could spray you. Let me go in, while you stay back. You got a rifle? Lay the rifle flat on the backseat and when you get out, open a back door and stand behind it, just in case."

★

WHEN HE FINISHED the briefing, and thought Ben and Dan understood the problem, he led the way through the dark to Slibe's. The farther in they got, the more the dark seemed to close down on them, like India ink spilling across the sky, and the more the trees seemed to hang down low over the road; and when they got on the gravel track, the narrower the road seemed to get, and the shorter the headlight beams, like the lead-in to a horror movie.

They went past the red mailbox that marked the last house before Slibe's, saw lights in a garage and what was probably the kitchen, and then they were at the end of the road. Slibe's house was dark, though an outdoor light cast a pink glow over the yard. Virgil could see a light in the kennel, up toward the peak of the roof, and a couple of lights in Wendy's double-wide. Two cars were parked outside the double-wide, and Slibe's truck was parked in front of his house.

Virgil tapped the brakes three or four times to tell the deputies that they'd arrived, then turned past the no trespassing sign, rolled by the sprawling garden, into the yard.

VIRGIL WENT TO THE DOUBLE-WIDE, lights trailing across the windows. He saw a curtain move as he got out of the truck, and a flash of Wendy's face, and then the door popped open and Wendy, with Berni behind her, asked, "Did you find him?"

"No." He was aware of the two deputies lounging behind their car. Good.

"Did he go back to Iowa?" Berni asked, over Wendy's shoulder.

"His plane's still at the airport," Virgil said. He looked around and then asked Wendy, "Where's your old man? And your brother?"

"Dad's down at the house, the Deuce, I don't know—but he was here earlier. He didn't have anything to do with this."

A door slammed on Slibe's house and Virgil turned that way and saw Slibe coming off the porch, and he glanced at the deputies—one of them nodded and said something to the other, in a low voice.

Wendy said, "Berni told us about you beating her up this afternoon."

Slibe came up and asked, "What the hell's going on?"

Virgil said, "Jud Windrow's gone missing."

"What's that got to do with us?"

The question was too sharp and too quick, Virgil thought, too defensive, and he could feel something uncoil in his brain.

"He was last seen here, talking with you people," Virgil said. "The night before McDill was shot, she spent with your daughter. Your daughter was going to sign with Jud once before, except her contact got strangled down in Iowa. That suggest anything to you?"

"Yeah, my daughter's getting fucked over by somebody," Slibe said.

"WHERE WERE YOU TONIGHT around seven o'clock—and where was your son?" Virgil asked.

"I was here. The meeting broke up, and Jud took off and the girls took off because they were playing. I fed the dogs and worked with a couple of them until it got dark."

"What about your son?"

Slibe glanced toward the kennel, then said, "He's gone walk-about. I saw him loading up his pack and told him I needed some help with the dogs. He said he didn't have time, and he got his rifle and headed out."

"On foot?"

"Yeah, of course on foot. They don't call it drive-about," Slibe said. "Anyway, Jud was okay when he left here, everybody saw him. How's the Deuce gonna follow him into town, on foot? Carrying a rifle?"

"Jud was going to the Duck Inn," Wendy chipped in.

Virgil looked at the three of them, running his tongue along his lower lip: goddamnit, they were lying. Had to be. Someplace along the line . . .

Berni said, "You know who did it? If Jud's gone? It's your girl-friend, Zoe."

Virgil said, "We've looked at Zoe and ruled her out."

"Why? Because of her ass?" Wendy asked. "Let me tell you, she doesn't do as much with it as you'd think."

"She's the one who told Jud to go to the Duck Inn, so she'd know where he was," Berni said, pressing.

"She runs all over the place up here, doing her taxes," Slibe said. "You see her car anywhere, you just think, she's doing her accounting."

"She might have heard I was with McDill," Wendy said. "She was all over the lodge the day after me and McDill got together and somebody might have seen us. She sure knew McDill well enough that she could have known that she went down to see the eagles every night."

Virgil thought about the bartender: the bartender had seen Wendy with McDill. Had somebody else?

Wendy looked at her father and Berni. "And that lady who got killed down in Iowa . . . that's when Zoe and I started hanging a little bit. That was . . . two years ago. It was." She turned back to Virgil: "Jesus Christ, Virgil: it was Zoe."

Virgil felt the corner he'd been pushed into: they were making a spontaneous case—maybe—but it sounded good, and he had no absolute rebuttal.

To Slibe, he said, "I want to see your son. I don't care where he's gone, you get him and tell him I want to talk to him. And if I don't hear from him by tomorrow, I'm gonna start a manhunt. We'll dig him out of the brush. . . ."

Slibe snorted: "Fat chance."

"I'll find him," Virgil said, holding Slibe's eyes for a moment.

Slibe didn't flinch, stared back, his eyes like black marbles: "What? You're gonna frame him? The Deuce didn't do it. And why would he, anyway?"

No speakable answer to that, Virgil thought. Because he wanted to fuck his sister? Because he was afraid she'd go away and never come back?

Virgil said, "I want to see him. Tomorrow." He turned and

headed back to his truck, nodded at the deputies, who got in their car. He climbed inside when Wendy screamed at him, "Zoe did it. Zoe did it, you asshole."

VIRGIL LED THE WAY out, drove until they were out of sight, then pulled over and the squad pulled over behind him. He walked back and asked, "Either one of you know, or could you find out, where Jan Washington lives?"

"Sure. She's out south of the river. . . ."

Virgil got directions and looked at his watch. Midnight. Well, screw it, if Washington's husband was home, he could get out of bed. He asked the deputies, "What'd you think back there?"

They glanced at each other, then one said, "I got this bad feeling about them."

"So do I—they're all a little too tangled up," the other one said. "I kinda wonder about Wendy and her old man. I wonder if he knocked off a piece of that, like, maybe, years ago, or something."

"Huh," Virgil said.

"On the other hand," said the first guy, who Virgil thought was Dan, "maybe you better take a closer look at Zoe, too. That whole family's always been a little off center. You know their mom was a lesbian? You know, became one?"

"Yeah? So what?" But he didn't say it. He stood up, slapped the door, and said, "You guys take it easy. Find that damn Windrow. Man, I'm gonna be pissed if he's off at one of these resorts. . . ."

"And that could be—there's only about a million of them," Dan said. "But we called in when we got out of there. No sign of him yet."

"The thing that messes me up is that we can't find the car," Virgil said. "I can't figure out why we can't find the car. I mean, even if they snatched him, we ought to be able to find that."

"Out in the bush somewhere," Ben offered.

"Find him," Virgil said, and he headed back to his car.

★

AND THE THOUGHT:

If somebody were going to snatch Windrow, with his car, and kill him and take the car out in the brush and ditch it . . . how would the killer get back to *his* car? It was possible that the killer was willing to walk eight or ten miles in the dark, and had left the car in an all-night parking lot somewhere. Or maybe had ditched it only a couple of miles out, so the walk back would be a half-hour or so. But how would he know that in advance? He had to know where Windrow would be eating, for one thing.

Unless there were two of them.

Like Slibe & Son.

And the Iowa cops thought the killer was male. . . .

THE WASHINGTONS LIVED FIVE or six miles out of town, on another country road, but not nearly as isolated as the Ashbach place. There were lights all along the way, and Virgil got glimpses of houses and sheds and cars and mailboxes on posts.

He drove past the Washington place and had to double back, shining his flashlight on the rural mailboxes, before he found it. They lived in a plain white one-floor ranch-style house with a two-car garage and white vinyl siding, with a shed around the back and a flower garden along the driveway. The only light looked like it might be a night-light, but the automatic yard light came on when Virgil drove down the driveway.

The front porch was a simple concrete slab. Virgil rang the doorbell, and a moment later he heard footfalls, and then the porch light flicked on. Washington looked out through the picture window, and came over and unlocked the door and said, "Jan? Is Jan okay . . . ?"

Virgil held up his hands and said, "I'm sorry to scare you, this isn't about Jan. I'm sure she's fine. But we've got a serious problem, and I wanted to ask you a couple of questions."

Washington, in blue pajamas, said, "Sure—c'mon in. What's going on?"

"We're looking for a guy . . ." Virgil said, and he quickly explained about Windrow. "I got a couple of questions. Have you or your wife had anything to do with Slibe Ashbach, or his son?"

"No. Can't say that we have. He's got that septic service, right? Our septic was done by El Anderson."

"Do you know them? Slibe and his son?"

"Slibe . . . the older one . . . I was on a tax adjustment board a couple of years ago, and he came in to ask for an adjustment, I believe. I can't remember what happened, but it wasn't a big deal. It seems like we might have referred it to the assessor for a reassessment. . . . I'd probably know him to see him. Maybe."

Then: "Okay . . . do you do your own taxes?"

"What?" Washington sat back.

"Do you do your own taxes? Or do you have somebody do them for you?"

"We have them done by a girl in town," Washington said.

Virgil's heart sank. "And that would be . . . ?"

"Mabel Knox is her name."

"Mabel Knox?" A reprieve.

"Yeah, she works for Zoe Tull," Washington said. "Zoe's got a big tax business downtown."

THE WASHINGTONS KNEW ZOE; and Zoe knew the Washingtons.

Probably meaningless, Virgil thought. But still, the only connection he'd found.

And he should have found it earlier; she should have mentioned it earlier.

Would have, if he hadn't known in his heart that Zoe was innocent. . . .

19

SLIBE ASHBACH SLIPPED OUT the back door of his house, stood in the dark, and listened. If you listened hard enough at night, you could hear a background crackling, as if the leaves of the trees were talking to each other, or the bugs were foot-racing through the long grass. . . .

He heard that, but didn't hear anything human. There was still light from Wendy's trailer; the light, Slibe knew, that pulled in the Deuce, like a moth.

He stepped out in the yard, in near pitch darkness, walking quiet in tennis shoes, along the back of the double-wide, his head below the bottom of the windows. He peeked at the corner and saw the Deuce standing there, on his cinder block, eye at the window. Slibe felt a clutch of anger at the sight of him; took a breath, got a grip, and asked, quietly, "See anything good?"

The Deuce didn't move. There was a circle of light on his eye, coming through the kink in the venetian blind, inside. He said, as quietly as Slibe, "I heard you coming from the time you closed the door. You sounded like an elephant coming through the grass."

Then he stepped down and moved closer to Slibe, eyes in shadow, and asked, "What do you want?"

"We need to talk, right now," Slibe said. "Go on up to the kennel, get out of the mosquitoes."

"Mosquitoes don't bother me none," the Deuce said, and he was telling the truth.

"They bother me. Go to the kennel."

They walked quickly, not shoulder to shoulder, but the Deuce trailing behind, so they moved single file, not talking. The dogs were mostly asleep, though one moaned at them as they walked past and up the stairs.

In the loft, the Deuce dropped onto a kitchen chair. "So talk."

"You saw the cops down there?"

"Yeah. I was sittin' up by the asparagus patch."

"That one guy, the state guy, Flowers, thinks you done it. Killed those people, and now this guy Windrow who was out here this afternoon. They can't find him anywhere, and they think he's dead."

"Didn't do it," the Deuce said.

"Listen, dummy. The cops don't care no more who did it," Slibe said. "They got one woman dead and one woman shot and one guy missing and all they want to do is arrest somebody so they can say it's over with. Flowers asked me where you were, and I told him you'd gone walkabout."

"Need some food, if I'm gonna walkabout," the Deuce said.

"I got food. Get it out of my cupboard. Get out of here."

"I dunno," the Deuce said.

"If you don't, they're gonna slap you in jail, bigger'n shit. I don't know when you'd be gettin' out."

"But I—"

"*Listen to me.* Didn't you hear what I said? They don't care. They just want to arrest somebody. The sheriff's got to get himself reelected. If they find somebody else, that's just fine—then they'll let you out. But if they don't, they'll try to hang it on you."

The Deuce put his head down, like he did when he was turning something over in his mind. After fifteen seconds or so, Slibe said, "I told them you were already gone. I believe if you stay out there for a while, they'll pick on somebody else."

The Deuce still didn't say anything, but he moved ninety degrees in his chair, and looked at a pile of outdoor gear that sat against the wall. "I got two boxes of shells at Martin's yesterday. I could stay out there for a while, if I had some Shake 'n Bake."

"I got a twelve-pack in the cupboard, never opened," Slibe said. "I got some cornmeal, I was down at the diner and got a bunch of those little packages of salt and pepper, twenty of them. You want to pack up, I'll go get them."

★

THE DEUCE WAS PACKED up in fifteen minutes—bivy sack, change of clothes, four pairs of socks, pump .22 with two boxes of shells, fifty rounds in each box, his knife, headlight, head net, gloves, bug spray. He thought about it for a minute, then added an ultralight fishing rod, a compact tackle box, and a yoga pad.

Slibe came back with a plastic sack full of food—Shake 'n Bake and cornmeal and a six-pack of beer. The Deuce said, "I'm not walkin'."

"What?"

"Takin' the canoe. You can drop me off on the river—I'll get down south of Deer River, in those swamps back there," he said. "Stay there as long as I want, eat sunnies and northern."

"I told them you went walkabout."

"If they ever ask, I'll tell them I keep the canoe hid out, and walked over."

Slibe said, "Okay. Okay. But we gotta get going. The girls have gone to bed. I want to move now."

THE DEUCE PACKED the food and tackle box, gathered up the rifle, fishing rod, and yoga pad, and carried them down to the truck. Slibe got two canoe paddles out of the woodshed. It was eight minutes out and over to the roughed-out landing at Big Dick Lake. The canoe, an old aluminum Grumman, was back in the woods, chained to a tree. They unlocked it, loaded it on the truck, and headed over to the river.

"Dark," Slibe said, as they turned off Highway 2 and rolled past a wild-rice processing place, and down to a boat landing.

"Not bad, when you get used to it," the Deuce said.

They put the canoe in the water next to the bridge, working with the Deuce's headlamp. He dropped in the pack, the rifle, the fishing rod, and the yoga pad.

Slibe said, "That pad, you're getting soft."

"Takes the hurt out of the roots," the Deuce said. "Sleep easier." He took the paddles from Slibe, and added, "I don't know what you're up to, Dad, but I'd 'preciate it if you'd leave me out of it."

He pushed off, pivoted the canoe, and disappeared into the night.

Slibe watched until he couldn't see or hear him, then spit into the water and climbed the bank back to the truck.

He stopped at an all-night gas station and bought a bottle of beer and drank it on the way home.

Thinking all the time.

Working the plotline.

20

VIRGIL STOOD ON ZOE'S front porch and pounded on the door like a drunk husband. The porch light came on, then the door popped, and Zoe peered at him through the screen. "Virgil?"

She was still fully dressed.

"Haven't found him. I was out at the Ashbachs'. Can I come in?"

"Sure." She stepped back, and Virgil pulled open the screen door and followed her into the living room and plopped on the couch, his pistol digging into his back. He'd forgotten about it. He leaned forward, pulled it out, and put it on the coffee table.

"You're carrying a gun," she said. Her voice was apprehensive.

"Not for you," Virgil said. "I was out at the Ashbachs' with a couple of deputies and we were ready to go."

"You mean 'kill somebody.'"

"I mean 'shoot back.' We're dealing with some loonies out there. That goddamn Slibe says his goddamn son's gone walkabout, whatever that means."

"It's Australian."

"I know that. I'm a cop, not an idiot," Virgil snapped. "Anyway, the Deuce is out wandering around with a gun, in the middle of the night. When I pushed them on it, all of them out there, Berni, Wendy, and Slibe, pretty much agreed on the killer."

"The Deuce?" She sounded skeptical.

"No. You."

She sat back. "Even Wendy?" she squeaked.

"Even Wendy. Though it started with Berni. Anyway, so here I am, ready to do what I should have done a long time ago, but didn't, because I like you. Go get a rope."

"A rope?"

"Yeah. Like a clothesline or something. Six feet long or so."

SHE HAD TO THRASH around for a while, but finally came up with a piece of electrical cord, which Virgil said would have to do, and he brought her back in the living room, looped it around his neck, put his hand under the cord, in front of his Adam's apple, palm out, turned his back on her, and said, "Strangle me."

"What?"

"Strangle me. Really go for it," he said.

"Virgil, I don't want to hurt you," she said.

"Well, if you start hurting me, stop."

So she tentatively pretended to strangle him, and he shook her off like a flea, said, "*Really* try, or I will kick your freakin' homosexual ass all over this living room."

That got to her, a little bit, anyway, and she tried harder, and he yanked her around and slapped her off the cord, and said, "Just like a little girl. What a fuckin' pussy. I'll tell you what, my third ex-wife was half your size, and she could've done a hell of a lot better job than that."

The goading worked. The third time, she finally went for it, and he had trouble getting loose, yanking her this way and that, and with one heavy heave, yanked her around and she lost her grip on the cord and cried, "My hands . . ."

He unwrapped the cord and asked, "You all right?"

"You almost broke my fingers." She was half lying on the couch, where she'd landed, looking at the reddening grooves across her palms.

He sat down and looked at her. "All right. You *could've* strangled Lifry, but I don't see you cutting her head off."

"I didn't strangle anybody," she said, tearing up.

"Why didn't you tell me that you do Jan Washington's taxes."

"I don't . . ." But then her mouth made an O. "Oh . . . *shit*. Mabel does!"

"You never said anything," Virgil said.

"But I don't *do* their taxes," she said. "I never even thought . . . Mabel does their taxes. They bring their stuff in an envelope, give it to Mabel. Or mail it; we send out an organizer with a mail-back envelope—and Mabel does them. I mean, I bet I talk to Jan Washington three times a year, and never in the office. On the street, I talk to her."

He looked at her for a minute, then said, "C'mon."

"Where're we going?" she asked.

"Out to the Eagle Nest."

"It's after one o'clock."

"If I needed the time, I'd look at my watch," he said. "Let's go."

They went out to the truck, then had to go back to the house so Virgil could get his gun, and he put it under the seat and they headed out to the lodge.

AUGUST NIGHTS GET COLD in northern Minnesota, and this one, not cold, was at least crisp. When they pulled into the lodge, a car full of women was just unloading, heading back to the cabins; coming in from the Wild Goose, Virgil thought. The cabins mostly trailed away from the lodge to the right, from the land side. Zoe took him around to the left, behind the lodge, to a cabin set on the highest ground around, with a green-screen porch.

"She's gonna be pissed," Zoe said.

"So what?"

"Just sayin'."

STANHOPE WAS MORE STUNNED than angry. She was wearing voluminous flannel pajamas with a flying-monkey pattern, with a ratty pink terry cloth robe tossed on top. "What?"

"Zoe here has been credibly accused of being the killer," Virgil told her. "I'm either going to clear her, or arrest her."

"What?" Stunned, not angry.

"Let's find a place to sit," Virgil said.

Stanhope's living room was comfortable in a lodge-like way, with shelves for old books, lots of *Reader's Digest* condensed novels from the sixties or so. A Bible was sitting on the arm of one chair. Virgil picked it up, tossed it from one hand to the other, like a softball, and said to the two women, "'Lying lips are an abomination to the Lord.' Proverbs twelve, twenty-two."

Stanhope: "Twelve, twenty-two?"

"How can you be 'goddamn this' and 'goddamn that' and go around quoting the Bible?" Zoe asked.

"Shut up," Virgil said. "Everybody sit down."

They sat.

To Zoe: "Now, on the day McDill was murdered, you were out here, right?"

"I came out, we were working on the books," Zoe said. "I finished the next day, when you were here. In Minnesota, you report your employee stuff each quarter, but the returns aren't due until the month after."

"What time did you leave?"

"About . . . I don't know. The middle of the afternoon."

She looked at Stanhope, who shrugged. "I don't know."

Virgil said to Stanhope, "I'm not looking for casual bullshit answers. Close your eyes. Concentrate, if you're capable of it. Think. When did you last see Zoe that day? What were you doing just before you last saw her?"

Stanhope closed her eyes, her fingers knotted in her lap, and finally said, "I saw her walking across the parking lot. I was in the office. I'd talked to Helen . . ." She looked up. "Okay. Helen was getting ready to leave, and I wanted her to finish her numbers the next morning, before Zoe came back. Helen leaves a few minutes before three o'clock because she has to pick up her kid at day care at three-fifteen. So, it was just before three."

Virgil to Zoe: "Is that about right?"

She nodded. "That's about right."

To Stanhope. "If I pull your ass into court, you'd swear to it?"

She nodded. "Yes. I suppose Helen would, too, because she was working with Zoe, and then she left to get Steve."

"Steve's the kid?"

"Yes. He's three," Stanhope said.

"What time do you think McDill left in the canoe?" Virgil asked.

"Early evening—six or so? I don't really know, because nobody really remembers seeing her leave. But that's not unusual, there are people paddling around all the time."

"So Zoe left at three o'clock, more or less, and McDill didn't leave for another three hours."

"Right," Stanhope said.

"Do you know the road that goes past the creek out of the lake?"

"Sure, I go up there in the fall," she said. "We try to be good neighbors with the people up there."

"Where would a killer hide a car?"

Stanhope had to think for a minute, and then said, "There are three houses that face out on the lake, but there are two more that are hunting cabins, not on the water. You could go through one of their gates, park behind a cabin. Or up the driveway. They're pretty overgrown, so you wouldn't see a car from the road."

"We looked up there, but didn't see much," Virgil said. "But the shooter would be taking a big risk. What if somebody was up there when he pulled in . . . ?"

Stanhope was shaking her head. "It's easy to tell. There's nothing much in the cabins—some beds, electric stoves, a pump, tables and chairs. Not much worth stealing. So the gates are closed at the road, but they're not locked up. You drive down there, and if the gate is closed, nobody's home. If somebody's up there for a couple days, getting ready for hunting season or something, they leave the gates open."

"So you could drive down there, open a gate, drive up the drive-way, close the gate, and you'd be out of sight."

"Yes."

Virgil asked Zoe, "Do you do taxes for anybody up there?"

224

She shook her head: "They're out-of-towners. From the Cities, I think. Maybe one from Alex . . ."

BACK OUT TO THE CAR. "Now where?" she asked.

"Down to your office. You must have a calendar."

"I do," she said.

They rode in silence, and not a particularly companionable one, back into town. On the way, Virgil called the sheriff's department, talked to the duty guy: no Windrow.

"You think he's dead?" Zoe asked in a small voice.

"I don't know. But I'm not sure he's alive," Virgil said. He pounded on the steering wheel. "I need to *do* something. I need to *do* something. I'm not *doing* anything."

IN TOWN, at her office, Zoe brought up her computer calendar, found two names, recalled both of them, and said, "That would have taken me up past five o'clock, for sure."

"But that's not far enough, Zoe," Virgil said. "You could make it out there with no trouble, leaving here at five o'clock. Think! What'd you do afterwards?"

"I walked over to Donaldson's and ate—I don't cook very much, neither does Sig—uh, then, let me see." She sat back and closed her eyes. "I ate . . . but first I went over to Gables and bought a magazine and looked in some windows, because I like to read while I eat. Then, I got gas."

"Did you pay for it with a credit card?"

"Yeah."

"And that would have been around . . . six?"

She thought about it. "Just about six. Maybe a little later, because I might not have gotten out of here right at five o'clock. I usually don't. Let me think. . . ."

Back to the closed eyes. After a minute, she said, "You know, I remember saying good-bye to Mabel that night. She came in to tell me something . . . mmm . . . I can't remember what, it was casual, but she would remember seeing me. Then I did work for a little bit.

225

Mabel leaves at five o'clock—she acts as a receptionist as well as an accountant, so she's in charge of closing up at five. You know, I bet I didn't get out of here until five-twenty or so. So it might have been six-fifteen or even six-thirty when I bought gas."

She shook a finger at him. "Credit cards. I pay for everything with credit cards, because then I have a record. Most accountants do that. C'mon, let's go back to my place."

They got back at three o'clock, and she took Virgil inside, past a little niche office with a filing cabinet, to a closet. Opening the closet, she revealed a stack of plastic file boxes with the years noted on them, going back to 2005.

She said, "Constance Lifry was killed two years ago . . . you have the date and time?"

"Yeah. Let me get it from the truck."

He came back with his notebook, and they found the relevant box. She found her American Express and Visa bills, and they ticked off the charges.

"Here," she said. "I went to Nordstrom's that day, too. They don't open until eleven o'clock. They know me—they wouldn't take my credit card from somebody else. Look, I went to Target, too, and I bought a bunch of stuff. . . . And the next day, I'm back . . ."

"You could have driven back by the next day," Virgil said. "But . . . these don't have exact time stamps on them."

"But they will have," Zoe said. "You can get them from Amex and Visa."

"I'm going to do that, Zoe," Virgil said. "Don't be bullshittin' me about this."

"Do it," she said. "Let's get it over with." And, she said, "You know I didn't do it."

THEY'D GOTTEN DOWN on their knees to search through the boxes, and now Virgil sat back on his heels and asked, "What gas card do you use?"

"I don't have one. I use my Visa," she said. "You can check that with a credit agency."

He thumbed through the Visa again, found charges for gas three days before Lifry was killed, and four days after. Nothing between. Of course, you could pay for gas with cash, though it never occurred to most people.

Huh.

He took his phone out of his pocket, looked up a number, and punched it up. It rang six times, and then Sandy, the hippie, said, "Virgil. Do you know what time it is?"

"Hang on a minute, I'll check," he said.

"Are you out on the town? I thought you were—"

"I'm up north, working a case," Virgil said. "Get a pencil. I need some information by the time I get up tomorrow, which will probably be about ten o'clock."

"I've got human osteology class at ten o'clock."

"So I'll call at nine-fifty," Virgil said. "We need to check the credit agencies for credit cards held by a guy named Slibe Ashbach. You got a pencil?" She did—he spelled the name. "And we need to see when and where he bought gas. . . ."

He gave her the dates.

"Virgil, you know, you are a real treat," Sandy said.

A male voice in the background mumbled something, and Virgil asked, "Who was that?"

"I have friends," she said.

"*Sandy* . . ."

"Virgil, shut up."

ZOE SAID, "Was that a special friend?"

Virgil said, "She's a researcher at the office."

"She ever done any research into Virgil Flowers?"

"Maybe," he said.

THEY SAT for a minute, and she asked, "Well, what's the verdict?"

"I never thought you did it. You're too stable. Though you have some stability problems when it comes to Wendy. If you were gonna kill somebody, you'd probably kill Berni. Or Wendy. Or yourself,"

Virgil said. He pinched his lower lip, thinking about it. "But it's complicated. If you figured that she was going to dump Berni anyway, eventually, like everybody does, maybe you wouldn't kill Berni. Maybe McDill was more of a threat, both to take Wendy away and to take the lodge away from you."

"Oh, for Christ's sakes, I'm going to bed," Zoe said, pushing up off the floor. "If you decide to arrest me, call ahead so I'll have time to wash my hair."

"That's what they all say," Virgil said.

Outside, sitting in the truck, he drew a line through Zoe: he'd make a few checks, so he wouldn't get bitten on the ass again, but she didn't do it.

21

VIRGIL SPENT SOME TIME with God that night, thinking about the way things were—about how somebody like Jud Windrow might now be lying dead somewhere, for no discernible reason—and why they were like that, and why a believer like himself would be going around cursing as he did: goddamnit.

Virgil held intricate unconventional beliefs, not necessarily Christian, but not necessarily un-Christian, either, derived from his years of studying nature, and his earlier years, his childhood years, with the Bible. God, he suspected, might not be a steady-state consciousness, omnipotent, omnipresent, timeless. God might be like a wave front, moving into an unknowable future; human souls might be like neurons, cells of God's own intelligence. . . .

Far out, dude; pass the joint.

Whatever God was, Virgil seriously doubted that he worried too much about profanity, sex, or even death. He left the world alone, people alone, each to work out a separate destiny. And he stranded people like Virgil, who wonder about the unseen world, but were trapped in their own animal passions, and operated out of moralities that almost certainly weren't God's own, if, indeed, he had one.

Virgil further worried that he was a guy who simply wanted to eat his cake, and have it, too—his philosophy, as a born-again once pointed out to him, pretty much allowed him to carry on as he wished, like your average godless commie.

He got to "godless commie" and went to sleep.

And worried in his sleep.

FIVE HOURS LATER, his cell phone went off, and he sat bolt upright, fumbled around for it, found it in his jeans pocket, on the floor at the foot of the bed.

"Hello?"

Sandy said, "Slibe Ashbach has a Visa card and a check card. He used the Visa card at an independent gas station in Grand Rapids early in the morning of the day Constance Lifry was murdered. He used the card again later that day in Clear Lake, Iowa, and at three o'clock the next morning, again in Clear Lake, and finally, later that second day, in Grand Rapids.

"It's about three hundred miles from Grand Rapids to Clear Lake. It's something between a hundred and fifty and a hundred and seventy miles from Clear Lake to Swanson, Iowa, depending on which route you take, or three hundred to three hundred and forty miles, round-trip. Then, another three hundred miles back to Grand Rapids. So, if you figure that his truck needs to be refueled every three hundred miles or so, which is reasonable, then it's quite consistent with the idea that he drove from Grand Rapids to Clear Lake, Clear Lake to Swanson, back to Clear Lake, and then on to Grand Rapids. In fact, it fits perfectly. Even the time fits, if Constance was killed at ten o'clock at night."

"You're a treasure beyond value," Virgil said. "E-mail that to me."

"Treasure beyond value, my ass," Sandy said. "That's not what you were saying the last time I talked to you."

"I don't have time for an emotional, ah, encounter, right now," Virgil began.

"You've never had time for an emotional encounter," she said. "If you ever find time, give me a ring."

She hung up; Virgil winced, sighed, and scratched his nuts.

SLIBE.

The good old Sliber. The Sliberoni. The Slibe-issimo.

"Slibe did it," Virgil said to the ceiling of the motel room, which didn't answer.

JOHN PHILLIPS was a short, balding, muscular redhead, wearing a blue suit that was, Virgil thought, silently punning to himself, ill-suited to his complexion. The lines in Phillips's face suggested a permanent skepticism, a guy who'd heard the phrase "I didn't mean to do it" a few hundred times too many. He was the Itasca County attorney, and he sat behind his desk, and in front of an American flag, his face growing more skeptical by the moment.

Sanders, the sheriff, sat with his legs crossed, to one side, looking at Virgil, while Virgil finished up: ". . . and that's about it."

"So you've got one thing—the Visa card and the gas station," Phillips said.

"No, I've got two and probably three dead, and one shot in the back, and a nut running loose. I *think* Slibe One probably did it, but it could be Slibe Two, and there's even a possibility that, for reasons we don't know, Wendy Ashbach did it. After I ran my strangulation test last night, it occurred to me that while Zoe isn't strong enough to have killed Lifry, Wendy might be. Wendy probably has thirty pounds on Zoe."

"But Wendy *wanted* to go with this guy Windrow," Sanders said.

"Yeah. And Wendy has an alibi, more or less, for McDill, though the alibi depends on exactly when McDill was killed, and we don't know that. Anyway, that's why I think it was probably Slibe One or Two, and not Wendy. But, if we can get a warrant for the whole property, we might as well take Wendy's place apart, too."

Phillips plucked a yellow pencil out of a Mason jar on his desk and used the eraser end to scratch his head. To Sanders, he said, "I can tell you what Don's going to say. It's a fishing expedition."

"Well, we do have the Visa card," Sanders said.

Virgil said, "That would be a huge coincidence, if Slibe, or Slibe Two, or Wendy, didn't use that to go down there and kill Lifry. That's solid. We've got opportunity on the others, McDill and Washington and Windrow. Neither Slibe One nor Two has a real alibi—and we have the fact that these killings seemed focused on the band."

"Except Washington," Phillips said.

"Well, yeah. But we've also got people killed," Virgil said. "Even if we're fishing, if we can find out which one is doing the killing, we can stop it. And if we can actually prove that one of them did it, I doubt that a court would throw out the evidence, if the search is only questionable. It's not *completely* unreasonable. Especially if it works out."

"Windrow plagues me," Sanders said. "We can't even *find* him. Avis has car locators installed on all their vehicles, and they're getting no signal, from anywhere in North America. The guy has gotta be at the bottom of a lake somewhere. The bottom of a bog or something."

"Probably off playing house with Little Linda," Phillips said.

"That's really funny, John, that's hilarious," Sanders said.

"Well, the Windrow thing is gonna be a problem," Phillips said. "We may not be able to get his name in front of a jury if we can't prove he's dead."

"Prove it? We don't even *know* it," Sanders said.

DISTRICT COURT JUDGE Don Hope was an older white-haired man with rimless glasses, and he said to Phillips, "John, there hasn't been a fishing expedition this big since Teddy Roosevelt went up the Amazon."

Phillips wiggled in his chair and said, "Judge, I hate to hear that phrase, you know? The piscatorial reference? I'm not sure—"

"Yeah, yeah, piscatorial my ass. Well, enough people been killed, and I'm so old, what the hell could they do to me? Get me the paper and I'll sign it. Not that it doesn't violate my principles all to hell and gone."

Virgil smiled and Hope asked, "What're you smiling about?"

"That was a smile of approval," Virgil said.

"You look like a smart-ass," Hope said. "What's that on your shirt?"

"A band," Virgil said. "The Appleseed Cast."

"Never heard of them," the judge said. "They sound like a smart-ass band."

"They *are* a smart-ass band," Virgil agreed. "Hey, thanks for the warrant, Your Honor. We'll make you proud."

"That Wendy is a buxom lass," the judge said. "Hope *she* didn't do it."

WITH THE WARRANT IN HAND, there was no huge rush to get out to Ashbach's place, and Sanders wanted to do it right, rather than do it fast. "We're not gonna arrive at the last minute and save Windrow," he said. "If they were gunning for Windrow, he's already dead."

"If Windrow isn't dead, if he's facedown drunk in some resort bar, I'll kill him myself," Virgil said. "You round up your guys, I'll get the crime-scene crew headed back this way. They'll be a couple hours getting here."

SANDERS GOT THREE COPS from Grand Rapids, plus five deputies. The crime-scene crew would make twelve, plus Virgil, and the sheriff decided to go along—Little Linda was dead in the water. Fourteen people should nail the place down pretty well, Virgil thought. They gathered in a courtroom, and Virgil ran them through what he expected—but he didn't expect much trouble.

"The main thing we're looking for is the gun, or any .223 ammo, or anything that suggests they own a .223 bolt action, like a hunting photo. Especially look for a prairie-dog-shooting photograph. Then, of course, blood. Take a long look at Slibe Junior, if he's back, for any signs of injury. Windrow was driving a Jeep Commander . . .

check car keys. We're gonna be out there for a while, so if you want to get a sandwich, or a couple of Cokes to take along, do it now. . . ."

THEY WENT OUT in a long rolling caravan, as soon as the crime-scene people showed up, the sheriff leading the way, Virgil bringing up the rear. By the time he pulled in, cops were spilling all over the acreage, and Wendy came out on the steps of the double-wide and shouted, "What the hell is this?"

The sheriff ignored her, knocked on Slibe's door, got no response, and Wendy came along, trailing Berni, and said, "Dad's gone into town."

"Then I'll give it to you, and you can pass it on," the sheriff said. "This is a search warrant for the premises of Slibe Ashbach and Slibe Ashbach LLC, doing business as Slibe Ashbach Septic & Grading. If you've got a key to the house, we won't have to kick down the door."

"I got a key. . . ." Then Wendy spotted Virgil: "What the fuck are you doing? Virgil? What're you doing?"

"Something came up. I can't talk to you about it. I need to talk to your father," Virgil said. "Is the Deuce back?"

"I don't know. You'll have to look," she said.

"In the house?"

"No, he's got the loft in the kennel." They all turned and looked at the kennel building, and Virgil remembered that there'd been a light on last night.

"There was a light on there last night," Virgil said. "I thought you guys said he'd gone walkabout."

"There's a light on there all the time," Wendy said. "It comes on at dark."

"What for?"

"I don't know—something to do with the dogs."

ONE OF THE COPS went with Wendy to get the key to the house, and Berni said to Virgil, "There's gonna be trouble about this. You guys are going to get sued all over the place."

"Do you know when Mr. Ashbach is expected to return?" the sheriff asked.

"I don't even know why he's gone," she said. "He took off a half-hour ago."

"All right." Wendy came back with the key, and the sheriff said, "Well, let's get to it."

THE CRIME-SCENE PEOPLE DID the basic search of Slibe's house, Wendy's trailer, and the Deuce's loft, while one cop kept an eye on Wendy and Berni. Three others walked the property and checked the outbuildings.

Virgil idled along with everybody, at one time or another, waiting for something to catch his eye.

The first thing he noticed about Ashbach's house was the neatness: a place for everything, and everything in its place, right down to a tall glass bowl, placed like a spittoon on the floor next to Ashbach's full-sized bed, to hold change—nickels, dimes, and pennies, but no quarters. He pulled out a couple of drawers in the bedroom and found the socks had been rolled; T-shirts were folded, dirty clothes were in a woven-willow hamper under a window; shaving gear, toothpaste, a couple of pill bottles, and a bottle of sunblock lotion were lined up like soldiers on the bathroom counter.

The pill bottles were prescription, and one of the crime-scene people told him they were two different kinds of statin.

VIRGIL REMEMBERED where Slibe kept the key to the gun safe, and they went through it, checked all the guns. They took all of the .223 ammo, which Slibe had said was for the Colt semiauto. The lab could check it all, to see if any might match traces found in McDill's skull; but the ammo was new, so there were no extraction marks to check, and there was no empty brass, no reloads.

"He told me once that they were thinking about going out west for prairie dogs—most of those guys are reloaders," Virgil said.

"Couldn't afford it otherwise," a crime-scene guy agreed.

*

THEY LOOKED through the firewood shed and found nothing but firewood, neatly stacked for the winter. The machine shed held two Bobcats, a front-end loader and a small shovel, and a larger shovel from Caterpillar. All three machines were older, but well tended. Behind the machine shed was a stack of white plastic pipe, of the kind used to build septic fields, and a concrete tank with a crack in it.

Nothing in the tank but long grass.

THEY FOUND a reloading station in Slibe II's loft.

The loft was just that: a wooden-floored second story in the metal kennel building; the dogs were quiet and friendly, looked well kept and well fed, but the place inevitably smelled of dog shit, and that was true up the stairs in the loft. The loft was heated with two 220-volt overhead electric heaters, and a potbellied woodstove at the far end. There was a sink, a bathtub, and a toilet in a walled-off area at the end of the loft, but there was no door.

Like the house, the loft was organized with military precision; everything neatly kept and clean, on the surface; but the insides of the drawers were a jumble of clothes and electrical and mechanical parts, hunting and fishing gear. When a cop opened the cardboard stand-alone closet, he found a tangle of hangers with winter clothes stuck this way and that, half of it hanging, half of it on the floor. Superficially like Slibe's place, but once you dug in, nothing like Slibe at all.

Four metal army-surplus ammo boxes sat on the floor next to the reloading station. Two contained shotgun shells, twelve- and twenty-gauge, and two contained empty brass. The crime-scene tech dumped the brass, and he and Virgil picked through it, found forty .223 cartridges, which they bagged.

Mapes, the head of the crime-scene crew, came up and took a look, and said, "We need the lab to check it, but I don't see any bolt-action extraction nicks. We need a closer look."

"All we need is one," Virgil said. He shook out the shotgun shells, hoping a stray .223 might be hiding in them, but there wasn't.

Virgil looked under the narrow bed and found a stack of old *Hustler* magazines, a plastic bag with five fading color photographs of a woman with eighties hair, and another plastic bag with perhaps a quarter ounce of marijuana.

He had the crime-scene guy bag the marijuana, then sat on the bed and looked at the photos. In one, the woman leaned on the front of a seventies or eighties Chevy with a much younger Slibe. They were in the driveway, with the road behind them. No garden, just an empty space. Wendy and the Deuce's mother?

Virgil took them to the end window, for the better light: she was a square-built dishwater blonde, busty, like Wendy, attractive in a country way. Slibe was blond. Virgil had noticed that he was blondish, behind the bald dome, but his hair was cut so short that it hadn't registered. In this old photo, blond hair covered his ears, as long as Virgil's was. Really blond. Rocker blond . . .

THE CRIME-SCENE GUY SAID, "Might have something here."

Virgil turned and saw him sitting on the floor next to the hamper, looking at a pair of denim coveralls, looking at the end of one sleeve.

"What?"

"Can't swear to it, but it looks like blood. Significant blood."

"Wouldn't he have seen it?" Virgil asked. He went over and peered at the stain, which was about the size of a half-dollar. The stain didn't appear to soak through; it was superficial.

"He picked it up from the outside, so it's probably not his." The guy held up the coveralls, and the sleeves fell to the side. "See, it's on the bottom of the sleeve . . . you know, like when you stick your sleeve in jelly, or something."

"Get it back to the lab, right now," Virgil said. This was something. This was good. "We'll eventually need DNA, but what I really need is to get a blood type, like, this afternoon. Gotta try to get Windrow's blood type. Like now . . ."

"Let's show it to Ron first. He knows blood."

*

THE CRIME-SCENE GUY bagged the coveralls and they carried them down the stairs and back to the house. Sanders saw them coming, asked, "What?" and Virgil said, "We might have some blood."

Mapes came out to take a look, said, "It's blood," and the word *blood* stuttered through the group of deputies.

Virgil got Sanders to send the coveralls to Bemidji with one of the deputies, and Virgil told the deputy, "Don't kill anybody, but use your lights and get your ass up there, quick as you can. They'll be expecting you."

"Abso-fucking-lutely," the deputy said.

Virgil called Bemidji on Slibe's landline phone, and told them what he needed, then called Sandy, the researcher, who was still a little stiff, but agreed to find out what Windrow's blood type was.

Wendy came over, attracted by the buzz. "What?" she asked.

Virgil: "Where's your brother?"

22

TWO PEOPLE ARRIVED IN the next ten minutes. The first came slouching through the police lines, a redheaded man wearing a rumpled black sport coat over jeans and long sharp-toed black city shoes that he called Jersey Pointers. He and his girlfriend had taught Virgil how to jitterbug—Ruffe Ignace, a reporter for the recently bankrupt Minneapolis *Star Tribune*.

Virgil waited arms akimbo, and Ignace came up, grinning like the Cheshire Cat, and said, "That fuckin' Flowers. When I saw your happy face, I went ahead and told the cops that I was here to consult with you."

"I oughta throw your ass out," Virgil said.

"That's right. I'm trying to save a bankrupt newspaper and you're piling on," Ignace said. "Thanks a lot, old pal. Forget everything you owe me."

"How you been?" Virgil asked.

"Tired of driving a hundred and fifty miles at the crack of dawn because some asshole twenty-three-year-old editor thinks I should," Ignace said. "I'm writing a crime novel."

"You and every other reporter in the state," Virgil said.

"Ah, they're writing screenplays. I'm writing a novel. I even got an agent." Ignace looked around, at the cops coming and going. "Catch anybody?"

"Just got a break. We're looking at a kid named Slibe Ashbach Junior, also known as the Deuce, son of Slibe Ashbach Senior, who runs this septic construction company, and brother to Wendy Ashbach, a singer in a local country band. We found some blood: it's on its way to Bemidji."

Ignace asked, "Blood from McDill?"

"No. She was killed at long range. . . . This was from yet another guy. We think there may be three connected murders and one non-fatal shooting. . . ." He took a minute to explain; he'd learned that Ignace had an eidetic memory for conversation, and would be able to write it all down later. The memory, Ignace had told him, was good for two or three hours before starting to fade. "Listen, I'm gonna have to introduce you to the sheriff. I don't know if he'll want you in here. Be nice, okay? We're also looking for the father, Slibe Senior. I'm gonna hang around here until he shows up, or until somebody says they've got him in town."

A truck came firing down the road, throwing up a cloud of dust. "Hell, here he comes now."

"But the son is the suspect?"

"Right now. The father was when we came in. Watch this . . . if the sheriff doesn't kick you out."

The cop at the end of the driveway had stopped Ashbach, and Virgil led Ignace over to Sanders and said, "Bob, I want to introduce you to Ruffe Ignace, he's a crime reporter from the *Star Tribune*. I let him in, but told him that it'd be your call to let him stay or go."

Sanders nodded at Ignace, didn't offer to shake hands: "If the local paper shows up, I'll have to kick you out, because I'm not letting those guys in. Otherwise, stand around with your hands in your pockets, and I don't care."

"Thanks, Sheriff. I appreciate it," Ignace said. "I'll stay back."

SLIBE'S TRUCK CAME rolling past the cop and into a slot along the garden fence, where it stopped, and Slibe got out, saw Virgil and the sheriff, and headed over, pushing an attitude. A couple of the deputies picked it up and vectored on him, but he slowed down as he came up, and shouted past a deputy, "What the hell is going on here? You're bustin' up my house?"

"We're searching it," Virgil said. "And Wendy's and your son's. Where's the Deuce? You find him?"

"I don't keep track of him," Slibe said. He looked wildly around, and said to Sanders, with a pleading note in his voice, "Don't fuck with my dogs, Sheriff. Don't fuck with my dogs."

Virgil said, "Come over to the house and sit down. I got a question for you."

The sheriff said, "Just to be on the up-and-up, we oughta read him his rights."

ONE OF THE DEPUTIES did that, and Slibe said to Virgil, "I don't want no fuckin' lawyer. And I don't want to be sittin' in my own house with you. Ask what you're gonna ask."

Virgil said, "You've got a Visa card. Let me see it."

Slibe looked at him for a second, then took his wallet out of his back pocket, thumbed through the card slots, found a Visa card, and handed it over. Virgil took the notebook out of his back pocket, looked at it: different number.

"How long you had this card?" Virgil asked.

"Thirty years? I don't know," Slibe said.

"Does the Deuce have one?"

"He don't," Slibe said. "He don't have a bank account. Wendy does."

"I've got a different card number for a Slibe Ashbach."

"But . . ." His eyes slid away, then came back and he said, "I got a business card. We keep it in the house, you know, for deliveries and such."

Virgil said, "Let's get it."

Slibe had a neat home office in a second bedroom at the back of the house, with a wooden desk. He pulled the left-hand desk drawer completely out, reached inside the drawer slot, and fumbled out four credit cards—a Visa, a Visa check card, a Target, and a Sears. Virgil checked the Visa number, and it matched.

He held it up. "On the morning of the day that Constance Lifry was killed in Swanson, Iowa, this card was used to charge gas in Clear Lake, Iowa, which is three hundred miles south of here. Early the next morning, it was used to charge gas at the same station, which means the driver probably put three hundred miles on his truck between those two gas-ups. Swanson is about a three-hundred-mile round-trip. The next charge was back here."

Slibe's eyes had widened, and now his Adam's apple bobbed, and he looked around the office, and at the sheriff, and said, "Jesus God. I knew that boy wasn't right."

"You think the Deuce did it?" Virgil asked.

"I don't know—I don't know," Slibe said. "But I didn't . . . I never stopped in no Clear Lake in my life, far as I know. I don't even know where it is. It's on I-35? I been to Texas down I-35, on my way to New Orleans, but that was after Katrina."

"The Deuce uses this card?"

"We all use it," Slibe said. He started to tremble and shake. "He's . . . used it for gas before. Without me knowin'."

Virgil said, "You don't know where he is, now?"

"No, but he's on foot, I believe. I saw him packin' up, he took some Shake 'n Bake out of my cupboard, got his gun and fishing pole." He was slack-mouthed. "Jesus God, you think he killed them people?"

Virgil said to the sheriff, "Now we *do* need to find him."

"We can do that," the sheriff said.

ITASCA COUNTY is a forest broken up by bogs and water and a few towns, twice as big as Rhode Island, three thousand square miles of pine, spruce, cedar, tamarack, birch, aspen, and maple. If all the Deuce did was sit under a bush, Virgil thought—Virgil was a prairie kid—he'd be almost impossible to find. The sheriff thought differently.

"You sit down on a stump, almost anyplace, and after a while, somebody'll come along. Damnedest thing. When somebody gets lost, the thing that keeps them lost is that they go wandering around. If they'd just sit on a stump, somebody would come along."

"That's great, Sheriff, except that he's carrying a rifle and he might've killed a few people already," Virgil said.

"That's a point," Sanders said.

Ignace stuck an oar in: "What're you going to do?"

"Well, if he's going to bump into somebody, that's what he's going to do," Sanders said. "What I'm going to do is, I'm going on the radio."

THE CRIME-SCENE CREW FOUND and bagged several kinds of ammo, a bunch of short cords and ropes that could have been used to strangle someone, and a dozen pieces of jewelry hidden in a box in an army footlocker full of comic books and the remnants of a set of giant plastic Tinker Toys.

The jewelry, including a strand of thin pearls, a small turquoise thunderbird, and several pairs of cheap earrings, went in a bag as possible trophies taken from the dead women. But when Virgil showed the bag to Wendy, her eyebrows went up and she said, "That's Mom's stuff. Where'd you find it? I used to have it and it disappeared."

Virgil checked with Davies and Prudence Bauer and neither knew of missing jewelry, of small pearls or thunderbirds. Bauer asked, "Where's Jud?"

Virgil said, "I don't know."

"You people are like a curse on us," she said, and she broke down and began to cry into the phone.

SANDY CALLED AND SAID that she'd spoken to Jud Windrow's ex-wife, and Windrow's blood type was A-positive, a common type. Slibe said that his was O, but Wendy didn't know hers.

The afternoon dragged into early evening. Ruffe was bored by the search, and finally said good-bye; he gave Virgil his cell number, said he planned to file, and then was off to explore the "erotic potentialities" of Grand Rapids. The cops started packing up and dispersing. Slibe spent the afternoon stomping around the acreage, cursing, worked with the dogs for a few minutes, watched the crime-scene people moving in and out of his house. Wendy huddled with Berni. At six, a tech from Bemidji called and said the blood on the sleeve was A-positive.

Virgil called Sanders: "I guess it's possible that Slibe Two is A-positive, if his mother was, but this makes me really think that Jud Windrow is . . . gone."

"We're going full bore on Slibe Junior," Sanders said. "If anybody in Bemidji County doesn't know who we're looking for, he's blind and deaf."

THE SUN WAS DOWN behind the trees when Sanders called back and said, "We've got a likely sighting. He's got a canoe, he's off the river in a swampy area down below Deer River. Some kids coming down the river spotted him heading back through the rice, and called it in."

"So what're we doing?" Virgil asked.

"Gonna be real quiet about it, set people up all along the river, put a couple boats up above him, down below him, so he can't sneak past," Sanders said. "Wait for daylight, go in with a helicopter. Run his ass down."

"Anything I can do?"

"Well . . . you up for a plane ride?"

*

VIRGIL WENT BACK through town, stopped at a Subway for a BMT and a Coke, ate it on the way to the airport. He was chewing on the sandwich when Sig called. She asked, "What you doing?"

"We're trying to run down Slibe Junior. . . ." He told her about the search, and about the credit card, about the upcoming plane ride.

She whistled and said, "Well, thank God. Be safe in the plane."

AT THE AIRPORT, he took a pair of binoculars out of his equipment bag, hooked up with a deputy named Frank Harris.

"Pilot's running late," Harris said. "He called and said his kid might have busted an arm in karate class. He'll be here as soon as he gets out of the emergency room."

"Ah, man . . ." Virgil didn't feel like waiting. He thought about Sig, sitting home alone, still unfulfilled. Looked at his watch. A half-hour passed, and then forty minutes, and Virgil decided if the pilot hadn't arrived by the end of an hour, he'd bail. He'd feel guilty about it, but he would.

The pilot, whose name was Hank Underwood, walked in five minutes later and said, "Sorry."

"Broken?" Harris asked.

"Yeah. Worse than we thought," Underwood said. He was a short, dark man about Virgil's age. "Not his arm, it's a wrist bone, the navicular. He could be in a cast for five months. He was supposed to start football practice in three weeks."

They were talking about it, walking out to Underwood's single-engine Cessna, and Virgil said the broken arm might be a blessing in disguise. "Maybe he'll turn out to be great at math and become a scientist."

"Rather play football," Underwood said. "All his pals will be . . . but you could be right." He sounded doubtful.

Underwood put Harris in the back, because he was shorter than Virgil, and as they took off into the darkness, the plane smelling of warm oil and cold air, said, "When we get up there, I'll roll a bit, to give you a view. We'll go up one side and down the other, using Deer River as our guide."

"How're we going to mark him?" Virgil asked.

"GPS," Underwood said. "We'll circle until we can get an azimuth that runs through him and some point in Deer River, and mark ourselves, and then do it again, from another angle. Won't be exact, but it'll be pretty damn close."

"As long as we've only got one fire," Harris said.

Underwood said, "Not many people camping in a swamp. It's usually dark as a coal sack along there. Our biggest problem will be if he's sleeping in his boat, and isn't cooking at all."

"Don't want to spook him," Virgil said.

"We'll be well off. We'll go up one side of the river, fool around for a while, then come back down the other," Underwood said. "If he's close enough to the highway, he might not even hear us."

THEY COULD SEE Deer River within a couple of minutes of taking off. "The place he's supposed to be is right down this way from the lights," Underwood said, gesturing. "See the line of lights? Now, ninety degrees towards us."

The river plain was pitch-black. They flew up the side, past the town, did a wide circle to the west, slowly, scanning the terrain, then came right back down the highway. On the second pass, Harris said, suddenly, "Got a fire."

"Where?" Virgil asked.

"About two-thirty . . . coming up on three . . . It flickers . . . lost it, goddamnit, got it, got it again . . ."

"Brush between us and it," Underwood said.

Virgil scanned down at the same angle as Harris, at three o'clock. "Got it," Virgil said. "I got it. It's small."

"No point in a barn fire to cook a weenie," Harris said.

UNDERWOOD TOOK THEM around the town, and they put azimuth lines from GPS markers through intersections of the highway, crossing at the fire. "Don't see another damn thing out there," Virgil said, scanning the darkness.

"There isn't anything else out there," Harris said. "You couldn't pay me five hundred dollars to camp out in there. No telling what you'd run into."

"Maybe even a crazy killer," Underwood said. *"Friday the 13th*, huh?"

"Never saw it," Harris said. "But that's the general idea."

THEY WERE ALL CRANKED when they landed. Virgil and Harris left Underwood to put the plane away, and after warning the pilot to keep his mouth shut, went roaring off to the sheriff's office. The sheriff and a couple of deputies were waiting for them, with a USGS topo map, and Virgil and Harris used a yardstick to draw out their lines.

"Not bad," the sheriff said, his finger on the map where the lines crossed. "Man, that's not more'n a mile from where the kids thought they saw him. Gotta be him."

"What time are you putting the chopper up?" Virgil asked.

"Sunrise is just about six o'clock—so, about six o'clock." Sanders looked at his watch. "Seven hours. You'll want to be on the ground, up in Deer River, by five at the latest. We'll put you in a boat."

"Who's in the helicopter?" Virgil asked.

"Me and the pilot," the sheriff said. "I'm paying for it, so I get the ride."

"He'll probably shoot you down," Virgil said.

"You just want the ride," Sanders said; and he was right. And he clapped his hands, once, and said, "Hot damn. This is something. I mean, I hate to say it, but I'm having a pretty good time right now. Wasn't having a good time this morning." He turned to one of the deputies. "I'll call you up if we spot him, and you get on to Jim Young, get his ass up to Deer River. I'll put down on the track up there, and I want a picture of me getting out of the helicopter."

And he said to Virgil: "Politics. He's the local newspaper guy."

"Gotcha," Virgil said.

THAT NIGHT VIRGIL THOUGHT about God some more, and about the Deuce, that lonely spark of fire out in the middle of a swamp, a single twisted soul believing itself safely wrapped in nature, with no idea of what was coming in the morning.

23

VIRGIL WENT BACK TO the truck and got a black nylon emergency jacket. August in Minnesota—chilly in the morning this far north, and this early in the day.

A river rat named Earl, drafted by Sanders, had just backed his eighteen-foot Alumacraft jon boat down the boat ramp into the water. Virgil would be riding with him, and with a cop named Rod. Rod was messing nervously with his AR-15, and kept looking downriver, where they expected the helicopter to show up. Two more jon boats were already in the water, and there were more both upriver and down.

"You going with your handgun?" Rod asked Virgil.

"Haven't decided," Virgil said.

Rod asked because he could see Virgil didn't have a long gun, and assumed his pistol was under his jacket; actually, it was under the front seat of the truck. All the guns were making Virgil nervous: they were heading into a swamp, without much visibility in some places, and six boats full of cops with rifles, converging on a central point from three different directions. Sanders's chief deputy was as nervous as Virgil, and worked back and forth through the deputies, talking about fire discipline.

Virgil went back to the truck again, looked back down the ramp, at all the deputies, at four cop cars and three trucks with trailers, watched Earl park his trailer, and thought that maybe the best idea would be to lie low in the boat; though lying low in a jon boat would shake your bones to pieces. The low, flat-bottom craft were fine when moving slow in flat water, but were no damn good in heavy chop; or in a heavy firefight, for that matter.

He thought about it some more, and finally pulled out his pump twelve-gauge, loaded three shells, and put seven more in his jacket pocket. If that wasn't enough, fuck him.

WAITED SOME MORE, in the mild stink of mud and rotting fish. One of the deputies borrowed a paddle and fished a plastic bag out of the water and threw it in a trash can. Somebody looked south and asked, "Wonder what they're doing down there?"

Then the chief deputy called, "Saddle up. Sheriff's on the way."

They all bustled down to the boats, climbed aboard, and the guys on the motors fired them up, quiet four-strokes, and eased out onto the lake, looking south. A minute later they heard the chopper, and then saw it, fairly high, coming fast, then slowing. And the shoulder radios went off and Rod said, "They got him! He's right under the chopper."

THEY ALL TOOK OFF, three boats carving long wakes in the smooth water, Rod holding his rifle straight up like a movie-poster commando, while Virgil sat on a cushion in the bow, back to the incoming wind. Rod, his fair face reddening with the cold wind, listened to his radio, and then shouted, "He's running for the trees, he's running for the trees."

The swamp was actually the remnants of a series of Mississippi oxbows, some of which could still be seen from the air, as long, curling cutoff lakes, separated from one another by wild rice flats, cattails, and brush. There was one big hunk of trees south of the flats. If the Deuce got into them, he'd be hard to dig out, especially if people were shooting at one another.

That had to be a ten- or fifteen-minute paddle, though, if he was still where he had been the night before. Sanders's flotilla was no more than two or three minutes away. . . .

They crossed the lake, running hard—hard for a jon boat, anyway—and cut into a channel that wrapped around in a hard curve. Earl stayed with the speed, though, familiar with the territory, juked once for a snag, and blew into an intersecting channel that Virgil thought might be the river, though it was only forty or fifty feet wide.

The chopper was drifting south, away from them, but they were coming up quickly. Virgil risked standing up for just a second, couldn't see much—but could just see the tops of trees to the south.

Rod shouted, "He's cutting through the grass, he's back in the weeds. . . ."

More noise, and Virgil looked back, saw the downriver boats coming up on them; now five boats running along, over a few hundred yards.

"Gotta be close," Rod shouted.

Another fifteen seconds and Rod shouted at Earl, and pointed, "Right there, right there . . ."

The chopper was probably no more than fifty or sixty yards ahead of them, and Virgil could hear a loudspeaker, but couldn't hear what was being said over the chop of the helicopter. Two more boats came in from the north, and Earl put them up against a bank of cattails; they drifted for a minute, then Virgil saw a small channel with flowing water, opening through the cattails. It wasn't more than eighteen inches wide.

"Can we push through there?" Rod asked.

"Tough," Earl said. He killed the motor, popped a pole mounted in brackets under the left gunwale, stood up, and pushed the boat back into the weeds. They got thirty feet, and that was it. "Too much drag," Earl said.

"Could we walk through it?" Rod asked.

"Nope. You might find shallow spots, but you'd be up to your neck every two minutes," Earl said. He started poling them back out, and Rod talked into his radio, and then said, "Back north—there's an open channel north. Shit, some guys are already going in, we're gonna miss it."

They got back out, and Earl fired up the motor, and they started north up the channel, and another boat backed out of the weeds and fell in behind them; Virgil could see more boats up ahead that had gone on while they tried to push into the cattails.

"He's at the trees," Rod shouted, and then, "They see him, they see him."

There were five fast pops, gunfire, and Rod shouted, "Holy cow, what was that?" and sat down, suddenly, and Virgil said, "Easy, easy, everybody, stay low . . ."

The helicopter was maneuvering overhead, and then they heard a long string of shots, semiauto fire, from two or three guns, and Rod shouted, "He's down, he's down, they got him," and Virgil thought: *Shit.*

THE HELICOPTER WAS RIGHT *there,* so close they couldn't hear themselves think, but they couldn't get into the shooting scene without threading through a quarter mile of beaten-down grasses and cattails, and finally they turned a last curve and saw the flotilla pulled up on a muddy bank tangled with brushy trees, and a cluster of cops by an aluminum canoe another fifty yards down the bank.

They had to get out in the water and stumble along the shore, up to their knees, before they got there, and Virgil pushed through the circle of cops to find two guys tying compression bandages on the Deuce's thighs and lower leg, and then one of the cops said, "Get him on the tarp, get him on the tarp," and four guys lifted him, and he groaned, and they put him on a blue plastic tarp and he began leaking blood across it, lots of blood.

Five other cops and Virgil got pieces of tarp and lifted him, and staggered back through the water to the first of the jon boats, the Deuce crying in pain, his eyes liquid and flashing white, and he asked, two or three or four times, "Why did you shoot me? Why did you shoot me?" They put him on the bottom of the boat, and the boatman fired it up and nosed the boat down the channel, and then, out of sight, Virgil heard the engine open up.

"Where're they going?" he asked a cop.

"Got an ambulance coming to the landing," he said. He looked haggard, though it was early.

"What happened?" Virgil asked.

"He tried to make it into the trees," the guy said. "I was in the third or fourth boat, and somebody in the lead boat took him out."

"Was he . . . did he have his gun?"

The guy cleared his throat and his eyes slid away. "His gun, uh, his gun's still tied in the canoe. I don't know, I think he was trying to pull the canoe up on the bank and make a run for it. . . . I don't know."

"How bad's he hit?" Virgil asked.

"His legs are all busted up, and he got one in the butt. Sideways in the butt. He's got some big holes."

Virgil looked around, lots of deputies standing back, now, talking in low voices.

Could be trouble, he thought.

THE DEPUTIES SAT on the scene, waiting for the BCA crime-scene people to show up. Mapes had had more business in Grand Rapids in a week than he'd had in the rest of his career, Virgil thought.

He moved around, talking to the deputies: two of them had fired their weapons. The first deputy had fired into the brush ahead of the Deuce to slow him down, to push him away from the trees. The second deputy thought the Deuce had opened fire, and fired at him, and as the Deuce had moved behind a tree from his point of view, then the first deputy fired again, confused about where the second burst had come from.

Virgil talked to a couple more deputies, then had Earl run him back to the boat ramp.

On the way, Earl said, "Don't think they shoulda shot that boy."

"If he'd gotten back in the trees with a rifle, could have got some people killed, digging him out," Virgil said, without much conviction.

Earl spit over the side. "He had plenty of chances to shoot somebody if he wanted to. Never untied that rifle."

"Not everything is simple to figure out," Virgil said. "Not everything is easy."

"That's the goldurned truth," Earl said. They were cutting through the channel with the early morning light coming on, throwing pale shadows on the water off the walls of wild rice, and Earl said, "God's country."

Virgil thought about Johnson Johnson saying the same thing, on Vermilion, and said, "Yes it is."

SANDERS WAS ALREADY AT THE HOSPITAL when Virgil arrived. He saw Virgil coming and walked toward him and asked, "Were you there?"

"Yeah, but I was the last boat in. I didn't see what happened. How's he doing?"

"He's hurt bad, they've got him in surgery, they're trying to control the bleeding. They're putting blood in him. I talked to one of the technicians, he's type O. You know, just remembering . . ."

"Yeah. That's gonna be important," Virgil said.

"I couldn't tell whether there was an exchange of gunfire down there."

Sanders used the *exchange of gunfire* cliché in a hopeful way, but Virgil was shaking his head. "He had a .22. It was still tied into the canoe when he was hit."

"Damnit. He didn't have a handgun or anything?"

"There was some confusion at the scene, but it was all complicated," Virgil said. "If he'd gotten back into the trees, with a gun, it would have been hell getting him out of there. Don't know what to tell you, Bob—but this might've been for the best. Nobody else got hurt."

"Tell that to Channel Three," Sanders said.

"They up here?"

"They called. I don't know if they're coming or not," he said. "How about your pal from the *Star Tribune*?"

"I don't know where he is; he's not exactly a pal—"

"Bullshit," Sanders said, showing a thin grin. "You must not have seen this morning's paper."

"Aw . . ."

"Smiling face right out there, on the front page," Sanders said. "Cracked the case."

"Aw, man."

*

SANDERS SAID THEY WOULDN'T know anything for certain until the surgeons came out to talk, and he thought that would be a while; an hour or two. "They gotta do a lot of work," he said.

He was going to wait. Virgil walked down to the front entrance and found a copy of the *Star Tribune*, paid for it, and looked at himself, standing, arms crossed, talking to Slibe. Not a bad shot; and he'd never seen Ignace shoot it, didn't even know that he carried a camera.

He looked pretty good, he thought. He was still thinking that when his cell phone rang. He pulled it out: Davenport.

"Yeah."

"You see the *Star Tribune* this morning?" Davenport asked.

"I'm looking at it right now. Let me tell you a few things; we had some trouble this morning. . . ."

When he finished, there was a moment of silence, and Davenport asked, "How strong's the case?"

"We're doing DNA on the blood on the sleeve, and we can get DNA on Windrow from his house . . . get the Iowa guys to do it. If we get a match, and with the credit card, we'll put him away."

"So, we're happy, right?"

"Not happy. The kid could have done it, but I went out there looking at his old man. His old man feels right for it, but I don't know about the kid. The kid doesn't seem like a planner, to tell you the truth. I don't know . . ."

"So you won't be back tonight."

"No. And probably not tomorrow night. Goddamnit, Lucas, this has got a mushy feel about it."

"Stay with it, let me know what happens," Davenport said. "A state senator, Marsha Williams, called about the McDill case. She's a friend of McDill's father, wanted to see what was up."

"You're taking pressure?"

"No, not really, she was doing a favor and she asked to be kept up-to-date," Davenport said. "If it's okay with you, I'll give her a ring, tell her where we're at."

"You can, but, uh . . . leave a little wiggle room."

*

HE WAS WALKING back toward the emergency entrance when Wendy Ashbach ran through the doors. She was dressed in a loose white blouse, jeans, and flip-flops, her hair uncombed; she stopped, looked around, saw Virgil, and cried, "Is he dead? Where's my brother?"

Virgil came up and said, "He's in the operating room. He was shot."

She began to weep, and pleaded with him: "He'll be all right? He'll be all right?"

"He was mostly hit in the legs, but he's hurt," Virgil said. "He lost a lot of blood before they got him here, but they're putting more into him. They've got two docs working on him."

"Where is he?"

He led her along to the emergency room, where Sanders was waiting with two more deputies, and Sanders saw her and came striding over and took her hand and said, "They're working on him. I can't tell you how he is, yet, but as soon as I know, I'll let you know."

She began getting angry, wanted to know what had happened, and Sanders put an arm around her shoulder and walked her down the hall. Virgil thought that he wasn't bad at that—at taking care of a relative.

THEY WAITED ANOTHER HOUR. Virgil took a call from Ignace, and asked, "When did you start carrying a camera?"

"Pretty neat, huh? It's about the size of your dick, so it's easily concealed. Fully automatic, point-and-shoot. How'd you like the picture?"

"Okay, I guess."

"I'll make you a print," Ignace said. "So, anything happen this morning?"

TWO HOURS AFTER the Deuce went in the operating room, a stocky dark-bearded surgeon came out and said, "We've stabilized things, but he's pretty messed up. We've stopped the worst of the bleeding, but he has multiple shattered bones in his leg and pelvis.

He's taken four units of blood. We've got a helicopter coming from Regions Hospital in St. Paul, we're going to lift him out."

"Will he be okay?" Wendy asked.

"He'll need a lot of rehab," the surgeon said. "And, uh, he's not totally out of the woods, yet. He's still in trouble, but we can move him."

THEY GOT MORE DETAILS, and Zoe came through the door, wrapped up Wendy. Half an hour later, the Deuce was rolled out to a waiting helicopter, saline and painkillers flowing into one arm, was loaded aboard, and was gone.

24

VIRGIL, SANDERS, AND JOHN PHILLIPS, the county attorney, met for a few minutes at Phillips's office. "If the blood works out, and with the credit card, and if his old man goes along, we're probably good," Phillips told Virgil. "But we could use a statement from Ashbach, when he recovers enough to give one. You should be right there. Get in there and read him his rights, and then see what he has to say. No big rush to get a public defender with him . . . wait until he asks."

"I wish I could find that damn .223," Virgil said. "He must have it hidden somewhere around the farm. I'm going to push Wendy and Slibe about it, see if he has a special place out there, in the woods."

"The gun would be the icing on the cake, if we could take a couple of prints off it," Phillips agreed.

VIRGIL CALLED DAVENPORT AGAIN, to fill him in on the meeting, and to impress on him the thinness of the case against the Deuce. "Gotta push that DNA, man. I know we're stacked up, but we need it."

Zoe called and said, "I'm at my house, with Wendy. You better come over here."

WENDY AND ZOE WERE sitting in Zoe's living room, both looking a little apprehensive, when Virgil arrived. The odor of marijuana floated softly through the room, and Virgil said, "Mellowing out, huh?" and Zoe said, "Not exactly," and Wendy said, "You're an asshole."

"I didn't like seeing your brother get shot," Virgil said. The two women were on the couch, side by side, and he sat down opposite, in an armchair. "I don't like seeing anybody get shot. The deputies were worried that if he got back in the trees with his rifle, he could pick them off one at a time."

"They could have just stayed back and waited—they didn't have to *shoot* him," Wendy said. "He was probably scared to death, with a helicopter coming down on him, and all those boats."

"You were out there?" Virgil asked.

Wendy shook her head and Zoe said, "No, but it's all over the radio. Everybody's talking about it."

Virgil said, "Wendy—I'm sorry."

Zoe: "Wendy: tell him."

Wendy started to cry. "Ah, God," she said, "this is so awful."

Virgil: "Tell me what?"

Wendy looked at Zoe, who nodded, and turned back to Virgil and said, "I don't think the Deuce did it. I think my dad did."

After a moment, Virgil asked, "Why do you think that?"

She said, "The day Erica got killed . . . I left out of there early in the morning, but I was feeling really up about everything. Excited about what we might do. We were recording at the Schoolhouse that afternoon, and the night before she seemed really into it. How we did that. How it all worked. So I thought, maybe I'd run by and invite her to come down and sit in. We took a dinner break and I ran out to the Eagle Nest."

"What time was this?" Virgil asked.

"Six-thirty, or so."

"You didn't see her?"

"No. She wasn't there. Her car was, but she was out somewhere, I didn't know where. Probably, I guess, she was already paddling down to see the eagles."

"Okay."

"Anyway, we had the session going, so I had to get back. When I came out of the lodge driveway, I thought I saw Dad's pickup going by. On the road. I went out after him, but the truck was really going fast, and I never did catch it. But it looked like his."

Virgil looked at her for a minute: "That's it?"

She turned to Zoe again, who said, "Better tell him the rest."

"What?"

Wendy was reluctant, but she said, "The next morning, I heard from Cat, who heard from a deputy, that Erica had been killed down in that pond, and that people were waiting for the state cops to come. I freaked out. I mean, I really freaked. I got in my car and I drove out there, and parked up in one of those driveways. I could see where somebody had walked back through those weeds so I went through and looked out on the lake and saw the boats . . . about a billion mosquitoes . . . so I watched them for a minute and then I snuck back to my car and took off. I was really scared."

Virgil rubbed his face with his hands. "Ah, man. What kind of shoes were you wearing?"

"Mephistos. Zoe told me that night that you were looking for Mephistos. I didn't want to throw them away, because they cost more than any shoes I ever had, so I hid them at the Schoolhouse in my equipment box."

"You told me I could talk about it," Zoe said to Virgil.

"Yes, I did," Virgil said.

"One more thing," Zoe said. She glanced at Wendy, then said, "The band was working on a song on Tuesday afternoon. . . . Slibe came looking for Wendy. McDill was there. Wendy got Slibe to order some pizzas, and they all sat around and ate them."

"Yeah."

"And Erica talked about the eagles, and about going down to the pond," Wendy said, finishing for Zoe.

"Oh, boy." They all sat around and Virgil thought he might've taken a toke or two himself, if it'd been offered. He said, finally, "You thought it was his truck. But you're not sure."

"I . . . you know how you see a truck, and they're all the same, but you know your friend's truck, the way he drives it, something about it? I thought it was Dad's. I was driving up to the road, and I thought, *What's he doing here?*"

ANOTHER SPACE, and Virgil said, "All right, Wendy. Constance Lifry was killed, Erica was killed, Jud Windrow's disappeared, and I think he's probably dead. All those seem to be connected to the band. But what about Washington?"

"I have no idea," Wendy said.

"Did the Deuce know Washington?"

"Not as far as I know. He doesn't really eat candy."

"How about your father?" Virgil asked.

"Same thing, I guess. I mean, she isn't friends with any of us."

"So why . . . I mean, if the Deuce is nuts, maybe he'd shoot Washington because he liked doing it. Because it was like hunting. He got a taste for it. But I don't see your old man like that. He seems too . . . tight."

"I don't know. I just don't know," she said. "It doesn't make any sense."

ZOE ASKED WENDY, "If it was your father, if he killed all those people, why'd he do it? To keep you close?"

Wendy nodded. "The only people my dad ever loved was my mom and me. And the Deuce, I guess. He's told me that a hundred times. When she left, it almost killed him. He says I act just like her."

"Your father never . . . ?" Virgil let the sentence fragment hang out there, instead of asking, "sexually molested you?"

Wendy took just a second to catch on, and then said, "Oh, no. No, no. Nothing like that."

"Never?"

"No. There was a time when I was thirteen, or twelve, I got kind of a bad feeling about him, like he was watching me, so I was kind of careful around him for a while. But nothing ever happened. Ever."

"What about with the Deuce?"

She smiled ruefully. "He liked to spy on me. You know, when I was coming out of the bathroom, peeking in my window and stuff. I didn't mind so much—he never did anything, either. He's really shy."

"What's your dad's relationship to the Deuce? He's seems to be pointing us at him."

She shook her head. "I don't know. He used to spank us both, because he believed in discipline. But Mom would jump in. . . . After she was gone, he beat up the Deuce pretty bad, a couple of times. That stopped a few years ago, when the Deuce started fighting back. It looked like maybe . . . like maybe Dad was taking on more than he could handle."

THEY SAT around for a minute, then Virgil asked, "Has your father ever talked to you about not leaving?"

She nodded. "Oh, yeah. He came from this really poor family—I mean, *really* poor. He had this brother who died young, supposedly of a heart problem, but Dad told me once that he thought it was because he didn't have enough to eat when he was a boy. There were times when they went hungry. They had a welfare program back then, where the government would give people peanut butter and lard and that kind of stuff. Leftover stuff, when the farmers grew too much. He said there were months when they ate peanut butter for breakfast, lunch, and dinner. He can't even stand the smell of it anymore."

She trailed off, and Virgil, trying to keep her rolling, said, "I can understand that."

She nodded. "Anyway, after high school he was a shovel man for another septic tank construction company, then he went in the army and learned heavy equipment. He was in for six years, saved every dime he could, and when he got out, he put a down payment on a

Bobcat and then . . . he worked and worked, and he met Mom and got married, and Mom worked and worked, all the time, and they finally got the business going. He doesn't think the Deuce can handle it; he wants me to. He thinks if I go running off to Nashville or somewhere, the business will . . ."

She shrugged.

"Go down the toilet," Zoe said.

"Not funny," Wendy snapped. To Virgil: "But I don't want to do it. I don't want to spend my life pushing some goddamned Bobcat around, or doing the office work for a bunch of rednecks."

"SO, why're you telling me this?" Virgil asked.

"'Cause if Dad did it, they should stop him," Wendy said. "And the Deuce . . . the Deuce can't help the way he is. Dad made him that way. After Mom ran off with Hector, it was like I was the mom, and I had to take care of the Deuce. Stand between him and Dad, as much as I could."

"The Deuce is what? Four or five years younger than you?"

"Seven," Wendy said. "You know, I think they'd kill him in prison. I think *being* in prison, in a cage, might kill him, all by itself. But he seems to attract attention . . . from people who like to make fun of him. If he went to prison, he'd die there, or get killed there. And it's not right, if he didn't do it."

"No, it isn't," Virgil said.

He leaned back and closed his eyes. If Slibe did it, and the Deuce was innocent, they had major problems. Once the police arrested somebody for a crime, it became almost impossible to convict somebody else, without a perfect, watertight case. Given the standard for a conviction—guilty beyond a reasonable doubt—a defense attorney would beat them to death with a prior arrest: "If you're so sure X is guilty, why'd you arrest Y two days before?"

They might be able to slide around that, since the two people involved were closely related, so the same evidence could point at either of them, but it'd be tough; especially if the only thing that pointed at Slibe was a "maybe" sighting.

Although he thought she was right about the truck. . . .

He opened his eyes and asked Wendy, "What would you say if you hit your dad with the accusation that he was there, with his truck, and he said, 'No, I wasn't. I was over at Joe Blow's house'?"

"Well, then . . . I guess I'd believe it," Wendy said. "Especially if Joe Blow backed him up. I'm not absolutely sure it was Dad's truck. I just thought so. At the time."

"Man. That's really soft," Virgil said. He leaned forward. "What would you think of the idea of wearing a wire . . . a microphone . . . and accusing him of killing Erica? Tell him about seeing the truck, see what he says? We could be right there, outside, if he tried anything."

"Ohhh, God." She brushed her fingers through her hair. "That would really be . . . traitorous, wouldn't it? He'd never forgive me, even if he's innocent. I mean, when Mom turned traitor, he never got over it. He did nothing but work, and come home and do the garden, and clean the house, and feed us kids. All the stuff that he used to do, plus all the stuff that Mom used to do, and then go to bed and get up and do it all over again."

"I can't think of what else to do but the wire," Virgil said. "Especially if that blood comes back as belonging to Jud Windrow. That points right at the Deuce. And I gotta tell you, honey, a singing career is looking pretty distant, if it turns out that your old man kills everybody who tries to help you along."

She said, "I've got to think about it."

"Think quick," Virgil said.

Zoe said to Wendy, "We could talk about it. Kick Virgil out, work through it together."

VIRGIL THOUGHT it might be a while. He called the sheriff and asked him for a couple of deputies. "I'm going out to talk to Slibe and I'd just as soon not be alone."

"I can understand that, what with his son being all shot up," Sanders said. "I'm up in Bigfork again. Swing on by the office; I'll have a couple guys waiting."

*

VIRGIL AND TWO DEPUTIES went out to talk to Slibe; but Slibe wasn't home. The dogs were fed and watered and happy, but the house, the loft, and the trailer were all empty, and Slibe's truck was gone.

When Virgil called Zoe, to get a verdict on the idea of bugging Wendy and having her talk to Slibe, Zoe said, "Bad news on that. Slibe called and she went out to meet him."

"Meet him? Zoe, if he's the killer, and they get alone—"

"They were meeting at Dick Raab's office," Zoe said.

"Who's he?"

"An attorney," Zoe said. "Probably the best one in town. Slibe told her it's time to shut up and save the family."

"Aw, that really makes my day," Virgil said.

"You want to know something?" Zoe said. "I think Wendy likes me again."

"Aww . . ."

VIRGIL CALLED SANDERS and told him they needed to get together with Phillips, the county attorney. "Trouble?" Sanders asked.

"Maybe," Virgil said.

THEY MET IN SANDERS'S OFFICE. Phillips looked unhappy; an older man sat in a corner with a carefully neutral expression on his face.

"Bob said there might be trouble," Phillips said, as soon as Virgil walked in.

Sanders nodded at Virgil, then gestured at the older man: "This is my dad, Ken Sanders. He was the sheriff here before me. Half the people in the county still think they're voting for him."

Virgil and Ken Sanders shook hands, and Virgil sat down and said, "I talked to Wendy Ashbach. She doesn't think the Deuce did it; she thinks her old man did."

He told them about the discussion with Zoe and Wendy, and about Slibe calling, and about the meeting with Dick Raab, the attorney. Ken Sanders looked skeptical, while his son and Phillips tended toward apoplexy.

"She's telling us now?" Phillips exploded. "After another woman is shot, and another guy disappears, and her brother gets shot up?"

"Slibe's her old man," Ken Sanders said. "He's the only one she's got, except for her brother. She was protecting him."

"If she's telling the truth, her old man's gotta be the biggest asshole in northern Minnesota," Virgil said. "He'd be framing his own kid."

Then Bob Sanders asked, "What if she's lying? What if she's protecting her brother? What if she's protecting herself? Have you talked to her father since the shooting?"

"No-no-no. I'll tell you what's happening. Jesus Christ, it's so clear," Phillips said. He got up and did a turn around the office, his hands pressed to his temples. "Wendy tells us her old man did it. We've already got a pile of evidence against her brother. Blood on the coveralls, he ran for it . . . So we put him on trial, and Wendy gets up on the witness stand and says she saw her old man at the lake. Not only that, it's his credit card on the way to Iowa. He could have hung the coveralls up in Junior's loft. The defense attorney puts Slibe on trial, and the evidence is as strong against him as it is against his son. The Deuce is acquitted, because, shit, let's face it, there's more than reasonable doubt. So then what? We arrest Slibe? His daughter gets all shaky on the stand, and we've got *blood* on the Deuce's coveralls. . . . Slibe's attorney puts the Deuce on trial, and . . . Wait a minute! Wait for it! They also put Wendy on trial, because Virgil has proof that she was down there. Those shoes. So Slibe gets acquitted. Ah, fuck me. Fuck me!"

Bob Sanders asked, "Are you serious?"

"Serious as a heart attack," Phillips said. "Dick Raab is going to take that girl and jam her straight up my ass. Ah, Jesus." He jabbed a finger at Virgil: "You get down to the Cities. You be sitting right next to the bed when the Deuce wakes up, and you suck a statement out of him. If he admits it, we're good. If he says his old man did it . . . well, we're not good, but it's something."

"And if he's already lawyered up?"

"Then we're fucked," Phillips said. "Wait a minute—*you're* not fucked. You caught everybody. It's me that can't get the conviction. *I'm* fucked. *You're* okay."

"That's a relief," Bob Sanders said to his father, who cracked a smile.

"Pretty fuckin' funny, Bob," Phillips said.

"I'll tell you what," Bob Sanders said. "Between the four of us . . . if the Deuce died, that'd settle things. We could let it go."

Virgil shook his head: "No. The killer is nuts. If it's Slibe—or even if it's Wendy—somebody else could get murdered. This is now the way he settles his problems. Because the guy is nuts."

THEY SAT IN SILENCE for a minute. Ken Sanders said, "Or the gal. Or the gal is nuts. I've seen that Wendy. She's a dead ringer for her mother." He chuckled. "I'll tell you what, everybody in town was watching *that* little romance, Maria Ashbach and Hector."

"You knew about it? I mean, did a lot of people know about it?"

"I don't know if a lot of people did, but Hector used to do the septic inspections for the county, and Maria Ashbach handled the inspection paperwork for Slibe—and pretty soon, you know, old Hector was inspecting more than the paperwork. Slibe Ashbach's wife with a Latino. Bound to blow up. And it did: Maria and Hector went and doomed the whole clan. They're all messed up out there. I wouldn't be surprised if Slibe had gone and diddled his little girl a time or two or three. That'd be why she's a homosexual."

"I asked," Virgil said. "She says no."

Ken Sanders sat up. "You asked? Must have more sand in you than you look like."

"He's the guy who massacred all those Vietnamese up in International Falls," Sanders said to his father.

Virgil got hot: "Look, I didn't massacre . . ."

Sanders laughed and waved him off. "Zoe told me that if I wanted to pull your weenie . . ."

Virgil relaxed. "I might have to spank her little ass."

"Could I watch that?" Ken Sanders asked.

"What is this? The comedy club?" Phillips asked. "Why are we all sitting around laughing? I'm telling you, they're all gonna walk."

Ken Sanders shook his head: "They're not going to walk. For one thing, we've probably got Wendy as an accessory, for withholding information. We've got those shoes, and if she's going to mess with you, she's got to admit that she saw her father out there, that she wore those shoes, and lied to Virgil about it. So we got her: you just have to figure out how to use her as a can opener."

Phillips considered the old man for a while, then said, "I knew there was a reason you got elected eight times."

"Damn right," Ken Sanders said. Then, to Virgil, "I read about that thing up in International Falls. You taking it hard?"

So they talked about it for a while, the old man listening attentively, asking a few intelligent questions. He said, finally, "I don't see that you had any better options, Virgil."

"I can't think of any," Virgil said. "I could have let it go, but . . . people get trials, you know? You don't make a deal with a bunch of foreign killers to come here and execute people."

Ken Sanders said, "I worry about cops with machine guns, though. We're turning ourselves into the military. Got machine guns, got squad cars that are like tanks, full of munitions and guys with armor. You get a situation like this morning, it's going to come to a bad end, all those guys running around with heavy-duty weapons. Hell, you get an ordinary car chase, and half the time somebody winds up dead. And half the time it's somebody who's completely innocent. Trying to cross the street . . ."

"I hear you," Virgil said.

"You know, old home week is fine, and all that—but we've got some shit to do," Phillips said.

Virgil stood up, stretched. "You're right. I need to break this thing down. I need to know who killed those people. Not so you can convict them; so I *know*."

"Then get your ass down to the Cities," Phillips said.

Virgil thought about Sig, and thought about going out there, and thought about the Deuce waking up in a hospital without an attorney right there.

He needed to go to Sig's.

He *had* to go to St. Paul.

25

VIRGIL CALLED SIGNY and told her that he had to go away for one more night, and though there might have been a thread of skepticism in her voice, she said, "You've got to get this done, Virgil."

He said, "Sig, honest to God, there's no place I'd rather be than up here."

"I believe that. . . ."

A CRAPPY, mindless drive down I-35 to the Cities; not much to look at in the afternoon, without even the romance of the night-time stars.

He caught Jimmie Dale Gilmore, with "Dallas," one of his favorites, and Lucinda Williams's cover of AC/DC's "It's a Long Way to the Top (If You Wanna Rock 'n' Roll)," and the music smoothed the flow, but when he drove into the parking lot at Regions Hospital in St. Paul, he hadn't thought of a single thing that could help.

BUT HE THOUGHT OF SOMETHING when he stepped into the room and saw the Deuce. The boy's slack face was a dark island in the middle of a lot of white sheets and white pillows and white bedcovers and electronic equipment that showed red and green numbers, and bags of clear stuff that flowed into his arms through plastic tubes, and flowed out of him through more plastic tubes. His eyes were closed, his breathing light and thready.

Virgil asked the nurse, "Has he been awake?"

"Yes. He was awake an hour ago, but he's in bad shape," she said.

"He hasn't said anything coherent. He doesn't know where he is. He's got painkillers running, I don't think he'll be back tonight."

"Is he going to make it?"

"Eighty-twenty," she said. "They had to repair his rectum, there were some bone fragments that went through. His legs and pelvis are gonna be held together with metal plates. His spine didn't get involved, but he's got a lot of damage in his legs. One of the surgeons said they might have to go back in a half-dozen times to get it all fixed. As well as it's gonna get fixed. And then there's infection. If that turns bad, it's all up for grabs."

Virgil said, "Thanks," and went down to the cafeteria and got a Coke and sat down to think about what he'd just seen. After a while, he looked at his watch and called Sandy, the researcher. She was getting ready to go home. "I need a bunch of information. I need to get it in the next few hours. I can get you the overtime. I you up for it?"

"Nice of you to ask, instead of ordering me around like your personal slave," she said.

"Sandy—"

"Shut up, Virgil. What do you want?"

"Okay, in order. There's a woman named Janelle Washington in a hospital in Duluth. I need to know which one. Her husband's name is James, they live in Grand Rapids. . . . I need to get a car registration. . . ." He gave her the rest of the list, which she said shouldn't be too much of a problem.

"Where are you going to be?"

"I'm heading up to Duluth. Goddamnit, I was up there two hours ago, down here for fifteen minutes, now I gotta go back."

"A little rain has gotta fall in every life," she said.

"You've got such a soft heart," he said.

"Lucas is just leaving. Do you want to talk to him?"

"Naw. He'd probably piss me off. Call me as soon as you get the information on Washington."

When he got off the phone, he went out to the truck, dug out his Nikon D3, carried it back up to the Deuce's room. The nurse wasn't happy about it, but Virgil got harsh, and she backed off. He stood on a chair and took several pictures of the Deuce, checking them on the LCD screen for sharpness, was satisfied and stepped down.

The nurse showed up with the nursing supervisor, and Virgil told them, "All done—and some things gotta be done. Screw the rules, and you can quote me."

HALFWAY TO DULUTH, as it was getting dark, he pulled into a roadside diner, parked in the side lot, and went to sleep for half an hour. Sandy woke him with the phone call, and told him where Washington was, and that she was awake and waiting, and then said, "You're right about the car. It was never registered, anywhere."

"Thanks, Sandy. See you in a couple of days."

He went into the diner and got a sticky bun, and headed north again.

JAN WASHINGTON WAS SITTING up in the hospital bed. He hadn't known her before she'd gotten shot, but she had the look of a woman who'd lost a lot of weight in the past few days.

"James is here someplace," she said.

"How are you?" Virgil asked.

"I hurt—all the time. They give me painkillers, but they're not working very well. Either that, or they knock me out. They can't seem to find a middle ground."

"I need to show you a photograph," he said. He took his laptop out of his bag, turned it on, loaded the Adobe Lightroom program, and brought up the best of the Deuce photos, the one that focused on the boy's face, and cut out the hospital gear. It looked almost like a driver's license photograph.

"Do you know this man?"

She looked at the photo for several seconds, then her forehead wrinkled and she said, "Oh—from a long time ago. That's Hector. What's his last name? He only worked there for a couple of years before they went off. . . . Hector Avila. That's it. He went off to Arizona with Maria Ashbach. They ran away together."

★

THEY SAT AND TALKED about it.

Hector Avila worked for the county as a civil engineer in the public works department, while Washington worked there as a clerk, before she quit to have kids. They were friendly, and she'd been around when Avila met Ashbach.

"Hector used to do the inspections on the septic installations out in the county. Maria handled the paperwork for Slibe's business. She was the office manager while Slibe did the excavation. I knew something was going on. I warned Hector about it. . . ."

"You warned him?"

"Well, you know . . . Slibe is a country guy, and this was his wife. You go messing around . . . there are a lot of dark country roads out there. You could get . . . shot. Like me."

"How long was the affair going on?" Virgil asked.

"Quite a while. A couple of years, at least," Washington said. "They were sneaky about it—after it got going good, they'd never talk to each other. I knew, because I knew Hector . . . He'd get a motel room somewhere, usually up at Hibbing, and she'd sneak up there. I don't know . . . it started out as pure sex, and then I think they fell in love. I hope they're happy, wherever they are."

VIRGIL CALLED RON MAPES, the crime-scene chief, at home, and told him what he needed. Called Sanders: "That search warrant out at Ashbach's was good for what, three days?"

"Yup. After that, we've got to go back. But we weren't required to finish the search the first day. What's going on?"

"If I tell you, you're gonna make fun of me when I fall on my ass," Virgil said.

"No, I won't—"

"See you tomorrow," Virgil said.

"Wait, wait—what about the Deuce?" Sanders asked.

"He was asleep. I never talked to him."

"John Phillips is going to be pissed. He needed that statement."

"Ah, the Deuce didn't do it," Virgil said. "You can tell John that for me."

"Virgil—"

"I'm going to need a couple more of your deputies. About nine o'clock," Virgil said.

VIRGIL GOT BACK to the motel at two in the morning and dropped facedown on the bed, and was gone.

Mapes called at eight o'clock and said, "We're down in the lobby."

"Go get a cup of coffee somewhere," Virgil moaned. "I'll get up in a minute."

"You don't sound like you'll be up in a minute," Mapes said.

"Ah . . . all right. I'm getting up."

THE MORNING was cool and quiet, with a sniff of rain in the air, and when Virgil got out to the parking lot, he found it wet: it had rained overnight, but not much—there were dry rain shadows under the cars. He walked across to the lobby, past the crime-scene van, and found Mapes and an assistant, Herb Huntington, looking at travel brochures.

"Lot to do around here," Mapes said. "I didn't realize."

"Your wife'll be happy to hear that," Huntington told his boss. "'Honey, we're getting out of Bemidji this year. Yes sir, we're going to Grand Rapids. Fishing, hunting, golf, whatever you want.'"

"You guys got your stuff?" Virgil asked.

"Virgil, I'm not saying you're crazy," Mapes said. "But I'm gonna hide in the back of the truck while Herb does the work." Virgil shook his head, a sad smile crossing his face, and Mapes asked, "What?"

"I'm not really guessing," Virgil said. "Let's go get some breakfast—we might be out there for a while."

"What do you got that I don't know about?" Mapes asked.

"We can't find Jud Windrow," Virgil said. "Not even with a LoJack on his car."

Mapes hitched up his pants. "Huh. Well, there is that. So—Log Cabin? Pancakes?"

*

THEY ATE AND PICKED up the two deputies, made a three-truck caravan out to the Ashbach place. They parked in front of it, which, for a moment, seemed abandoned, a cloud hanging over it. Virgil banged on Slibe's door, got no answer, and one of the deputies walked around to the garage, looked inside, and called back, "His truck's gone."

"Check the loft." To Mapes: "Might as well get going."

Virgil started toward Wendy's double-wide, and halfway there, the door opened and Wendy, barefoot, in jeans, came out on the concrete steps. "What're you doing?"

"Where's your father?" Virgil asked.

"He's . . . our attorney said we weren't supposed to talk to you, no matter what you said," Wendy said. Berni came up behind her, put her hand on Wendy's shoulder.

"You gotta do what your attorney says," Virgil said. "But I'll tell you, Wendy, if your father is here, and he pops up and he shoots somebody, I'll send you to prison for murder."

"Let me . . . what are you doing out there?"

Across the yard, Mapes and Huntington were pacing across the garden. "Continuing the search," Virgil said. He looked at Berni: "Berni, the attorney hasn't told you anything because you don't have an attorney. So I'm asking you, do you know where Slibe is?"

"That's not fair," Wendy protested.

"Fuck fair," Virgil said. "Berni, if you know, you better say, or you're gonna be in as deep as Wendy."

Wendy said, "I'll tell you—don't pick on her. He's working a job south of town, on the Wendigo farm."

"When did he leave?"

"Usual time, I guess—six-thirty or so. I heard him go," Wendy said.

"Didn't you think it was a little odd, him not going to see the Deuce?"

"I think he was too freaked out, and then they took the Deuce away," Wendy said. "Berni and I are going down to St. Paul today, maybe he'll come. What're you doing out there, Virgil?"

*

HUNTINGTON WAS AT THE BOTTOM of the garden with a metal box slung around his shoulders, holding what looked like a basketball hoop at the end of an eight-foot pole. As they watched, he pushed the hoop out in front of him, so it hovered over the top of the potatoes, and started walking up the length of the garden, Mapes pacing along with him.

"Wendy, you oughta go see your brother," Virgil said. "I was down there last night. He could use some support."

She turned back to him: "Is he bad?"

"Bad enough. They can fix him, but it's going to take time. The biggest threat is infection." He told her about the visit, turned back, and saw Mapes walking toward them. Huntington was wandering in a circle, stepping on tomato plants and cucumber vines, heedless of the damage, killing them.

Mapes said, "We got a mass, Virgil. And it's big."

"No question?"

"Well, we got a mass. You think you know what it is; and it's consistent. That's all I can tell you at this point."

Wendy asked, "What?"

Virgil sighed and stepped up on the top step and put his arm around her shoulder and squeezed her tight. "Ah, God I hate this."

"*What?*"

"Wendy . . . I believe your mom is down there, under the garden."

SHE FROZE, as if all the muscles in her body contracted at once. Then she pushed him off, and Berni, agape, stepped away and said, "You're crazy."

Wendy, horrified, looking from the garden to Virgil, repeated it: "You're crazy."

Virgil said, "These guys are using a top-end metal detector. They say there's a big buried metal mass out there, under the garden.

"You told me that when your mother left, she left her car here, and took off with her boyfriend, Hector Avila. I had a BCA researcher look up Avila's car, which was a 1990 S10 Blazer. It was never reregistered anywhere in the United States. There was no sign of it in

Arizona, New Mexico, Texas, California, Nevada, Colorado . . . no place in the Southwest.

"You told me that when you came back from school, that your father told you that your mother had gone away, and that day he started a garden. . . ."

She shook her head. "No . . . no, no, no, not right. Mom's out in Arizona."

"Can't find her," Virgil said. Can't find a Hector Avila, either. Can't find a Maria Ashbach getting a divorce anywhere in Minnesota or Arizona or anywhere else."

"Dad told me when they got divorced . . ."

"And he told you that he got a letter that said your mom didn't want to see you anymore. Did that sound like your mom?"

She looked at the garden, a sense of dry-lipped desperation about her. "But that . . . but that . . ."

"Your brother. I took his picture and showed it to Jan Washington, in the hospital in Duluth. She thought it was a picture of Avila. The Deuce is Avila's son, and your father knows it. That's why he's framing him."

"It can't . . ."

"There's only one way to find out," Virgil said. "We know we've got a big metal mass down there. We know your father had excavation equipment that he could have used to bury it. You're out here at the end of the road, with nobody going by. He could have pulled it off. We gotta look."

WENDY STARTED TO CRY, and Berni wrapped her up and led her back into the trailer, Berni looking at Virgil with fear on her face, and Virgil said, quietly to the deputies, "Hang around, keep an eye on them."

He called Sanders: "You better get out here."

Mapes showed him the space in the garden where they were getting the best responses. "You can't tell exactly how big it is, but it's probably car-length, and probably car-wide, and not too deep."

WENDY CAME OUT of the house, tears streaming down her face: "How're you going to dig it up?"

"Get some guys out here."

"I can run the Bobcat better than anyone in the county."

"Wendy, that's a really bad idea."

She shrieked at him: "I can't stand this. I can't stand it. I can't wait. You understand that? Mom's in Arizona. Mom's in Arizona, and she might come back. She can't be in the garden. . . ."

Virgil said to Berni, "You better take her—"

Wendy pushed Berni away. "Bullshit. I'm going for the Bobcat." She stalked away, and one of the deputies moved to cut her off, but Virgil gave him a shake of the head, and the deputy stepped back. Virgil followed her, and Berni followed Virgil, and the deputy came after them, leaving the second deputy, Mapes, and Huntington standing in the garden.

THERE WERE TWO BOBCATS in the machine shed, one with a front-end loader, the other with a shovel. The larger Caterpillar shovel was gone. Wendy climbed into the Bobcat with the shovel and fired it up. She said to Virgil, "Out of the way."

"Not a good idea, Wendy," Virgil said.

"I don't care. . . ." She idled the machine for a moment, said, "When Mom left, something must have busted in his brain. He told me once that he'd taken her into town, and they bought gravesites together. I mean, they were thirty."

"I think that's why he was holding you so close," Virgil said.

She ran the power up a bit and said, "Out of the way."

VIRGIL FOLLOWED THE BOBCAT across the yard, and Mapes came up and said, "You think this is a good idea?"

Virgil said, "We're going with the flow. Give her an outline to work with."

MAPES MARKED OUT a perimeter, and Wendy went to work. She was good with the shovel, cutting down a foot at a time, over the whole perimeter, dumped the dirt to the side, out of the garden, the black-and-tan soil piling up as she went deeper and deeper. At two feet, Virgil could see her crying, and stepped up next to the Bobcat and called, over the engine beat, "You okay?"

"Somebody's been digging here, deep. The soil's all cut up. Get back . . ."

Sanders showed up with another deputy, and Virgil walked over. The sheriff got out of the car, gawked at Wendy in the Bobcat, and asked, "What the hell's going on?"

"I think Hector Avila and Maria Ashbach are down there."

"*What?*"

VIRGIL EXPLAINED and Sanders said, "You can't be having her dig them up. Get her out of there. What the hell . . ."

But they were down three feet, and as Sanders was speaking, there was a shriek of metal. Wendy lifted the shovel and backed off, and one of the deputies jumped down into the hole, dug around with a spade, then stood up and looked at Virgil and asked, "What color was the Blazer?"

"Blue," Virgil said.

"We got blue," the deputy said.

WENDY WAS IN CONTROL now, her face tight, cold. After a short argument with Sanders, she moved back up to the hole and removed two inches of dirt, and then another inch, and then began to hit metal along the whole length of the hole.

She backed off, and the deputies climbed down into the hole with a long-handled shovel and a spade.

Wendy wandered away, through the picket fence around her father's house, and sat on the porch, her feet on the porch step. Virgil and Berni sat on either side of her.

"Dad used to whip her ass. I remember it. I remember her fighting him and crying. He used to cry after he did it—but he said he had to, because she'd screwed something up. I thought that was . . . the way men acted. Most of the time, everything seemed all right. . . ."

"We got a letter from Mom. Dad showed it to me, he read it to me. All about she was going to have a new life, and it was better if we didn't get involved. She said good-bye. I remember Dad telling the Deuce that she wasn't coming back, and the Deuce starting to cry because he didn't understand where Mom went. It was like she was dead or something. . . . And then Dad told me a couple of years later that they were getting a divorce, and then they had gotten one, and I told all my friends. . . ."

"And I told my mom," Berni said. "And the way things are here . . . everybody knew they'd gotten a divorce, and what happened."

"He was building a story," Virgil said.

They sat and watched the deputies dig, and then Virgil asked Wendy, "Why'd you lie to me about that lipstick card? The kiss mark you made for McDill?"

She said nothing for a moment, then turned her face toward him: "I don't know. I was scared of you. I was going to deny everything. . . . I don't know. It was stupid."

Across the drive, in the hole, one of the deputies knelt, and started working with his hands. Virgil got up and said, "Wait here."

"Bullshit," Wendy said.

THE DEPUTIES HAD CLEARED off a roof, and in another few minutes, had cleaned off a foot-long patch of windshield. Sanders got a flashlight from his car and handed it down, and the deputy, on his knees, shined it through the glass, pressed his face closer, moved the light, then stood up and looked at Wendy and then at Virgil.

"Got some clothing."

"Some clothing," Sanders said.

"Got some clothing and . . . some bones and hair."

WENDY SAT DOWN, suddenly, in the raw dirt, then flopped backward, her irises rolling out of sight.

"She's fainted, or something," Virgil said, holding her head up. "We better get, uh, what do . . ." He'd never dealt with a woman who'd fainted.

Berni came to hold her head and shouted at Sanders, "Get her to a hospital, get—"

Then Wendy stirred and Virgil said, "Don't move. You fainted, is all, just stay like that."

But Wendy rolled to her hands and knees and looked in the hole. "All these years," she said. "All these years, I thought she'd come back someday. Or I thought I'd be famous, and I'd have a show in Arizona, and she'd come up and talk to me. . . . I still have that dream. All these years . . ."

26

SANDERS WALKED OVER, a radio in his hand, and said, "They're there—and he's gone. The Caterpillar is still there and the lowboy, but he's gone. The people at the site said he was going to lunch."

"Probably back in town," Virgil said.

"We'll sweep through there. . . ."

An intermittent drizzle had begun, coming with the occasional ragged black cloud, going with brighter gray ones. They all stood hunched in it, watching the work.

There were four cop cars on the road outside the fence, a couple more trucks down the driveway, and three civilian cars, as well as Virgil's truck and the crime-scene van parked in front of the house. Mapes and Huntington were directing the excavation, and half the truck was now clear, sitting in the bottom of the widening hole. One of the civilians was a Bobcat operator from Grand Rapids, and he was carefully digging down the sides of the vehicle, while deputies with shovels did the close work.

Full circus mode, Virgil thought.

PHILLIPS, THE COUNTY ATTORNEY, wearing a yellow rain jacket, climbed out of the hole, scraped mud off the bottom of his shoes on the lawn, and brushed off his hands and came over and said, "Goddamnedest thing. The woman's in the backseat, the guy's across the front. It looks to me like he shot them in the head. The skulls are right there, faceup, grinning out at you. . . ." He shivered and said, "I won't be trying to sleep tonight. Or maybe the rest of the month."

"How did this happen?" Sanders asked. "Why didn't anybody know?"

"A lot of people did know. They knew it before it happened—knew that Hector and Maria were going to run off," Virgil said. "And then they were gone . . . and they'd gone to Arizona. Everybody knew that. Slibe apparently didn't make any secret of it. Now that I think about the way it worked, he must've started a few rumors himself. About the letter from Maria, and all that. People *knew* she'd written back . . . because Slibe told people."

"Her family . . . her parents?"

"Don't know," Virgil said. "I'll ask Wendy when I have a chance."

THE SHERIFF WATCHED the excavation, then sidled over and asked quietly, "How in the hell did you figure this out?"

Virgil said, "People kept talking in the background, about Hector Avila and Maria, and I never concentrated on the Hector part. But when we were searching the Deuce's loft, I found some pictures of Slibe and Maria when they were young. They were blond. And Wendy is flat, pure blond: she's so white she's transparent. I got down to the hospital, and the Deuce was propped up on these white sheets, and he was so dark . . . and it all tripped off. Hector Avila, a Latino name. An affair; a dark kid; a father who seemed willing to frame his own son. It occurred to me, the Deuce wasn't his son. . . .

"I thought about that, and then I thought about the fact that we can't find Windrow's car. Not even with a LoJack on it. Maybe somebody found and disconnected the LoJack, but there was another explanation. You said it yourself—that it must be in a lake somewhere. Or something. Like, buried."

"And you thought about those goldarned Bobcats. . . ."

Virgil nodded. "And that Slibe started a big garden the day his wife disappeared forever."

THEY WERE TALKING when Virgil saw Slibe's truck coming, burning up the road, and he said, "Oh, shit. Slibe."

The cops turned and looked, and a couple of them ran for their cars. Slibe's truck slowed, stopped, and Virgil could see a figure in the driver's seat, taking them all in—taking in the hole in the garden. The truck started to back up, to turn around, and a cop yelled, "He's running," but then it straightened again, came on, accelerating, moving too fast to make a good turn at the driveway, took out the mailbox and then came on, straight at the deputies in the drive, who scattered, the truck accelerating, throwing wet gravel, coming straight at Virgil and Sanders and Phillips.

Virgil yelled, "Get out of the way," and Phillips ran for the garden hole and Virgil and Sanders ran for the concrete steps, got on the steps as the truck brushed by, Slibe's face framed in the side window of the truck, and then he was past them, continuing past the house and the crime-scene van, past the kennel. The truck crashed through a board fence and into the back pasture.

Wendy'd heard the commotion and came to the door, and saw the truck disappear. The cops were pulling vests from their cars, and Sanders was pointing the deputies after the truck, and Virgil asked Wendy, "What's back there?"

"Nothing. He can't get out of the pasture. . . . There's a shortcut down to Hourglass Lake. A trail . . ."

"There's a boat?"

"No, there's a place you can fish, but it's not our property. There's swamp on both sides of it, there's a creek that goes in there. . . . I don't know. He can't swim that good, so . . . There's a cabin that way." She pointed. "Left when you get to the lake. If he got to that road I guess he could get out. It'd be a long walk."

Phillips had heard the last part of it, and he said, "It's wet country back there. I don't see where he's going. There's hardly any way out."

Cop cars were going in on Slibe's trail, and Sanders hurried up: "I called for the state patrol chopper. It's gonna be a while." A cop car headed out of the driveway, and he added, "I got guys going over to Hourglass; they can seal off the landing, and the roads."

Virgil said, "Why didn't he run? He seemed to know what he was doing."

Berni, who'd come up behind Wendy, said, "We'd go swimming down on Hourglass sometimes. Slibe's got an old plastic toolbox, you know, like a truck toolbox, hidden back in the woods. It's got fire-starter and a minnie net and some fishing poles."

"But how's he . . ." Sanders began.

Berni said, "It's big enough for a gun. I never thought of it when you were here looking for the gun, but it's big enough for one, easy."

VIRGIL TO SANDERS: "Get your guys. If he's out there with a .223 with a scope, they gotta back off. Those vests won't work. Gonna get some guys shot up if they push him."

Sanders was already jogging toward his car.

"You know what we need?" Berni asked.

Virgil: "What?"

"We need the Deuce to track him down."

THE COPS WERE ALL gunning up, and Wendy asked, "They'll kill him, won't they?" and Virgil thought that was probably the case, but didn't say so.

"Where's the lake?" he asked. "Exactly?"

Wendy pointed to a low spot in the skyline. "Right down there. But it's more than half a mile."

Virgil said, "I gotta go out," and, "I'll try not to hurt him, if I see him."

He went to his truck and got his vest and his shotgun, slapped the Velcro tabs in place, walked over to Sanders, who was directing traffic. "I'm going up on that high spot." He pointed to a place thirty degrees to the right of the tree line dip that marked the lake.

"You think that shotgun's gonna work? I can get you an AR-15 if you'd rather," Sanders offered.

"I'm okay—but tell your guys where I'm at. I don't want to get shot up by a friendly."

"Take a radio." He yelled at one of the cops: "Bill—give me your radio."

VIRGIL TOOK THE HANDSET, hung it on his belt, climbed into the truck and followed the rest of the crowd through the broken fence, and bounced over the pasture. At the far end of the field, he could see where Slibe's truck had crashed through another fence, this one barbed wire, and had gone into the trees. The cop cars were stopped short of that, and most of the cops were standing behind their cars, while two more did an end run to the left, into the woods.

Virgil didn't like it: there'd be some dead people for sure, if they pushed Slibe. He drove as far as he could, but well to the right of the others, got out of the truck and on the radio.

"Your people are crashing into the woods. If he decides to fight, he'll kill some of them," Virgil said. "They gotta let him move before they do. They gotta calm down, or he's going to hunker down somewhere and ambush them."

"Gotcha. I think they've got a good idea where he went, they're just keeping him moving."

"They're moving too fast, way too fast," Virgil said. "If he's got that rifle—"

"Gotcha."

VIRGIL THOUGHT, *Dumbass.*

The sheriff hadn't struck him as a dumbass, but the chase was hot and he was caught up in it. Cops watch movies like everybody else, and sometimes, it gets them killed.

Virgil pumped three shells into the shotgun, put the rest in his pocket, and jogged over to the fence, did a leg lift over it, careful not to get snagged, and headed through the woods. He didn't know exactly where he was going, but he'd know it when he saw it.

There was no high land nearby, but there was *higher* land, and a man running from guns instinctively took one of two paths—he ran through gullies or along creeks that concealed him from view, or he ran along the high ground, so he could see what was happening, could see the pursuit.

Or, if he was smart, he ran just below the crest of a ridge, so he could move up, make a quick check around, and still be out of sight with a step or two.

But higher ground was involved in all of it—either as concealment or for the view. Virgil was headed for the only nearby higher land. That ridge would also bring Slibe back past his acreage, while still in the deep woods—probably the land he knew best.

Virgil could set up on high ground, he hoped, and catch Slibe as he went by.

Because the cops weren't going to get close, not unless Slibe was on a suicide run. If he was, the cops wouldn't need Virgil to help handle that. . . .

VIRGIL MOVED up the hill; the brush was thick, mostly small aspen, cut maybe ten years earlier, and he couldn't see fifty yards. At the top, the land sloped away, and though he couldn't see it, he sensed wet ground that way—there was more light coming through the trees than there should be, if it was all solid forest, which meant the trees ended somewhere downslope. The lake, probably, or a marsh.

He backed up the hill, trying to find a spot with good sight lines. None of it was really open; he finally found a root hole where an old aspen had been blown over, and eased down into it, and sat on a chunk of rotting log. He was wearing his gray rain jacket, which wasn't bad; he shouldn't be too visible.

Then settled down and listened, heard nothing, except some distant shouting. Not even squirrels—thought he'd probably spooked the squirrels himself, and they wouldn't start bashing around again for another ten minutes or so.

He'd turned the radio down when he got out of the truck, and now put it to his ear, picking up the electronic whisper of shouts and calls: this guy was moving left, that guy was moving left, the other guy didn't see anything, nothing was moving out there, this guy was going to make a move farther around, that guy had come down to a swampy area and couldn't go any farther.

Virgil couldn't quite picture it in his mind, because he didn't know the ground well enough, but he got the impression that the deputies had pushed well out to Slibe's left, and they now had a line that extended from the pasture down to the lake. So Slibe couldn't go that way without shooting somebody. The deputies thought they had him pinned against the lake.

Maybe they did; and maybe they didn't. Slibe had known where he was going, and was moving fast.

Virgil put the radio down and listened . . . listened . . .

Listened for gunshots. Or footsteps.

SLIBE CAME SNEAKING along the right side of the high ground. Virgil thought first that it might be a squirrel, because there wasn't much sound. But it had been raining, a little, enough to wet the leaves, and mute the usual crinkle and thrash. When he heard a stick break, he thought it must be Slibe; squirrels don't break sticks.

Slibe could have been quieter, if he'd moved more slowly, and he probably knew that; but he couldn't afford to. Virgil listened to him coming in, and wondered what was going through his mind. Where did he think he could run to? Was he going to kill somebody else, somebody back in the woods, somewhere—at a cabin, steal the car and an ID, maybe some money? He could be in Canada in a few hours, and that would slow down the search. . . .

Kill somebody there, in another cabin, head north and west. Get up north of Calgary, in the oil fields. There were people from thirty countries up there, it *was* the Wild West.

SLIBE WAS CLOSE, picking his way through the trees.

Virgil peeked, thought he saw movement, lost it, but had an idea where he was. Saw it again; nothing was exposed but his left eye, and he tracked the other man coming in. Slibe was dressed in jeans and a long-sleeved shirt, was wet, had a scoped rifle in his hand. Stopped, fifty feet out, looked around, looked back along the line he'd come, back where the deputies were.

Listened, then came on, his face grim, his hair wet and stuck to his forehead, the rifle loose in his left hand, his right hand pushing through the trees.

When he was close, Virgil said, not too loud, "Don't make me kill you."

Slibe froze.

Virgil said, "I've got a twelve-gauge aimed at your stomach. I can't miss."

Slibe turned his head, looking for Virgil, finally found him, saw the gun.

"Drop your rifle," Virgil said.

Slibe didn't.

Virgil said, "People keep talking about me massacring those Vietnamese up in International Falls. I'm not afraid to kill you, Slibe, but I don't want to. Now drop the gun, and let's go into town."

Slibe looked back along the line where the cops were and said, "You were the one I was worried about. I could have dodged Sanders's boys."

Virgil said, "I'll tell you what, Slibe. You're going to prison—but you'll get out. You're young enough. You get a good attorney, you can deal. We don't have anything solid on McDill or Lifry, and we got no idea about Washington or Windrow, where you put him . . . so it's down to your wife and Hector, and you can deal. Ten years, maybe. When you get out, Wendy'll be here with the business."

Virgil was lying through his teeth. Slibe would never see the outside again, not this side of eighty, anyway.

"Wendy and that fuckin' Deuce," Slibe said.

"Hey—he's Wendy's brother."

Slibe still had the gun in his hand; the drizzle picked up, and was dripping off the aspen leaves and soaking both of them. "You know about that?"

"Yeah. People kept telling me about your wife running off with a Mexicano, and I finally took a look at the Deuce. He doesn't look much like an Ashbach."

Slibe laughed, shortly. "I would've been okay if you hadn't shown up. I had it under control."

"Ah . . . maybe," Virgil said. "Why don't you just toss that gun over there—"

"You're not really giving me a chance here, are you?" Slibe asked.

"Not really," Virgil said.

Slibe looked back toward the shouting cops and said, "Ah, fuck it," and tossed the gun to the side.

Virgil didn't move. "I worry a little about you having a pistol, so why don't you just walk down the hill with your hands on top of your head, back toward the pasture."

Slibe nodded, and turned down the hill. Virgil followed behind, well back, called Sanders on the radio, and said, "I've got him. We're coming down to the pasture, off to the right of my truck."

"Gotcha," Sanders said.

SLIBE LED THE WAY down the hill, then up the fence line to the left, saying, "There's a hole in the fence up the way. I always meant to fix it; but it was a good spot to set up during deer season, so I left it."

"Did you break into Zoe's one night?"

"You recordin' this?"

"Nope. Just you and me. And given what else has happened, nobody's gonna give a shit. I'd just like to know."

Slibe almost laughed. "I just wanted her to shut up. I went in there thinkin' . . . I don't know what I was thinkin'. I'd had a few bourbons, down at Jack's. Anyway, I went sneakin' in there, quiet as a mouse, and all of a sudden this voice says, in the dark, 'I got a shotgun. I'll blow your fuckin' head off.' I was drunk, but not that drunk—I snuck right back out of there."

VIRGIL SAW THE HOLE in the fence, and Slibe crossed over into the pasture. Virgil followed, and down the hill, saw cops running for their cars. Slibe took his hands off his head, and Virgil said, "Hands on top of your head."

Slibe said, "Go ahead and shoot me down, right in front of all them witnesses. I don't have a gun." He pulled off his jacket. He was wearing a T-shirt, which was soaked and stuck to his body. He turned around, hands up: no gun.

He said, "I got no gun, and you're gonna have to shoot me down. Either that, or get your ass kicked. Because you are the one that done this to me, Virgil. Bigger than shit. I'm gonna kick your ass."

He came at Virgil with a rush, and Virgil tried to butt-stroke him with a shotgun—he'd once had a two-minute butt-stroke lesson in the army, and it didn't seem any more useful then than it did now, as Slibe dodged the shotgun butt. Virgil twisted away, heard people yelling, almost lost his footing on the wet pasture grass, and then Slibe came back again, low, tackling, and Virgil tried to move around him, but couldn't, and when Slibe hit him, he heaved the shotgun over the fence into the woods, and they both went down, rolling in the grass and the mud.

He only had to hold on for a minute, Virgil knew, and the deputies would be there. Then Slibe clouted him on the side of the head and Virgil punched him in the kidneys a couple of times, best he could, but Slibe got over him on one of the rolls, and hit Virgil in the face with an elbow and Virgil felt his nose break.

Then Virgil was on top, bleeding, and *really* pissed, and he gave Slibe a shot in the eye, and they rolled again. Slibe twisted, so they were facing each other, Slibe on top, and Virgil got an arm around Slibe's neck and squeezed the other man close, with Slibe flailing away at Virgil's ribs and trying to pull free.

If he pulled free, he'd be on top with both fists loose, and in a position to really pound Virgil; and his head was slippery, and he was pulling out of Virgil's hold. But Slibe's ear was right there, and Virgil bit into it, hard as he could, and squeezed with his arms. Slibe started screaming and thrashing, and Virgil bit harder and they rolled around again, Slibe on top and then Virgil, and Virgil was thinking that the cops had to be close, and his eyes were full of blood and he couldn't see. . . .

And the deputies landed on Slibe, a couple of big Scandinavian kids, and yanked him loose and Slibe screamed again, and Virgil realized that while Slibe was over there, being pinned to the ground, most of his ear was still in Virgil's mouth.

Virgil spit it out and groaned, and one of the cops screamed, "You been shot?"

Virgil said, "Ah, man," and sat up. He was covered with mud and grass and maybe, if his nose was still working right, a little dog shit.

Slibe was sitting on the ground, his hands cuffed behind him, blood pouring down the right side of his head. He said to Virgil, "Kicked your ass."

Virgil said, "Tell your ear that, motherfucker." He looked around on the ground, couldn't see it; crawled around for a minute, blood streaming out of his face, spotted it in a wet footprint. He picked it up, and held it up so Slibe could see it.

"It was worth it," Slibe said.

Sanders arrived, looked at Virgil, and said, "Your nose is bent."

"Ah, it's busted," Virgil said.

"Does it hurt?" Virgil looked at him, and Sanders held up his hands and grinned and said, "Sorry."

A COP with a medical kit gave Virgil a gauze pad to hold to his nose. He retrieved the shotgun and pointed the deputies to the spot where Slibe's rifle was. Waited until one of them came up with it, then staggered over to his truck. Slibe was put in the back of a cop car, and they all rolled slowly up the pasture back to the house.

Virgil got out, head tipped back, still pressing the bandage to his nose. Wendy was there, and said, "You didn't kill him."

"No, but I beat the shit out of him," Virgil said.

She looked at the blood running down Virgil's face and chin, and said, "Yeah. You look like it was pretty one-sided." She could see Slibe through the side window of the cop car, looking out at them. "Can I say good-bye?"

"I don't care," Virgil said. Still bleeding. "Yeah, why not?"

One of the cops popped the back door of the car, at Virgil's request, and Wendy bent over and said, "I'm sorry, Daddy."

Slibe, soaked, muddy, bleeding, looked at her and said, "All I wanted to do was love you women. That's all I ever wanted," and Wendy began bawling again.

Virgil thought he saw a flicker of satisfaction cross Slibe's face, as he watched his weeping daughter; and Virgil slammed the door again.

27

VIRGIL GOT OUT OF the hospital with an aluminum splint holding his nose straight, and a crisscross splotch of tape holding the splint in place. His face hurt, his neck hurt, his ribs hurt, and he'd pulled a muscle in his groin, he thought. He sat in his car and called Davenport, and filled him in.

Davenport said, "Uh-huh," about six times, and then, "So how soon can you get back here? We've got some serious shit going on."

"I'm going fishing," Virgil said. "I've got my vacation and I'm taking it, and not only that, I'm putting in for time-and-a-half, for all my overtime. I'm putting in for thirty hours of overtime, god-dammit. You guys are gonna pay for a trip to the Bahamas."

"I've been to the Bahamas," Davenport said. "They're really . . . flat. And hot. Flat and hot. You won't like it. I recommend a quick trip to Mille Lacs, catch some walleyes, you know, have a couple of margaritas. Get wild with some of those outstate women."

"Bullshit. I'm going to the Bahamas," Virgil said. "But first, I'm going to take a week right now, sick leave, to get my nose straight, and maybe do some fishing on the side. And we've got things to do up here. We haven't found Windrow."

"That's a detail best left to the people who know the countryside," Davenport suggested. "You know *where* he is—he's buried. Now they just have to find the exact spot."

"They don't consider a dead man a detail up here," Virgil said. "So. If somebody dies, feel free to call me for a funeral donation. Other than that, I'll see you in a week or so."

"Seriously, Virgil, you all right?" Davenport asked.

"My nose hurts worse that I can possibly believe," Virgil said. "My nose hurts so bad my front teeth hurt."

"I know how that is," Davenport said. "I'm on my fourth nose. If you like to fight, that's what happens."

"I don't like to fight," Virgil said. But maybe he did, a little; he'd absolutely kicked Slibe's ass, he thought, not counting the nose.

"Could have shot him," Davenport said.

"No, I couldn't."

"Then quit bitching about it," Davenport said. "See you in a week. Take some time at night to get all the paper done. I'll okay the overtime—you can even add a little to it. Take it easy."

"Okay."

Virgil was about to hang up when Davenport said, "Hey—wait a minute."

"Yeah?"

"Weather wants to know—what happened to the ear?" Weather was Davenport's wife, and a plastic and reconstructive surgeon.

"I don't know. It was all ripped up, and we didn't treat it too well. It got stepped on, and got some dog shit smeared on it. . . ."

"Dog shit?"

"Yeah, this was just down from the kennel, in a field they used to train the dogs. Anyway, it was pretty messed up, and they couldn't get it to go back on," Virgil said.

"So . . . what'd they do with it?" Davenport asked.

"I don't know. Disposed of it, I guess."

"How do they do that?"

"Hell, I don't know," Virgil said. "Throw it in a ditch?"

*

SLIBE WAS TAKEN UNDER the wing of his attorney, who didn't allow him to say anything about anything; but Phillips was happy. "We've got him. We know it and they know it. We don't need anything else—Lifry or Washington or McDill."

"We're gonna get Washington and McDill, because of the rifle," Virgil said.

"We'd have to prove that he was the one that used it, and not his son," Phillips said. "Now, we don't really have to do it. We can pack all that information into the sentencing recommendation, to clean it up for the relatives of the dead people."

"What about the Deuce? He's all shot up?"

"Well, we'll have to see," Phillips said. "I anticipate further court proceedings."

"Yeah. I anticipate a court order that says, 'Dear Itasca County: Please drop your shorts and bend over.'"

"Maybe. We've got further issues with the Ashbach family that are still outstanding," Phillips said. He seemed happy at the thought of the further issues. "Like Wendy lying to you. All those issues could go away in a proper settlement."

"I love talking to lawyers," Virgil said. "It gives me a fresh, clean view of life."

VIRGIL RAN INTO SANDERS'S father, Ken Sanders, in the hall outside the sheriff's office, and the old man said, "I missed all the excitement. I understand Slibe beat the crap out of you."

"Ah, I had him," Virgil said. "I didn't want to hurt him, when it wasn't necessary."

Sanders smiled: "I guess that's one view. And I guess I'd rather have a broken nose than one ear. Though, I gotta tell you, you look a little odd with those white things sticking out of your nose."

"I can take them out in an hour," Virgil said. "I'll be good as new."

"Except for the nose brace and the tape."

"Well, yeah."

Sanders stuck an index finger in Virgil's gut, said, "Check you, cowboy," and went on his way.

VIRGIL WENT BACK to his motel and found Zoe walking down the hall, apparently having gotten no answer when she knocked on his door. She looked miserable. "Well, it's all over for me and Wendy. I rushed out there when I heard, but she's back with Berni. Big-time."

"Zoe . . . give it up," Virgil said. "She doesn't love you. She loves herself. I mean, you're not going to be able to compete with that."

"Oh, I know it," Zoe said. "Sig keeps saying that I ought to get more in the scene over in Duluth, or down in the Cities."

Virgil patted her on the shoulder. "Look. You're planning to buy the Eagle Roost . . ."

"Eagle Nest."

". . . Nest. You want to turn it into a lesbo destination, right?"

"We don't use the word *lesbo* that often," she said, "but that's correct."

"You're going to meet somebody. Somebody who's successful, like yourself, and you're going to have a terrific relationship," Virgil said.

"You think?"

"It'll happen," Virgil said.

"You going over to see Sig?"

"Oh, yeah. If you show up tonight, by the way, I guarantee that you won't be buying the Eagle Nest, or having a great relationship with anybody, because I'll choke the life out of you."

"Come have coffee with me tomorrow morning," she said. "I'll want all the details, about what my sister does in bed. I know she's been getting ready." She stood on tiptoe and pecked him on the cheek. "See you tomorrow; and good luck."

LIFE, AND CRIME, were complicated. There was a lot of work yet to be done: statements to be taken, evidence to be marshaled, reports to be written. Expense accounts to be submitted.

But not tonight.

Tonight, he was heading for Signy's.

HE'D JUST PULLED off his shirt when his cell phone rang. He looked at the number: Sanders. Damn. Well, he was going to Signy's, he didn't care what else had happened. He pressed the "talk" button: "Yeah?"

"We had people walking through the woods on the other side of the fence from Slibe's—looked like some machinery had been through there," Sanders said. "We've got a patch of roughed-up dirt, about car-sized. Bunch of dead trees and brush pushed over it, but . . . we got your crime-scene boys coming out in the morning. I think it's probably Windrow."

"Sounds like it," Virgil said. "I'll be out there to watch."

He hung up, and caught the image of himself in the dresser mirror: his eyes dark, sad. Windrow had been a good guy, full of life. If Virgil hadn't told him about Wendy . . .

NOW HE NOT ONLY *wanted* to go to Signy's, he *needed* to. Needed a human touch; and a little physical pleasure. He was not a man to boast, Virgil thought to himself, but he was going to turn the woman every way but loose. They'd been dancing around each other for a week, and she'd as good as told him that she hungered for Dr. Flowers's Female Cure.

Virgil got cleaned up, carefully pulled the cotton packs from his nostrils—that hurt like fire—and shaved and perfumed himself, although he didn't call it that. Old Spice was a manly deodorant, not a perfume, even if you did put a small splash under the testicles.

When he was ready, he checked himself in the mirrored door of the motel room: tapered long-sleeve shirt, sleeves rolled up to the elbows, second button casually undone, boot-cut faded jeans over high-polish cowboy boots with the decorative teal-colored Thunderbird stitching up the sides. Women went for men with polished boots.

I am a genuine piece of crumb cake, he thought, admiring his image in the mirror; there was that thing about the aluminum brace on his nose, and the tape, and the incipient black eyes, but a woman of quality could see past all that.

★

THERE WAS A KNOCK on the motel room door, and he thought, *No*.

And he thought about turning out the lights, so they wouldn't shine around the curtains, or under the door. . . . He could lie on the bathroom floor, and stop breathing. . . .

Another knock, louder. "Officer Flowers, please, I need some help."

A genuine piece of crumb cake, Virgil thought. He opened the door.

He'd never before seen the woman standing on the walkway. She was older, in her fifties, wearing walking shorts and a Hawaiian shirt, and pink plastic-rimmed glasses with a retainer cord. She said, "They told me you were here."

"Who?"

"The desk clerk. He told me you were here."

"I was just going out. . . ."

"Look," she said. She pointed across the way, at another motel, a taller, bigger one, that called itself a lodge. "I'm staying over there, my husband and I are up for the week."

"I really don't work town calls—"

"I think it's Little Linda," she said.

A long moment, then Virgil said, "Little Linda."

"Yes. My husband didn't think we should get involved, but we've been here for four days now, and they *never stop*. They just go at it *all the time*. I saw the boy come out of the room a few times, and saw him come back, with food, but I never saw her. I could only hear her, *all the time*. Anyway, I saw you in the parking lot, and I recognized you from the newspaper, and I thought you'd be the best one to tell."

"If you haven't seen her . . ."

"But I did. Ten minutes ago, coming back to the lodge, and she had a big hat on, but I was looking out the window and they were walking right toward me, and she pushed the hat back and looked up and I thought, 'Little Linda!' I recognized her right away. Then, they came up the stairs, and they started in again."

"You're sure it's Little Linda."

The woman stopped talking, her mouth hanging open, then her

eyes slid to the side for a moment, as she thought about it, then snapped back: "Yes. I'm sure. And she's not being held captive, I promise you that. She's there with a boy who looks like he's about sixteen. They know each other *very* well."

Virgil had talked to a lot of cops in the past week, but he remembered the one called Service, because Service had been a friendly guy, and had said something about living in town all of his life. He didn't want to call Sanders, because Sanders could ask that Virgil stick around. . . .

He called the sheriff's administration line, identified himself, and got a home phone for Service. Service's wife answered, passed the phone to her husband. Virgil said, "I can't tell you why, because it would cause me some trouble, but get your ass over here."

Service took ten minutes. Virgil regaled the woman, whose name was Debbie, with the story of the buried couple at Slibe's place.

Service arrived, and Virgil said, "I want you to meet Debbie. Debbie, this is Service."

DEBBIE AND SERVICE DISAPPEARED into the lodge. Five minutes later, sirens started simultaneously in several parts of town, and Virgil went back into his room and rebrushed his teeth. When he came out, a pod of cop cars had gathered at the lodge.

He wanted to go to Sig's . . . couldn't help himself. Got in his truck, rolled across the parking lot, left the car running, walked into the lodge, found a cluster of cops. Service was coming down the hall, looking happy, spotted Virgil.

"Got 'em," he said. They slapped hands. "And thank you. The kid's her secret boyfriend from Apple Valley. The sheriff's on his way back from Bigfork. I'm smelling like the biggest rose in Minnesota. Clean bust, all mine."

"Pretty good service, huh, Service?"

VIRGIL GOT CRANKED DRIVING out to Signy's, heart beating harder, that wash of adrenaline working through his arteries; and though he was tired from the day, the fight itself put an edge on him.

Must be like when the barbarians came home from battle, he thought, and jumped the old lady.

And in addition to polished boots, women also liked to care for injured guys, he thought.

THE ANTICIPATION OF IMMINENT sex, some argued, was as good as the sex itself, but Virgil thought they were wrong about that. *Nothing* was better than sex. Not even a forty-pound musky. A fifty-pounder, he'd have to think about. . . .

And thinking about it amused him, and he turned on the satellite radio where, by chance or by God, ZZ Top was running through "Sharp Dressed Man."

An omen, and a good one.

He was still pounding the steering wheel in time with the ZZs when he got to Signy's, where some of the air came out of his balloon; a strange and battered pickup was parked in the yard, which was truly inconvenient.

In his mental approach plan, he'd thought to drag her ass through the kitchen and throw her on the bed. Now they had to get rid of somebody first. He parked the 4Runner, climbed down, looked around once, and headed for the door.

Signy banged through it before he could knock, and then pressed her back against the closed door.

She looked wonderful: the slightly tired green eyes, the messed-up hair, the bruised lips, the slack cast of her face . . .

The bruised lips?

"Ah, Virgil," she said. She put her hands flat on his chest. "Ah, guess what?"

"Ah, what?"

She looked up with her sleepy green eyes, the eyes of a woman whose brains were anything but tight.

"Ah, jeez," she said. "You know Joe? Joe came back."